The Satanist

Is Black Magic still practised in Britain and other civilized countries today? Judging by the reports of unsavoury happenings that appear every few months in the Press the answer is definitely yes; there cannot be so much smoke without any fire Not very long ago the police raided a Satanic Temple in London, W.2, and while this story was being written the Customs actually seized Satanist regalia that was being imported into Australia.

Dennis Wheatley has always regarded Magic as a thing too dangerous to dabble in himself; but he has discussed it with many people who have – among them the late Aleister Crowley, the Rev. Montague Summers and Rollo Ahmed – and he has steeped himself in the ancient basis of the cult by most extensive reading.

Few writers could therefore be better qualified to describe how Satanists secure their recruits and blackmail the unwary, and the sort of thing that goes on in their secret Temples.

No one unprepared to acquiesce in appalling blasphemies and take part in the sexual rites by which Satanists obtain their occult power could possibly hope to penetrate a Satanic circle. In this story a man and a woman determine to pay that price in order to solve a foul and brutal murder.

The man, young Barney Sullivan – a secret agent working under Colonel Verney – is drawn into it while investigating Communist activities. The girl, Mary Morden, has a past which enables her to put moral scruples behind her, as she knows she must if she is to triumph over evil and bring a vile crew of Devil worshippers to justice.

This story is not for the young or the squeamish. But it may prove a warning to the innocently curious who are tempted to dabble in the occult.

For originality and ingenuity of plot, scene after scene of tense excitement, and its brilliant climax, *The Satanist* would prove hard to equal. In our view it surpasses even *The Devil Rides Out* and, like it, will become a classic of occult fiction.

T H E   S A

Dennis Wheatley

HUTCHINSON OF LONDON

TANIST

HUTCHINSON & CO. (*Publishers*) LTD
178–202 Great Portland Street, London, W.1

London Melbourne Sydney
Auckland Bombay Toronto
Johannesburg New York

First published 1960

*This book has been set in Times type
face. It has been printed in Great Britain on
Antique Wove paper by Taylor Garnett
Evans & Co. Ltd., Watford, Herts, and
bound by them*

*To the memory of
that most illustrious story-teller,*

ALEXANDRE DUMAS PÉRE

Whose books gave me enormous pleasure when I was a boy.

Whose heroes, while subject to normal human frailties, set a splendid example to the young of courage, loyalty and endurance – for which reason I have modelled the heroes of my own books on them.

And whose very slender short story, 'The Corsican Brothers', while having no resemblance whatever in period, subject, background or plot to *The Satanist*, gave me the idea of using identical twins as two of my principal characters in it.

Dennis Wheatley

Contents

1

A dangerous assignment

COLONEL VERNEY'S office was on the top floor of a tall building in London. He was sitting at his desk looking at a photograph of the naked body of a man of about thirty. Dark marks on the wrists and ankles showed where they had been tightly bound; the head lolled back and the neck was half severed by a horrible gash from ear to ear. Laying the photograph down, the Colonel said:

'The Devil's behind this. I'm convinced of it.'

'Several devils, if you ask me, Sir,' replied Inspector Thompson, who was sitting opposite him. 'Must have been, to have trussed poor Morden up like that before cutting his throat.'

'I didn't say "a devil" but "the Devil" – Lucifer, Satan, or whatever you care to call the indestructible power of Evil that has sought to destroy mankind ever since the Creation.'

The Inspector had been transferred to the Special Branch only a few months before; so he did not know much about the work of Colonel Verney's department. Like the other branches of the Secret Service, its function was to secure information; it never took legal proceedings. Whenever these were required the case was passed to Special Branch for action. Morden had been one of Colonel Verney's young men, and Thompson had come over from Scotland Yard to report on the case. The report was negative as, although it was over a week since Morden's body had been found in an alley leading down to a Bermondsey dock, the police had so far failed to secure a clue of any kind to the murder. But

Thompson had also brought with him the results of a second post-mortem held to answer certain specific questions raised by the Colonel.

Now, he gave a slightly uneasy cough, and said: 'I should have thought it a pretty plain case, Sir. Morden was after these Communist saboteurs, they rumbled him and knocked him off. I can't see how the Devil comes into that. Not from the practical point of view, anyhow. But, of course, if you've got any special theory we'd be only too happy to follow it up.'

The Colonel shook his head. 'No, I've nothing you could work on, Thompson. I'm about to brief another man to carry on in Morden's place. He might pick up something, and naturally your people will continue to check up on all the roughnecks who might have been involved. We can only hope that one of us will tumble on a lead. Thank you for coming over.'

As the Inspector stood up, the Colonel rose too. He was a rather thin man and tall above the average, but his height was not immediately apparent on account of a slight stoop. His hair was going grey, parted in the centre and brushed firmly back to suppress a tendency to curl at the ends. His face was longish, with a firm mouth and determined chin; but the other features were dominated by a big aggressive nose that had earned him the nickname of Conky Bill – or, as most of his friends called him for short, C.B. His eyebrows were thick and prawn-like. Below them his grey eyes had the quality of seeming to look right through one. He usually spoke very quietly, in an almost confidential tone, and gave the impression that there were very few things out of which he did not derive a certain amount of amusement; but at the moment his thin face was grim.

Having politely seen the Inspector to the door, he paused on the threshold and said to his secretary in the outer office, 'I'll see Mr. Sullivan now.' Then he returned to his desk.

Barney Sullivan was twenty-eight years of age, and, in contrast to his Chief, made the most of his five foot nine inches by carrying himself very upright. He was broad-shouldered, rather round-faced and had a nose that only just escaped being snub. His mouth was wide, his brown eyes merry, and his hair a mass of short, irrepressible dark curls. Those merry eyes, a healthy bronzed skin, and his swift movements, showed him to be a young man endowed with abundant *joie de vivre*.

As he came in, Verney, now faintly smiling, waved him to the

10

chair the Inspector had vacated, offered his cigarette case, and asked:

'Well, young feller, how's the world treating you?'

With a word of thanks, Barney took one of C.B.'s specials – they were super-long Virginians that he smoked occasionally as an alternative to his beloved thin-stemmed pipe – then he replied.

'Not too badly, Sir. I had a grand run with the Pytchley on my day off last week. We killed three times, Apart from that, only the usual complaint; too much desk work. I'm sick of the sight of card-indexes.'

C.B. shrugged. 'Has to be done. Backbone of our job. But I've got something for you that should mean your being out and about for quite a while. That is, if you care to take it.'

'Orders is orders, Sir.' Barney gave a wide-mouthed grin. 'All that matters is if you think I'm up to it.'

'I do. Otherwise I wouldn't offer it to you. But I've never yet asked a man to gamble his life with his eyes shut. The risk involved in this case is far greater than any of us are expected to take in the normal course of our duties; so I'll not hold it against you if you say you'd prefer to stick to routine work. Before you reply you'd better take a look at that.'

Barney picked up the photograph that C.B. pushed across to him, stared at it a moment and gave a low whistle. 'So that's what happened to poor Teddy Morden! I knew, of course, that he was dead, but understood that he'd died of a heart attack.'

'We don't broadcast such matters,' remarked the Colonel quietly, 'or even let on about them in the office to anyone who is not immediately concerned. Now; how about it?'

'I'll play, Sir.' Barney's reply came after only a second's hesitation. 'I hardly knew Morden, except to pass the time of day with; but he was one of us and I'm game to have a cut at the swine who did that to him.'

'Good show, Sullivan. I had a hunch that in you I'd picked the right man to carry on from where Morden left off. The chance of your running down his murderers is pretty slender, though. The police haven't got a clue. Of course, you might strike a lucky lead but, anyway, that isn't really your job. I showed you that photograph only so that you should know the sort of thing to which you will be exposing yourself by stepping into Morden's shoes .'

C.B. got out his pipe and began to fill it. 'This is top-level stuff. Last December a high-power meeting was held with the P.M. in the chair. Among those present, as well as several Cabinet Ministers, were the leaders of the Opposition and some of the big shots of the T.U.C. They met to discuss a matter which for a long time past has been giving a lot of responsible people headaches; namely, the hold that Communism still has on Labour. As a result of that meeting the Prime Minister sent for me and ordered me to carry out a special investigation.'

As he paused, Barney remarked, 'I was under the impression that the savagery with which the Russians put down the Hungarian revolution had resulted in a major set-back for the Communists all over Western Europe; and that here, especially, owing to the strong line recently taken by the T.U.C. Chiefs, the Reds have been finding the going much more difficult.'

'You were right about the effect of the Budapest massacres, but that was quite a few years ago. The Communists get most of their recruits from among young people who are discontented with their lot, and for many of them the Hungarian purge is now only an episode in history. Anyhow, we have good grounds for believing that support for Communism here is again on the increase. You are right too, of course, that for some time past the T.U.C. has been taking active steps in an attempt to check the influence wielded by Communists in the Unions; but it's an uphill game. Did you happen to see a booklet published last year that was called *The British Road to Stalinism*?'

'Yes. It was a warning to trade-unionists put out by the Industrial Research and Information Service about the danger of Communist infiltration.'

'That's right. And the I.R.I.S. is no Tory-backed set-up. Its Chief is Jack Tanner, a former chairman of the T.U.C. and president of the Amalgamated Engineering Union. The booklet was issued in an attempt to impress on the ordinary workers the importance of attending Branch meetings and using their vote in the election of shop-stewards and Union officials. If anything could have woken up the rank and file of Labour one would have thought a broadside from such a source would do the trick; but it failed to make any noticeable impression.'

Having lit his pipe, the Colonel went on. 'There are eight million trade-unionists and only twenty-five thousand Communists, yet the Communists hold posts out of all proportion to their numbers. The average British working man is as sound as a bell. If only we could get a quarter of them to face up to their responsi-

12

bilities, we could check the rot in no time. But they won't. And only the comparatively few, who have political ambitions, will stand for election as officials because the work entailed would mean giving up some of their evenings instead of watching T.V., working in their gardens, or going to the pub.'

Barney nodded. 'Yes, apathy's the root of the trouble; but from what one hears, it's not only that. A lot of the elections are rigged.'

'Ah! Now you're talking, young feller. That's one of the things I want you to find out about. As you will have seen from the papers, the T.U.C. have been toying with an investigation into ballot rigging for a long time past; but they don't seem to be able to get down to brass tacks, and it is a real menace. Once one of these Red gentry succeeds in getting himself into a key post, such as secretary of a branch, he is in a position to do all sorts of fiddles. He can call snap meetings at a time when those who would oppose him are sick or on holiday; he can nominate his pals to act as tellers when votes are counted, and get up to a dozen tricks which result in others of his kidney getting seats on the committee. The process is cumulative and before the ordinary members of the branch wake up to what is happening they find that it is Communist controlled. And once they're in, it's next to impossible to get them out. Anyone who tries is either beaten up or, in some way or other, put on the spot.'

'Like that Union official they accused of raping the typist,' Barney grinned. 'If the girl hadn't proved a decent sort and refused to lie for them, he would have been out on his ear and his private life wrecked into the bargain.'

'That's it. No game is too dirty for them to play, even against one of their own kind if he shows signs of disagreeing with the Party line – and the other name for that is "orders from Moscow".'

The Colonel sat forward and went on in his low conspiratorial voice. 'Now, we can't do much about the general apathy at the moment. But if we could get the low-down on these rigged elections and other crooked dealings it would provide really valuable ammunition for the T.U.C. in the purge they are attempting. Not only could they get the boys we had the goods on sacked from their posts, but full publicity about what has been going on would raise the dander of the honest majority men and make them more conscious of their responsibilities. Greater numbers of them would attend meetings and the odds then would be on honest chaps instead of saboteurs being elected. Get the idea?'

'I certainly do, Sir.'

'Good! Then there's another angle to it. Since the war, Britain has been fighting for her life economically. Industry has done marvels in increasing our exports, and the Government did a wonderful job a while back in saving the pound. But the country has been deliberately robbed of a big part of the benefit it should have derived from these stupendous efforts.'

'By unofficial strikes,' hazarded Barney.

'You've said it, my lad. In the past ten years they've cost the country untold millions, and at times thrown as many as a hundred thousand people, who had no part in the dispute, out of work for several weeks. It's their repercussions that prove so costly and there seems no way of altering the pattern they follow. A group of Reds get a dispute going on some little point of procedure in a small plant where they have control. The installing of a new machine, or an alteration in schedule to improve efficiency, is all they need to start an argument. They persuade one category of workers that it may lead to their getting smaller pay-packets, or cause redundancy, so they down tools. If it ended there that wouldn't be a very serious matter. But it doesn't. The agitators get busy with the cry that a threat to one category of workers is a threat to all, and out come other categories in sympathy. Yet even that is not the worst. After a week or two the stoppage in that factory begins to affect others. Nine times out of ten the thing it is making is not a finished article, but a part or material essential for putting the completed product on the market. That means far bigger plants have to put their hands on short time, or are brought to a standstill.

'It's time everyone realized that every man who joins a strike that has not the approval of his Union is a Public Enemy; because these wildcat stoppages eat into profits like rats into corn, and profits mean taxes. If it had not been for all this downing of tools without real justification, by now we could have doubled old-age pensions and child allowances, and had a shilling off the income-tax into the bargain.'

'Bejesus, you're right, Sir!' The touch of Irish slipped out owing to Barney's spontaneous agreement. 'Look at that B.O.A.C. strike. It must have cost the country millions; and largely because the men let themselves be carried away by the brilliant oratory of

14

Sid Maitland – in spite of the fact that, according to the Press, he openly declared himself to be a Communist. They just wouldn't listen to Jim Matthews but howled him down, and when he tried to get them to accept the Union's ruling and rely on its negotiations they called him a traitor. It's a shocking state of things when they won't be guided by their own Union officials.'

'That's what is giving the responsible Labour leaders such a headache. For the past year or so they have been doing their utmost both to oust the Communists from key positions in the Unions and to get a firmer control over the shop stewards. But it is uphill work, because it lays them open to accusations of attempting to browbeat the workers and of being secretly in league with the Tory government; and it is difficult for them to convince the rank and file that they are not.'

'Yes, I see that. They're between the devil and the deep blue sea; and owing to the size of the Unions it is impossible for their top men to keep in personal touch with all their tens of thousands of members. That is where the shop stewards have such a pull.'

The Colonel nodded. 'True enough. But don't run away with the idea that all the shop stewards are bad hats. The great majority of them are good chaps doing a very valuable job of work maintaining good relations between the management and their mates. The trouble is that the bad ones are in a position to do an immense amount of damage by formenting these wildcat strikes. Those are the boys we want to get the low-down on; so that we can expose them and help the T.U.C. in its big campaign to purge the British Labour movement of Russian influence.'

'And where do I come in on this, Sir?' Barney asked.

Again C.B.'s voice sank to a conspiratorial low. 'Sinews of war, young fellow. That's our line of attack. Men who come out unofficially don't get strike pay. Yet some of these unofficial strikes go on for months. Meantime the strikers have got to live and feed their families. How do they do it? We know the answer to that one. At least we know it to apply in some cases, and have good reason to suppose that it applies in many more. They are given enough cash to keep going on the side from secret funds controlled by the Reds.'

'Don't some of the better types query where it comes from?'

'Those who do are told that it is from subscriptions raised among sympathizers.'

'But, in fact, it comes from Moscow.'

15

'For such considerable sums, that seems the only possible source of origin. One of Russia's prime objects is to disrupt our industry, in order to create the unemployment and discontent which always results in the spread of Communism; so they could hardly spend their money to better purpose. Yet the fact remains that we have failed to uncover any link between the leaders of these unofficial strikes and any of the Iron Curtain country Embassies, or any other Soviet-controlled set-up.'

'Quite a number of the top Reds go to Russia from time to time, Sir.'

'Yes, and although they give out that they go there only for a holiday, I don't doubt they return with plenty of ideas that don't do British industry much good; but they could not bring back any considerable sums of money with them – not without our knowing about it.'

'And you want me to try to find out the source of supply?'

'That's it; then we could think up some way of cutting it off.' C.B. pulled at his pipe for a moment, then said with a change of tone, 'Now, a word about yourself. What led you to join this outfit?'

Barney grinned. 'I was broke. My creditors in Dublin had made Ireland too hot to hold me. I decided that I'd got to take a steady job, but I knew that I'd never settle down to a humdrum office routine. It had to be something that would provide me with a bit of excitement now and then, and my uncle, General Sir Geoffrey Frobisher, got me in here.'

'So that was it, eh! Of course, I knew that old "Frosty" Frobisher had vouched for you, and looking up your file the other day reminded me that you are the Earl of Larne. How come that you have never used your title?'

'Well, it was this way, Sir. I've practically no family, only my mother's brother, the General. Both my parents died when I was quite young and he became my guardian. He did very little about it, though; but I can't really blame him for that. I lived in Ireland and he lived in England. During most of the time I was at school he was up to his eyes in the war. Then for the greater part of the next six years he was stationed abroad – doing tours of duty in the Middle East, then in Germany. No one else had any right to call me to account, so I'm afraid my high spirits led to my becoming rather a bad hat. I got sent down from Trinity for leading a pretty hectic rag, but I had quite a generous allowance and plenty

16

of friends. The fathers of several of those with whom I used to stay in the holidays reared bloodstock, and I've always been good with horses; so I naturally gravitated to that as a means of earning a living. I won quite a few steeplechases and received handsome presents from the owners. But it was a case of easy come easy go, and most of what I made over the sticks I lost by backing losers on the flat.

'Thanks, Sir.' Barney took another of C.B.'s long cigarettes, lit it and went on. 'They were an expensive crowd to live with, too, so I was soon up to my eyes in debt. But I was in my last year at the University when I was sent down, and becoming twenty-one a year later saved me from disaster. My father didn't leave me a fortune, only a few thousands, and if I'd had any sense I should have pulled up then. As it was, like a young ass, I started to really hit up the town. What with the gee-gees, the girls, and throwing expensive parties, I got through the lot in a couple of years.'

'You would have been twenty-three by then. That's about the time you came into the title, isn't it?'

'Yes, Sir. But I had never expected to. When my father died there were seven people between myself and the Earldom, and we didn't even know that branch of the family. One was drowned in 1939, two more were killed in the war, and another met his death while climbing in Switzerland in 1951. That still left three; the late Lord Larne and his two sons. They had lived in Kenya since before the war, so I'd never met any of them and never gave them a thought until one day in 'fifty-four. I learned then that all three had crashed in their private plane and been killed.'

'Didn't you come into any money with the title?'

'No. The place in Ireland had been sold way back in the 'twenties, and all the money Lord Larne left went to his widow, who still lives in Kenya. All I came into were the heirlooms – some good family silver and a few pictures – but unfortunately they weren't worth much.'

'What happened then?'

'The General sent for me. I came clean with him about my debts in Dublin and he said some pretty caustic things to me; but, by and large, he behaved extremely well. He declared that as I came of an ancient and honourable family, I was under a definite obligation not to disgrace the title; that if I took it up, it would certainly lead to my continuing to mix with people whose style of life I could not afford, and that, in any ordinary job, it

17

could only prove a handicap to me. Therefore, he argued, I ought not to use it until I had lived down my raffish past. By then I had realized that if I did not turn over a new leaf I was riding for a really nasty fall; so I agreed to forget the Earldom for the time being, leave Ireland, and make a fresh start. He said that if I'd do that and promise to go straight for five years before using my title, he would pay my debts and make me an allowance of £300 a year until I got on my feet.'

'So that was the way of it.'

'Yes. Then we talked about all sorts of jobs and eventually he hit on the idea of getting me in here. That appealed to me more than going off to one of the Dominions or into industry. I went back to Dublin, hardened my heart about saying good-bye to any of my friends so as not to have to lie to them about my future plans, packed up my things and simply told my landlady that I was going to the United States. I imagine my sudden disappearance was no more than a nine days' wonder, and I've never been back there since. Naturally I missed the hectic parties, the racing, the girls and the champagne for a bit, but I soon became so intrigued by the work here that I didn't miss them any more; and I can never be sufficiently grateful to the General for what he did for me.'

C.B.'s long face broke into its most friendly smile. 'Yes, he certainly did the right and handsome thing by you; but you've yourself to thank even more for having the guts to snap out of the sort of life you had been living for so long. About this title of yours, though? The five years are nearly up, aren't they?'

'Yes; only another three months to go.'

'Do you propose to use it then?'

'No, I don't think so. Having a title these days doesn't get one anywhere. It only costs money and I'm not all that well off. I might if I married though, as the girl would probably like it, so it wouldn't be fair to her not to.'

'Are you thinking of getting married?'

Barney grinned. 'No, Sir. I prefer to love them all a little bit.'

'Good. You're wrong, though, about a title never getting a man anywhere. There are times when it can be very useful, and that might well prove the case, in certain circumstances, during the course of this job I'm putting you on.'

'What! While I'm posing as a Red among manual workers and

18

technicians?' Barney opened his brown eyes wide in surprise. 'Surely not?'

'That will be your role for most of the time, of course, but there may turn out to be another angle to the business. I'm not telling you about that at present, because it is only a theory of my own and I don't want to start you off with preconceived ideas that might both warp your judgment and be wrong. But if at any time you do feel that the use of your title might help to open a door to you, use it. I'll take the responsibility for your breaking your promise to the General and, if need be, square matters with him.'

'Very well. That's O.K. by me, Sir.'

C.B. pushed a thick file across the desk, and said: 'Here is all the dope we've got so far. Take it to your office and spend the next two or three days going through it very thoroughly. Naturally I have a dozen other members of the firm hard at it, ferreting out the pasts of various fellow-travellers, attending meetings, checking figures, and generally gathering information, but you'll be the only one to be planted on the inside in London as a real red-hot Red. Your line will be that you've just come over from Ireland. We'll provide you with all the background stuff – a Party card, membership cards of half-a-dozen Unions, and a list of the most promising branches at which to use them. Don't start anything until you have mastered that file, and when you have, let me know. Can I take it that you are clear on what I want you to do?'

'Yes, Sir. I've to get you all I can on the methods used by Communists to become officials in the Unions, about rigged elections and where the money comes from to finance unofficial strikes.'

'You've got it, young feller. Good luck to you.'

'Thank you, Sir.' Barney Sullivan tucked the file under his arm and, with his cheerful face more serious than usual, left the room.

As Barney went out, Verney again picked up the photograph of Morden's body. With set mouth he stared at it while thinking of the points that had emerged from the second autopsy, for which he had asked.

Morden's ankles had been lashed together, but his wrists had not; they had been lashed separately to thick pieces of wood or iron. The marks of the cords that had bound his ankles did not make a straight line; they made a V pointing towards the feet, as though pressure had been exerted between them to drag the

19

cords down where they met in the middle. Immediately below the point of the V there was severe bruising of both ankles, as though a thick stake, or peg, had been thrust between them. There had been no blood on the body when it was found, so obviously it had been washed after Morden's throat had been cut; but the second autopsy had revealed that while there was no trace of blood on Morden's body, there were still tiny particles of blood under his eyelids and in his hair.

Inspector Thompson had been aware that Colonel Verney had given most of his time before the last war to checking up on the activities of Fascists, and that since the war he had given most of it to checking up on those of Communists. What the Inspector had not known was that, as C.B. was responsible for keeping tabs on all groups which might be engaged in any anti-social activity, it had included a number of secret societies that practised Black Magic. The knowledge that he had gained of such matters was, therefore, considerable.

With a heavy sigh he put away the photograph. It was the marks on the legs that had first led him to suspect that Morden had been hung by his bound ankles from a stout peg between them, and now the particles of blood found in his hair confirmed that. Verney did not believe that the killing was the work of thugs in the dock area. In his own mind he now felt certain that Morden was the victim of a ritual murder, and had been crucified upside-down.

2

A widow seeks revenge

COLONEL VERNEY lived for a good part of the year as a grass-widower. That was not because he was lacking in affection for his wife, but both of them had been over forty when they married and she had been loath to give up the charming little villa near St. Raphael, in the South of France, where she had made her home for the previous seven years.

During those years, as Molly Fountain, she had built up a reputation for herself as a very competent writer of adventure stories and her work brought her quite a comfortable income. Had that been added to the Colonel's – since in Britain the incomes of husband and wife are assessed as one for tax purposes – the result would have been that they would have been compelled to pay away a big proportion of their joint earnings in income and super tax. By continuing to be domiciled in different countries they were better off by at least a thousand a year, which more than paid for frequent trips by one or other of them between London and St. Raphael and, moreover, enabled Molly to go on writing her books in the sunny, secluded retreat where inspiration seemed to come to her much more easily than in a city.

The law allowed her to spend up to three months a year in England without becoming liable to tax, and Verney spent his leaves with her in France; added to which his work often necessitated his going to the Continent for consultations with his opposite numbers in other capitals, and sometimes she flew from Nice to Geneva, Paris, Rome or wherever it might be, to be with him. In consequence, a month rarely passed without their being able to have a few nights together or longer sessions of a fortnight or more; and for two middle-aged people, both of whose minds were largely occupied with their work, the arrangement had proved very satisfactory.

Verney, too, was particularly fortunate as by this arrangement he had not even had to forgo the benefit of leaving his bachelor quarters, for a London home where he was made much of. The same month that he had married Molly, her son John had married Ellen Beddows, and Ellen had just inherited a handsome fortune from her father. John was doing well as a junior partner in a firm of interior decorators, but it was Ellen's money that had enabled them to start their married life in much better style than he would have been able to afford.

They had bought one of the delightful new houses that were being built in Dovehouse Street, Chelsea; and behind it, at the far end of a pleasant little paved garden, it had another building which was virtually a self-contained flat. It consisted of a large, lofty studio with a small bedroom, bathroom and tiny kitchenette. As the house itself contained ample accommodation for the young couple, and they both adored C.B., they had insisted that he should come to live in the studio.

This proved an admirable arrangement, for he enjoyed all the amenities of a home without always being on top of them. Moreover, as he continued his old practice of dining two or three nights a week at his club, they could when they wished ask other young couples to dinner without having him too as odd man out; and when they had larger parties he was always happy to place the big studio at their disposal.

It had been on Monday, March 7th, that he had briefed Barney Sullivan, and on the following Sunday afternoon he had just settled himself down in the studio to read the papers, when John Fountain came across, put his head in at the door, and said:

'C.B., a young woman has called and is asking to see you. Her name is Mrs. Morden. What about it?'

With a sigh C.B. lowered the paper. He knew that it must be Teddy Morden's widow, and felt that an interview with her would certainly be most painful for them both, the odds being that she had come to upbraid him for sending her husband to his death; but he quickly resigned himself to it.

'All right, John. I'll see her.'

22

John gave him a wicked grin. 'She's quite an eyeful – a ravishing blonde. Poor old Mumsie. What's it worth to you for me not to let on to her that you've got yourself a lovely girl-friend?'

C.B. grinned back. 'That's quite enough of that, young feller. Bring her along.'

'O.K. Chief. But my silence will cost you a case of Moet N.V.'

Two minutes later Mrs. Morden stepped across the threshold of C.B.'s spacious book-lined sanctum. From behind her shoulder the irrepressible John winked at C.B. and made the V sign; then he quietly closed the door upon them.

Mary Morden was twenty-three and John had not exaggerated her good looks. A small black hat enhanced the gold of her ripe-corn coloured hair, which she evidently kept long, as it was done up in two thick plaits at the back of her head, leaving fully exposed two unusually pretty little ears. Her eyebrows were rather thick, and she left them like that because they were so fair that, had they been plucked, they would hardly have shown; but below them were two almond-shaped eyes of that deep blue colour which is most usually seen in combination with the dark beauty of an Irish colleen. Her nose was straight, her mouth firm and her pointed chin slightly aggressive. She was fairly tall with a good bust that nicely balanced her hips, and she carried herself well. C.B., who had an eye for such things, decided that her black and white check suit, although it fitted her well, was ready-made; but that her nylons were of fine quality. As she took the chair he placed for her, she crossed a pair of legs of which she had good reason to be proud, and he saw that they ended in small, neat feet.

He had seen her before on two occasions. The last had been at Morden's funeral, and there he had only bowed to her as a veiled, pathetic figure. The first had been when he had had to go down to her flat at Wimbledon to break the news of her husband's death to her. It had been a Monday morning; she had been busy doing the weekly washing, and so had come out from the kitchen with her hair tied up in a scarf, wearing a faded blouse, tight blue jeans and a pair of down-at-heel slippers. She had little make-up on now, but she had had none at all on then, and a wisp of hair that had got loose from under the scarf had given her a slightly sluttish appearance. He had been struck by her fine eyes but failed to realize that she was a beauty before the news he brought confirmed her fears for Teddy, who had not been home since the afternoon of Saturday; upon which she had buried her face in her hands and burst into a passion of tears. To make the horrible job he had to do a little easier, he had first sought out Morden's brother and sister-in-law, and taken them with him. Having told Mrs. Morden of her husband's death as gently as he could, and provided her with ample money to meet any immediate necessities, he had left her with her relations by marriage.

Now, as soon as she was seated, she said briskly: 'I do hope you will forgive me for spoiling your Sunday afternoon like this, Colonel Verney, but I thought it a likely time to catch you and, that in view of what I want to talk to you about, it was better that I should come to your home than to your office.'

'You're not spoiling it,' he assured her with a smile. 'I was only glancing through the papers. I'm glad to see you and, if I may say so, looking so, er . . .'

'You mean recovered from the shock,' she helped him out, 'Well, it's a fortnight now and one can't go on weeping ones eyes out for ever. It was a choice of either letting myself sink into a sort of morbid coma that might have gone on for months, or getting down to something that would occupy my time and mind, and I decided on the latter.'

'Well done you. I'm delighted to hear it.' Offering her his cigarette case, he added: 'Tell me about this job you've got?'

'What lovely long ones.' She took a cigarette and, after he had lit it for her, said: 'I haven't got it yet. That's why I'm here.'

He raised his prawn-like eyebrows a fraction. 'I see. Well, if it's a reference you require I'd be delighted; but if you want me to find you a job that's rather a different matter. Still, if you'll tell me what qualifications you have, I'll do my best to . . .'

'Thanks, but this isn't a case for either. I followed your wishes in telling my friends and neighbours that Teddy died of a heart-attack, but we know that he was murdered. You couldn't have concealed the truth from me, even if you had wanted to, because I had to be given his death certificate. I don't think that by nature I am vindictive, but Teddy meant . . . meant a lot to me. I want to help bring his murderer to justice.'

'That's very understandable,' said C.B. gravely, 'but I'm afraid you would only be wasting your time. The police are doing everything possible, and even with all their resources they haven't yet got a clue.'

'Then that is all the more reason why you should let me try

24

my hand. If in a fortnight they have failed to get anywhere, it means that the trail has gone cold by now, so they are not very likely to. Fresh crimes are calling for the attention of the police every day; so they will give less and less time to Teddy's case, and after another few weeks shelve it.'

'No case is ever closed until the criminal is caught.'

Mary Morden made an impatient gesture. 'No, but after a while the file joins the hundreds of others on unsolved crimes and no one does any more about it.' Her strong jaw hardened suddenly and she added: 'But take me on and that won't happen. I'll stick to it for years if . . .'

'Take you on!' C.B. repeated, then he quickly shook his head. 'No, Mrs. Morden, I'm sorry, but that is quite out of the question. Even if I wanted to I couldn't. There are very definite rules governing procedure in my department.'

'Oh, I didn't mean officially. That's why I thought it best to come here to see you. Then no one could suspect that I was working for you. And I don't want any pay. I'm not rolling in money, but I can manage on what I've got.'

For a moment C.B. looked straight at the beautiful earnest face opposite him; then he shook his head again. 'Honestly, it's not possible. For you even to make a start I'd have to disclose to you the mission Teddy was employed upon, and that would mean letting you into all sorts of official secrets. I could lose my job for that. Besides, you would be exposing yourself to grave danger and that's a responsibility I'm not prepared to take.'

She pulled a face, shrugged and made a move to stand up. 'Very well, Colonel Verney, I'm sorry to find you so un-coopera- tive and sorry to have wasted your time. I'll just have to set about the business on my own.'

'Hey! Wait a mo', lady.' Conky Bill gestured her back into the chair. He was trying desperately to think of some way in which he could dissuade her from entering on an investigation that, at best, would mean months of futile endeavour and, at worst, the chance that she would run up against real trouble which would end in her becoming a lovely corpse.

'Well!' she smiled suddenly. 'Are you thinking of changing your mind?'

'No, M'am,' he replied promptly, getting to his feet. 'And I'm not likely to in a matter like this. I'm just going to make you a cup of tea.'

25

'That's nice of you,' she conceded, and her smile broadened, showing two rows of strong, even teeth.

He rather prided himself as a brewer of a good cup of tea, and some minutes later he emerged from his kitchenette with a tray on which reposed a pot of Earl Grey, milk, lemon, sugar and a plate of shortbread biscuits. Setting it down he said, 'You must be "mother". Lemon for me and three lumps of sugar.'

As she poured out, he went on, 'So you're going to play the lone wolf, eh? Or rather the unshorn lamb going into the forest to put the fear of God into the great big hairy bears. I've had the best part of thirty years at the game, but most times I've gone in a tank with plenty of air cover. All the same, I still look on myself as a learner, and I'd be awfully interested to hear how you propose to set about it.'

She passed him his cup. 'Elementary, my dear Watson! I shall find out all I can about everyone with whom Teddy had anything to do these past few months.'

'Did he tell you anything about the job he was on?'

'No, not a thing. He was terribly security-minded.'

'Then that won't get you anywhere; because you can have no line on the people he was after.'

'You can't be certain that it won't. And I have got one line that might lead to something. It wasn't at all in keeping with his character, but some time back he suddenly became deeply interested in Spiritualism.'

Had it not been for his long training at suppressing all signs of emotion while interrogating people, C.B. might well have dropped his tea-cup. As it was his long face remained impassive as he said, 'Really; and he made no secret about that?'

'He would have, but a mutual friend of ours happened to see him at a séance, and told me about it. When I tackled him he came clean and admitted that he had been to several. I tried to persuade him to drop it. After all, his work took him out at night often enough without his spending an evening or two a week attending séances. Besides, I am a Roman Catholic. Not a very good one, I'm afraid. In fact, we were married at a Registry Office and I haven't been inside a church for years. All the same, I still believe in its teaching, and that Spiritualism is wrong. Teddy knew that, of course; otherwise he would probably have suggested my going with him. As it was, he seemed absolutely

26

fascinated by this new interest. He wouldn't listen to me and continued to go to the meetings in spite of all I could say.'

'But what leads you to think that his interest in Spiritualism had any bearing on his death?'

Mary Morden's fair eyelashes fluttered and for a moment veiled her deep blue eyes as she replied, a shade uncomfortably: 'Because there was something behind it – something very unpleasant.'

C.B. had to keep a tight hold on himself in order not to show the intense interest which gripped him as he asked in his low voice: 'What sort of thing?'

'I don't really know. Teddy used to talk in his sleep. He never gave away any office secrets, and mostly it was incoherent muttering. But during the last few weeks he began to have nightmares. He seemed to be struggling in a sort of medieval hell. He raved about the Devil taking the form of a small black imp, and of a Temple where animals were sacrificed. An Indian was mixed up in it, and someone whom he referred to as "the Master". When he woke from these nightmares, or I woke him, he was drenched in sweat. But he wouldn't tell me their cause. He used to shrug them off by saying that he was making a study of the occult and had been reading a lot about the bad side of it.'

'That may have been true. On the other hand, one can't rule out the possibility that he had got in with some bad hats at these séances and that they introduced him into a Black Magic circle.'

'That's what I think.'

'And you intend to follow this up?'

'Yes.'

For a moment C.B. was silent. All she had said fitted in so well with his own theory of what lay behind Morden's death that he was greatly tempted to tell her to go ahead. Yet few people knew better than he did the terrible danger to which she would be exposing herself if she did. Having decided that he must do his best to stop her, he said:

'Listen, lady. In my work I've been up against this sort of thing before;[1] yet I've never succeeded in bringing a big Black to justice. They are incredibly cunning and utterly unscrupulous. If I, with all the resources of my department, can't get the goods on them, how can you, a woman working on her own, hope to? Supposing you are right, you'll get no further than the fringe of

[1] See *To the Devil – a Daughter*

it; then they'll catch you out, and the odds are that you'll end up as poor Teddy did. It isn't on! You've got to put this idea right out of your head.'

She gave a slight shrug. 'Of course there's a risk. I know that. But in my case I think you exaggerate. If these people did kill Teddy, it must have been because one of them found out that he was working for you. As you have turned me down that could not apply to me. Anyway, I'm a free agent, and, if I choose to do this, you can't stop me.'

'No, I can't. But I can give you some idea of the sort of situation you will be faced with from the very start.'

'I'd be interested to hear it.'

'Well, all Black Magic rituals are based on sex or, to use more appropriate words, unbridled lust, perversion and obscenity. If you ever succeed in getting inside a Satanic Temple, you will be expected to witness and applaud acts which would turn the stomach of a member of the vice-squad, let alone a decent young woman like yourself. But that would be only after your own initiation. And that's the hurdle you'd have to take before you could get anywhere. You don't need me to tell you what a lovely person you are, and they are not going to give you a ring-side seat for nowt. Your entry ticket would be having to give yourself to the man who introduced you into the circle.'

Mary Morden dropped her eyes again. 'I can only hope that he wouldn't be too repulsive.'

'What!' C.B. sat forward suddenly. 'D'you mean you would?'

'Yes.' She looked up and met his glance squarely. 'I'd better be frank with you, Colonel Verney. I grew up in the back streets of Dublin and became a cabaret girl. For reasons with which I won't bother you there came a time when I had to have more money than my pay. Cabaret girls get plenty of opportunities to earn money the so-called easy way, and those who do don't think of themselves as prostitutes. But, to be brutally honest, that's what I was for the best part of a year. And, believe me, even with girls such as I was, who don't have to go to bed with every man who asks them to, it's not easy money. There are times when men who seem to be decent sorts turn out to be absolute swine, and to earn a few pounds that way is like suddenly finding oneself in hell.

'Four years ago Teddy took me out of that. He knew the sort of life I had been leading, but all the same he married me. I'm

28

not going to tell you that he was my one great love. The fact is, I've never had one; but I was terribly fond of him. He gave me security, a decent home, respectability, everything that any reasonable woman could want except a child, and I made him a good and faithful wife.

'But now that is all over. I've no family. I'm on my own again. With his pension and a little capital he inherited from an uncle I'll be free from want; but by killing Teddy some fiend robbed the world of an honest, decent, kindly man, and robbed me of everything that made life worth while. So I'll not stick at using my looks, and my body too, if need be, in an attempt to get even with his murderer.'

For a moment C.B. was silent again, then he said: 'If that's the case, Mrs. Morden, there's no more I can say; except to express my admiration for your determination and courage.'

'Thank you,' she said gravely. 'I'm glad my confession hasn't made you think too badly of me.'

'Far from it. None of us has much choice about the sort of life we have to lead when we are young; and, frankly, it is a small grain of comfort to me to know that at least you are prepared for the sort of thing it's certain you'll have to face.'

'That's that, then.' She picked up her bag. 'Well, I won't keep you any longer. Thank you for seeing me and giving me such a nice tea.'

Waving her back, he said: 'No, don't go yet. Although I can't give you any official help, maybe I can suggest a way to lessen these risks you are determined to run.'

Her mouth twitched in a faint smile. 'I'll bet that it is to try to make myself look old and unattractive.'

He laughed. 'No; there would be no chance of your succeeding in that. Even a make-up expert couldn't alter your face enough for people not to detect at close quarters that it was a painted mask. Then, how about your figure, and those legs? But I was thinking of the risk to your life, not to your, er – virtue. You won't be able to disguise the fact that you are an extremely attractive young woman, but you could radically alter your appearance and give yourself a different type of beauty.'

'What would be the point of that?'

C.B. put his index finger alongside his big aggressive nose and spoke almost in a whisper. 'Before poor Teddy was done in you can be certain that the people who did the job first found out all

29

they could about him. From the moment they began to suspect that he was spying on them they would have had him followed. That would have led them to his home. It is a thousand quid to a rotten apple that they know you and all about you. The moment you went among them – that is, as your natural self – they would recognize you and realize that you were on their track. Then your number would be up before you had even started. If you are to stand any chance at all you must assume a completely new identity.'

'I see. Yes, of course, you are right. Well, I'll turn myself into a brunette, change my hair-style and do everything else I can think of to alter my appearance.'

'Good! But that is not enough. You must also change your place of residence and live in new quarters under a different name. Would that be difficult for you? I mean, although you tell me you have no family of your own, there are your in-laws. Could you think of a plausible excuse for going away for a while without leaving them your address?'

Mary's mouth tightened, and her voice held a trace of bitterness. 'I won't have to think up an excuse. Teddy's people are the worst type of middle-class snobs. God knows, I've done nothing to antagonize them. It is just that they had pinned their hopes on Teddy marrying some little piece vaguely connected with the peerage, or at least a girl whose parents had money; and I didn't fit into either category. They had no time for me from the beginning and if I took a running jump into a pond tonight, it wouldn't cost any of them a wink of sleep. I have only to shut up the flat and give out that I'm going back to Ireland for the Mordens to count themselves well rid of me.'

'I would advise you to do that then. Move into furnished rooms or a small hotel in some district where you know no one. Take a new name and open an account in it at a local bank, then instruct your own to pay your funds into it as required and to forward your letters there enclosed in envelopes bearing the name you have taken. Shut yourself off as completely as you can from all past associations, and communicate with no one. That includes myself. If these people know that Teddy was working for me they may be watching this place; so don't come here again or to the office, or telephone either. That is unless one of two things happens. One, you have succeeded in getting something definite for me to act on; two, you believe yourself to be in danger of your life. In the latter case, evidence or no evidence, you can count on me to come with all the King's horses and all the King's men racing to your rescue.'

'Thank you, Colonel Verney. I don't expect you will hear any more of me for quite a time; but when you do, I only hope it will be on the first count and not the last. You've been very kind, and at least I can promise not to call for your help without good reason.'

Five minutes later he let her out of the side door into the narrow alley that ran between the studio and the garden of the house next door. As he watched her, a trim figure, head held high, walking with firm step swiftly away, he wished more than ever that he had been able to dissuade her from entering on this dangerous undertaking, or at least to give her some protection.

Back in his armchair he pondered for a long while whether he should pass on to Barney Sullivan what she had told him, inform him of her intentions, and tell him to co-operate with her. But, each working on his own, neither could bring the other into danger, and they provided two sources through either of which he might learn the truth about the murder of Teddy Morden; whereas, if they were associated, should one become suspect, the other would also. So he decided against letting Barney know anything about Mary's proposed activities.

It was a decision that he was to look back on later with bitter regret.

3

A scientist becomes queer

It was three weeks later – to be exact, late in the afternoon on Monday, April 4th – that Colonel Verney received a visit from Squadron Leader Forsby. They were old friends as they had worked together during the war, and afterwards Forsby had been seconded to special Security duties. For the past two years he had been responsible for security at the Long Range Rocket Experimental Establishment, which was situated on a lonely stretch of coast down in Wales.

The Squadron Leader was a small, grey-haired man with a kindly face and a deceptively meek manner, for he could be extremely tough when the necessity arose. As he set down his brief case and took a chair, Verney said: 'Glad to see you, Dick. What sort of trouble has brought you up to the great big wicked city?'

'It's a funny one, C.B.,' the little man replied. 'May be nothing in it, maybe a lot. One of my science babies has gone a bit queer.'

'I thought they were all slightly nuts, anyhow.'

Forsby smiled. 'They're a special breed and live in a different world from us. Ethically many of them are quite irresponsible; but this is a bit out of series.'

'Don't tell me we've got another Nunn May or Fuchs on our hands!'

'I hope not, but he just might be. His name is Otto Khune. He's of German extraction but born American, in Chicago. In 1945 he married an English wife. She was a young Wren signals officer, and they met while she was doing a tour of duty at one of the Naval repair bases that we set up in the U.S. during the war. Evidently she didn't fancy the idea of living in the States, as they both came to England in 1946, and he took British nationality. As he had already been working for the Yanks on Rocket projects, and was fully vouched for, he was given a job by the Ministry of Supply; but the marriage didn't last. His wife divorced him in 1951. His speciality is fuels, and for the past eighteen months he has been top man in that line at the Station.'

'What's he been up to?'

'Nothing. It is simply that his colleagues are worried about his mental state. They all have their own quarters, of course, but the unattached ones feed and spend a good part of their leisure hours in a mess. For some weeks past Khune's behaviour there, particularly when it is getting late at night, has puzzled the others. They say that for short periods he talks and behaves as though he were an entirely different person. Did you happen to read that book *The Three Faces of Eve*?'

C.B. shook his head. 'No, but I heard several people talk about it. I gather it was a report by two professional psychiatrists on an American woman who suffered from split personality.'

'That's right. I found it absolutely fascinating. Normally she was a prudish, dowdy little housewife with a shy, retiring nature, but at times she changed into a gay, bawdy-minded, come-hither girl, bought herself expensive clothes, made herself up fit to kill and went out to hit up the night spots. Then a third individuality emerged when she appeared to be a grave, sensible, responsible woman. And these changes in personality took place not once, but many times actually under the eyes of the men who were examining her; so one can hardly write the whole thing off as a hoax.'

'No, schizophrenia is a mental state now fully accepted by the medical profession. If that's the trouble with this chap Khune, I take it your worry is that while dominated by this new personality he may commit some breach of security?'

'Exactly. When in his normal state we have every reason to believe him to be a patriotic naturalized Briton, but when he has these queer fits he appears to be anything but that. The sort of thing he says is that the only hope for the world is a new deal, starting with the elimination of all the old Imperialist and Capitalist governments; that the United States' oil interests and big business are at the bottom of all the ills that are afflicting mankind, and that true freedom for the individual can only be achieved by complete equality for all.'

'That sounds like the old Communist gags. Do you think he is being got at by the Russians?'

'Maybe, but somehow I don't think it's that. His ideas seem to be more on the old anarchist lines—the complete abolition of all rule with everyone muddling along in little share-and-share alike communities. Anyhow, as he was away this weekend, I decided, on the off-chance that he is in communication with some no-goods and that I might find something that would throw light on the matter, to search his quarters.' Forsby opened his brief-case and taking from it a typescript, added: 'There was nothing of any interest among his correspondence, but in his desk I found a document in his writing, and this is a copy that I took of it.'

Verney put on his spectacles, spread out the paper and read:

I, Otto Helmuth Khune, am making this statement of my free will and while of sound mind in case anything should happen to me, or my sanity later be questioned.

I was born in Chicago on February 8th, 1918, of naturalized American parents who had immigrated from Germany in 1910. They had had six children before the birth of myself and my brother Lothar, we two being my mother's third set of twins. Of the others, three died in infancy, or early childhood, and neither pair of twins was identical, whereas Lothar and I were.

We were the last children born to my parents and the three earlier ones who survived were all girls. One met her death in a fire in 1933, the two others married and live in Detroit and Philadelphia respectively. It is now nearly fifteen years since I have seen either of them and neither plays any part in the matter of which I am about to give an account. Both my parents are now dead.

When I state that Lothar and I are identical twins, I mean that literally. Our physical resemblance was so exact that even people who knew us intimately, at times mistook one of us for the other. Mentally, too, we were extraordinarily alike. We had the same tastes in food, recreations and clothes, and almost invariably shared our likes or dislikes of people. As we grew into our 'teens the latter trait began to show some divergence, but mentally we continued to be remarkably attuned.

Neither of us had any difficulty in reading the other's thoughts

34

and frequently we started to say the same thing at the same moment, so that the similarity of our minds became a joke among our acquaintances. The bond was still closer than that for, if one of us felt ill, the other invariably was, almost at once, subject to the same symptoms. This even extended to the demonstrably physical. On one occasion in a fight at school I had my eye blacked; Lothar felt the blow and soon after his eye also closed and coloured up. On another he fell and broke his ankle, upon which I suffered such acute pain in mine that I had to have the same treatment for such a mishap.

Another thing that we had in common was a highly developed psychic sense. It is said that the seventh child of a seventh child is often endowed in this way; and Lothar and I stood in this relation to my mother, who had been a seventh child. She, too, was psychic to some degree. To a limited extent she could see things in a crystal and tell fortunes by cards, and she had had several death warnings that proved true foreknowledge of the event. But her psychic faculties were not so highly developed as those of Lothar and myself.

We could assess people's characters by the colour of the auras round their heads, which are invisible to the great majority of persons, but were perfectly visible to us. We had hunches about matters which would affect ourselves that invariably proved correct, and could often foretell good or ill fortune that would come to our friends.

We could 'see' things. Our first experience of this was when we were quite young, and was the spirit-form of a dog with which we used to play, without thinking there was anything strange about it, in our bedroom at night. Later we saw several ghosts, and for that reason neither of us would ever pass a cemetery after dark, although in due course we found out that ghosts are more generally pathetic than malignant.

These psychic faculties came to us quite naturally. When young we accepted them as normal and made no special effort to develop them, except in one particular; this was the ability to hypnotize. Both of us possessed it, but Lothar in a much greater degree than myself; perhaps because from the beginning he used to practise on me. To incite me to do ordinary things in this way was, of course, easy, because without any special effort he was able to convey to me his thoughts. But the test of his powers came when he willed me to do things that I was naturally averse to doing. Often he failed, but

35

he was extraordinarily persistent and gradually he gained an ascendancy over me in all things except matters about which I felt particularly strongly.

Lothar and I were both clever and ambitious. We did well at school and later secured degrees with honours in maths and chemistry at the University of Chicago. Our father had been a young professor of mathematics at Leipzig before he decided to emigrate, and afterwards held a post as a senior examiner in the employ of the Chicago Schools Board. In our early days we owed a lot to his private tuition but in due course we entered fields which were beyond his sphere, and after we had taken our finals promising careers were open to both of us.

I secured a well-paid appointment with Weltwerk Schonheim Inc., the big industrial chemists, but Lothar, to most people's surprise – as such posts are not well paid – accepted a junior professorship at the University. His reason for doing so was, however, no secret from me. Beyond all things he loved power; and whereas had he gone into industry he would, for some years at least, have had to knuckle under to his seniors, by becoming a professor he at once achieved a position in which he was able to dominate and mould the minds of a group of mostly intelligent young people.

In the mid-1930s, while still in our 'teens, we had both become members of the Youth Corps of the Deutscher Bund, which was particularly strong in Chicago and was then rapidly expanding there, owing to the vigorous activities of a group of pro-Nazis. Lothar rapidly became prominent among them and by the time the war broke out in Europe, our age then being twenty-one, he was recognized as one of its leaders!

Naturally our sympathies were with Germany, but Lothar felt much more strongly on the matter than I did. He threw himself into a campaign aimed at giving Germany all the help that was possible; whereas my attitude was isolationist, and I maintained that as American citizens we ought to use such influence as we possessed to keep the United States strictly neutral.

In America the repercussions of Pearl Harbour were terrific. Isolationism disappeared overnight and almost to a man the people were behind the Government in its declaration of war on Japan. But in Chicago opinion was far from being so unanimous about the U.S. also entering the war against Germany. On this, for the first time in our lives, Lothar and I not only differed fundamentally, but quarrelled violently. I held that, although it might be distasteful to us, our duty lay in loyalty to the United States and, if need be, we must fight for the country in which we had been born and reared and under whose just laws we had been enabled to earn an honourable living. He held that blood counted for more than the accident of being born outside Germany, that in the triumph of the Nazi ideology lay the only cure for the decadence which infested the great democracies, and that it would be shameful to cling to our easy way of life instead of doing our utmost to help Hitler in his struggle. In short, the United States having declared war on Germany, he declared himself to be personally at war with the United States.

Of course, he was not such a fool as to say so openly, but he obtained exemption from continuing his lectures at the University on the excuse that he intended to join the U.S. Air Force, and shortly afterwards disappeared from Chicago.

The telepathic tie that united us kept me to some extent informed about him as, from time to time when I happened to think of him, I had visual images of his surroundings and people he was with. I felt certain that he had gone to South America and from there, via North Africa and Italy, succeeded in reaching Germany.

Then I saw him working on graphs and scientific data in one of many cubicles that formed a concrete warren underground. One night when I had just got off to sleep, I woke with a start to find myself actually with him. At least that is what it seemed like. He, or I, for I suddenly realized that my ego had got into his body, was lying flat on the ground in pitch darkness. But the darkness lasted only a second, then I was aware of a hideous din and blinding flashes momentarily lighting up the scene all round. I knew then that I was in the middle of an appalling air-raid and that he had been knocked out by blast. The flashes showed a flat countryside, broken only by some groups of hutments and several long mounds with concrete entrances. I was absolutely terrified, but I picked myself up, ran like a hare for the nearest bunker and threw myself inside. In my panic I tripped, went head over heels down the steep stairs and knocked myself out at the bottom.

When I came to I was back in bed in Chicago, feeling like death and with frightful bruises on my head and body. Next day I heard over the radio about the great air-raid on the German Research Works at Peenemünde, and I had no doubt at all that it was there that I had been. I can only imagine that in the instant Lothar passed out he sent a spiritual SOS to me, and that on finding his body empty I entered and saved it.

On another night during the final phase of the war, Lothar called me to him. By then, of course, I had long-since realized that he was one of the scientists working on Long Range Rockets, as at times I had had brief visions of him both at work and taking his pleasure with several different German girls who had jobs at the Establishment. Owing to his hypnotic powers, few women could resist him; but his mind was always too much occupied with serious matters for him to become a slave to that sort of thing, and it has no bearing on what followed.

I think it was again fear that had caused him to call for me, but there was nothing I could have done to help him on this occasion, for he was fully conscious and I remained only an invisible presence by his side, sharing his desperate anxiety. The Russians had just surrounded the Station and entered it, and he was terrified that they would shoot him. But they didn't. They marched him off with a number of other scientists to a railway siding and they were all locked into cattle-trucks.

This experience had no more immediate effect on me than others when I had had mental pictures of Lothar in all sorts of situations, pleasant and unpleasant; but during the next few weeks I became unaccountably ill and suffered from bouts of acute depression. Normal grounds for depression I had none. On the contrary, I had every reason to be extremely happy as, only a few months earlier, I had married Dinah Charnwell, a lovely English girl with whom I was passionately in love, and I had no financial or other worries. The reason for my wretched state was undoubtedly my picking up Lothar's vibrations while, half-starved and desperately uncertain about his future, he was being transported as a prisoner by slow stages into Russia.

By midsummer I began to recover. Subconsciously I was aware that he was receiving better treatment, and not long afterwards, in a dream in which we met, he told me that he had become completely reconciled to putting his knowledge and abilities at the service of the Soviet Union.

I should make it plain that during all this time neither I, my family, nor anyone else with whom we were acquainted had heard from Lothar direct, or through any other source. Yet, when I did meet him again, on his coming to London in 1950, he confirmed that all I had learned of his activities through our psychic tie-up was substantially correct, and I found that in a like manner he had followed the general outline of what had been happening to me.

38

Of that visit of his to London I will postpone writing for the time being, as I am too tired to write much more for the moment. In due course I will include an account of it in a further passage of this document, since I intend to continue it as a record of the mental disturbances with which I have recently become afflicted. I will confine myself now to stating that I feel certain that Lothar is again in England, and that for some sinister purpose of his own he is endeavouring to dominate my mentality. But I will not allow him to succeed. I will not.

'Extraordinary story,' C.B. commented as he laid the document down. 'D'you think there's any truth in it, or that he's just got bats in the belfry?'

'It's true as far as I've been able to check up,' replied Forsby. 'I looked in at the Ministry of Supply before coming here and got them to show me the confidential report that was compiled on Khune when he applied to be taken on for the sort of hush-hush work he's still doing. Most of it was from American sources. It confirms what he says of his family and early life in Chicago, and that he had an identical twin named Lothar. It also confirms that Lothar disappeared from Chicago early in 1942, and states that as he was known to be a rabid Nazi it was suspected that he had left the U.S. with the intention of joining the enemy. The close association of the twins up to that time led the F.B.I. to keep our man under careful observation for a while, but they satisfied themselves that he and his family had lost touch with Lothar; so he was written off as a security risk and O.K'd. for employment in a Government Research Establishment. By the time our Ministry of Supply came into the picture he was married to an English girl, had taken British nationality, and the war with Germany was over; so, without hesitation, he was accepted for secret work.'

'Then it's on the cards that the rest of his story may be true. Telepathy has been scientifically proved beyond question, and it's common knowledge that twins are apt to develop that faculty between themselves much more readily than other people.'

'That's so; but this business of one showing the physical marks of injuries received by the other takes a bit of believing.'

C.B. pulled thoughtfully on his thin-stemmed pipe. 'I think one must admit that it is possible. Mental disturbances can certainly produce physical results. There have been plenty of cases in which neurotic young women have believed themselves pregnant and shown all the symptoms, until a doctor has been called in and examination shown that their swollen tummies contained nothing but a bubble of air. One can't laugh off the religious fanatics, either. There are numerous well-authenticated accounts of nuns who from intense concentration on our Lord's crucifixion have developed stigmata – actual wounds in the palms of their hands and on their insteps, similar to those suffered by Jesus when he was nailed to the cross.'

'Yes, I hadn't thought of that; and, of course, you are right. That certainly makes Khune's story more plausible. Anyhow, we must play for safety by assuming that his brother is trying to get at him, and that makes him a security risk. How do you suggest that I should handle the matter?'

'I don't see that there is much we can do at the moment.'

Forsby smiled. 'Neither do I. That's why I came to you. The work he is doing is too important for me to persuade the Director to take him off it without a much more down-to-earth case than this.'

'I wouldn't advise that, anyway, for the moment. "Satan still finds evil work for idle hands", etc. Much better to keep his mind occupied as much as possible. Naturally you'll keep him under observation. If you think he is likely to give us real trouble you could use these dual personality fits of his as an excuse to have him vetted by the medicos, and get them to lay him off. But if he only continues to simmer, take no action except to try to get hold of the next chunk of this statement that he is writing. From it we might get a bit more data on this Nazi-cum-Bolshie twin of his, Lothar. He sounds a dangerous type, and if he really has come to England the odds are that he's up to no good; so we must do our best to locate and keep an eye on him.'

'Right-o!' Forsby stood up. 'I'll be off now, then, C.B. I've made an early drinks date as well as a dinner date with old friends for this evening, as I so seldom get up from Wales.'

On the following afternoon Verney had a talk with Barney Sullivan. The latter had already put in three progress reports and C.B. had sent for him to discuss the latest. Together they went through it.

Provided as he had been by the office with Union cards and a suitable identity, Barney had met with no difficulty in attending a number of branch meetings, presenting himself in each case as having just moved into the district and wishing to make his number before actually taking a job; and the Communist Party ticket he carried had enabled him to get acquainted with several Union officials who were known Reds. Ample money to stand rounds of drinks to such gentry after the meetings, and his vital personality, were now leading them to treat this new Comrade from Ireland as one of themselves and to talk fairly freely about Party matters with him.

His principal discovery so far had been that the Communists were far from happy about the way their affairs were going. The savage suppression by the Russians of the Hungarian uprising had proved a serious blow to them and cost them several thousand members. During the many months that had since elapsed, although they had worked extremely hard, they had not yet succeeded in making up the loss. For this they were able to take some consolation from the fact that they had engineered many unofficial strikes and that their plans for infiltrating into Union offices had gone better than might have been expected; but now, suddenly, this latter most important item on their programme had become subject to a serious threat.

For many years past the post of General Secretary to the great C.G.T. had been held by a Communist. In a month's time he was due to stand for re-election and a vigorous labour leader named Tom Ruddy, who held strong anti-Communist views, had been nominated to stand against him. Ruddy was far from being a newcomer to labour politics or a nonenity. Although, in 1939 past his first youth, instead of remaining at home in protected employment he had wangled his way into the Army, become a sergeant-major and been decorated with the D.C.M. for knocking out one of Rommel's tanks in Africa. After the war he had stood for Parliament, got in, and made quite a name for himself as a Socialist with plenty of sound common sense; then, on losing his seat in the 1951 election, he had resumed his work as a Union official and steadily mounted in the esteem of his more responsible colleagues. His war record guaranteed him the support of the greater part of the old soldiers in his union; he was a good speaker, had a bluff, forthright manner, and a sense of humour.

All this added up to make him such a popular figure that the Communists were beginning to fear that, in spite of all the secret machinations they might employ, by mid-May it was highly possible that he would have ousted their own man from the key post in the C.G.T. And their anxiety did not end there; for they were afraid that, if Ruddy proved victorious, it would have widespread repercussions throughout the whole Labour movement, leading to many other Communists losing future elections to their opponents.

Verney naturally knew of Tom Ruddy and the forthcoming election, but he was surprised and pleased to hear that Ruddy's prospects seemed so good, and he urged Barney to keep his ears well open for any plot that might be brewing to sabotage Ruddy's chances.

They spent the next half-hour going through a list of the Communists with whom Barney had got into touch at branches of other Unions. In some cases he had been able to pick up small items of information about their private lives which would be added to their dossiers; about others C.B. was able to pass on to him further particulars that might be helpful which had been brought in by the department's network since Barney had started on his mission. Both of them knew that it was this careful collation of a mass of detail, rather than some spectacular break, that usually brought results in the long run.

When they had finished, the Colonel leant back and said: 'I take it you haven't tumbled on anything which might give us a line on poor Morden's killers?'

'Well . . .' Barney hesitated. 'Not exactly.'

'Come young feller!' For once C.B.'s voice held a suggestion of asperity. 'That's no reply. Yes or no?'

Barney pulled a face. 'Sorry, Sir. I ought to have known better than to hedge with you. But it's such an unlikely bet that I thought you might think I'd gone a bit goofy and was wasting my time.'

'Nothing's unlikely in this business. Let's have it.'

'Well, last week I thought I'd go down to Wimbledon and call on Mrs. Morden. I've never met her, but I intended to introduce myself as a member of the firm and say that I'd been sent along to enquire how she was bearing up, and if there was any way in which we could be of help to her. My idea was that now five weeks have elapsed since her husband's death she might be sufficiently recovered from the shock not to mind talking about him, and she might say something about him that hadn't seemed to her to have any bearing on the case, but would to me.'

Verney nodded. 'Good idea. What came of it?'

'She wasn't there. I got it from her neighbours on the other side of the landing that nearly three weeks ago she shut up her flat and went off to Ireland without leaving an address.'

'I see.' To himself, C.B. was thinking, 'So my warning about what she'd be up against didn't shake her, and she's probably putting her lovely head into some hornets' nest by now. Anyhow, it's some comfort that she's taken my advice about going somewhere else to live and severed the ties by which she could be connected with Morden.' Aloud, he added: 'It was from her neighbours you picked up a lead, then?'

'No. It so happened that, while I was still talking to the woman across the landing, the local parson put in an appearance. He had come to call on Mrs. M. for the same sort of reason that I had intended to give. Having drawn a blank we went downstairs together and I offered to give him a lift back to his vicarage in my car. Naturally, we discussed Morden's tragically early death in general terms and it transpired that up to a few months ago he looked on Teddy as one of the ewe-lambs of his parish. Mrs. M. is an R.C. so he hardly knew her. That's why he hadn't called before; and he'd done so then only as a Christian act, to see if she was getting over things all right. But Teddy had been brought up as a staunch Protestant and, although he married out of his own Church, he had continued to attend it regularly and to act as a sidesman.'

Barney paused and ran a hand through his mop of short dark curls. 'That is, up to a few months ago; but quite suddenly he stopped going. At first the padre thought he must be away on holiday, but he ran into him one evening, learnt that he had not been away and naturally enquired the reason for his backsliding. Teddy seemed a bit embarrassed but was persuaded to come to the vicarage for a glass of sherry; then he came clean. Apparently he had become a Theosophist, and could no longer fully believe in the doctrines of the Church.'

Instantly Verney's interest quickened, but he only said: 'That certainly sounds rather queer in a well-balanced chap like Morden. Where do we go from there?'

'The padre tried to argue him out of it; but Teddy wouldn't budge. Apparently he had been attending a course of lectures and séances. He maintained that the things that took place there could not be faked, and he was convinced that the Theosophists held the true key to the after-life. As luck would have it, he mentioned the name of the woman who runs the circle at which these miracles are performed, and the padre remembered it. She is a Mrs. Wardeel.'

'Have you managed to trace her?'

'Yes, Sir. I got her address through the Society for Psychical Research. It is 204 Barkston Gardens. I gathered from the man I got her address from that Theosophists and Spiritualists don't usually hold the same beliefs; but this Mrs. Wardeel seems to be running a cult of her own that combines the two, as at her meetings lectures on the theory of the thing are followed by actual demonstrations of being able to get into touch with the spirit world.'

'And you intend to follow this up?'

'I shall if you don't think it a waste of time Sir. Actually I wrote off to Mrs. Wardeel at once and asked if I could attend one of her meetings. As I couldn't provide any introduction, I thought she might prove a bit cagey about letting a stranger into these mysteries; so I took your tip about using my title to add a bit of snob value to my request. Anyhow, it worked. I had a typed letter back from her secretary saying that Mrs. Wardeel was always happy to spread enlightenment among people of sufficient education to be fitted to receive it, and that I should send a cheque for five guineas as the fee for a course of six lectures. I sent my cheque, and the first is tonight.'

'Go, by all means,' smiled C.B. 'It might lead to something; one never can tell. I wonder, though,' he added after a moment, 'what the real explanation is about Morden. Did he really get bitten with this mumbo-jumbo, or did he deliberately desert his Church because he thought he was being watched and wanted to convince these people that he had fallen completely for the line they were selling him?'

Barney shook his curly head. 'I fear that's a thing that now we'll never know.'

'True enough, young feller. Anyway, don't let them turn you into a spook addict.'

'No fear of that, Sir,' Barney grinned. 'The odds are, though, that I'll get no more than a good laugh over the fun and games by which a few small-time crooks make a living out of the bunch of loonies that I'll find at this place tonight.'

When Barney had gone, Verney took from a drawer in his desk the photograph of Teddy Morden's body. After staring at it for a moment, he thought to himself: 'It ties up. The moment Mary Morden told me about these séances, I felt certain it tied up. She doesn't stand much chance, poor kid; but, if Barney's as astute as I believe him to be, we'll get Morden's murderers yet.'

4

Out of the past

 T HAT evening Fate took a hand, for it was decreed that a few minutes before eight o'clock Barney Sullivan and Mary Morden should meet on the doorstep of 204 Barkston Gardens.

They had approached from different directions and, until they came face to face, she noticed him only as a youngish man wearing a soft hat and a loose-fitting grey tweed overcoat that hung from broad shoulders, while he registered her as a tallish girl with her head well up and a fine springy walk. Then, as they turned together into the square brick porch, the electric light in its roof suddenly revealed clearly to each the face of the other.

Barney had no more than a vague feeling that he had seen Mary somewhere before; after which his mind switched almost instantly to speculate on why such a good-looking young woman should be dabbling in spiritualism instead of spending her evening at some cheerful party, or dining and dancing with a boy-friend.

That he did not know her again was perfectly understandable; for, apart from the fact that it was five years since they had met, Mary had changed her appearance in every way that was possible. Her smooth plaits had gone; she now wore her hair shoulder length and curled at the ends, and had had it dyed a rich, dark brown. Her thickish eyebrows had also been dyed, and plucked so that they remained fairly thick at the inner ends but tapered away to points which gave the impression that they turned up slightly at the ends. She was wearing more make-up: a much

45

heavier shade of powder, that gave her fair skin the bronze tint
of a brunette who has recently been sun-bathing, mascara on her
lashes, eye-shadow, and a magenta lip-stick with which she had
succeeded in changing a little the shape of her mouth. Her
experience of making up while in cabaret had stood her in good
stead, and even her ex-neighbours at Wimbledon would have been
unlikely to recognize the quietly turned out Mrs. Morden in this
new presentation by which she had deprived herself of her golden
hair, but become much more of a *femme fatale*.

On the other hand, at the first glance, Mary recognized Barney
and her heart gave a jump that seemed to bring it right up into
her mouth. Her face would have betrayed her had he not at that
moment turned to ring the front-door bell. It was answered almost
immediately by an elderly woman servant. Barney politely
stepped aside for Mary to enter, then followed her in.

As the servant took his coat and hat, Mary walked on towards
a middle-aged woman who was standing in the middle of the
square hall. She was a large lady with a big bust on which dangled
several necklaces of semi-precious stones. From her broad, flat
face several chins sloped down into a thick neck, the whole being
heavily powdered. Her eyes were a very light blue and unusually
widely spaced. Upon her head was piled an elaborate structure of
brassy curls, and her whole appearance suggested to Barney the
type of rich Edwardian widow whose Mecca used to be the Palm
Courts of Grand Hotels. He assumed, rightly, that she was
Mrs. Wardeel.

To Mary she extended, held high, a carefully manicured and
heavily beringed hand, as she said in a deep voice: 'Ah, Mrs.
Mauriac; or perhaps, now that you have become a regular
attendant at our little gatherings, you will allow me to call you
Margot?'

'So, she is French,' Barney was thinking. But actually Mary
had been mainly governed in the choice of a *nom de guerre* by
making it fit with the initials on her handbags, and other personal
belongings, that it would have been a nuisance to have to alter.
It was only as an afterthought that it occurred to her that, as she
had to take another name for a while, it would be rather fun to
assume the sort of one that might have been chosen for a foreign
film-star. Meanwhile, Mrs. Wardeel continued to gush at her.

'You know, I always take a special interest in the young who
seek the great truths – young physically, I mean; for, of course, we

46

are all young whenever we get away from these wretched bodies that anchor us here. Not, of course, my dear that that applies to you. But there is no escape from the advancing years, is there? And for the young to learn early that they will never really grow old is such a marvellous protection against the time when one's looks begin to fade. I am sure that one of the Masters must have you in his particular care to have guided you to us so early in your present incarnation.'

As Mary smiled and murmured a few appropriate words, Barney came up behind her. Mrs. Wardeel turned to him, again offered the beringed hand, and made a gracious inclination of her big synthetically-gold-crowned head.

'Ah; and now a new seeker after the Light. But we have two tonight. Are you Mr. Betterton or Lord Larne?'

Barney pressed the slightly flabby fingers and replied with a gravity that he felt the occasion called for. 'I'm Lord Larne, and I am most grateful to you for allowing me to – er – come here and learn about the sort of things that really matter.'

'You are welcome,' she said in her deep voice. 'I welcome you in the name of the Masters. All who come here are sent by them; but only upon trial. Do not expect too much at once. Those who show scepticism and demand proof for everything reveal by that that they are not yet sufficiently advanced to be worthy of approaching the higher spheres. But, if you are patient and receptive, stage by stage the great truths will be unveiled to you.'

Three more people had arrived so, turning to Mary, she added, 'Mrs. Mauriac, would you take our new friend, Lord Larne, through to the meeting room?'

Mary's heart was still pounding, but her face now showed nothing of her inward agitation. On Mrs. Wardeel's introducing her to Barney, they exchanged a conventional smile, then walked side by side towards a room at the back of the house. As they did so, she was wondering what could possibly have brought to such a gathering the type of man she knew him to be, and, even more extraordinary, why he should be using a title to which she believed he had no right.

The room they entered was long and fairly broad and looked larger than it was in fact because all its furniture – except a desk at one end – had been removed and replaced by seven rows of fold-up wooden chairs. Some twenty people had already taken their seats. Most of them were middle-aged and fairly prosperous looking; there were more women than men, and among the former were two Indian ladies wearing caste marks and saris.

Barney ran his eye swiftly over such of their faces as he could see from where he stood and decided that they looked a more normal crowd than he had expected – in fact, they might all have been collected in one swoop by clearing and transporting the occupants of the lounge of any of the better-class South Kensington hotels. Mary nodded a greeting to a few of them, then took the chair that he was holding for her. As he sat down beside her he said:

'I gather that you are one of the older inhabitants of this village, Mrs. Mauriac?'

'Oh, I . . .' her mouth felt dry and her voice threatened to rise from nervous tension. With an effort she got it under control. 'I'm far from that. This is only the third meeting that I've attended.'

Barney noted that she had no French accent, then he replied: 'Even that puts you quite a bit ahead of me. Do you find the teaching easy to follow?'

'Some of it.' To cover her confusion Mary hurried on. 'I find the arguments for believing in Reincarnation simple and convincing, and I've become terribly interested in that. But I'm still a long way from understanding the Theosophical doctrine.'

'Really!' He raised his eyebrows. 'I was under the impression that Theosophists were anti-doctrinaire. I thought they concerned themselves only with getting at the original wisdom that is said to lie at the root of all the great religions, but most of which has since been obscured by the teachings introduced by many generations of ignorant priests.'

'That's quite true; Theosophy does not conflict with Christianity or Buddhism in their best sense. But all the same it has its own doctrine, and much of it seems awfully complicated to me. You see, it isn't as though this was a course of lectures in which one starts at the beginning; each is on a different aspect of the ancient teaching, and newcomers like you and I have to do our best to pick up what we can as we go along.'

Having by this time had a chance to take full stock of Mary, Barney was congratulating himself on his luck in acquiring so unexpectedly such a glamorous companion with whom to listen to what he anticipated would be a lot of twaddle; but he was temporarily prevented from developing the acquaintance further by the arrival of an elderly lady, leaning on an ebony walking stick, who greeted Mary with a smile, took the chair on her other side, and began to talk to her about the last meeting.

During the next five minutes another dozen or so people arrived, including a fat, squat Indian wearing thick-lensed glasses, and with protruding teeth, who from his bowing and smiling to right and left seemed to know nearly everyone there. Then Mrs. Wardeel came in followed by a small, bald man in a dark grey suit who looked as if he might have been a bank manager. He walked round to a chair behind the desk while she paused beside it. Silence fell and she said:

'Dear followers of the Path, Mr. Silcox is well known to most of you. We are blessed in having him with us again. Old friends and new alike will, I know, benefit from another of his talks. This evening he is going to speak to us on the True Light to be found in the Gospels.'

Mrs. Wardeel took a seat that had been kept for her in the front row and Mr. Silcox stood up. Without any unctuous preamble he went straight into his subject, which was to place a new interpretation on many of the sayings of Jesus Christ, given the assumption that He believed in Reincarnation, was Himself in His last incarnation, and was really referring to such matters most of the time.

According to Mr. Silcox, when our Lord spoke of His 'Father', He was referring not to a father either physical or divine, but to His own complete personality built up during countless incarnations, only a fragment of which He had brought down with Him to earth.

This argument was based on the Reincarnationist belief that everyone's parents are chosen for them only to ensure that they are given the sort of start in life best suited to provide them with an opportunity to learn whatever lessons are decreed for them in their new incarnation; and that they are their own father in the sense that their egos have already been formed by certain of their experiences during a long succession of past lives.

In support of this contention the speaker drew attention to that passage in the Second Commandment to the effect that God would 'visit the sins of the fathers upon the children even unto the third and fourth generation'.

'Could any sane person,' Mr. Silcox asked, 'believe a just god capable of showing such vicious malice as to threaten the innocent

49

and unborn with dire chastisement for evil done by their physical parents or grandparents?' Clearly the explanation of this apparently harsh decree was that, each of us being spiritually the child of the personality we had created for ourselves in previous lives, if we did evil in our present incarnation we should have to pay for it in the future, and it might take us three or four more incarnations before we had fully worked off our debt.

All this was new to Barney and, far from being bored as he had expected, he found it deeply interesting; so for the next half-hour he gave his mind almost entirely to following Mr. Silcox's interpretation of the sayings of Our Lord.

Mary, on the other hand, was hardly listening. The main arguments for Reincarnation were already known to her, and her thoughts had gone back five years to the last time she had seen Barney. That had been in the grey dawn of early morning in a room of a small hotel in Dublin. He had not long got out of the bed they had shared and, having dressed, he had kissed her goodbye with the cheerful words:

'I'll see you again soon, sweetheart, and we'll have better fun next time.' But there had been no next time and, although she had searched high and low for him, she had never seen him again until tonight. With a sick feeling she went back in her mind over the whole sordid story of her life as Mary McCreedy.

Her mother had earned a precarious living as a small-part actress in musical comedy, vaudeville and anything else that offered. About her father she knew nothing except that, according to her mother, he was a naval officer and had been lost at sea while she was still an infant. As no reference was ever made to any of his family she suspected that he had never married her mother. In any case, whether or not she was illegitimate, she knew that to have been the case with her brother, Shaun, who had been born three years after herself. His father had been a Dublin business man, known to her during her childhood as Uncle Patrick. She assumed now that in those days he largely supported the household, as they had lived in reasonable comfort and she and her brother had been educated privately. But when she was fifteen 'Uncle' Patrick had died, and they had had to move to a much poorer part of the city.

Shortly afterwards her mother had taken her away from the Convent she was attending, to have her taught dancing. The following year she appeared in Pantomime and, as she was a well-

50

developed girl for her age she had, by lying about it, got herself a job when barely seventeen in the Cabaret of a Dublin night-club.

Meanwhile her mother, having failed to find another permanent protector, and harassed by debt, had taken to the bottle; then, before Mary had been many months in Cabaret, on the way home one Saturday night in a state of liquor her mother had been knocked down and killed by a bus. After that Mary had had to move with her young brother into two rooms, and had become the sole support of their little household.

The night-club where she worked would not have been worthy of the name by continental standards, so hedged about was it with restrictions imposed by a Municipality under the moral influence of the Roman Catholic Church. There were no near-nude floor shows, nor was drinking permitted till the small hours of the morning. In fact, it was little more than a restaurant that hired a troupe of girls to sing and dance in little numbers which would not give offence to family parties and, in theory at least, the girls were all respectable. But, of course, between shows they were expected to act as dance-hostesses to any man who might ask them and so, inevitably, they were inured to receiving certain propositions.

Mary had been aware that some of her companions owed their smarter clothes and expensive trifles to accepting such offers, and she had not got on less well with any of them on that account; but at eighteen the teaching of the nuns still had a strong influence upon her. Moreover, she cherished romantic ideas that in due course a Prince Charming would come along, and that she would be shamed if, on his marrying her, she were not still a virgin. Yet, with a young brother to keep as well as herself, although the Church school to which he went had waived his fees since their mother's death, she found it ever harder to make ends meet.

That had been the situation when she met Barney Sullivan. He had come in one evening with several other young roisterers and picked her out to dance with. She had been attracted at once by his merry smile and carefree gaiety, but at the end of the evening he had casually given her a handsome tip and made no suggestion of seeing her again, However, in the weeks that followed he had come in on several occasions after dinner with three or four other well-off young fellows out for a good time, danced with her, and given her the impression that he had fallen

51

for her. Then one night he had turned up with the same little crowd of friends, this time slightly tight, but most cheerfully so; and, after sharing a bottle of champagne with her, he had suggested that she should sleep with him. On her making her usual reply that she was 'not that sort of a girl' he had refused to believe her, declaring with a laugh that all the girls there did if a chap could make it worth their while; but he had not pressed her further.

A few nights later he had come there again, and that night it so happened that she was in desperate trouble. Her young brother, who was in his last term at school, was the treasurer of the football club, and he had confessed to her that afternoon that he had spent the money entrusted to him. If he could not replace it by the following day he would be found out and branded as a thief. It was only a matter of six pounds odd, but she had not got it and had already had from the management an advance on her wage to pay the rent. She had intended to humiliate herself by attempting to borrow from some of the other girls, but that would have meant a further debt round her neck that it would be a struggle to repay. Barney, flushed with champagne and with a pocket full of money from a lucky day at the races, had offered her twenty pounds if she would do as several of the other girls had, and go to bed with him. Attracted to him as she was, and harassed by her anxiety about her brother, she had given way to his pleading.

No sooner had they left the club than she began to regret her decision and, for her, the next hour was one of misery. Although she was a normal healthy girl fully capable of passion, she was totally inexperienced; so a combination of panic, guilt and – much as she needed the money – shame at having succumbed to earning it in this way, temporarily rendered her frigid. Barney, feeling on top of the world, and his finer senses dulled by the wine he had drunk, swiftly set himself to overcome her unresponsiveness. It was only afterwards, as she lay weeping in his arms, that he realized to his considerable distress that she had been a virgin.

But for her matters had not ended there. At first she had put down his non-reappearance at the club to disappointment in her; then, to her horror, she realized that she was going to have a baby. Instantly she jumped to the conclusion that he was purposely avoiding her because he suspected that he might have given her one. She did not know his address and, although she asked all sorts of people, none of them knew it either. It was not until

52

some weeks later that a friend of his came to the club and was able to tell her that he had gone off to America quite suddenly, without even saying goodbye to his circle of boon companions.

Meanwhile her life had become one long agony of anxiety and fear. In vain she lit candles and prayed morning, noon and night to Our Lady for a natural release from her condition; her prayers remained unanswered. At length she confided in one of the other, older, girls and learned that she could be got out of her trouble; but it was going to cost a lot of money. As she was as hard-up as ever, and the matter was urgent, there was only one thing for it; her friend arranged for her to borrow the bulk of the money from a money-lender, and she had to begin accepting the offers of men who came to the club, whether she liked them or not, as the only means of repaying the instalments on the loan.

She soon learned that such encounters were not always unpleasant, but in most instances she found them loathsome and degrading. Moreover, as the club was very far from being thought of as a centre of prostitution, advances of that kind were made to the girls there only occasionally, and it soon became apparent to her that Barney had treated her with exceptional generosity; which meant that a considerable time must elapse before she was entirely free from her debt.

Those months remained vivid in her memory: the horror and pain of the illegal operation; her misery at having to give up practising her religion because she could not bring herself to confess to having committed so grievous a sin; the nausea that had at times assailed her from having to submit to the caresses of half-drunken men; the awful strain of having to pretend to enjoy it when, tired from a long evening's dancing and aching for her bed, she had been driven miles out into the country by some stranger to be made love to in the back of his car; and the shame aroused in her by the sneering looks or lecherous grins of slatternly chambermaids who had shown her up with men to tawdry bedrooms in dubious little hotels.

And her penance had lasted longer than it need have done, since, to bring some cheer into her life, she had given way to the understandable weakness of using part of the money she earned to buy better clothes and many small luxuries which she could not before afford. With the interest on her debt, it had been ten months before she had managed to get clear finally. Then, shortly afterwards, during a fortnight's holiday at the seaside, she had met Teddy Morden; and he had taken her to London, freeing her from her past, and giving her his love, his name and a happy married life.

Yet even four years as a contented wife had not made her feelings about Barney Sullivan less bitter. It was his act which had resulted in those ten months during which she had hardly known a day free from anxiety, or disgust with herself at the life she had been forced into leading! It never entered her mind that if a man paid a girl to go to bed with him he was entitled to assume that she knew how to look after herself, and was not responsible for what might become of her afterwards. As she saw it, he should have known that he might have put her in the family way and come to the club again to find out if she was all right; instead of which, as it appeared to her, he had deliberately refrained from doing so from fear that she might be pregnant by him, then gone off to America leaving her to her unhappy fate. In consequence, in her mind he had become the symbol of all that is mean and contemptible in a man.

With a little start she suddenly realized that Mr. Silcox had come to the end of his talk. During the ten minutes that followed several members of the audience asked him questions, which he answered with easy assurance. Then Mrs. Wardeel moved a vote of thanks to him which met with decorous applause, after which she said:

'Now, dear fellow followers of the Way, let us rearrange the chairs and see what Mrs. Brimmings has in store for us. No doubt some of you will have heard of Mrs. Brimmings. From the accounts I have had she is a remarkably gifted medium and under her control, the Chinese Mandarin Chi-Ling – whose last incarnation took place some two hundred years ago – she is able to make contact with not only the first, but also the second and third, astral planes. We are most fortunate in having her with us tonight.'

Everyone stood up. The unoccupied chairs were put back against the wall and the rest formed into a large circle, in the middle of which a chair was placed for Mrs. Brimmings. As Mrs. Wardeel led her forward to it, Barney saw that she was a small, faded elderly woman with grey hair scragged back into a bun, and wearing rather shoddy clothes. It occurred to him that she might easily be taken for a charwoman, and a moment later she said to Mrs. Wardeel in accents that reinforced that impression:

54

'May I 'ave a rug, dear. Me poor feet get so cold when I'm out of me body.'

A rug was duly fetched and wrapped round her, then the company settled down and, crossing their arms, all linked hands with their neighbours. Before taking her place in the circle Mrs. Wardeel switched out all the lights except one with a heavy blue shade, thus darkening the room to a faint bluish gloom, in which the medium could be seen only as a dark shape; then she said in a deep whisper:

'For the two new friends who are with us tonight, I shall give the usual warning, Whatever may happen, no one must break the circle by letting go the hand of his neighbour. To do so would be to place the medium in grave danger by bringing her spirit back to her body too suddenly. And no one should address her unless called on to do so.'

After that, silence fell, broken only by an occasional half-suppressed cough or the faint creak of one of the wooden chairs as someone eased his position. To Barney the silence seemed to continue for a long time, which he judged to be about twenty minutes, although in fact it was little more than ten. But it had the effect of creating a definite atmosphere of tension and expectancy.

At length a faint blob of light appeared high up in a corner of the room. It flickered about uncertainly for a little then, to Barney's surprise, descended on his own forehead. With difficulty he suppressed an exclamation; but, almost instantly, it moved again and came to rest for a moment on the forehead of a man nearly opposite to him, after which it disappeared.

'Ah!' Mrs. Wardeel gave a heavy sigh of satisfaction, then declared in an audible whisper. 'All is favourable. Our two new friends are accepted on probation to sit with us in the mystic circle.'

Again silence fell. It lasted for about five minutes and Barney was becoming a little bored when, without the least warning, an illuminated trumpet appeared a few feet above the medium's head and from it there came a long musical note.

In a flash it was gone, but the faintly seen form of the medium seemed to be writhing from side to side and she was breathing heavily. After a moment she became quite still and from her came a voice utterly unlike her normal one, which said with a slight foreign accent, but clearly and with authority:

'Once more you disturb my meditations. Beware that you do not do so without good cause. Yet I will always descend among those swathed in the bonds of a present incarnation to bring them that need me comfort and reassurance.'

There was a pause, then the voice went on. 'You who are now called Josephine Carden. Why do you still seek to get into touch with him who was your husband? You have already been told by a companion of mine, known as Little Violet, that all is well with him, and that he wishes to forget his last time here, so that he may the sooner make progress towards a higher state.'

A low sob came from a fat woman not far away from Barney on his left, and her body threatened to slump forward, but was held back by her neighbours keeping a firm grip on her hands.

'Hush, dear,' murmured Mrs. Wardeel. 'That was most unkind of the Mandarin; but another time some other guide may bring you comfort.'

'Silence woman!' shouted the Mandarin. 'My time is not to be wasted or my judgment questioned by such as you. Silcox! Henry Silcox, I have good tidings for you. The Master K.H. has consented to your passing the Second Grade of Initiation.'

The little man who had given the talk gave a gasp and murmured, 'I am humbly grateful. I shall do my utmost to be worthy.'

There came a short pause, then the voice spoke again. 'Betterton. There is one here named Betterton?'

'Yes, yes!' exclaimed the other newcomer, opposite Barney, on whose forehead the light had also rested.

'You seek knowledge of the wife who recently cast off her fleshly envelope. She is happy. She is united again with the girl child who was sufficiently filled with grace to leave you while in her last life still young in years. Your wife bids you marry again for the sake of the other children.'

So it went on for about twenty minutes, the strong, vibrant, slightly foreign voice throwing out bits of information or commands to some dozen people in the audience. Then silence fell again. Some minutes passed and the medium began to groan. Mrs. Wardeel broke the circle, went over to her and softly stroked her forehead until she came round, then asked:

'Are you feeling all right, Mrs. Brimmings? Can we put the lights up now?'

'Yes, dear.' Mrs. Brimmings spoke again with the voice of a

56

cockney char. 'Mister Chi-Ling always takes a lot out of me; but I'll be meself again soon as I've 'ad a cup-o'-tea an' a bite to eat.'

As Mr. Silcox switched on the lights, Barney made a quick assessment of the performance he had seen; and he was fully convinced that it was a performance. It had been well put on and superficially convincing; but he had little doubt that the light and the trumpet were permanent properties of the room frequently put to use at these meetings. So, too, could a sound apparatus be installed beneath Mrs. Brimmings's chair through which someone outside the room had made Chi-Ling's pronouncements; or else the medium was quite a different personality from that which she normally appeared, and was a clever actress, highly skilled in voice production. As for the Mandarin's messages, suitable ones could easily be cooked up to sound impressive to the older members of the circle with whose circumstances Mrs. Wardeel should have had little difficulty in becoming acquainted. That, too, doubtless applied to the newcomer, Betterton, whereas to himself, about whom Mrs. Wardeel had had no means of finding anything out, no message had been given.

Counting heads, he reckoned that Mrs. Wardeel must have netted about thirty guineas on the evening. Silcox, he thought, was probably honest and had given his talk for nothing, while Mrs. Brimmings's rake-off for her collaboration was, perhaps, a fiver; so that left a handsome profit and, as the meetings were held weekly, he decided that Mrs. Wardeel was running quite a useful little racket.

As the circle broke up he released Mary's hand and asked her, 'Have you ever received a message at one of these sittings?'

She shook her head. 'No, not yet; although I always concentrate during them, hoping to hear something of a person I knew who has not long been dead.'

'Passed over, you mean,' he corrected her with a grin.

She gave him a queer look, his levity giving her cause to wonder more than ever what had brought him to such a gathering. But she turned away without reply, and they mingled with the others who were now filing out of the room.

Crossing the hall, the little crowd entered a smaller room at one side of which there was a buffet with tea, coffee and light refreshments. There a babble of conversation had broken out, and two other men, one the fat Indian with the pebble glasses and hideous protruding teeth, and another whom Mary greeted as

57

Mr. Nutting, came up to her. Anxious not to lose touch with her, Barney swiftly forestalled the others in getting her a cup of coffee and a plate of sandwiches. When he rejoined her she asked him if she had heard aright that he was Lord Larne, and on his smilingly confirming that, she introduced him to Mr. Nutting and the Indian, whose name was Krishna Ratnadatta.

For a short while the four of them talked together about the séance, then Nutting, who proved to be an earnest bore, button-holed Barney and, to his annoyance, entered on a long description of how he had been led to take the Path of Discipleship. But Barney listened to him with only half an ear so, although Ratnadatta was speaking to Mary in a low confidential voice, he happened to overhear him say:

'These meetings off Mrs. Wardeel's, they are for the young enquirer very well. Yes, very well for those who, in this incarnation, are at the beginning off the Path. But you, Mrs. Mauriac, I am told by the insight that I haf been given, are already well advanced upon it.'

Barney's interest at once being aroused, he managed to keep Mr. Nutting going with an occasional appreciative nod, while concentrating on the continuance of the conversation between Mary and the Indian, to whom she replied:

'I should like to think so, Mr. Ratnadatta.'

'That it ees so, I know, Mrs. Mauriac,' were the Indian's next words. 'At the two previous meetings after weech we haf talked together I haf by your quick understanding been much impressed. Such understanding ees not given to those who in previous incarnations haf not learnt a lot. Haf you at times perhaps had glimpses off your previous lives?'

'No,' said Mary, 'I'm afraid I can't claim that I have.'

'No matter. Some off us bring down with us from our Vase of Memory much more than others. But that ees no criterion off how well filled up with past experience a person's vase may be. In some case the Great Ones decree that far memory be obscured, for a while, for good purpose. So it ees with you I think. To yourself you owe it to reopen your waking mind to the sub-conscious, so that you may bring new strengths for progress on the astral plane.'

'I am endeavouring to recall my dreams and write them down, as the lecturer last week told us that we should.'

'Good; very good. Such training ees valuable; but to succeed that way require much time.' Mr. Ratnadatta paused for a moment then went on. 'There are other roads; channels by weech a person can reach the astral plane with swiftness, but such are great secrets and you will not learn off them here.'

'Could you perhaps . . . ?' Mary said hesitantly.

'It ees possible. But on yourself everything would depend. You would haf to give all your mind to the great work. Perhaps your circumstances do not permit that, eh? Your husband, you haf tell me, passed on two years ago; but perhaps you haf children, or parents to take great part off your thought?'

Out of the corner of his eye, Barney saw Mary shake her head. 'No, I have no family and am quite alone in the world.'

'Good, very good. Then, if you haf the will to devote yourself, I will giff thought to introducing you to another circle. Not like this, but one in weech power can be called down; real power by those who haf penetrate far into the mysteries.'

'I'd be most terribly grateful if you would.'

'First we must talk more together, before I can make final decision. For this are you agreeable to meet me on Saturday evening?'

'Yes; at any time you like.'

'Good; very good. Meet me plees then at entrance to Sloane Square Tube Station at eight o'clock, and I giff you dinner.'

Flashing his protruding teeth at Mary in an oily smile, Mr. Ratnadatta bowed to her politely and moved away. Murmuring an apology to the verbose Mr. Nutting, Barney swiftly recaptured her and, seeing that the party was beginning to break up, asked:

'May I see you home, Mrs. Mauriac; or, anyhow, to your Tube or bus stop?'

She hesitated only a second before replying, 'Yes, if you like. Thank you. I shall be walking; but it's no great distance as I have a flat in the Cromwell Road.'

Having made their adieux to Mrs. Wardeel, they collected their coats and left the house together. Barney was a fluent and amusing talker, but on this occasion he confined himself to serious comment on the evening's events, as he feared that if he showed levity about the séance, or showed curiosity about his companion's private life, she might resent it. But while he talked his mind was functioning independently and again assessing Mrs. Wardeel's set-up.

He knew well enough that, apart from the typical old lag, it is extremely difficult to pick out, simply by their faces, criminals from law-abiding citizens. But from the general behaviour of the people at the meeting, he had come to the conclusion that the majority were either quite harmless, serious students of the occult, or sensation seekers. Only the Indian had struck him as possibly being a dangerous type, and his view had been reinforced by Ratnadatta's saying to Mary that he could introduce her to another circle of much higher-powered occultists. It seemed just possible that the Indian had made the same proposal to Morden, and that through accepting it he had got himself involved in Black Magic, then tried too late to break away and been murdered to prevent him betraying the dark secrets of the cult.

Mary, with still vivid memories of her late husband's night-mares, in which he had mentioned an Indian, had encouraged Ratnadatta's advances from her first visit to Mrs. Wardeel's, in the hope that he might be the man Teddy had had on his mind; and now, while listening to Barney's small-talk about the meeting, she was congratulating herself on being, as she believed, on the right track, and having an appointment to meet Ratnadatta privately on Saturday, which might enable her definitely to link him with the crime.

Barney had already decided that he, too, must cultivate the Indian with the object of also putting himself in the way of securing an invitation to join this more secret circle; but that would take time, and the lovely Mrs. Margot Mauriac, with whom he was walking, was already on the brink of receiving such an invitation. If, therefore, he could keep in touch with her, that might prove a short cut to learning a lot more about Ratnadatta. And in this instance, he felt with pleasurable anticipation that, for once, duty opened a most attractive prospect.

In consequence, when they reached the tall old house half-way along the Cromwell Road, in which Mary had rented a furnished flat on the fourth floor, he said with his most winning manner:

'You know, I really have found this evening thrilling. It has opened up all sorts of new speculations and ideas in my mind. But I don't know a soul with whom I can discuss them – that is, except yourself. Would you . . . I know it's awful cheek on such a short acquaintance . . . but would you have dinner with me one night? I've got to attend a business meeting tomorrow evening, but what about Thursday or Friday? Please say yes?'

For a moment she looked straight at him; then, with a rather tight-lipped smile, she said, 'All right then. If you like. Let's make it Thursday.'

'Splendid!' he laughed. 'I'll call for you here at seven-thirty.'

A shade awkwardly they shook hands. She turned away, and as she walked up the steps to the porch, he waved her a cheerful 'Good night'.

Mary had not been taken in by his apparent eagerness to discuss the occult. She knew too well the way a man looks at a woman when she has suddenly aroused a physical interest in him. As she went upstairs to her flat, she was thinking:

'You rotten little cad. So you'd like to try to seduce me again! Lord Larne indeed! I suppose you've found that posing as a Lord makes it easier for you to put girls in the family way then leave them in the lurch. All right, Mr. Barney Sullivan. This time it is I who will lead you up the garden path. I'll play you until you're near crazy to have me, then drop you like a brick.'

5

The Brotherhood of the Ram

BARNEY gave considerable thought to where he should take Mary to dinner on the Thursday. It had to be a restaurant at which he was not known as Mr. Sullivan. That left open to him most of the more expensive places; for although his salary, coupled with the allowance his uncle made him, enabled him to live quite comfortably, he was not well enough off to go to them except occasionally when he was on a job and the bill, or a good part of it, could be charged up to his expense account. In this case that applied, and he wanted to do Mary well; moreover, he wanted to dance with her afterwards. But he had said nothing about that and spoken only of a quiet dinner; so, even if he turned up in a black tie, the odds were that she would not be wearing the sort of clothes in which she would be happy for him to take her to the Berkeley or the Savoy. At length he decided to go in a dark suit and take her to the Hungaria, as he had been there only a few times as a member of other people's parties, the food and band were good, and evening dress optional. So, using his title, he rang up and booked a table.

She was ready for him when he called for her in a taxi, and, as he expected, was dressed in a cocktail frock. At the sight of her his pulses quickened slightly, for she struck him as even better looking than as he had seen her in his thoughts during the past two days. Nevertheless, their evening together did not run with anything like the smoothness that he had hoped.

The reason for that was not far to seek. Ostensibly they were

62

a well-matched young couple out for the sole purpose of enjoying one another's company; but actually each of them was deliberately deceiving the other, and finding it necessary to lie about nearly every question that cropped up.

Both, in preparation for the meeting, had thought out a false past and present for themselves. Barney had decided to take the role of the late Lord Larne's eldest son, who had been killed with his father in the aeroplane crash. He said that he had spent most of his life in Kenya and was over in England only on a long visit to go into the possibilities of opening a new Travel Agency, with London tie-ups, in Nairobi.

Mary, one of whose fairly regular and more pleasant sources of income during her black year in Dublin had been a Customs Officer, now gave her late husband that role; adding, as an explanation of her name, that he had been quite a lot older than herself, come to England with the Free French and, after the war, taken British nationality. She said that he had died two years earlier as a result of a heavy crate, not properly secured to a crane, falling upon him; and, lest her faint suggestion of an Irish accent should stir old memories in Barney's mind, she told him that she was 'Liverpool' Irish and had been brought up in that city.

Her occupation she gave as a free-lance model, and in that there was a substratum of truth. She had picked up the rudiments of such work from her mother, who had eked out her earnings as an actress in that way, and had herself a few times earned a small fee for showing dresses in one of Dublin's less expensive shops; so, during the past fortnight, she had taken it up again to supplement her pension and, now that she was older and had more poise, the agent she had gone to had already found no difficulty in getting her several bookings.

But on both sides the past was a subject giving constant rise to unexpected questions calling for swiftly thought up lies by way of answer; so neither of them could be natural and at ease. Moreover the ostensible reason for their meeting – to talk of the occult – failed to bridge the gap because she knew little more about it than he did. In consequence, finding her decidedly reluctant to say much about herself, he was reduced during the latter part of dinner to giving her accounts of the doings of the Mau-Mau, while praying that she had not read the book upon which he was drawing for experiences as though they were his own.

However, when they took the floor, matters improved somewhat, for he was a naturally good dancer and she had been a professional. They spoke little but each found in the other an excellent partner and thoroughly enjoyed the smooth rhythm. While they danced the best part of two hours sped swiftly by, and by then the fact that they were both playing a part had slipped to the back of their minds. Feeling now that he could open up on a matter that concerned her personally with less chance of her resenting it, a little before midnight Barney ordered more coffee and liqueurs then asked her:

'How well do you know that Indian chap who was at the meeting?'

'Mr. Ratnadatta?' Her voice was casual. 'Oh, he's just one of several acquaintances I've made at Mrs. Wardeel's; although, as a matter of fact, I've learnt more from talking to him after the meetings than at them. But why do you ask?'

'Well . . .' Barney hesitated a second. 'I suppose I ought not to have listened to your conversation with him; but I couldn't help overhearing him offer to take you to some much more advanced occult circle, of which he is a member.'

'He didn't. He only said he would consider doing so after he had had another talk with me.'

'Yes. I gathered that. But he asked you to have dinner with him on Saturday, didn't he? And it's unlikely that he would have done that unless he had pretty well made up his mind already that you were a suitable candidate.'

She smiled. 'I hope he does. He implies that Mrs. Wardeel's parties are only kindergarten stuff, and I'm sure he knows what he is talking about. It would be terribly exciting to belong to a group possessing real power.'

Barney gave her an uneasy glance. Now that he had spent an evening at close quarters with the beautiful 'Margot' he was beginning to feel an interest in her that had nothing to do with his job; and as he thought it highly probable that Ratnadatta's circle practised Black Magic, he did not at all like the idea of her getting herself mixed up with that kind of crowd. On the other hand, he did want her to lead him to it. How to handle this dilemma worried him considerably; but, after a moment's thought, he decided that, even if it meant prolonging his investigation, he ought to try to head her off, so he said:

'I don't know much about the occult, but one thing about it is clear. There are only two ways of obtaining power by supernatural means. One is by leading the life of a Saint; the other is by becoming a disciple of the Devil. Like you, I'm talking of real power now; and you may be right in believing that this chap Ratnadatta can lead you to it. If so, maybe he's a saint, but I'd lay a packet that he and his pals turn out to be Black Magicians.'

Mary was also of that opinion, but she did not admit it. Instead she said, 'Not necessarily. They may be advanced practitioners of Yoga.'

'Yes; I suppose that's a possibility. Still, the idea of your letting him become your, er – guide, philosopher and friend, worries me.'

'That's nice of you.' Her voice held only a suspicion of sarcasm.

'I mean,' he persisted, 'that you might get yourself involved in something pretty unpleasant if you keep this date with him on Saturday.'

'I am not in the habit of breaking dates, once I've made them. Anyway, he is only giving me dinner.'

'You never know. He might suggest taking you on to this circle of his afterwards.'

'I hope he does. I'm full of curiosity about it.'

'Look Margot,' he said, using for the first time the Christian name by which he knew her, and hedging slightly in an attempt to get in on the game now she had made it clear that she could not be persuaded to drop it. 'I'm curious about it too. You may be right about its being a Yoga party, and if so it could be the real path to developing one's higher faculties. Anyhow, I mean to cultivate old Ratnadatta until I can persuade him that I am also a suitable candidate to be let in on his mysteries. But that will take time; so, just in case it is a Satanist set-up, if he does offer you a chance to join his circle, I wish you would stall for a while. Then, if I can get on the right side of him after another couple of meetings at Mrs. Wardeel's, we could fix it so that I go with you on your setting sail into these unknown waters.'

Mary felt a little secret thrill of satisfaction. During the first part of the evening the false personality she had had to build up had made her feel so awkward with him that she knew that she was far from making herself a charming and interesting companion. She had even begun to fear that her plan to ensnare and pay out this plausible roué who had brought such misery upon her was about to become still-born, and that he would never ask her out again. But now, here he was already showing deep concern for her, and anxious to become her protector in case she ran into danger. All the same, she had no intention of delaying for a single day if she was given the opportunity to follow up this possible lead to Teddy's murder. And if Barney was left to wonder what was happening to her on Saturday night, so much the better. That was just the sort of thing to make him all the keener.

She shook her head. 'No, I'm afraid I can't do that. If I once turned down an offer from Ratnadatta he might not ask me again. But I assure you I'm perfectly capable of taking care of myself. And now, I think I ought to be getting home.'

'O.K. then!' With a light-hearted shrug he appeared to dismiss the matter, but after a moment he added, 'I haven't enjoyed dancing so much with anyone for a long time. If your friend the Fakir hasn't turned you into a pretty white nannygoat, what about having dinner with me here again on Sunday?'

Mary smiled back at him. 'I enjoyed it too, and I'd like to do that. You'll have to take the risk, though, that by then I'll have acquired the power to turn you into a horrid black toad.'

'I'm awfully flattered that you should feel like that about me!'

She gave him a puzzled look. 'Unless you're being sarcastic, I don't quite see what you mean.'

His eyes suddenly danced with devilment, and his teeth flashed in a grin. 'Surely you know that a witch has to take her familiar to live with her?'

The waiter brought the bill at that moment; so Barney did not see her flush, as she thought angrily, 'He hasn't changed a bit. How like him to seize the first chance to throw out that sort of suggestion under cover of a joke.' And it was that angry thought which was largely responsible for precipitating her into a stupid action very soon afterwards.

Ten minutes later, as their taxi moved off, Barney, with the assurance of a man who is rarely repulsed by women, put an arm round her shoulders. She let him, and predicted to herself what his next move would be – he would begin at once to tell her how beautiful she was, then when they came opposite the Ritz he would attempt to kiss her and, if she allowed him to, by the time they reached Hyde Park Corner he would put his free hand on her knee.

In her first two assumptions she proved right, but as he drew her towards him she swiftly jerked her head away, and snapped, 'Stop that! How dare you treat me as if I were a tart!'

66

Next moment she could have bitten her tongue out. It was an absurd thing to have said, simply because he had tried to kiss her, and she had been impelled to say it only because she was already visualizing in her mind the sort of thing she expected him to attempt later, if she let him.

Sitting back quickly, he exclaimed: 'What on earth are you talking about? Treat you like a tart! I've done nothing of the kind.'

'Yes you have.' She took refuge in angry contradiction. 'To try to make love to a woman who has given you not the least encouragement, and whom you hardly know, the very first moment you are alone with her, is as good as telling her to her face that you think she's the sort who can be had for the price of a dinner.'

'Nonsense!' said Barney, firmly. 'Men don't kiss tarts in taxis. They wait till they get back to their flats, do what there is to do, give them a few quid, and, nine times out of ten, go home and forget all about them. Whereas I want to see you again. You know I do; and I wouldn't be such a fool as to spoil my chances of our becoming really good friends.'

Her mind fixed on his words 'and forget all about them'. They acted like a can of petrol poured on the fires of her Irish temper and, ignoring the rest of what he had said, she stormed at him:

'So that's how you treat girls who are reduced to giving themselves for money, is it? And what about afterwards? Say you've put the wretched girl in the family way. I suppose that's no concern of your Lordship's?'

'Really, Margot!' he protested. 'I can't think what's got into you. A tart is a tart, and is doing a job of work like any other, even if at times it is not a very pleasant one. It is up to her to learn how to take care of herself. If she doesn't bother and gets caught, you can't hold the man responsible.'

'As he did it, he is.'

'I don't agree. If a chap is having an affair with a decent girl that, of course, is different. It is up to him to see that nothing goes wrong, and should they have the bad luck to have an accident, obviously it's his responsibility to get her out of trouble. Listen, I'll give you a parallel. When I was younger and lived in . . . out in Kenya, I often used to ride for other people in steeplechases. Say an owner had a really fractious horse and asked me as a favour to ride him, if the brute had thrown me and I'd broken a leg I'd have had the right to expect the owner to cough up my doctor's fees and hospital expenses. But if he had paid me for the job, and I'd taken the risk for money, it wouldn't even have occurred to me to ask the owner to foot the bill. In the same way, with tarts, getting in the family way is simply an occupational risk; that's all there is to it.'

'But supposing the girl is young and ignorant?'

He shrugged. 'If she's been paid I don't see that that makes much difference. These girls always have older friends to whom they can go for advice, or know of some old woman who'll do the necessary. But what beats me is why you should have become so het-up about all this.'

Mary saw the red light. She had already been dangerously near to stating her own case. If she pursued the subject further it might easily ring a bell in his mind and cause him to recognize her. Then goodbye to all hope of getting her own back on him. With an effort she pulled herself together and said in a calmer voice. 'You are quite right. It is only that I'm sorry for girls who have to earn their living that way and, as a woman, resent the fact that men's lust should force them to it.'

'Oh come! I admit that prostitution could not exist if there were not the demand that keeps it going. But the majority of these girls are just lazy sluts who prefer to lie late in bed in the morning, deck themselves out in clothes they could not otherwise afford, then spend most of their time drinking or dancing in bars and clubs, rather than do an honest day's work.'

'Perhaps that is so; but there must be exceptions.'

'No doubt there are. But what has that got to do with the fact that I tried to kiss you? In the most respectable circles, from their 'teens on, when boys and girls like each other they kiss without any thought of going to bed together afterwards. I can only suppose that you've got some awful Freudian complex that turns you into an icicle at the touch of a man.'

'It's not that,' she said with an effort. 'I'm quite normal. I enjoy being kissed by a man I like. But . . . well . . . I do need a chance to make up my mind if I like him enough first.'

The taxi had just pulled up outside the house in which she was living, and Barney said with a smile, 'Then I haven't blotted my copy-book irretrievably. I'm glad about that. May I take it that Sunday is still on?'

68

'Yes,' she nodded as he helped her out. 'I'm afraid I've behaved rather stupidly. I didn't mean to. Please forgive me. And thank you very much for this evening. Good night.'

Still much puzzled by her outburst he watched her go up the steps and let herself in, then he told the taxi to drive him to his rooms in Warwick Square.

While undressing, Mary did her best to reassess the relationship between them, of which only she was aware. The views he had expressed, obviously with complete honesty, on a man's obligations, or lack of them, to a girl with whom he had slept, depending on whether she had given herself to him for love or for money, had made a considerable impression on her. In fact, as a general principle, she found it difficult not to accept them. But, having for five years nurtured a bitter grudge against him as the author of all her personal sufferings, she found it impossible to dissociate him from them overnight.

The carefree attitude that he still displayed to life, his passing himself off as a lord, and his taking it for granted that she would let him make love to her after only a few hours spent in his company, all combined to reinforce her belief that he was cynical, unscrupulous, heartless, and a menace to any woman who was fool enough to fall for him. But in this case it was he who had fallen for her. The anxiety he had displayed about her meeting Ratnadatta on Saturday evening, and his eagerness to see her again, was, she felt, ample evidence of that; and as she dropped off to sleep she was savouring in advance the triumph she would enjoy when she had led him on into a state in which she would make him utterly miserable with frustrated desire.

On the Saturday evening she duly kept her appointment with Ratnadatta at Sloane Square Tube Station. Sleek, paunchy, his brown eyes expressionless behind the pebble lenses, but his rabbit teeth protruding in an ingratiating smile, he greeted her most politely, then beckoned up the leading taxi on the rank.

He was dressed as she had seen him on previous occasions, in a pale blue suit of thinnish material, over which he now had a light fawn overcoat. Apart from the colour of his skin, the only indications of his Eastern origin were that his hat was of the kind habitually worn by Mr. Nehru, and that he smelled strongly of scent. As they got into the taxi Mary caught a pungent whiff of it; but to that she was far from objecting, as during their talks together at Mrs. Wardeel's she had several times had to suppress an impulse to back away from him on account of his breath. It had a curiously sweet yet unpleasant odour like that of bad lobster, and she hoped that his having scented himself so lavishly this evening would help to counteract it.

The taxi took them only half-a-mile then pulled up outside a small restaurant in Chelsea. Its Eurasian proprietor welcomed Ratnadatta as a valued patron and, bowing them to the back of the restaurant, led them upstairs to a small room in which a table was laid for two.

Although her host was on the youthful side of middle-age, it had somehow not occurred to Mary that he might have amorous designs upon her. But from her black year she was well aware of the use to which such private dining-rooms were usually put and, as her glance fell on a sofa against one wall, she was seized with swift revulsion at the thought of such an encounter with him.

Catching her uneasy look, he said quickly, 'You haf no objection, plees; the things off weech we shall talk are not for other ears.'

Momentarily reassured, she replied: 'Yes, of course. I quite understand.'

When the menu was produced he urged her to order whatever she fancied, so she chose potted shrimps, a tournedo and Coupe Jacques; on which he said that the same would suit him too.

As the proprietor left the room, she remarked, 'I thought that Theosophists who have achieved initiation had to become vegetarians.'

He chuckled. 'Those who are Theosophists only are little people. They know nothing. We off the Brotherhood haf passed beyond such senseless taboos. Off commandments we haf but one, "Do what thou wilt shall be the Whole off the Law".'

She smiled back at him. 'That sounds an easy philosophy to follow.'

'It ees good, very good. It frees the mind from all care – all inhibitions. With the shackles off convention thrown aside, life becomes all pleasure. That ees as the Great One wishes for us.'

'You speak as though the three Masters in whom the Theosophists believe were one.'

'Yes, plees. As in much other things, they make great error. There ees only one Supreme Entity and he can give us all our wishings.' At that moment a waiter came in with the first course

70

and Ratnadatta added quickly, 'We talk of this more later, yes. Eat now and enjoy.'

During the meal he plied Mary with questions, sometimes direct, and sometimes oblique, so that she could not be quite certain at what he was driving. Mostly they concerned her past, her religious beliefs, and the life she was leading at present. Owing to the practice she had had in answering similar questions put by Barney two nights before, she found herself able to answer much more readily and even embroider convincingly the picture she had built up. On the subject of religion she took special pains to assure him that although she had been brought up as a Roman Catholic, she had long since ceased to be a practising one, and now regarded the hard and fast beliefs demanded by that faith as quite unacceptable to an intelligent individual.

At times she tried to lighten her replies to his catechism in the hope of bringing a little humour into their conversation; but the Indian did not respond and continued to regard her steadily from behind his thick-lensed spectacles. However, the food was good, if not pretentious, and he proved an attentive host. When the pudding had been served he poured her another glass of wine and asked her about her sex life.

Again she felt an inward shudder at the thought that he might be leading up to attempting to make love to her; so she replied coldly, 'I don't think we need go into that.'

'Indeed yes.' His voice for the first time held a note of sharpness. 'To judge your fitness for advancement all your personality you must reveal to me. The secret life as well as the open life. Speak now of your first experience.'

Realizing that she would have wasted her time, and get no further with him, if she refused, she told a plausible lie about it. 'Apart from cuddling, and that sort of thing, with a few young men, I had none until I was married.'

'And then?'

'Well, I got no pleasure from it at first, but after a while, like any normal girl who loves her husband, I came to enjoy it.'

'Since your husband's death what, plees? Haf you a lover?'

She felt sure of the answers he would like to that, so she gave them. 'No,' then added, 'not at the moment, but I have had several.'

'You take them why? Because you fall in love with each, or for some other reason?'

71

'I liked them all, naturally. But it was really because I felt lonely. Besides, I'm young and healthy and, having got used to that sort of thing, after having been deprived of it for a while I felt the need for it.'

'Good, very good. Most sensible. This shows that you are already free from the false bindings you received as young from Christian teaching. Instead you haf taken your own will for guide. What now off women? Haf your own sex sometimes attraction for you?'

Mary shook her head.

'You haf perhaps a strong feeling against homosexuals?'

'No. I'm sorry for them, that's all. But if they are made that way I think they have as much right as other people to enjoy themselves in their own fashion.'

'Again you show the broad mind weech tells me that your incarnations haf been many.'

They had finished the bottle of Chianti that Ratnadatta had ordered, and now the waiter arrived with coffee and liqueurs. When he had gone the Indian said:

'For your understanding I must now speak off things that are hidden from most. Perhaps you haf heard sometime off the reply savages in dark Africa make to white men who ask "Why do you make prayer to the idol, the waterfall, thunder, and what else. Such can do you no good. Haf you never heard that there ees a great God high up in the sky who created all things and ees all-powerful. It ees to Him that you should make your prayers."'

'No,' said Mary, 'I've not. What do the savages reply?'

'They say, "Yes, we know off the great god who created the world and all that ees in it; but to him it ees useless to make prayer. Our ancestors did so and found he did not answer. That was because he no longer hear. Having finish the world he loose interest in it and go far far away to make other worlds. But in the idol he leave a little part off his power and to the river and the fire-mountain we make sacrifice because if not they become angry; then perhaps they destroy our crops, our cattle, ourselves."'

Ratnadatta solemnly nodded his head and went on. 'Those savages haf preserve a truth long lost to nations civilized. The Creator did after completion go away to think only off making new worlds. To worship Him ees foolishness; a waste of time.'

'Surely, though, you don't suggest we should worship idols?' Mary asked.

'No, no! Yet the Creator did leave power behind Him. He delegate it to one off his sons.'

Hardly believing that she could have heard aright, Mary murmured, 'You mean Jesus Christ?'

The dark face opposite her took on a contemptuous look. 'What an idea! He was a prophet only, one off many and not a very good one. I speak off Prince Lucifer.'

'I . . . I see. He was an Arch-angel, wasn't he; before he became the Devil?'

'An Arch-angel, yes. A true son off the Creator. Devil ees a term used only by those who fear Him. It came to use with the spread off the Christian heresy. If you are to progress you must forget such foolishness. Those who haf true knowledge reverence Him as Our Lord Satan. For off this world he ees the Lord. All power over it ees His. He was given it as His Principality. The Bible, even, makes admission of that.'

Mary thought to herself, 'Well, now we know where we are. Both Barney and I were right in believing this horrid little man to be one of a circle of Satanists.' Aloud she said, 'I remember the passage now. What you say throws an entirely new light on everything.'

'Good, very good.' Ratnadatta smiled at her. 'Another passage I recall to you. On the high mountain He offered Christ all cities and the plains. Not the world, off course, but as far as he could see. That we know to haf been because He think Christ could haf been useful servant and wish to save him from taking wrong Path. Christ being conceited fool refuse; so, instead off becoming a great Lord, he died horrible death. But my point ees that Prince Lucifer's offer would haf made no sense if the cities and plains were not His to give.'

'Yes; I suppose that is so.'

'You suppose!' snapped the Indian. 'Understand plees, that if you wish for advancement you make no questionings off what I tell.'

'Oh, I wasn't doubting you,' Mary assured him hastily. 'Please go on and tell me how I can become one of the favoured of . . . of Him who is Lord of this world.'

He smiled again. 'The Path ees not difficult for those who are willing to embrace life with whole heart. Remember, the Creator told Adam that He had made all things for his delight. The same wish has also been that off His great son, Our Lord Satan, for all descendants off Adam up to present day. At first, perhaps, inhibitions from youthful upbringing may unexpectedly make troubles in your mind. You must practise to be rid off them; yes ruthlessly. Only so will you fit yourself to take part in secret rituals. It ees by these we call down power to ourselves. Without taking part in them all else ees off no use.'

'What sort of rituals are they?' Mary enquired.

'The most ancient off all. They haf been practise since the beginning off the world. Most religions preserve relics off them; submission, communion, in some also offering off sacrifice. But in all the meaning off them has been obscured by evil or ignorant priests. Most haf become so distorted to be now unrecognizable. This in the West more than in the East, or even dark Africa. People still primitive haf preserved greater degree off truth. Good example ees sacrifice. To make sacrifice ees to pay tribute, and it ees proper that those who are protected should pay tribute to their Protector. Also blood ees the life force. It must be spilt so that its spiritual essence may be returned in form off renewed vitality to persons who take part in such ritual. But perhaps you haf not yet strong enough desire to progress for overcoming prejudice off Europeans against rites off this kind?'

Under her bronze make-up Mary went a little pale. The appalling thought had suddenly struck her that Teddy's terrible end might be due to his having been offered up as a human sacrifice. To find out if Ratnadatta and his circle had had any part in bringing about Teddy's death was her sole object in cultivating the Indian, and it looked now as if, should he prove willing to take her to a meeting of Satanists, she might have to become an unwilling accomplice at some other hideous crime. Yet the only alternative to steeling herself to face such a possibility was to throw her hand in; so she said:

'The reason you give for making sacrifices is quite logical; so I should feel no qualms at witnessing such a ritual. Are they . . . are they performed often?'

'Four times a year we sacrifice a ram,' he replied quietly. 'That ees because the circle to weech I belong ees one off many Lodges scattered all over the world weech form the Brotherhood of the Ram.'

She suppressed a sigh of relief, but a moment later wondered if he was telling the whole truth, or only a part of it from fear

74

of disclosing too dangerous a secret to her before he had better reason to feel confident he could trust her with it.

Leaning forward across the little table he went on, 'I haf now judge you and believe you are ripe for advancement. But first answer me plees. Question one. After what I haf tell you ees it still your earnest wish to receive enlightenment?'

Mary could now smell again the sweetish bad-lobster odour of his breath, but she showed no sign of the queasy feeling it gave her, and she replied firmly, 'It certainly is.'

'Question two. Do you agree to giff your whole will to developing your mind to a state in weech power can be entrusted to you?'

'Yes,' she nodded. 'To be given occult power is my dearest wish.'

'Question three. To achieve that are you willing to surrender yourself absolutely to Our Lord Satan for the furtherance off His work – the bringing off happiness to those who follow Him?'

Again she said, 'Yes.'

'Good, very good,' he purred, much to her relief sitting back and sparing her further distress from the ill-conditioned interior of his fat little paunch. 'I haf instinct about you. I was right. And now I give you pleasant surprise. Tonight ees Saturday. It ees on Saturdays that my Lodge holds its meetings. You will not be made initiate tonight. No; not yet. Not till you haf seen for yourself something off the ancient mysteries. After, perhaps you feel fear to go on. Then ees still time to withdraw. Such decision show only that, after all, you are not yet ready to accept full truth. No harm done. But if after you again affirm will to proceed at a future meeting I introduce you as neophyte.'

Suddenly he again sat forward, and the hard little brown eyes behind the pebble glasses bored into hers. 'One thing more. You will mention never to anyone what you haf seen. Should you do that we will know off it. The ear off Our Lord Satan misses nothing. You would do better to commit suicide than live to face His retribution.'

'I . . . yes. I quite understand,' she said in a low voice. 'It is very good of you indeed to give me this opportunity of . . . of advancing along the true Path. Whereabouts is the meeting being held?'

He stood up. 'Until you become initiate, that I must keep secret from you. But soon I am now hoping that you will be a

Sister off the Ram. If so, you will haf had great good fortune that it ees my Lodge that you join. For this year it ees granted power greater than all others, because the Great Ram has come to us from distant land to act temporarily as our earthly Master.'

After the unspecified but terrible fate with which Ratnadatta had threatened her should she betray them, Mary had been seized with sudden panic. Already she had made up her mind that, even if she failed to secure any evidence that they were connected with Teddy's death, but found that they were actively engaged in evil practices, she would give chapter and verse about them to Colonel Verney. Yet the threat brought to her mind the powers they might possess. It seemed certain, at least, that among them would be clairvoyants of far greater abilities than the sort of semi-amateur she had seen crystal gazing the first time she had gone to a meeting at Mrs. Wardeel's; and, perhaps, true mediums. If they were capable of overlooking her and traced her to Colonel Verney that might really place her in danger of her life.

The thought of the Colonel brought back to her the warning he had given her about the seriousness of the risk she would be running if she attempted to penetrate the secrets of a Black Magic circle; and Barney, too, had shown acute concern at the idea of her doing so. Although she had refused to recognize it before, she knew that they were right, and that it was madness for her to pit her wits against a whole group of clever, unscrupulous people who, she was now persuaded, could call on evil occult forces to aid them. Swiftly she began to seek an excuse by which she could back out while there was still time.

But with equal suddenness to the panic which had seized her, a memory now flashed into her mind. It was of one of Teddy's worst nightmares. In all of them he had muttered and raved, mostly incoherently, about Satan and hell, and even such absurdities as being chased by a black imp, but sometimes he cried out short sentences aloud. Once, just before she had woken him, he had shouted, 'The Ram! The Great Ram! Smoke is coming from him! He must be the Devil!'

At the time, she had hardly registered the words, taking them for just one more of Teddy's nightmare fantasies. But now, following on what Ratnadatta had said only a few moments before, they came back to her. And they made sense. The Great Ram was a man; the Master of Ratnadatta's Lodge. Here was the proof of what she had previously only suspected. Ratnadatta *was* the Indian Teddy had mentioned in his ravings and *had* taken him to the place where she believed he had met his death.

Like a bugle call rallying the remnants of a decimated squadron of cavalry to charge again, the knowledge that she had really hit on the right track caused strength and determination to flow back into her. Now, whatever might happen to her she knew that she must go through with it.

6

The Satanic Temple

T EN minutes later Mary was again in a taxi with the Indian. He had spoken to the driver in so low a voice that she had been unable to overhear it; so she knew only that they were going in a northerly direction. Then, when the taxi had carried them only a few hundred yards, he produced a clean white handkerchief from his pocket, folded it carefully on his fat knees, and turning to her said:

'I haf told you that the place off meeting must be kept secret from you until you become initiate. Plees now, I put bandage over your eyes.'

Relieved, at least, that as he leaned towards her she had an excuse for turning her head away from him, she submitted, holding the handkerchief in place while he tied its ends behind over her brown dyed hair.

After the taxi had taken a few turnings she lost all sense of direction, and the drive seemed to her to last a long time; but, during it, she was saved from becoming a prey to nervous speculation by Ratnadatta's carrying on what almost amounted to a monologue upon matters of such interest that it soon engaged her mind.

His theme was ancient religions and, although Mary's knowledge of them was decidedly sketchy, she had read sufficiently to appreciate that the views he expressed threw a new, even if distorted, light on many things.

He explained to her that, just as the early Christians had been

78

forced to go underground to avoid persecution by the government in Rome, so, when Christianity had later gained a hold on other governments, the followers of the Old religion had had to seek safety from the laws enacted against them by going underground. He said that the word 'witchcraft' had originally been 'wisecraft', derived from 'craft-of-the-wise', and that the belief that witches and wizards were necessarily evil people was a most mistaken one. Some had been charlatans, but a high percentage of them had been people who had passed through many incarnations, were initiates who understood the great truths, and so enjoyed occult power. And it was the recognition that they wielded such powers, and fear of them by the ignorant Christian priests, which had led to their persecution.

He then talked to her of the heavenly bodies, the influence they exerted on human beings, and how those influences could be made use of to further the interests of initiates who had learned the secret of timing their acts to coincide with cosmic rays most favourable to their success. By such means, he said, money could be acquired without working for it, positions secured, and either fertility or sterility made certain. But, he added, such operations needed to be undertaken only by initiates who were temporarily isolated from the Brotherhood, as at the meetings of its Lodges each Master was invested with the power to give swift aid to followers of the Path in achieving all their reasonable desires – as she was about to see for herself that night.

He was describing to her certain rain-making and fertility rites, still practised with success by peoples remote from civilization who had had handed down to them a little of the old wisdom, when the taxi at last drew up.

Quickly untying the handkerchief that blindfolded her, Ratnadatta got out. As he paid off the taxi she looked about her and saw that they were in a dark street, lined on both sides by mean houses. There was a little group of men in caps talking together outside a public house on the corner, but otherwise few people in sight.

Taking her arm, Ratnadatta hurried her along in the other direction. They turned a corner into another mean street along one side of which there was a high blank wall. At its end the wall continued at a right angle as one side of a narrow lane. Entering it they walked on for about a hundred yards. Mary saw then that it was a cul-de-sac, with an end that broadened out into a small court in which, with their lights out, half-a-dozen cars were parked.

On the left side of the court the wall merged into a large square brick house. Its tall windows showed not a chink of light, but a single low-power electric bulb made a pool of dim yellow radiance from over the stone pediment of its porch. Five steps, two of them cracked, led up to the porch which was flanked by fluted pillars. Above the broad front door, from which the paint was peeling, Mary noticed a fine Adam fan-light. It reminded her of the many in the older streets of Dublin, and she realized that this mansion, now surrounded by slums, must date back to Georgian days.

Ratnadatta pressed a bell push several times, as if he was using it to send a morse code signal. The door was opened and, stepping in, they came face to face with a heavy curtain that screened the interior as though it was a black-out precaution to prevent light shining into the street at a time when an air-raid threatened.

An end of the curtain was lifted and they sidled through, emerging into a small pillared hall with a wrought-iron balustraded staircase leading up from its centre. After the decayed appearance of the outside of the house, its inside came as a striking contrast. The hall was brightly lit by a sparkling crystal chandelier that hung from the centre of its ceiling, the cornices were gilded, the furniture was the finest Chippendale and two negro footmen in plain liveries bowed silently to Ratnadatta as he and Mary came in, then took their coats.

She wondered where the house was situated and, as the taxi had set off from Chelsea towards the north, she thought it might be in Islington, or one of those districts no great distance from the City in which rich nobles had long ago had their town residences. In any case it seemed probable that some wealthy family had held on to it for several generations, always hoping that the value of its site would increase, whereas it had gone down and down as the district in which it lay had gradually deteriorated into a slum area.

Before she had time to speculate further, Ratnadatta took her up the broad staircase and along a corridor to a curiously shaped room. It was low ceilinged, very long but quite narrow. Half way along it stood a table on which were several decanters and some light refreshments. Along the far wall were a row of half-a-dozen elbow chairs, all of which faced an unbroken line of heavy brocade curtains.

After a glance round, Mary assumed from the position of the chairs that the curtains must screen windows out of which anyone seated opposite them could look when the curtains were drawn back. While she was wondering how, in such a place, there could possibly be a prospect worthy of such elaborate arrangements for looking at, Ratnadatta had gone to the table and filled a wine glass from one of the decanters. Offering it to her with a bow he said:

'This you will like. It ees a rare wine coming from Greece. In old times it was great favourite with priestesses who serve the oracle at Delphi.'

On sipping the near-purple coloured liquid, she thought it tasted like a rich sherry in which aromatic herbs had been steeped. Finding it very pleasant she drank about half the contents of the glass. Ratnadatta meanwhile had helped himself to a lighter golden coloured wine, and remarked:

'For me something drier. Off this wine off Cyprus I am very fond. Come now. Be seated, plees, and soon I shall show you that I haf made no idle boast off the powers bestowed by Our Lord Satan on those who serve him well.'

They sat down side by side in two of the elbow chairs and for some ten minutes the Indian resumed his discourse on ancient rites; then, having glanced at his watch, he leaned forward and pulled a cord that drew back the pair of heavy curtains facing which they were seated. To Mary's surprise this did not reveal a window; only a blank wall covered in patterned satin; but in it, opposite each of the chairs, was what she at first took to be a ventilator, as it was an aperture about six inches square, covered with fine mesh wire netting.

Ratnadatta signed to her to look through it, and when her eyes came close to the wire she found that these secret observation posts gave an excellent view of a large and lofty room. She guessed that at one time it had probably been a banqueting hall, and the curious shaped room in which she was sitting a minstrels' gallery, opening into it. But now the former had more the appearance of a chapel. At its far end, covered with a broad strip of blood-red silk, was a long raised slab, that looked as though it might be used as an altar. Beyond it stood a great carved throne of ebony, and behind that, tall red silk curtains having embroidered upon them in gold a design of two drop-shaped sections with curved tails interlocking to form a circle, which, although

81

Mary did not know it, was the Yin and the Yang – the Eastern symbol for the male and female principles. In the body of the hall, to either side of a central aisle, instead of pews were ranged a dozen or more divans plentifully stocked with cushions of many colours, and from somewhere out of sight came the sounds of a band tuning up.

Down in the hall some twenty people were already assembled, and were being joined by others. They were coming in by a door that Mary could not see, as it was below the balcony in which she was sitting, but just within her range of vision there was a large table on which stood an array of bottles and glasses; and each newcomer helped himself to a drink from it before joining the earlier arrivals.

From the groups down below there came up a gentle murmur of conversation and from their behaviour they might have been guests at a perfectly respectable cocktail party. But one glance was enough to see that this gathering was far from being anything of that kind. Everyone present was wearing a small black satin mask, a narrow black velvet garter below the left knee and silver sandals, but little else. They had on only long cloaks of transparent veiling, sparsely decorated with silver suns, moons or signs of the Zodiac; so that the bodies of all of them were almost as fully revealed as if they had been naked. The party consisted of roughly equal numbers of both sexes; among the women there was an enormously fat negress and a young Chinese girl; among the men, two negroes, one of whom had white hair, an Indian and two who looked like Japanese.

The company was a mixture of all ages and although about a third of them had well proportioned figures the bodies of the majority were far from attractive. But there was nothing to suggest the obscene either in the decor of the temple or the attitudes of the people in it, and Mary decided that the single silver-spangled garments they wore, by softening the lines of thick hips, lean shanks, hanging breasts and pot-bellies, made the ugly ones considerably less repulsive to look at than if they had been morally irreproachable eccentrics standing about quite naked in a nudist camp.

Feeling uncertain what sort of reaction Ratnadatta would expect her to display at the sight of this spectacle, she played for safety by remarking: 'What a huge woman that negress is. I should think she must weigh twenty stone.'

82

He turned from his grille to nod to her. 'Yes, perhaps. She ees on a visit to London from Hiati. There she ownes factories and a great estate. She ees a Lesbian and her riches enable her to indulge her tastes. At our last meeting I speak with her and she tell me that she keep twenty young girls in a harem for her pleasure.'

Mary suppressed a shudder of disgust and asked: 'Who is the very tall man with the fair wavy hair?'

'That I cannot disclose to you, because he has not spoken to me off himself. It ees our rule never to question one another, or speak off what we may learn by accident. I inform you about the negress only because she make no secret off who she ees or what she does.'

The unseen band was still apparently tuning up, as only a jumble of discordant notes came from it; so Mary remarked: 'The band seems to be taking a long time to get going.'

Ratnadatta turned to her again with a look of surprise. 'It ees not a band. It ees a recording off a piece by a young musician off great promise.'

'Then I don't think much of it,' she declared. 'It has no tune or rhythm. Like so much of this ultra-modern music, it's just a senseless series of discords that I should have thought anyone could throw together.'

'You are wrong,' he told her severely. 'And you must learn to like it. In recent times the arts haf made great strides. Musicians, painters, sculptors, haf broken away from tradition. That ees good; very good. They no longer follow slavishly tastes set by bourgeois society. This shows that they are persons fitting themselves for advancement and acceptance off the hidden truths. To all such, encouragement must be given. The work they do helps much to break down other conventions which strangle happiness off mankind.'

In any other circumstances Mary would have argued hotly that the beauty given to the world in the past by its great artists had made a contribution to the happiness of mankind that it was hard to equal, and that the monstrosities in stone, meaningless daubs on canvas, and ugly compositions of sound now being produced could bring pleasure to few people other than those with twisted minds; and that she believed that in most cases it was a wicked racket to get money out of wealthy fools who could be persuaded that such crudities would have a lasting value. But she naturally refrained from expressing her views and, to change the

83

conversation, asked: 'Why do they all wear a single garter below their left knee?'

'It ees insignia off power,' Ratnadatta replied. 'Old as the world. To be seen as indication off priests even in Altamara cave drawings off primitive peoples.'

At that moment the recording came to an end and the crowd below began to settle themselves on the divans. On some two or three sat down together facing the altar, on others single individuals lounged at full length, their heads supported on one hand in the manner of Romans about to enjoy an entertainment or a feast. Suddenly a cracked trumpet sounded a single note. Complete silence fell and lasted for about three minutes. Then the trumpet sounded twice more and everyone stood up.

From under the balcony on which Mary and Ratnadatta were sitting a tall figure emerged, walked with slow stately step up the aisle and turned at the altar to face the congregation. Unlike them, he had no mask and was wearing a heavy robe of black satin, richly embroidered with mystic symbols in many colours. He also had on a high, pointed fool's cap similarly decorated. His face was that of a man in his sixties and judging from it he might have been a bishop, for it was round, smooth, pale and benign.

Ratnadatta said in a whisper, 'This ees not the Great Ram, but the High Priest that he haf temporarily replace. He holds the title Abaddon and has much power. But the Great Ram has more, far more. Presently he will come and grant wishes off all who desire.'

While he was speaking the congregation bowed to Abaddon and he bowed to them in return. In a melodious voice he said: 'Exalted Brethren of the Ram, as followers of the True Path, in the name of Our Lord Satan, I bid you welcome. Be seated and at your ease.'

The congregation bowed again and resumed their seats or lounging postures on the divans. He seated himself on the throne, then spoke again. 'I, Abaddon, am an ear of the Great One. Through me He listens to all you have to tell and through me He will distribute praise or blame.'

A scrawny middle-aged woman stood up, stepped quickly towards him and began to speak in a low voice. Mary strained her ears to catch what she was saying, but at that moment Ratnadatta pulled the curtain cord, so that the heavy curtains swished together, shutting off her view and all sounds from below.

'I regret,' he said, sitting back, 'but in turn they now make report off work each has carried out for pleasing Our Lord Satan since they last attend a meeting. Such it ees not fitting that you should hear until you are initiate. But haf patience, plees. Presently we look again. Meantime I get you another glass off wine.'

For the comfort of the nearly naked congregation the whole place had been thoroughly well heated, and up in the gallery it was almost stifling; so Mary's throat was a little parched. Yet, as he stood up and moved towards the table, she wondered if she ought to drink any more. She had found the herb-flavoured wine delicious, but felt sure that it was unusually potent stuff and suspected that the slight dizziness she had been feeling for some while past might be due to it, rather than to the overheated atmosphere. Caution prompting her to play for safety, she said, 'Would you mind if I had a soft drink instead?'

'If you prefer,' he replied without a trace of hesitation. 'We haf here a drink weech ees made from mangoes and other fruits. It ees good, very good. I mix you some with soda, and a lump of ice, yes?'

It proved another strange but delicious drink and, acquitting him of the suspicion that the wine he had given her might have contained a small dose of some subtle drug, she quenched her thirst gratefully with the iced fruit drink.

During the next half-hour he talked to her about the old gods and goddesses of several countries and the truths which lay behind the mythology concerning them. He told her that they had all been actual people, on earth in their last incarnations, and so capable of calling down supernatural powers; that the word Pagan, as a term of opprobrium, had not been applied to them until much later, and then by misguided priests who taught that salvation could be achieved only by leading a dreary life of chastity, humility and self-denial; but that in fact they had been enlightened beings, bringing great happiness to the world when it was young and so for many generations afterwards rightly venerated by their peoples.

As Mary listened to him the time sped swiftly by. Her head continued to be a little muzzy but the sensation had no resemblance to the feeling she normally had on occasions when she knew that she ought to refuse another drink. She felt wonderfully alert, her nerves were steady, and the fears about what might happen to her that had agitated her mind on her first entering this hidden mansion had entirely vanished.

In the last few minutes Ratnadatta had twice taken a quick look down into the temple and when, after a third reconnaissance, he again pulled the curtain right back, she sat forward eagerly to see what was going on.

The congregation was still spread about upon the divans and some were talking in hushed voices, but there was an air of expectancy about them and many kept glancing in the direction of the altar. The High Priest, Abaddon, was now seated to one side of it on a low chair. He had taken off his fool's cap and Mary saw that he had a big dome-shaped head that was completely bald. Another low chair on the opposite side of the altar had been taken by a tall fair-haired woman with fine classical features who, Ratnadatta told Mary, was the High Priestess of the Lodge.

The cracked trumpet blared out its single note. Instantly those who had been whispering together fell silent. One minute passed, two, three, four, five, without anything happening. Those minutes seemed to drag interminably while an utter silence was maintained and the strain of expectancy mounted. Two more full minutes passed, then the trumpet blared out six long blasts. At the first the whole congregation rose, Abaddon and the High Priestess with them, and stood with bowed heads.

The blood-red curtains behind the altar moved slightly but did not appear to part. Afterwards Mary wondered if her eyes had closed for a few seconds, though she felt sure they had not. Yet at one minute there was nothing to be seen between the curtains and the back of the throne, and the next a man was standing there.

As he moved out from behind it she drew a sharp breath and her heart began to beat furiously. The man was tall and slim. His body was encased in black tights from shoulder to wrists and ankles. Round his waist he wore a loose, narrow belt which was entirely encrusted with flashing precious stones and weighed down to one side by a jewelled dagger. Upon his breast dangled a golden winged phallus suspended from a necklace of large pearls alternating with equally large rubies, and below his left knee was buckled an inch-deep garter shimmering with the green fire of priceless emeralds. Only the lower part of his face could be seen. It was thin, with an aggressive, deeply cleft chin above which

86

was a full, startlingly scarlet mouth. His upper features and the top of his head were hidden under a mask fashioned to represent the big black bulbous nose, the slit eyes and the great curling horns of a Ram.

Seating himself on the carved ebony throne he leaned back, crossed his long legs, and cried in a harsh, intolerant voice: 'Children of my Office. From High matters I spare time to preside over this Lodge again. By the favour of Our Lord Satan I have the power to grant your wishes, should it please me to do so. Waste no moment in unnecessary babbling or you will incur my anger. Now; lift up your heads and tell me your desires.'

His English was correct and fluent but he spoke with a curious accent that Mary could not place, and she thought it unlikely that he had been born an Englishman.

As though he had threatened to leave before half the congregation had had a chance to crave something from him, they all launched themselves forward, tumbling over one another in their endeavours to be first at the altar. A cynical smile twisted his scarlet lips for a moment; then, lifting one hand, he cried, 'Stop! Remain still!'

Instantly the crowd halted, and seemed rooted where they stood.

Pointing a finger at an elderly woman who had succeeded in nearly reaching his throne and was now on her knees beside it, he said, 'You! What do you ask?'

'My sight, Master!' she wailed. 'It is almost gone and the specialists can do nothing for me.'

Leaning forward he ripped the mask from her face and spat first into one of her eyes then into the other.

She cowered back, blinked for a moment, then gave an hysterical shriek of delight. 'A miracle! A miracle! I can see clearly again! Praised be the name of our Lord Satan! Blessings on the Great Ram!'

Still gibbering her thanks she began to slobber kisses on his feet, but he kicked her away and turned to a weedy looking man on his left.

'Master!' said the man hoarsely, 'I am a Harley Street psychiatrist. Through overwork I am losing my power to hypnotize, although I always guide patients in the way Our Lord Satan would wish me to.'

The Great Ram touched him between the eyes with one finger, and said, 'Your power is restored.'

87

A haggard woman at whom he next looked cried: 'Master, I need heroin. My supplier has been arrested. I beseech you to direct me to a new one.'

'Fool!' he snapped at her. 'If you have neither the wit to secure it nor the will to do without it, you are no longer fitted for Our Lord Satan's service. Return here in seven days and if your condition is not satisfactory, I will cause you to die in a fit.'

As the woman reeled away sobbing, the huge negress got her turn. In a deep voice she rumbled, 'I'se a stranger in London. My voodoo don't work well here. I's got a yen fer a little white gell, Master. Give me a love charm so I'll get her.'

With a smile the Great Ram plucked a hair from a part of his mask that was made of ram's wool, gave it to her, and said, 'Cause her to swallow that and she will be yours.'

A thickset man cried, 'Me too, Master! I am half crazy for a stubborn woman and I beg a love charm.'

The mouth of the fearsome figure on the throne drew into a hard line, then opened to reply, 'The last was a special case. Because she is a stranger to England her vibrations do not beget reactions here. If yours are too weak to accomplish your object, consult with Abaddon. You should know better than to trouble me about such a minor matter.'

The younger of the two negroes begged to be cured of a lung complaint that he had contracted owing to the damp climate of Britain. The Great Ram laid a hand upon his chest and told him that he was cured.

One of the more attractive women said that she was pregnant, and that as she had a weak heart she was afraid either to use drugs or have an illegal operation. She was told to stand aside until the rest had been dealt with.

Another of the younger women said, 'Master, I am the secretary of a junior Minister. He may go far, and if I could induce him to fall for me I could make use of him in furthering Our Lord Satan's work. But I am not good-looking enough to tempt him.'

The Great Ram stood up, drew the girl into a close embrace and gave her a long kiss on the mouth. Mary was too far off to see the full details of the transformation, but that one had taken place was beyond dispute. As the girl stepped back her hips looked slimmer, she held herself better so that she seemed taller, her previously slack breasts had filled out, and her lank lustreless hair had become a crown of shimmering curls.

A gaunt, middle-aged man said, 'Master, I am a publisher. Everything that I have published since joining the Brotherhood has in some form been slanted against either capitalism or Christianity or accepted conventions. But such books do not sell well with the people who can best afford to buy; and I have nearly exhausted my capital. What shall I do?'

After looking straight into his eyes for a moment, the Great Ram replied: 'I can see that you have had an interesting life, so I bestow upon you the gift of writing. Write a book based on your own experiences. Abaddon will arrange that it shall be made into a film. Its rights will bring you several thousand pounds.'

One of the two Japanese put a hand to his sleek dark hair, gave a pull and, as it was a wig, it came off, revealing a completely bald skull. 'Master!' he said in a sibilant voice. 'Through an illness two years ago I lost all my hair. Rude people mock at me, and it is a great handicap when making love to women. I beg you make it grow again.'

The Great Ram laid a hand on the man's head. When he withdrew it the bald pate was no longer shining but faintly coloured with a first sprouting of fine dark fluff. 'Do not brush it for a month,' he said. 'By then it will have grown an inch, and it will continue to do so.'

So it went on, cures and favours being distributed to all, except for a few who were turned away on account of their requests being either ill regarded or considered too trivial. Mary sat spellbound, her gaze riveted on the scene. She now felt certain that both the wine and the fruit juice she had drunk must have contained some drug, as every few minutes she found some difficulty in focusing her eyes, but the thought did not worry her, for the drug had also made her feel happy and exhilarated. The sight of the uglier of the semi-nude people down below no longer filled her with revulsion; they now inspired in her only a wish to know more of them as interesting human beings, and to miss nothing of these extraordinary proceedings.

She had not long to wait before she witnessed a more astounding manifestation of the Great Ram's powers than any she had yet seen. When the last request had been dealt with, he spoke to the pregnant woman whom he had told to stand aside, and ordered her to lay herself at full length on the altar. Now, standing in front of his throne, and about a yard away from her, he let his chin fall on his chest so that the lower part of his face became hidden by the mask, from either side of which protruded the fearsome curling horns. For some minutes, while the congregation watched with bated breath, he remained quite still, a tall black-clad figure, either deep in contemplation or concentrating intensely. Almost imperceptibly at first, a faint mist began to obscure his legs from the knees down. It thickened, becoming like smoke, and increased in height until it formed a dark oval cloud hiding his limbs from the feet to half-way up his thighs.

Suddenly it solidified. Mary gave a gasp of astonishment and horror. She blinked her eyes, sat back, rubbed them, then looked again. She could still hardly believe it, yet she knew she was not dreaming. The dark cloud had become a grinning black imp; the imp of Teddy's nightmares.

The creature was not like a child, but was a perfectly formed manikin, about thirty inches high. It had a pot belly, long pointed ears, but no hair, and its red eyes glowed like live coals in its pitchblack face.

Neither it nor its creator moved for what seemed an immensely long time, but was in fact about two minutes. Then the small supernatural monster began to disintegrate, but only so far as to become again a dense black cloud. In that form it began to oscillate and lengthen until it turned into a swiftly whirling spiral of thick oily looking smoke. The spiral straightened to a five-foot long upright streak. Its upper point curved over, shot downwards like a diving aircraft and entered the body of the woman lying on the altar.

Her eyes were shut, there had been no sound, and evidently she remained unaware that anything was happening to her – until the whole of the evil spirit had disappeared inside her. Then she began to writhe and murmur, but her paroxysm was of short duration. In less than a minute her dark invader streaked out of her, spiralled, reformed into a cloud, solidified and again became a black imp standing in front of its master.

With a gasp she sat up, looked round in astonishment then, catching sight of the imp, gave a cry of terror.

'Silence woman!' It was the voice of the Great Ram, still clear but now seeming to come from a long way away. 'I have destroyed the new life in your body. Go home at once and do what there is to do. In an hour's time you will have been freed from your trouble.'

Getting up from the altar, the woman made a movement as

though she intended to throw herself at his feet in gratitude, but evidently she was too frightened of the imp, which stood between her and him, to do so. Instead she made an awkward curtsey, called out, 'Oh, thank you! Thank you! Blessed be Satan's name!' Then, her hair dishevelled and her muslin cloak flying out behind her, she ran from the temple.

The voice of the Great Ram came again. 'Prepare to receive through me the Benediction of Our Lord Satan, that you may be fitted to honour the Creator by the rite symbolical of His work.'

At this order the congregation swiftly formed up in two lines facing the altar. For a few moments complete silence and stillness reigned again. Then the imp moved forward from the dais on which the Great Ram was standing, jumped soundlessly down on to the floor of the temple and, like a General inspecting troops, moved slowly along the front rank, but pausing for a moment in front of every individual. As it did so each was shaken by a sudden shudder, and some uttered a low cry.

As the two lines of men and women had their backs to Mary, and the imp was so much shorter than they were, she could catch glimpses of it only as it passed from one to another; so in a whisper she said to Ratnadatta:

'What is it doing to them?'

The Indian whispered back. 'He ees touching the genitals off each. Through him, in this way, their sexual powers are restored or increased. It enable them to enjoy with more frequency than others, yet without tiredness.'

When the imp had completed its round it returned to its place in front of the Great Ram; its outline began to quiver, slowly it disintegrated into a ball of smoke, then the smoke faded into mist and the mist dispersed, leaving the air clear. Since producing this terrible familiar the Great Ram had remained with bowed head and as still as a statue. Now he raised his head, gave himself a slight shake and in a few swift strides walked round the throne to take up his first position with his back to the tall blood-red curtains. The congregation bowed their heads. With his left hand he made the sign of the cross upside down. There came a faint movement of the curtains and he disappeared as mysteriously as he had arrived.

An audible sigh of relief went up from the congregation. Abaddon then rose from the seat to one side of the altar, which he had occupied all this time, and addressed them:

'Brothers and Sisters of the Ram. Tonight there will be no further ceremonies. Seven nights hence we meet again. All should attend unless engaged that evening on the work of Our Lord Satan. I need hardly remind you that three Saturdays hence is Walpurgis Nacht, and a feast of obligation. As is customary, that night we shall symbolically sacrifice ourselves by offering up the life-blood of a ram to Him who has illimitable power. Now, be at your ease, and rejoice while appeasing those appetites given by the Creator to mankind with the object of making the world a happy place to live in. Do what thou wilt shall be the Whole of the Law.'

As he ceased speaking, the congregation broke its ranks, resumed its early carefree chatter, and some of them began to move the divans so that they should form a big circle. Others carried low tables from the sides of the hall, setting one down in front of each divan, while others again fetched dishes of food and bottles of wine to set upon them.

Before the arrangements for this next phase of the Satanists' activities was completed, Ratnadatta again pulled the curtains, then said to Mary: 'Now they make jolly feasting and afterwards they enjoy to dance. But that there ees no point in your remaining to see. Also I wish soon as possible to join them. So now we go.'

Mary thought it highly probable that the party would end in an orgy; so she would have liked to stay on in order to find out if those who wished were allowed to leave before it took place, and if the rest paired off in couples or they all became involved in a general drunken mêlée. But as Ratnadatta had announced his intention of joining the party as soon as he was rid of her, she had no option but to let him take her away.

Down in the front hall they retrieved their coats, then went out into the dark courtyard. The half-dozen parked cars were still there and Ratnadatta remarked to her, 'Only those who live at a distance outside London are permit to park cars here. Otherwise too many make for undesirable comment in neighbourhood. But I haf ordered taxi weech meet us not far off.'

Again they walked through the mean, now deserted, streets, until they emerged opposite one of the new, featureless blocks of flats that since the war have been erected in all the poorer parts of London. On the corner a taxi was standing with its flag down. As they approached it the driver leaned from his cab and said:

'Would you be Mr. Smithers?'

'Yes,' nodded Ratnadatta. 'I regret if we haf kept you waiting for long.'

'That's all right,' the taxi man replied gruffly. 'The garage wot sent me guaranteed my fare, and said you was a generous gent as would give me a good tip. 'Op in. Where d'you want ter go?'

The Indian handed Mary into the cab then, in a low voice, gave the driver his instructions. Within a few moments of the taxi moving off Ratnadatta again produced the folded handkerchief and Mary once more submitted to having her eyes bandaged.

'Now,' said Ratnadatta, as soon as he had knotted the handkerchief behind her head, 'what feelings haf you about what you haf witness tonight?'

'I was positively staggered,' she replied. 'For a lot of the time I felt frightened, of course. I'd have been terrified if I had not had you with me. And I'd never have believed such things could happen if I hadn't seen them with my own eyes. But I was fascinated; absolutely fascinated.'

'You haf not then too great fears to wish to proceed?'

'No. If other women can screw up the courage to face things like . . . like that black imp, I don't see why I shouldn't too.'

'Good, very good,' he purred. 'But there ees one other matter on which I must talk with you. Earlier I haf spoken much this evening upon subject off fertility rites performed by primitive peoples. I now giff you reason why they still practise such rites. It ees because they haf had great truth handed down from generation to generation that sex ees the most potent off all magics. By act off it alone can men and women enter into communion with Him who represents Creator. This explains why custom was in ancient times for every maiden to go to temple and offer her virginity to first stranger. That way, you understand, she make her first communion, Not to plees self with lover off choice. That to come afterwards. But first with whoever Our Lord Satan may choose for her as His representative. In my country are many fine temples open to public where this tradition ees still observed.'

'It is what is known as sacred prostitution, isn't it?' Mary asked in a low voice.

'Yes plees; you are right. But proper expression ees Service to Temple; and all who wish to become Sisters off the Ram must observe this ritual before they become initiate. You understand?'

93

'But I am not a virgin,' she objected quickly.

'No matter. The offering off yourself will be accepted as symbolic off act weech you would haf performed had you received right teaching when younger.'

Much that Ratnadatta had said over dinner had left no doubt in Mary's mind that initiation into the Brotherhood of the Ram would be a very different business from the purely spiritual promotion with which the leading Theosophists encouraged their most earnest adherents, and all she had seen in the past hour had confirmed her belief that an assurance that she was willing to submit herself to some form of sexual baptism would be demanded of her before she could get much further. From the beginning she had recognized that if Teddy had been murdered by Satanists, and she was to succeed in penetrating their circle, that would almost certainly be the price she would have to pay; but it had then been only a possibility for future consideration. Now she was called on to decide whether she really would go to such lengths.

She was not in love with, or pledged to, anyone; and to give herself to a man she had only just met would be no new experience. To some extent she was still affected by the mild aphrodisiac that Ratnadatta had given her in her drinks, and the image of the very tall man, with his splendid torso, rippling muscles and fair wavy hair, came into her mind, making her feel that, as a purely physical act, service to the temple might well prove enjoyable. At worst she would find it no more repugnant than one or two particularly unpleasant nights which she could recall having had to spend with half-drunken men during her black year in Dublin, and it would be over much sooner.

Nevertheless, there were limits beyond which she was not prepared to go. She had never even spoken to a coloured man until she had met Ratnadatta, and had all a normal white woman's prejudice against physical contact with them. What if one of the negroes or orientals who had been at the meeting was selected as the stranger to whom she had to offer up her symbolic virginity, or – worse – Ratnadatta himself. At the thought of his hot little hands upon her and his foul breath in her face, her stomach nearly turned over.

A shade impatiently, he asked: 'Well, haf you made up your mind? Since you are not a virgin and haf had several lovers why do you hesitate? You haf nothing to be frightened off. Come plees; tell me your decision.'

94

Suddenly she saw a possible way to safeguard herself from the sort of ordeal she felt that she could not possibly face, and answered shrewdly, 'While we were at dinner you told me that the sole creed of the Brotherhood was "Do what thou wilt shall be the Whole of the Law". That does not square with the possibility that I might find the first man who wanted me repugnant, and so intensely dislike the idea of having to give myself to him.'

Before replying Ratnadatta, in his turn, hesitated for a moment, then he said in the reassuring tone that a father might have used to a child afraid to enter a swimming pool: 'About that you need feel no concern. Our Lord Satan wishes joy to all who are prepared to serve Him. His High Priests decree matters so that partners in the Creation rite are well suited to one another.'

'In that case,' said Mary, 'I still wish to be accepted as an initiate.'

'Good; very good.' He sounded pleased, although not particularly so. 'You may congratulate yourself. Wisdom acquired in your past lives has again conquered inhibitions with weech your upbringing shackled you in this. I shall set your feet firmly on the Path for good life obtained by power to influence minds off others.'

A moment later she felt his fingers at the back of her head, untying the handkerchief that blindfolded her, and he added: 'Now you haf taken decision it ees not necessary to drive long way round about. Excuse plees that I shall drop you here; but so I am sooner back.'

On looking about her Mary saw that the taxi was moving eastwards and running up towards Hyde Park Corner. As they neared the bus stop, Ratnadatta said, 'I see you at Mrs. Wardeel's on Tuesday, yes? After that again on Saturday. You meet me plees at Tube Station as before. But this time later; at nine thirty o'clock.' Then he tapped on the window for the taxi to stop. They wished each other good night, she got out and the taxi carried him on in the direction of Piccadilly.

It was not yet quite midnight so the buses were still running. After a wait of five minutes she got one, and as she looked round at her fellow passengers she wondered what they would think if they knew how she had spent the evening. Had she told them, she knew that they would never believe her, and would put her down as mad. But she was not mad, and the possession of such a secret gave her a feeling of superiority over them. All the same, by the

95

time the bus set her down in Cromwell Road, the excitement that had buoyed her up for the past two hours was rapidly draining away.

Making as little noise as possible she crept upstairs and on reaching her little flat made herself a cup of coffee. As she drank it she visualized again the extraordinary things she had witnessed. On a sudden impulse she gave her arm a hard pinch to make certain that she was not dreaming.

She was not. That hideous black imp and the pregnant woman had not been part of a nightmare. She had really seen them. And she had arranged to go to the temple again with Ratnadatta next Saturday. If she did, she would have to submit to initiation. While the Indian had been talking to her about it that had not seemed too high a price to pay for the chance of identifying Teddy's murderers. But now, at the thought of those evil near-naked servants of the Devil, with whom she would have to feast and dance, a wave of panic and revulsion swept through her. Teddy was dead. Nothing she could do would bring him back to life. It was madness to place herself in the power of such people for the slender hope of being able to revenge him. Her nerve would break and she would give herself away. Suddenly she reversed her recent decision. She would not go on Saturday; or to Mrs. Wardeel's on Tuesday, either. She would make a clean break while there was still time, and try to forget the whole awful business as soon as possible.

7

An unfortunate – accident (?)

On Sunday morning Mary lay late in bed. The emotions that had agitated her the previous night had taken a lot out of her, and she felt tired and listless. As she thought over all that Ratnadatta had told her of the ancient cult, she had to admit to herself that many of his arguments in its favour were logical and, perhaps, contained a sub-stratum of truth. Yet that did not alter the fact that the advantages obtained by its few unscrupulous adherents must be gained at the expense of many honest decent people, and its amoral teachings be a menace to family life, high principles, and everything that went to make a well-ordered world.

But, in any case, she had not been seeking to obtain power for herself, and her resolution to be done with Ratnadatta and all to do with the occult remained unchanged.

That left her with a new problem. What was she now to do with herself? She could not yet pick up the threads of her old life where she had left them, because before leaving Wimbledon she had gone to an estate agent, told him she was going to Ireland, given him the keys of her flat and asked him to let it furnished for her for three months for the best price he could get.

Thinking of the flat turned her thoughts to Teddy. It was now six weeks since his death, yet, at times, she still missed him terribly. It was not that he had ever been for her the world's great heart-throb, but he had been gentle, generous and reliable and she had come to count on his companionship. He had been quite good-looking, too, a very adequate if not terribly exciting lover, and always most appreciative of all she did to make their home a place to which he could be proud to bring his friends.

Since he had had so many fine qualities, she wondered now why she had never felt more deeply about him, and decided that probably it was because he had been too transparently good to keep a woman intrigued for long by his personality. It seemed a sad commentary on life that the best men often failed to do so, whereas gay, irresponsible deceivers like Barney Sullivan could so often make women adore them.

It occurred to her then that at least she had Barney left over as a legacy from her abortive investigation into Teddy's murder. Planning the moves for her revenge on him would give her something to think about between the occasional jobs she was getting as a model. She would be seeing him again that night and this time she would give him some encouragement, anyhow to the extent of letting him kiss her.

At midday she got up and cooked herself an egg dish in the tiny kitchenette. It was very sparsely equipped and as she stood at the minute gas-stove she wished, not for the first time, that she were back in her own well-furnished kitchen at Wimbledon. It gave her the idea of going out there. Not to the flat, as by this time it was certain to be occupied by strangers; but she loved the Common. It was a sunny day and now that it was mid-April the silver birches would be putting out their tender young green leaves. The chance of her running into anyone she knew was small; and, suddenly recalling the way in which she had completely changed her appearance, she realized that they would not know her if she did. Anyway, now she had decided to stop playing the detective it was no longer necessary to avoid all contacts with life as Mrs. Morden.

As usual she took ample time to make herself up and dress with care, then she went out and took a bus up to the Green Man on the corner of Putney Heath. Owing to the fine weather there were quite a lot of people about, and twice single men driving slowly by in cars attempted to pick her up. But she was used to such unwelcome attentions when alone and, ignoring them, struck out with her long firm stride across the common. In turn she visited all her favourite spots; the old Windmill, the dell where William Pitt the younger, while Prime Minister, was said to have fought a duel, and the ponds on which the children were sailing their boats.

The fresh air and the long walk did her a power of good, the healthy sights and sounds around her drove from her mind haunting thoughts of the Great Ram, and after making a hearty tea at a little place just off the Common, to which she had been on a few previous occasions, she returned to London in excellent form for her next encounter with Barney.

They had arranged to meet at seven-thirty, and when she arrived at the Hungaria there he was in the foyer looking as devil-may-care as ever, but with an eye-shade over his left eye, and the curve of his cheek below it badly discoloured.

With a slightly amused grimace she said: 'It looks as if you have been mixed up in a fight.'

'I have,' he laughed. 'I'll tell you all about it when you've parked your coat.'

When she came out of the cloakroom he took her downstairs to the cocktail lounge and, as soon as they had ordered drinks, she asked, 'Now! What have you been up to?'

'I hit a man smaller than myself, and got the worst of it!'

'Then you deserved your lesson,' she said, although she did not believe him. He might be a thoroughly bad hat where women were concerned, but she felt certain he was not the type of man to do anything cowardly. All the same, it intrigued her that, instead of producing some cooked-up story about having defended a child or a dog against ill-treatment by a gang of toughs, he should elect to pretend to have been in the wrong.

'As a matter of fact,' he told her with a lopsided grin, 'I got it in a free-for-all. Last night some pals of mine suggested that we should try our luck at a gambling joint that one of them knew of up in St. John's Wood. After a bit of a binge we went along there and played *chemi* for a while. Of course the game was rigged, as it always is in those sort of places; but the bloke who runs it made it a bit too obvious that he took us all for suckers. When we caught him out red-handed, we decided to break the place up. By ill luck I found myself up against the chucker-out. He was only a little runt of a man, but I suppose he had served in the Commandoes or something. Anyhow, before I knew what was happening, he had given me this whopper, and a couple of minutes later he bundled me out into the street.'

The truth was very different. The previous night he had attended a Union meeting down in Shoreditch and come up against one of the casual risks inseparable from his investigation.

His work entailed his covering the activities of several Branches, each of a different Union, for all of which his office had provided him with forged membership cards, and he could, at most, have taken a regular job in the area of only one of them. Since it would have been pointless to devote eight hours a day to working as a docker, busman or some other category of labourer, having told the Secretary at each branch that he had recently come to London from Ireland for family reasons, he had registered himself at them all as unemployed and since skilfully evaded, on one excuse or another, taking such jobs as had been offered him.

The Party ticket he carried was evidence enough for the Communist members on the committees of the Branches to which he belonged that he was to be trusted, but to induce them actually to confide in and make use of him, he had lost no opportunity of putting himself forward at every meeting he attended as an active trouble-maker. It followed that the more conservative members of the branches had come to regard him as the type of hot-head who is a menace to regular employment and good relations with the bosses. The night before, on his leaving the meeting, three such anti-Communists had followed and later tackled him in an ill-lit street. They had charged him with being a 'professional out-of-work' and a 'bloody agitator' who wanted to see everyone else out of work in support of his Communist opinions. Then, while two of them had stood by, the third stalwart, a man with the build of a blacksmith, whom they referred to as 'good old Ed', had made him put his fists up and sailed into him.

As Barney was nowhere near the weight of his opponent, and in such circumstances pulling one of the fast tricks he knew was out of the question, he had had the sense to let himself be knocked down early in the encounter; so he had got off fairly lightly. Actually, too, he was more sorry for the man who had attacked him than for himself, since the two other men who had been present might talk about 'old Ed's' exploit; so he dared not refrain from reporting the affair to his Communist friends on the committee, which meant for certain that they would put 'old Ed's' name on their black list and, sooner or later, find an excuse to victimize him.

Mary, of course, knew nothing of all this, and she readily

100

accepted Barney's story of the gambling joint, because it fitted in with the picture of him, as an unprincipled young roisterer, that she knew of old. After a moment, she remarked with a smile:

'See what comes of being one of the idle rich and staying up half the night to throw your money about.'

'Have a heart!' he protested. 'I'm only one of those poor Irish Earls who has to get his robes out of pop when there's a coronation. As for being idle, I spent hours and hours last week trying to persuade Civil Aircraft lines to run tourist flights to Kenya.' He then launched into an account of established flight schedules and the numbers of passengers carried, from information he had mugged up since last they had met, the better to establish his cover-story with her.

After a second cocktail they went up to the restaurant, and she told him about two model shows for which she had been booked in the coming week; but all the time she was wondering why he had not yet asked her about her meeting with Ratnadatta. At length the temptation to broach the subject proved too strong for her and she said, a shade coldly: 'It seems you are no longer interested in learning how I got on last night.'

He had deliberately refrained in order to pique her, and now he laughed. 'I guessed you were bursting to tell me; so I've been holding out on you. But to tell the truth I'm itching to hear, and near as damn it gave you best only a moment ago. How's the form for your becoming a pretty white nannygoat and me a big black toad?'

'In your case, pretty good,' she replied lightly, 'though you needn't flatter yourself I'd have you as my familiar. Last night Mr. Ratnadatta took me to a place in Chelsea and gave me dinner upstairs in a private room!'

'What!' he exclaimed. 'Of all the nerve! And you let him?'

'Why not? He is a nice little man, and extremely learned.'

'Nice little man, my foot!' Barney stuck his chin out aggressively. 'He's a smarmy no-good Babu. It was damned impertinent of him to take you to a place like that, and I'd like to kick his learned bottom.'

'Really Barney!' It was the first time she had used his Christian name, although he had asked her to when she had dined with him the previous Thursday. 'You sound as though you had only just climbed out of the bog. It's silly to take such a primitive view of it. He wanted to tell me about the secret doctrine and he couldn't

101

do that in a restaurant with other people nearby who might overhear him.'

'Oh, all right then. What had he to say about it?'

For the best part of half-an-hour, between mouthfuls of food and wine, she gave him the highlights of Ratnadatta's discourse, and as they discussed them Barney had to agree that much of it made sense. Just after the main course they had chosen – a Hungarian *goulash* – had been served, he enquired: 'And when you had finished dinner, what happened then?'

She gave her sweetest smile. 'He took me to a Satanic temple.'

'The little swine! That's just what I feared he might do. Still, it seems you came to no harm, otherwise you wouldn't be looking so cheerful.'

'No; I enjoyed it. I found it absolutely fascinating.'

Barney was on the point of giving way to an outburst but, his duty coming uppermost in his mind, he checked it and asked, 'Whereabouts was this place?'

'I've no idea,' she replied lightly. 'He took me to and from it in a taxi, and both ways he insisted on putting a bandage over my eyes. Going there took a long time and for no very good reason I got the impression that it was somewhere in north-east London. But I'm sure the distance we covered coming back was much shorter, and when he dropped me at Hyde Park Corner the taxi had just come up the slope from Knightsbridge; so it may be anywhere.'

'You must have seen something of it when you got out of the taxi. What was it like outside?'

'It was an old Georgian mansion with a high wall all round it, except for its front; and there it faced on to a semi-private courtyard. But it was in the heart of a slum district. That's all I can tell you.'

'That doesn't get us far. In a great area like London there must be dozens of derelict places like that in districts that have gradually deteriorated into slums.'

'Oh, but it wasn't derelict. Inside it was beautifully decorated, and furnished in keeping with its period.'

'That doesn't surprise me. Those sort of crooks have oodles of money. What happened after you arrived there?'

For a second Mary hesitated. She had not forgotten Ratnadatta's threat that he and his friends would know about it if she betrayed their secrets, and take steps to exact a grim penalty. But now that she had made up her mind to break with them, and would soon have lost touch with him altogether, she felt that she need no longer take serious notice of his threat. Besides, she was thoroughly enjoying Barney's reactions to the dangers she had courted and was tempted by the urge to see him becoming more wrought up on her account.

'Well,' she said, 'if I do tell you I must ask you to keep it to yourself. You see, I'm not supposed to speak about these people's doings to anyone, and if it leaked out that I had they might make trouble for me.'

'I fully appreciate that,' he nodded. 'So the last thing you need be afraid of is that I'd let you down.'

'All right then. He took me up to a gallery where without being seen we could look down on the interior of the temple. There were about thirty men and women in it, all masked and wearing only gossamer-thin cloaks, through which one could see absolutely everything.'

Barney's face had become grim, and he muttered, 'That's more or less the kind of form I expected. But, damn it all, Margot! You mustn't let yourself get involved further in this sort of thing. You really mustn't!'

'I don't know.' She gave a shrug that implied sophisticated detachment. 'I haven't yet quite made up my mind. I wouldn't have missed this show last night for anything. By comparison, the sort of things one sees at Mrs. Wardeel's is child's play. Ratnadatta and his friends really can call down power, and I'm awfully tempted to go with him again next Saturday. It depends on whether I can screw up my courage to go through the initiation ceremony.'

'What form does it take? Something pretty beastly, I bet.'

'Not necessarily. But once in, I might be expected to take part in the, er – social activities of the Brotherhood.'

'I don't quite get you?'

'Well, Ratnadatta let me watch them do their serious stuff, but then he said that I'd seen quite enough for a first visit. Just as we were leaving they were about to sit down to a feast, and I've rather uneasy suspicions about the kind of fun and games they may have got up to afterwards.'

'Suspicions! Be your age, Margot! You'd get yourself raped for a certainty.'

She turned her big blue eyes on him with an innocent look. 'D'you really think so?'

'Of course I do! You mustn't even think of going to this place again. You've got nothing to offer them except your body, and that's what they're after. They might even dope and white-slave you. Let's hear now about what you did see – their serious stuff?'

With secret amusement at his agitation, Mary replied: 'First of all they made their reports to the High Priest about what they had been up to since last attending a meeting. He looked a charming old man; the sort of priest that no woman would mind confessing anything to. Then, after a long period of silence, came the manifestations of genuine occult power. Somehow, I didn't see exactly how it happened, but the Arch-Priest of the Brother-hood appeared from some curtains that hung behind the altar.

'They all seemed a bit scared of him, and so was I. Apparently he is the big-shot of a world-wide organization, and only in London on a visit. The greater part of his face was hidden under a horned headdress, he was dressed in black tights – just as one sees pictures of the Devil – and he was wearing a fortune in jewels. He listened to the requests made by the congregation, and granted nearly all of them what they asked for – beauty, ways to make money, restoration of sight and all sorts of other favours and cures.'

Barney stopped eating and a slow smile spread over his face as he said, 'Oh, come on; you're pulling my leg?'

'No, really! And after that there came the most extraordinary and terrifying thing of all. A small cloud of smoke formed down at his feet and from it there materialized a hideous black imp.'

While she was speaking, Barney had picked up from in front of him the wicker cradle in which lay the bottle of Burgundy they were drinking with their *goulash*. With his other hand he took her glass and refilled it. As she was about to take it from him, somehow, they fumbled it. At the moment she said the word 'imp', the glass slipped from between their hands and precipitated the whole of its contents into her lap.

With exclamations of dismay, both of them stood up. A passing waiter quickly pulled out the table and muttered expressions of sympathy while Mary hurried off to the ladies' room. The splashed table cloth was replaced, the remains of the *goulash* taken away and fresh places laid.

Mary was furious. As an aid to her designs to ensnare Barney she had put on her best semi-evening frock. It was brand new, and of a yellow material which she had chosen because, now that she was a brunette, she knew that the colour would set off her dark beauty to perfection.

In the cloakroom she quickly wriggled out of it and the attendant did her best to remove the stain by sponging with hot water. But when they had rough-dried it in front of an electric fire, the edge of the great circular splodge, where the wine had soaked in, was still plainly visible, and to their dismay they found that some of the wine having trickled through between Mary's legs, there was a smaller stain on the back of the skirt. As the wine there had had longer to penetrate the material, sponging the place had less effect and the woman glumly declared that she doubted if even proper cleaning would get it out.

Conscious of the many pairs of eyes taking stock of her misfortune as she recrossed the restaurant twenty minutes later, and still seething with rage, Mary rejoined Barney. He accepted the blame, and apologized profusely. She, out of good manners, did her best to make light of the matter and said that it had been her fault; but she was unable, altogether, to conceal her annoyance, and when new portions of *goulash* were served to them she petulantly told the waiter to take hers away as she had had enough.

Barney ate some of his in an uncomfortable silence; then in an endeavour to take her mind off her misfortune, he said: 'I didn't really mean it when I said I thought you were pulling my leg. Do go on and tell me more about the extraordinary things you saw last night. You'd got as far as the appearance of the black imp.'

As though she had received a mild electric shock, Mary stiffened slightly. It had flashed into her mind that the spilling of the wine might not have been an ordinary accident. In defiance of Ratnadatta's warning, she had been giving away the secrets of the Brotherhood. Was it possible that she was being overlooked and some occult force had been set in motion to check her? Thinking about it again she knew that the mishap had been more her fault than Barney's, because it was through her hand that the glass had actually slipped. Momentarily it had seemed as if her fingertips had lost their sense of touch, and next second the wine had cascaded into her lap. Suddenly she felt convinced that the temporary paralysis, although it had come and gone in less time than it takes to draw breath, could have been caused only by supernatural means.

Striving to conceal the fear with which the thought filled her,

105

she stammered: 'The . . . the imp! Yes, I . . . I. But, of course, I *was* pulling your leg. There was no imp or priest who used it to perform an abortion. . . .'

Barney shot her a swift, shocked suspicious glance and broke in, 'You never mentioned that.'

'Oh . . . didn't I? Well, it doesn't matter. I was making the whole thing up. I mean about them all wearing masks but having no clothes on, and about an Arch-Priest they called the Great Ram performing miracles.'

'D'you mean that? Honestly?'

'Of course.' She forced a smile. 'I was just seeing how much I could get you to swallow.'

He smiled back. 'I boggled at the miracles, and the black-clad gent producing an imp was a bit too much; but you sold me the general set-up. Anyhow, praise be to God you were only fooling. What did Ratnadatta's game turn out to be after all, though?'

'It was as I thought – Yoga.' Mary quickly tried to recall the little she had heard about Yoga, and went on: 'It really was rather thrilling. One of them, wearing only a loin cloth, lay down on a bed of nails, and another walked on live coals without burning his feet. It can be of practical use, too, if one works at it hard enough. Ratnadatta swears to me that through having learnt to breathe in a certain way he can keep himself warm on the coldest day without wearing an overcoat. It is also the royal road to getting out of one's body; so I mean to take up practising the exercises.'

'Does that mean that you are going to this place again next Saturday?'

Mary still had no intention of doing so; but the temptation to re-arouse Barney's concern for her, even to a more limited extent, led her to reply, 'Yes, why not?'

His reaction was just what she had hoped for. 'And that, I suppose, commits you to having dinner again in a private room with this slimy Babu?'

Recalling all she had told him of Ratnadatta's arguments in support of the ancient worship of Satan as the Lord of this World, she suddenly saw the red light. That did not fit in with the new aspect she had given the Indian as an innocent practitioner of Yoga. To forestall Barney's possibly asking her to explain this obvious contradiction in the story she was now anxious that he should believe, she said:

106

'I was fooling about that, too. We dined downstairs in the restaurant, and next Saturday he is not even giving me dinner. I'm not to meet him at the Sloane Square Tube until half-past nine.'

'What about his blindfolding you, though? Did he, or was that just another taradiddle to get a rise out of me?'

Mary saw that she was cornered. As she had no idea in what part of London the temple was situated, she could not tell him its locality; on the other hand, to admit that she had been blindfolded was to imply that there really was something sinister about it. In desperation, her nerves still barely under control, she exclaimed:

'Oh, for goodness' sake leave it! You've no right to catechize me about where I go or what I do.'

'Sorry,' said Barney, 'but seeing we're friends, I'm naturally interested.'

For a few minutes they ploughed into the Peach Melba that they had chosen as a pudding. When they had finished, Barney said: 'Come on, let's dance.'

His proposal brought back to her the stained condition of her frock. 'How can I?' she snapped. 'The wine not only went through to my belt, but dripped off it on to the back of my skirt; so both from the rear as well as from the front, I look a shocking sight.'

For a moment Barney considered whether he ought to offer to buy her a new dress. But he decided that as this was only the second time he had taken her out, he did not know her well enough, and she might regard the suggestion as an impertinence. After a moment he said, a shade resentfully:

'I'm terribly sorry about your dress. But really it wasn't my fault. I handed your glass to you and you seemed to be gripping it firmly before I let go of it.'

Again the terrifying image of the imp came into her mind. Renewed fear mingled with resentment caused her to give an angry shrug. 'What's it matter whose fault it was? My dress is ruined anyway; and I'm not going to make an exhibition of myself just to please you.'

Barney also had an Irish temper and at this, as he felt, unjustified attack on him, he said: 'Well, if you don't want to talk, and you won't dance, there's not much point in our remaining here, is there?'

'No,' she agreed. 'And the sooner I can get my dress into soak the better chance there will be of the stains not showing after I've had it dyed a less attractive colour.'

'O.K. Let's go then!' Abruptly he stood up and pulled out the table for her. 'Go and get your coat. I'll settle the bill later.'

She had hardly had time to think before he put her into a taxi. And he did not follow her into it. He gave the driver her address and some silver then, with a casual wave, he wished her an unsmiling 'good night' and stalked off back into the restaurant. They had been on edge with one another for three-quarters of an hour, but when the blow-up came it lasted less than four minutes.

On her way home Mary cursed herself whole-heartedly. She had meant to play the siren with Barney that evening, and so convert the interest he had shown in her from the first into a much warmer feeling. But now, for the second time, she had behaved in a manner which could only lead him to believe that, attractive as her looks might make her, she was so stupid, prudish, and naturally ill-tempered that it would be folly to cultivate her further. From the manner in which he had left her, it was clear that he did not mean to ask her out again.

Since she had lost Teddy everything had gone wrong. She had given up her home, and the friends who might have comforted her, to set out on a wild-goose chase; or at least one that fear had forced her to abandon. And now she had thrown away the last human link which could provide her with an interest. She was, and must continue to be for some time to come, as utterly alone in the world as if she had become marooned on a desert island. Unless, far worse, when she least expected it, Ratnadatta appeared on the scene to exact payment from her for having ignored his warning. Her day had started with such promise, yet ended with catastrophe. That night she wept herself to sleep.

8

A prey to loneliness

THE saying that 'hope springs eternal in the human breast' certainly applies to most healthy people, and there was nothing in the least wrong with Mary, either mentally or physically. In consequence, after a sound sleep, she began to view her situation more cheerfully. The occult manifestations she had witnessed on Saturday night were of a potency sufficient to have struck terror into anyone's mind; so it was hardly to be wondered at that only twenty-four hours later her nerves were still so jumpy that she had accepted an accident as evidence that the Brotherhood was keeping watch on her by supernatural means, and had the power to make her let drop a glass of wine.

But when she had woken and thought about the matter for a while, she decided that she had panicked unnecessarily. For the Satanists to keep a round-the-clock watch on her, they would need to employ a whole team of clairvoyants, and surely that was rating her importance to them much too high? To suppose that when anyone was about to betray their secrets an occult alarm bell rang to inform them of it was hardly credible; and, if they did have some such telepathic control, why should they have let her go on for several minutes describing the temple, its congregation and the things she had seen happen in it, before stopping her? On top of that the idea that they had the power temporarily to paralyse her fingertips from a distance seemed altogether too fantastic. The truth of the matter must be that she had simply been careless in taking the glass, and the fact that she had dropped

109

it just as she was on the point of telling Barney about the black imp had been no more than a coincidence.

Much comforted by this logical banishing of her overnight fears, while she lay in her bath she sought again for some interest to occupy her mind now that she had abandoned her crusade to bring Teddy's murderer to justice, and some weeks must elapse before she could restore her old appearance to a point when she could take up once more, without embarrassment, with the people they had known.

The modelling work on which she had started only recently had, as yet, brought her few new acquaintances. It would bring more in time, but she knew that the majority of the men in the so-called 'rag' trade regarded the models they employed only as dummies to display clothes on, and the girls themselves, enjoying a much higher than average standard of good looks, all had either husbands or numerous boy-friends, who kept them fully occupied.

The previous night she had resigned herself to having lost Barney and had not been able to make up her mind if she was glad or sorry. Despite her long nurtured grievance against him, while in his company she enjoyed his gay, intelligent conversation and, subconsciously, was still strongly attracted to him physically. To know that she would not now have the satisfaction of making him fall for her, then being thoroughly beastly to him, was a sad disappointment; but she tried to console herself with the thought that two wrongs did not make a right, so perhaps it was as well that her plan to avenge herself on him had been nipped in the bud.

Yet the thought of him was like a worrying tooth and as she lay in her bath she toyed with the idea of trying to get in touch with him. Had she known his address she would have written him a line of apology for her behaviour, and so tried to start the ball rolling between them again that way, but she did not. It then occurred to her that he would be in the telephone book; so, getting out of the bath, she dried herself quickly and got the book, but no Lord Larne was listed in it. Throwing it down she upbraided herself for a fool for having even bothered to look, as she ought to have realized that, having no right to the title, he would not have had the face to use it publicly. That settled the matter. She must accept it that he had once more gone out of her life.

110

The only other people she had met after changing her personality to Margot Mauriac were those who attended the meetings at Mrs. Wardeel's. She now knew several of them by name and could, if she chose, develop a friendship with them. As they were nearly all considerably older than herself, and earnest seekers after truth, that would not prove very exciting. But at the thought of whole days, when she had no modelling engagements, spent in aimless window-gazing, and with no prospect in the evening but going to a cinema on her own, she decided that such human contacts would be better than nothing.

She had not meant to go to Mrs. Wardeel's again, because that would entail meeting Ratnadatta. But if the spilling of the wine had been, as she was now convinced, a normal accident, she had nothing to fear from him. Instead of simply not keeping her appointment with him next Saturday she would tell him on Tuesday night that, having thought the matter over, she had now decided that she was still too conventionally minded to prove a suitable candidate for initiation into his Brotherhood.

She began to wonder then if, from anger at her having wasted his time, he might bring some form of trouble on her. But suddenly a new thought entered her mind. Barney would be at the meeting too. Why hadn't she thought of that before? Here was her chance to recapture him. She would get him to walk home with her afterwards, tell him that as a compensation for having spoilt his evening on Saturday she had prepared a little supper for them, and bring him up to her flat.

The more she thought over this new plan, the more it pleased her, and the urge she felt to carry it out soon overcame her vague fears of meeting Ratnadatta again. That afternoon she went up to the West-End to model some swim-suits for the coming summer season, and in the evening thoroughly enjoyed a film. Tuesday she had no engagement; so she spent the morning turning out her sitting-room and in the afternoon spread herself at Harrods, buying smoked Westphalian ham, cold salmon, materials for a salad, cheese straws and fruit. As she laid the table she again regretted her own much nicer things at Wimbledon, but she had bought plenty of flowers to make the room gay and the wine-salesman had assured her that the bottle of Hock he had recommended was really good.

Filled with happy anticipation, she set off for Mrs. Wardeel's and arrived there a little before eight o'clock. When she entered the lecture room neither Barney nor Ratnadatta had arrived. The latter did so just before the proceedings started, but Barney had still not put in an appearance.

The lecture that evening was on Maya religious beliefs and how they tied up with Theosophy, but she hardly took in a word of it. Every few minutes she looked towards the door, hoping that she would see Barney slip in and quietly take a seat at the back; but her hopes were disappointed.

She then tried to persuade herself that, having heard the subject of the lecture at the last meeting, he thought it would bore him, so meant to come later in time only to see another medium perform. But the lecture finished, the chairs were arranged in a circle, and still he did not come.

On this occasion the medium was a tall, thin man. Having taken his chair in the middle of the circle, he was wrapped up to the chin by Mrs. Wardeel in a voluminous sheet, then two members of the audience were chosen to assure the rest that no hidden wires or other apparatus had been connected in his vicinity. All the lights, except for one small bulb, were turned off, the spectators linked hands with their neighbours, there was a long, long silence during which nothing happened, then a gentle radiance in the neighbourhood of the medium's mouth became perceptible.

Gradually it increased until the whole of the lower part of his face could be seen by it. Opening his mouth wide he began to breathe stertorously and a pale yellow foam formed round the inside of his lips. The foam increased until it became a solid bubble, hiding both his upper and lower teeth and his tongue. For a while the bubble ballooned and deflated in time with his breathing, and as he strove to force it out the radiance was sufficient to show that sweat was streaming down his face. At last it lapped over, covering his chin then, looking like a thick band of dough, slowly made its way down the slope of the sheet that covered his chest until it reached the level of his stomach. There it stopped, but more and more of the stuff oozed down till a lump as large as a medium-sized melon had formed. The lump flattened out and five roundish points began to protrude from it. These lengthened until the whole thing had roughly the shape of a huge hand attached by a curved arm to the medium's mouth.

Mary had never before seen an occultist project ectoplasm, and cause it to take on the likeness of human limbs or a rudimentary human body; so normally she would have been much impressed by the strange exhibition. But having, three nights before, witnessed the far more hair-raising spectacle of the Great Ram conjuring up a cloud of smoke that turned into a perfectly formed manikin capable of movement, although unattached to him, she found the long slow performance somewhat wearisome. Moreover, her mind was still on Barney and his failure to attend the meeting.

When they had last dined together, he had frankly declared his disbelief in the genuineness of the medium they had seen the week before, so she thought it possible that scepticism about Mrs. Wardeel's parties as a whole had decided him against giving any more of his evenings to attending them. But she was more inclined to believe that, feeling certain she would be there, he had refrained from coming so as to avoid any possibility of being drawn into a resumption of their, so far, most unsatisfactory, tentative moves towards entering on an affair.

Her disappointment was naturally proportionate to the hours she had given to musing over the way in which that evening she would make Barney take a much better view of her, and those she had spent in preparing that delightful little supper. But by the time the medium had re-absorbed his ectoplasm she had made herself face up to it that, if it was to avoid meeting her again that Barney had failed to attend this meeting, the odds were all against his coming to the one next week, so she would be wise to write him off for good and all.

When the party moved into the dining-room for coffee, Ratnadatta sidled up to her, gave his toothy smile and said in a low voice: 'Mrs. Mauriac, I haf another person with weech I wish to talk here tonight. But I also wish to talk with you. As it ees private matter, better that we talk in street; so plees I walk part off way home with you.'

His friendly greeting at first confirmed her belief that she had nothing to fear from him; but his words sent a sudden chill through her. Perhaps he did know that she had spoken of the Brotherhood to Barney. If so, his proposal to walk home with her suggested that he wanted to get her on his own in a situation where he could do her some injury. Then, after a moment, she dismissed the idea as highly improbable, and reassured herself with the thought that, anyway, he would not be such a fool as to attempt to harm her while walking through a respectable district

113

at an hour when there would still be plenty of people about on whom she could call for help.

Taking her consent for granted, he had left her at once and quickly attached himself to a heavily made up, middle-aged woman, wearing valuable jewels, whom Mary had not seen there before, and he remained talking to her for the next twenty minutes. Meanwhile a retired General, who had singled Mary out on a previous occasion, brought her a coffee and sought to entertain her with an account of marvels he had seen Fakirs perform in India many years before she was born.

When the party began to break up, the bejewelled lady took herself off, Ratnadatta rejoined Mary, listened with her to a final story by the General, then tactfully prised her away from him. Five minutes later they were walking side by side towards the central stretch of the Cromwell Road, and he said:

'I haf forgot to tell you that when we meet on Saturday you must wear no make-up. None at all, you understand? Scrub your face clean. Also your hair must be done as plainly as possible, scrag back flat with ends done as bun at back off head.'

Mary gave him an astonished look, then faltered: 'As a matter of fact, Mr. Ratnadatta, I . . . I've been thinking things over and I . . . well, I've come to the conclusion that I'm not really advanced enough to accept initiation yet.'

In turn he shot a surprised look at her. But his voice held no trace of anger as he replied: 'Initiation! You haf flatter yourself. At best some time must pass before you can hope for so much. First stage ees neophyte. Acceptance on probation only, after taking oath of loyalty to the Brotherhood. Next the neophyte must perform some act for token off willing service. . . .'

He had been about to go on, but she cut in quickly, 'Do you mean that in the case of a woman it is then that she performs her service to the temple by, er – offering herself to a stranger?'

'No, no.' He shook his head. 'That does not come until initiation. It ees part off the initiation rite. By act off willingness I refer to performing satisfactorily some work for furtherance off aims off the Brotherhood weech the neophyte is giffen order to do by our High Priest Abaddon. Only by passing such test does a neophyte become qualified for initiation.'

They walked the next fifty yards in silence, while Mary was thinking, 'It looks, then, as if I could go with him again to the Temple next Saturday without having anything much to be afraid of. If they had designs on me the last thing they would want is for me to do my hair up in a bun and make myself look like a scarecrow. And it would give me one more chance to see if I can learn from them anything about Teddy.' Yet caution urged her to try to find out a little more before committing herself; so aloud she asked: 'What exactly would I have to do to be accepted as a neophyte?'

'I haf already tell you,' he replied a shade impatiently. 'You promise obedience to our High Priest and take oath to keep secrets off the Brotherhood. Then you are welcomed and well-wished by all present and ceremony is concluded. The rite takes only a quarter-of-an-hour – perhaps twenty minutes.'

'And afterwards?' she enquired.

'Why, as you are not initiate, you must go home, off course. I take you again to Hyde Park Corner. You wait then two, three, perhaps four weeks, till occasion arise when Abaddon has use for you, and requires from you token act off willing service.'

'What would happen if I failed in that?'

'You would haf lost your chance to become initiate. Most regrettable; for whatever you may feel yourself, I know you to be ready for advancement. But there ees no reason why you should fail. The task provided ees always suitable for the neophyte to weech it ees given.'

Now that he had made it clear to her beyond all question that she must still pass through two preliminary stages before having finally to commit herself, she felt very differently about the matter from the way she had on getting home from her visit to the Temple the previous Saturday night. The thought of the long empty days and lonely evenings that lay ahead of her played their part, and once more there rose in her the urge to try to find out about Teddy.

'Very well, then,' she said impulsively. 'To be honest, I was a bit scared and meant to back out. But I don't mind going through this short ceremony if I am to be given plenty of time to get used to the thought of facing the big one. So I'll meet you as we arranged on Saturday.'

'Good; very good,' said Mr. Ratnadatta.

9

A fiendish plot

THE following morning, while Mary was disconsolately making a late breakfast of the Westphalian ham she had bought as a first dish for the supper at which she had planned to entertain Barney, Colonel Verney was already in his office hard at work sorting the papers in his 'In' tray. On the previous Monday he had had to attend a N.A.T.O. conference in Naples; so he had flown down to Nice on Friday night, in order to spend the weekend with his wife, gone on to Naples and got back only the night before. He had found Molly in good form and had thoroughly enjoyed relaxing among the orange trees and oleanders in the garden of their villa. Such breaks he knew to be a sound insurance against strain from overwork but, all the same, they had to be paid for on his return by an accumulation of matters requiring his attention.

Putting the longer documents aside he dealt first with letters needing a prompt answer; then, having sent his secretary off to type them, he got down to an hour's reading of reports. Among them there was one from Squadron-Leader Forsby. In a brief letter he said only that Otto Khune's behaviour during the past week had continued much as before and as yet gave no grounds for suspicion that he was communicating with any questionable person. But sometime during the week he had completed the account of his past, and a copy of it, which had been taken after a further search of his quarters, carried out when he was absent

116

from the Station on Sunday, was enclosed. Spreading out the typescript, Verney read:

It was in May 1950 that, after an interval of eight years, I again saw my brother Lothar. I was at the time living with my wife Dinah at Farnborough, and engaged, as an official of the Ministry of Supply, in tabulating the results of new fuels then being tested at the Experimental Aircraft Establishment there.

We occupied a pleasant little house on the outskirts of the town, had made a number of friends in the neighbourhood, and our life was a very happy one until, early in May, I began to be plagued by constant thoughts of Lothar.

For a long time past, thoughts of him had come to me only infrequently. I was aware, although it had never been confirmed as a fact by a communication from him or any other source, that he was in the U.S.S.R., and now content to carry on his scientific work there under his Russian masters in one of their research establishments. It distressed me that he should be working for the Communists, but there was nothing I could do about it, and I had come to accept it that, as our paths in life had diverged so widely, it was unlikely that we should ever meet again.

Yet, having once more started to think about him, try as I would I could not get him out of my mind. In fact, I became the victim of a mental disturbance of the same nature as that I have suffered recently. I found that I could no longer concentrate fully on my work or take pleasure in the social life that my wife and I had been leading. Then too, as now, I gradually became convinced that Lothar was in England and wished to see me.

My visions of him increased in clarity until I became familiar with the surroundings in which he was living. He had two rooms on the ground floor of a rather shoddy apartment house. It was number 94, in a long dreary street which I knew to be in North London somewhere beyond St. Pancras Station. The next development was my becoming aware of the way to find it on starting from the Station, and that Lothar was willing me to come there to meet him.

I knew instinctively that no good could come from such a meeting; so for some days I resisted the urge to go there. But Lothar gave me no peace; and both Dinah and my fellow employees at the research station became greatly alarmed by my mental condition. They said that at times I talked as if I were a different person, and urged me to see a doctor.

117

To have done so would have been futile. Medical science now accepts telepathy, but I doubt if any doctor would have believed my story and, even if he had, it would have been beyond his power to help me. The probability is that he would have had me put into a mental home, if only for a period of observation, and, as that could have brought me no relief, I were not prepared to submit to it.

At length, towards the end of the month, on May 26, to be exact, I decided that, if I was not to lose my job owing to a complete breakdown, I must give way to Lothar's urging. So I took the day off and went up to London.

From St. Pancras I had no difficulty in finding the street in which Lothar had his rooms, and it proved in all respects precisely the same as I had seen it in my visions. On going up the steps of No. 94, I saw that the front door was ajar. Walking in I entered the first room on the right. As I had felt certain he would be, he was sitting there and expecting me.

To begin with, my fears that such a meeting would bring misfortune on myself were stilled, because he greeted me with great affection; and few people can exercise more charm than Lothar when he is in a mood to do so. I learned that he had periodically overlooked me and so had followed the outline of my career just as I had his. He had known of my marriage and that I had left the United States to settle in Britain, and was aware of the type of work that I was then employed upon; and he confirmed my belief that he had gone by way of South America to Germany, been captured by the Russians at Peenemünde and later reconciled himself to continuing his scientific research on rocket development under the Soviet Government.

It was this, he admitted frankly, that had been his main reason for not having got into touch with me openly, as he had entered Britain by clandestine means and, to minimize the risk of being found out, left his lodging only when the mission he had come upon necessitated his doing so. His other reason was that, since we still resembled one another so closely, it would have been impossible for him to conceal the fact that he was my twin and, as I had no doubt told my wife that he had deserted the Allied cause during the war, for him to have turned up at Farnborough might have greatly embarrassed me.

He produced a bottle of wine, and over it we talked for a long while about our youth in Chicago and our devotion to one another in those days, then of the lives we had made for ourselves in Russia

118

and Britain respectively. From what he told me it was clear that upper-crust scientists fared far better there than here. We were then thirty-two years of age and he was already receiving an emolument in the form of excellent accommodation, transport, holiday, and priority goods vouchers which, added to his cash salary, enabled him to live at a standard that, with British taxation at its present level, I could never hope to equal.

It was this which led me to make some remark to the effect that not only had the men in the Kremlin abandoned all attempts to make the Marxist ideology work in practice, but they were deliberately creating a new aristocracy with such cynical disregard for even a semblance of equality that Britain's Welfare State brought her much nearer to being a Communist society than the revolution had Russia.

He entirely agreed, remarking that true Communism could never work in any country and, realizing that, although they could not openly admit it, the men in the Kremlin had, in fact, become Nazis. It was that which made him willing and happy to work for them. He went on to say that he still believed the Hitler doctrines to be the only ones by which, in the modern world, the masses could be made to work the hours they should and be controlled effectively; that, by the application of those doctrines, power could be concentrated in a few hands in a way that was impossible in the democracies, and that power ultimately used to establish a world order – call it Communism or anything else one liked – ruled over by a single governing body.

When that day came, he declared with complete self-confidence, he meant to be a member of it – and it would not be many years in coming. The Western Powers could not compete effectively in the armaments race because the expenditure of their governments was limited by the reluctance of the voters, to whom they had to go, cap in hand, to retain power, to provide sufficient money; and as each of them, again at the dictation of these masses, had to place the individual interests of their countries before those of maintaining a united front, capitalist-democracy was doomed. Innumerable jealousies and divergent policies inherited from the past could be made afresh into bones of contention and played up into serious national issues, which would keep them from ever combining wholeheartedly; so, one way and another, when Russia struck they would be incapable of mobilizing even a third of their potential strength against her.

119

Power, he contended, was the only thing really worth having. And what could equal playing a part in decreeing the way of life to be followed by the whole human race when the new World State was established? He meant to do so, and out of his old affection for me he wished me to share his exalted station.

It then transpired that the object of his visit, which was being kept secret even from all but one high official at the Soviet Embassy, was to take me back to Russia with him. He said that immediate employment could be arranged for me with a remuneration which would enable me to enjoy many luxuries that I could not afford here, and that if I wished it my wife could be brought over later to join me. But that was only the beginning of the programme. He was already well on the way up the ladder to political power and in due course would have a special use for me. What exactly that was, he would not specify; but it hinged upon the fact that, as identical twins, once I became fluent in Russian we could easily pass for one another.

Even while he was still describing this, apparently, alluring prospect to me, I had made up my mind to refuse. Quite apart from the fact that I believe enslavement and the destruction of individuality, which is the policy of the Soviet Government, to be the most evil fate that could befall mankind, and that I am a loyal British subject with a deep sense of gratitude for the freedom and security I enjoy as a naturalized citizen of this country, I was not in the least tempted to accept temporary affluence as the price of the uncertainties of aiding him in his political career in Russia. Brilliant as I knew Lothar to be, there could be no guarantee that his ambitions would not bring him up against some, perhaps, less gifted but more powerful rival; then, as there were plenty of examples to show, it would need only one slip by him on some interpretation of Marxist doctrine for us both to land up in Siberia, or even find ourselves facing a firing squad.

On my declining his proposal he tried sweet reason and, exerting all his charm and will-power, argued with me for over an hour. Then, finding that I still stood firm, his manner changed and he began to threaten me. He said that secret plans he had made for the furtherance of his ambitions could not be carried out unless he had a double to appear in his stead on certain important occasions and that, as I was the only person who could pass as himself without question, like it or not I had got to return to Russia with him.

When I still refused he issued an ultimatum. He gave me three days in which to think it over and said that, if by the third day I did not come to him again prepared to do as he wished, he would give me no further chance but bring about my ruin.

On that we parted and I returned to Farnborough. As can be imagined, I was greatly worried. It did not occur to me that, living in hiding as he was, he was capable of upsetting the well-ordered life I was leading, but I did fear that he would use the occult link between us to badger me and make me miserable. To my surprise the contrary proved the case and for a whole week I remained free from those mental invasions of my consciousness by him with which I had been afflicted from the beginning of the month.

This lulled me into a false sense of security. I began to believe that his threats had been only idle ones, and that he had resigned himself to my refusal to go to Russia with him. I was to learn differently.

I belonged to a group of scientists who met once a month for an informal dinner – for which, as a number of us came up from the country, we did not change – at the Connaught Rooms. A distinguished guest always addressed us on some subject of interest and there was a debate afterwards. Sometimes the debates were of such interest that a number of us congregated in the downstairs bar after the meeting had broken up to continue the discussion. If I joined the party in the bar, lingering there made it too late for me to catch the last train back to Farnborough; so I had formed the habit of taking up an overnight bag with me as I had found that I could always get a room at one or other of the small Bloomsbury hotels if need be. Governed, therefore, by my degree of interest in the subject discussed, and how I chanced to be feeling, I either stayed the night in town or got home soon after midnight.

It so happened that a week after my meeting with Lothar, I attended one of these dinners, and stayed on afterwards talking to some of my friends. When I went to the cloakroom to get my night-bag the attendant declared that I had already collected it. In vain I produced my ticket and vowed that I had not. The attendant protested that I had said I had mislaid my ticket, and that on my giving my name, which was on a label attached to the bag, and signing a slip, the bag had been handed to me. She also produced another attendant to confirm that I was the gentleman to whom the bag had been given.

Supposing that a professional thief had impersonated me, I registered a complaint and, as it was by then too late to catch the last train, after trying several hotels that were full I secured a room at

121

one in which I had stayed only once before, and slept in my underclothes.

Next morning, as was my custom on such occasions, on arriving back in Farnborough I went straight from the station to my office. At the midday break I went home for lunch. As I greeted Dinah I expected her to ask me how I had enjoyed my dinner in London. Instead, looking more radiant than I had seen her for a long time, she threw her arms round my neck and cried:

'Darling, you ought to go to those dinners of yours more often if you always come home after them. I don't think we've had such a wonderful night since our honeymoon.'

As she was holding me to her I was able to conceal my astonishment. Then, over her shoulder, I distinctly saw Lothar's face, and it was sneering at me. Instantly the explanation of what Dinah had said became clear. Lothar had impersonated me and slept with her the previous night.

My distress and fury can be imagined; but realizing the shattering effect the truth would have on her, I felt that I must prevent her from getting the least suspicion that anything was wrong. Controlling my emotions with an effort, I told her how much I loved her and what a joy she was to me. Later, I found my night-bag in a cupboard in the hall. That was concrete evidence that Dinah had not dreamt my return, and I had no doubt that Lothar had gone to some trouble to collect it, so that he might use it as a sort of sign-manual that he really had been there and taken my place as Dinah's husband in our bed.

One would have thought such an act, causing me the sick misery that it did, would have been enough to satisfy his resentment at my refusal to fall in with his plans; but it was not.

Three weeks elapsed, during which I gradually became less troubled by thoughts of him and the criminal deception he had practised on Dinah; then one morning I received a solicitor's letter. It informed me that I was to be cited as co-respondent in an action for divorce.

Knowing myself to be guiltless, I went up to London and demanded from the solicitors an explanation of the unjustified charge that had been brought against me. They gave it to me, chapter and verse.

Soon after six o'clock in the evening of the day that I had attended the dinner, a Mr. Wilberforce had caught me in flagrante delicto with his wife in the bedroom of their flat in Bayswater. He had forced me to give him my name and address, and a woman who cleaned for them was prepared to give evidence that, not only had she let me into the flat that evening, but had also done so on two previous occasions. The fact, as I learned later, that Mrs. Wilberforce was a woman of dubious reputation, who frequented night-clubs, made no difference to the legal aspect of the matter. As I had arrived in London that evening at five o'clock and spent the best part of the next two hours watching a film that I had particularly wanted to see, I could produce no alibi.

The only possible explanation was that Lothar, having read my mind and knowing my intentions, had impersonated me with this woman before going down to Farnborough, as a means of being further revenged upon me.

Hardly able to contain myself for fury, I jumped into a taxi and drove straight to Lothar's rooms. This time the front door was shut. My ring was answered by a blowsy woman who gave me a surly nod and said:

'Hello Mr. Vintrex, I'd begun to think you wasn't coming for that envelope you left with me. Hang on half-a-mo', and I'll go and get it for you.'

It was obvious that she took me for Lothar, so I let her continue to think so, and she slouched off down into the basement. The moment she had disappeared I tried the door of the room in which I had seen him. It opened at my touch and I walked in on the off chance that I might find something there which would give me a clue to his whereabouts.

A young man with long hair was seated there tapping away at a typewriter. I asked quickly if he happened to know the address of the previous tenant and how long it was since he had left. With a shrug, he replied, 'No, I don't even know his name. But I've been here a fortnight.'

I thanked him and backed out just in time to meet the landlady as she reappeared up the basement stairs. She handed me an envelope and with a murmur of thanks I left the house.

It had jumped to my mind that Lothar had left some paper with the woman because he thought it too dangerous to carry about with him, so he was still in this country and, with luck, it might be something which would enable me to trace him; or, rather, enable the police to do so, as, by then, I had made up my mind to put them on to him as an enemy agent.

With trembling fingers I opened the envelope. It contained only a single sheet of paper with the following words printed on it in

123

capitals – 'Congratulations on Dinah. She must love you a lot, and I'm sorry I won't be in England when you have your next night out. I wonder how she will take it when you have to tell her about the Wilberforce woman?'

My feelings can be imagined as the full implications of the swinish double trick he had played me sank in. And as he had evidently left the country it was useless to go to the police.

Desperately I wondered what to do. At first I felt inclined to tell the truth, both to Dinah and to a solicitor as my defence in the divorce case now pending against me. But since Lothar could no longer be laid by the heels and brought into court as evidence of my innocence, I knew that I should never be believed. I had told Dinah about Lothar, and his being my identical twin, during our engagement, but I don't think his name had been even mentioned between us since. If only I'd told her about my seeing him in London, or gone to the police then, I would have had some sort of case, but to state now that my twin brother had turned up out of the past and impersonated me would sound laughably thin.

One thing I could do was to subpoena the woman with whom Lothar had lodged because, obviously, I could not have been living in her house and at Farnborough at the same time; and that, in due course, I did, but it did not save the situation.

For some days I said nothing to Dinah, but I became so ill from worry that I decided the only way to escape a nervous breakdown was to come clean with her. Of course, I did not tell her that Lothar had slept with her that night I was in London, or that he was a Russian agent, as the first would have inflicted grievous pain on her unnecessarily and the second, if it now got out – my not having reported that at the time – might have cost me my job to no good purpose. I told her only that I had seen Lothar in London and that he had used my name when caught with the Wilberforce woman.

Dinah behaved very well; but it was obvious that she did not believe my story. She took a night to think things over, then told me that our future must depend on what transpired when the case was heard. If I could prove my innocence she would most humbly beg my pardon for having doubted me. If I'd suffered a temporary aberration and it was a single slip, she would forgive me. But if it emerged that I had been having a regular affair with this woman, she would have to think again. In the meantime she meant to go back and live with her parents.

As the case could not be heard until the autumn session, I spent *a miserable summer. At last it came on and in court I saw Mrs. Wilberforce for the first time. She was a Spanish type black-haired and good looking, and had plenty of sex appeal. I suppose I should have expected it, but to my horror she greeted me as an old friend, and said, with a reproachful smile:*

'I do think, Otto, you've behaved awfully badly in not writing or coming to see me all this time. What's done's done, and it couldn't have made matters any the worse for you.'

All I could do was to make no reply and give her a stony stare.

The case did not take long, as my only witness, the lodging-house woman, let me down completely. My solicitor had told me that she had proved extremely awkward and refused to sign a statement; and now in court she declared on oath that she had never before set eyes on me.

Her reason was not far to seek. She must have been in the pay of the Russians to take lodgers that they sent her, ask no questions and keep her mouth shut. Evidently she believed me to be a Soviet agent and, for her own safety, had determined to deny all knowledge of me, so that should I later be arrested she would escape being involved in the case.

The verdict, of course, went against me; but after that I thought my fortunes were changing for the better. The cross-examination of the Wilberforces' cleaning woman had disclosed that her mistress frequently entertained men alone in the flat when her husband was absent; so the damages awarded to Wilberforce were much less than I had feared I should have to pay and, as this also revealed her as unlikely to be the kind of woman I would have had a regular affair with, I had good hopes that Dinah would return to me.

Alas, I had underestimated Lothar's vindictiveness. With diabolical cunning he had left a hidden landmine to make more certain the wrecking of my marriage. Like so much else about us, our writing was so similar that he had never had any difficulty in forging mine, and he had made most skilful use of a letter purporting to have been written by me to Mrs. Wilberforce.

In it he referred with filthy delight to certain obscenities in which they had indulged on his previous visits to her, and said how greatly he was looking forward to another session of the same kind when he came to see her at six o'clock on the evening of my dinner in London. But instead of sending it to her he had sent it to her husband with an anonymous note to the effect that the writer had found it in a handbag that she had left behind in a night-club. It was this which had led

Wilberforce to turn up at their flat unexpectedly at the hour given, as Lothar had evidently planned he should, and so catch them in bed together.

Fortunately for my reputation, as the case against me appeared such a clear one the contents of the letter had not been disclosed in court but only mentioned as the reason for Wilberforce having surprised his wife. But the solicitors who were holding a watching brief for Dinah requested a sight of it afterwards, and their report to her proved my final undoing. She started divorce proceedings against me and early in 1951 was granted her decree nisi.

I have not seen Lothar in the flesh, or heard anything of him, since our one meeting in May 1950. But I feel certain that he is now in England, and have the impression that he is living somewhere near the East Coast. Anyway, he is endeavouring to condition my mind to a state in which I would be prepared to meet him again. Should he succeed, it is quite possible that this time I shall murder him. It is in case I should do so that I have set all this down; as it may be regarded as some justification for my act, and stand me in better stead than would the same account if extracted from me, piece by piece, under police examination after the crime had been committed.

Apart from the poignant tragedy unfolded in it, this second instalment gave Verney considerable concern. From it there could be no doubt that Lothar had completely gone over to the Russians. Therefore, if he was now in England and endeavouring to get hold of his brother, the odds were all against his wanting to do so only for personal reasons; it was much more likely that he hoped to induce him to give away information connected with his secret work and was, in fact, a Soviet agent.

That being so, no effort must be spared to secure his arrest. But with the information so far to hand, there was no more chance of finding him than a needle in a haystack. Owing to Otto's justifiable hatred of Lothar, it seemed unlikely that he would be persuaded to agree to a meeting but, if he did, Lothar would have to disclose his whereabouts to him, and then would come a chance to pounce. Perhaps at that point Otto might be persuaded to co-operate; but, in asking him to do so, Verney saw a snag. If Lothar was overlooking him he might learn of his brother's intention to betray him and so avoid the trap.

After some thought C.B. decided to await developments for a

while, but to take the precaution of sending Forsby two extra assistants with instructions that, should Otto leave the station, they were to tail him and, if he met his twin, arrest both brothers.

For another three-quarters of an hour the Colonel rapidly read through an assortment of documents, then his buzzer went and his secretary said over the inter-com: 'Mr. Sullivan is here and would like to see you. He says it is rather important.'

'Send him in,' replied Verney, and a moment later he was greeting Barney. 'Hello, young feller! Been in the wars?'

Barney's eye was getting back to normal, but the flesh round it still showed discolouration. 'No, Sir,' he grinned. 'Just a tiff with a stout fellow who didn't like my politics.'

'Well, what's the news? It had better be pretty good, because I've got my plate extra full this morning.'

'It is, Sir. I tried to get you Friday night, but they said you wouldn't be back till this morning. I've got the low-down on the source from which the Commies draw their secret funds to prolong unofficial strikes.'

'Have you indeed! Good work. Sit down and tell me more.'

'There are about fifty men at a small factory out at Hendon who have been on strike for some weeks without Union backing. My Red pals on the District Committee haven't made any secret of it from me that they are giving unofficial assistance to the strikers. On Friday, as I'm an out-of-work, I managed to get myself picked as one of the two body-guards against a possible hold-up to go with the official who draws the money from the bank. We drove in a car to Floyds branch in Tottenham Court Road. There were two big bags of silver, so I and my opposite number took those while the Chief Scout locked up the notes in his brief case. To my disappointment he had pushed the cheque across the counter face down, but after the cashier had paid out a clerk came along to speak to him. He was still holding the cheque in his hand, but not looking at it. Without thinking he turned it over and I succeeded in getting a squint at the side that mattered. It was drawn on the account of the Manual Workers' Benevolent Society.'

'Well done, partner. Nice work.' C.B. flicked open his case and offered the long cigarettes. 'I'll see the right chap at the Treasury and ask him to find out for us who finances this Workers' Benevolent. Under the Currency Regulations the banks are now obliged to disclose certain information when it is applied for officially.

127

Copies of the Benevolent's passbook sheets will give us its source of income, and that may well lead to something I'd very much like to know. Tell me now, what's the latest on Tom Ruddy's chances for Secretary-General of the C.G.T. ?'

'I'd say they're jolly good. He was down here addressing a meeting of London delegates last night. Not being a delegate I wasn't entitled to attend, but I thought it important to find out the form from a ring-side seat if I possibly could, and I managed to wangle my way in on the ticket of a chap whose pocket I'd picked outside. It was pretty lively; plenty of heckling, of course, but Ruddy is used to that and, by and large, he put up a first-class performance. When the meeting was wound up, there could be no doubt that the majority of the delegates were all for him.'

'That's good to hear. If he can get himself elected I'm sure it will have a most stimulating effect on the workers who would like to oust their Communist representatives from other Trade Unions. Anything to report on your second string?'

'I don't quite get you, Sir?'

C.B. shrugged. 'Your main assignment is to get me all the dope you can on Communist secret procedure – like running this account in the name of the Workers' Benevolent. By second string, I mean following up any lead that might help us to solve Morden's murder. When you were last here you had a hunch that his sudden interest in Theosophy would be worth investigating.'

'Sure, and I did, Colonel.' The Irishism came out quite spontaneously, as Barney ran a hand through his short dark curls. 'And I've made a start on it. I couldn't go to old Mother Wardeel's last night, because of Ruddy's meeting. But I went the week before. She is running what I'd guess to be quite a profitable racket with no harm to it. No doubt most of the stuff she puts on is faked, but it provides something to natter about for a bunch of mostly worthy types who have more time and money than sense. I made two contacts that may prove worth cultivating, though: a Babu and a very attractive young woman.'

An image of Mary immediately sprang to C.B.'s mind. As a lead to checking up if it were she that Barney had encountered, he raised a prawn-like eyebrow and remarked: 'I shouldn't have thought that sort of thing held much appeal for young people; she must have been quite an exception.'

'Not as regards age. Of the twenty-odd women there, four or

five were under thirty; and one was a tall blonde who might quite well have been a film starlet.'

This coincidence made Verney think it probable that Mary had balked at taking his tip to dye her beautiful golden hair, so was the blonde Barney had referred to; but, seeking to confirm this impression, he asked, 'What type is this young woman in whom you are interesting yourself?'

'She is a brunette. Brown as a Mediterranean mermaid, shoulder length hair that curls at the ends, eyebrows with a slightly satanic tilt, and a mouth as red as a pomegranate. She is a Mrs. Mauriac, and the widow of a Frenchman who was a Customs Officer.'

The description differed so greatly from C.B.'s memory of Mary Morden that he decided that, if she had carried out her intention of going to Mrs. Wardeel's, she must be the film-starlet. Meanwhile Barney was going on, 'She certainly is a poppet. That is, to look at. But she's one of the most puzzling pieces one could come across in a long day's march.'

'In what way?'

'Well, she talks in a most sophisticated manner about the sort of games one would expect Satanists to get up to, yet acts as if she were sweet seventeen and had never been kissed.'

'It seems that she is very forthcoming to strangers; or else you must be quite a psychologist to have found all this out about her in one meeting at which a lot of other people were present.'

Barney grinned. 'Oh no. Twice since I have taken her out to dinner.'

'I see. And is it your intention to charge these outings up on your expense account?'

'Certainly, Sir.' Barney's voice was firm. 'And since she knows me as Lord Larne I had to do her jolly well. Besides, all work and no play, you know. But, joking apart, it really was for the good of the cause.'

'Seeing how infernally tight the Government keeps us for money, you'll have to justify that.'

'I learned that she had been to a place that I believe to be a Satanic temple.'

C.B. smiled. 'If it is, and you can take me to it, I'll certainly have that chalked up to you as the price of one dinner.'

'I can't. I don't know where it is. Neither does she.'

'Was she doped before being taken there?'

'No; blindfolded. And I may be barking up the wrong tree.

Over dinner on Sunday night she was getting quite chatty about it. She described the interior of the place, a Brotherhood of masked, near-nude men and women, and various wonders performed by a priest dressed up like the Devil whom they call the Great Ram. Then she suddenly closed up like a clam; told me she had been pulling my leg and that really the place was only a joint where they practise Yoga.'

'Do you know who took her there?'

'Yes, Sir. That's just the point. It was one of Mrs. Wardeel's regular supporters: an Indian named Ratnadatta. He is the other bird I am interested in, because he's too intelligent to waste his evenings stooging around with that sort of crowd unless he has some ulterior motive.'

'You think he might be a sort of talent scout, keeping an eye out for likely suckers who could be made use of, one way or another, by some Black fraternity?'

'That's it, Sir. I heard him disparaging Mrs. Wardeel's outfit to Mrs. Mauriac as no better than a children's circus, and saying that, if she was really interested in the occult, he could show her some real grown-up stuff. That was a week ago last Tuesday, and on Saturday night she went to this place with him.'

'And what do you deduce from all this?'

'Well, Teddy Morden became a regular attendant at Mrs. Wardeel's parties, didn't he? Perhaps this Indian gent introduced him, too, into this sixth-form set-up. Maybe the whole thing is a mare's nest, and Mrs. Mauriac really was pulling my leg about it being a Black Magic circle. But if she wasn't, I think it's on the cards that it was there that Morden got up against trouble.'

'That's fair enough. All right. I'll O.K. both your dinners. What is your next move to be?'

Barney grinned. 'I'm going after Mr. Ratnadatta. I'm certain he's up to no good; and I mean to have the pants off him before he is much older.'

10

Ordeal of a neophyte

ON Saturday Mary could settle to nothing. She had no engagements during the day, so after tidying her flat and doing her week-end shopping she had nothing to occupy her. In turn she tried the radio and reading a thriller, and abandoning both went out to see a film; but even that failed to hold her interest for more than a few minutes at a time. She simply could not keep her mind from speculating on what might happen to her that evening.

She endeavoured to fortify herself by remembering that Ratnadatta had been quite definite in his assurances that she would not be required to offer herself in service to the Temple until her initiation, and that before that there was a second stage to be gone through in which some token act of work in the interests of the Brotherhood had to be performed.

But how much reliance could she place on his word? She would have to trust herself to him again in that old mansion hidden in a slum, which was now the secret meeting place of depraved men and women. For the ceremony it was certain that she would have to go down into the temple among them. She would, almost certainly, be expected first to undress and don their uniform of only a mask, silver sandals and a transparent muslin cloak. She had no illusions about the emotions that the sight of herself aroused in men, often even quite respectable ones, when they saw her in a swim-suit on a bathing beach. What if some of the Brotherhood followed their own dictum, 'Do what thou wilt shall be the Whole of the Law' and set upon her? Even if

Ratnadatta had the will to protect her, would he be able to do so? And why should they refrain from demanding of a neophyte what they might expect to be given willingly by an initiate?

Yet in the end, soon after nine o'clock, she found herself in a bus on the way to Sloane Square; for, late in the afternoon, several thoughts had come to her to allay her fears. Depraved as the members of the Brotherhood might be individually, they were under the orders of their High Priest Abaddon, and from his benevolent looks she believed he would protect her; they clearly set great value on the proper observance of their ceremonies, so were unlikely to depart from a set ritual; and surely Ratnadatta would not have spent so much time indoctrinating her unless his object was to make her a permanent disciple of the Devil, whereas that would be defeated if she were so treated that night that she refused ever again to go to a meeting. Moreover, once a neophyte, the probability was that she would be permitted to talk to other members of the Brotherhood, and that would give her a chance to pursue her original intention of trying to find out if the Satanists had been responsible for Teddy's terrible end.

At the Tube Station Ratnadatta was waiting for her. As he had directed, she had no obvious make-up on and had had her hair scragged back tightly into a bun; so, although she had tied a silk scarf round her head, she felt quite a sight. But his comment was one of approval.

They got into a taxi and again she allowed him to tie a handkerchief over her eyes. The drive seemed much shorter than when he had taken her to the Temple the previous Saturday and during it he said little, except to reaffirm that the ceremony would be quite a brief one and add that, as it was to be the first item on the evening's programme, he hoped to be able to drop her at Hyde Park Corner well before eleven o'clock. Again she wondered, with a nasty sinking feeling inside her, if he was telling the truth; but it was too late to back out now.

The taxi set them down in a different place from that at which they had got out before, but after a few minutes' walk through streets that stank from the garbage that littered their gutters, they again turned into the cul-de-sac at the end of which lay the old mansion.

As soon as they were inside, the Indian led her across the fine hall to a room on the ground floor. Its walls were lined with books, some of which were handsomely bound and others that

132

looked as if they were very old. It was heavily carpeted and richly furnished, so had the appearance of a wealthy man's study, but some filing cabinets and a dictaphone and typewriter on a side table suggested that it was also used as a business office. Behind a heavily carved desk, which was bare except for a bronze copied from that retrieved from Pompeii and now in the secret museum at Naples, which depicts a satyr raping a goat, sat Abaddon.

The High Priest was wearing a dark lounge suit, and Mary thought that he looked more than ever like a Bishop. He stood up as she came in, came forward to meet her with a charming smile, took her by the hand, led her to a chair, and said:

'Welcome, my child.' Then, with a glance at Ratnadatta, 'Our Brother Sásín, here, has told me a lot about you. He believes that you are one of those who are old in time, and that your feet are truly set upon the right Path; so that you are worthy of advancement and to be granted, in due course, powers which will enable you to be of value in the service of Our Lord Satan. But first, I must examine you myself; for my consent to our acceptance of you as a neophyte is dependant on my confirming Sásín's opinion.'

For some five minutes he put to her a number of questions which she answered in a low voice, replying to them all in the way she thought he would wish, on the basis of the instruction Ratnadatta had given her during their numerous talks.

Abaddon's eyes were large, pale blue and steady. Once or twice, when she found a lie difficult to tell convincingly, she had a subconscious urge to look away from them, but found she was unable to. Under that intent gaze she almost panicked, feeling certain that he must detect the fact that she was not telling the truth about her convictions. But at last the catechism ended, and he appeared satisfied. Turning to Ratnadatta, he said:

'My reading of our young friend is that she is troubled by certain fears and still has lingering doubts. But both are not unusual in applicants of her age. The unknown is always more frightening to the young, and she has not yet had long enough to free herself entirely from ideas acquired during a conventional upbringing. Yet neither of these encumbrances to a happy state of mind are, in her case, so considerable that they will not soon be dissipated now that she has come among us. Our High Priestess will not be with us tonight, but any Sister of the Ram is qualified to prepare her. Go, Sásín, and bring here two of our Sisters from among the early arrivals.'

133

As Ratnadatta left the room, Abaddon took from a drawer in his desk a black satin mask, gave it to her and said, 'Take off your scarf and put that on. The identities of all the Brothers and Sisters of a Lodge are known to its High Priest and High Priestess; but it is not required that they should disclose them to one another. Some do so in order that they may develop outside in their everyday lives, friendships they have made here; others prefer to keep their identities secret. For that reason, from beginning to end of all our meetings everyone except myself and our High Priestess remains masked.'

When she had adjusted the mask, he went on: 'For the same reason no one is ever addressed while here by the name by which they are known outside. The ceremony of initiation includes baptism into the initiate's new faith. Each receives a Satanic name by which he is in future known among the Brotherhood. It must be a name associated with the service of Our Lord Satan. The names of His great nobility – the Seraphim who surround His throne and receive their orders direct from Him – such as Asmodeus, Uriel, Zabulon, Nebros, and so on, may not be taken by initiates. Like my own, Abaddon, they are reserved as titles for the High Priests of the different Lodges. But you may choose your own from those of all the witches and wizards who have actually lived in the past in this country or any other; and, since all of us in our past incarnations have many times inhabited both male and female bodies, a man may choose a witch's name or a woman a warlock's, should they so desire.'

Having said what he had to say, he fell silent and seemed quite content to sit, his long, beautiful hands folded on the desk in front of him, regarding Mary with a faint smile. But she found the continued silence and this unwavering gaze vaguely disquieting; so she searched her mind for some remark to break it and, after a moment, said:

'Circe was a famous witch, wasn't she. It's a pretty name and I think I'd like to be called after her.'

'By all means, my dear.' His smile deepened and he slightly inclined his high domed head. 'The name of the Greek enchantress will go well with your dark beauty. But think the matter over. There will be ample time to do so before your initiation, and by then you may have decided that you prefer some other.'

At that moment Ratnadatta re-entered the room. He now had on a mask and with him were two masked women. Both were wearing the sort of clothes in which they might have gone shopping in Bond Street or to a smart luncheon party.

The elder had grey hair and was small, but carried her well-preserved little figure very upright and had an air of great self-confidence. Her clothes were good but vaguely shabby, as though she did not bother with such matters overmuch. She was wearing a rope of good-sized pearls, a wedding ring, and a diamond half-hoop that did not appear to be of any great value.

The other was the Chinese girl. One glance was enough to tell Mary that her suit must have cost all of sixty guineas, her little hat near twenty and her hand-made shoes again as much. She had a diamond and platinum clip in the lapel of her coat, of the kind that could have come only from a jeweller of the first rank. She wore no wedding ring, but on her left hand there blazed one of the largest diamond solitaires that Mary had ever seen.

Standing up, Abaddon bowed to them, said, 'Greetings my children', then gestured with his right hand towards Mary. 'Here is one who aspires to join us in serving Our Lord Satan, and who I have good hopes will prove herself fitted to become our Sister. For the time being we shall refer to her as Circe.'

With a glance at Mary, he waved his left hand towards the two women. 'The Countess of Salisbury, and Tung-fang Shuo, honoured Sisters of the Ram.' Then, to them, he added, 'In cell number ten you will find all things ready for apparelling Circe suitably for her first ceremony. Be pleased to escort her to it and do all that is necessary.'

Both women gave Mary an appraising look. Very conscious that her clothes were 'off the peg', her face un-made-up and her hair done most unbecomingly, Mary wilted under their glance. But, next moment, she saw that beneath their masks the mouths of both of them were smiling, and the older one said briskly, 'Don't look so worried, child. There is nothing to be frightened about. Come with us, now.'

Somewhat reassured, Mary gave a half-smile to Abaddon and Ratnadatta, then accompanied the two women from the room. As they walked, one on either side of her, up the broad staircase, the elderly Countess remarked: 'Perhaps Abaddon's mentioning a cell scared you. But it need not. In Victorian times this house was a nunnery and the big reception rooms on the first floor were converted into a number of small cells. They come in quite useful now as they provide us with a range of private changing rooms.'

135

Half way down a broad corridor they entered one of them. It no longer had any resemblance to a cell. A fitted carpet covered its floor; on its panelled walls hung several small, but beautifully executed, coloured erotic French prints of the eighteenth century. It was furnished with a wardrobe, dressing table, electric fire, and chairs, on one of which reposed a strange collection of items consisting mainly of iron and sacking.

'Get your clothes off, my dear,' said the Countess, and Mary began to obey. As she did so, impelled to show that she was not completely overawed, she said: 'Abaddon told me that everyone here goes by the name of a witch or wizard, so why do you continue to use your own name, Lady Salisbury?'

The little grey-haired woman gave a sharp laugh. 'Outside these walls I have no title, but if you had read the old historical chronicles you would know that the Countess of Salisbury, who lived in Edward the Third's time, was the Queen witch of England. She was the King's mistress and it was from her that he snatched the emblem of Satan's power, her jewelled garter. Far memory tells me that I lived her life in a previous incarnation; so I took her title.'

'And you?' Realizing now that she must not neglect the opportunity to get these women to talk, Mary looked at the Chinese girl. 'I'm afraid I did not catch your name, but I'd be interested to know about its associations.'

The girl smiled. 'I am Tung-fang Shuo, and take my name from the great Chinese magician who lived in the second century A.D. But tell us, what impels you to wish to become a Sister of the Ram?'

'A desire for power,' replied Mary promptly.

'What kind of power?' enquired the Countess.

After hesitating a second, Mary answered, 'Power over men.'

A beak-like nose projected from the Countess's mask and she wrinkled it in a suggestion of contempt. 'Then I think you stupid. You have looks enough already to get most men you might want. Power can have more interesting uses. Fifteen years ago my husband was no more than a fairly rich industrialist with no worthwhile social connections. Now, if I unmasked I should be surprised if you did not recognize me. Hardly a week passes without my photograph appearing in the *Tatler*, or some other paper. I am one of the best-known hostesses in London; and that brings far more satisfaction than just being able to lure any man you want into bed with you.'

'I do not agree,' declared Tung-fang Shuo. 'Your life of constantly entertaining important people must be one long round of anxiety and trouble. Regard myself. Three years ago I was brought to London as a typist to work in the Chinese Embassy. Behold me now. I toil not, neither do I spin. I am the mistress of a millionaire. He must kiss my feet before I will allow him to make love to me, and if I were fool enough I could make him squander his whole fortune on my whims.' Suddenly she raised her hand, flashing the huge diamond on her finger. 'But I am wise enough to be content with such presents as he of his own will buys me.'

By that time Mary had taken off all her clothes. The Countess picked up the sacking from the chair and held it out to her. To her amazement she saw that it had been fashioned into a rough two-piece garment. The upper part was simply a sack with holes cut in it at one end through which head and arms could be passed; the lower, another sack, slit down one side and along its bottom, so that by a string threaded through its top it could be tied round the waist as a skirt.

Tung-fang Shuo's black almond eyes smiled at Mary through the mask she was wearing. 'I am sad for you at this moment. You are very beautiful, and it is a hard thing for a beautiful woman to have to put on clothes that lessen the desire of men for her. But you are still a Christian; so you must wear a Christian's livery.'

Obediently Mary wriggled into the coarse, scratchy sacking, while Tung-fang Shuo pulled out from under the chair a pair of shoes so ugly, and made of such thick leather, that they resembled men's football boots from which the top few inches had been cut off. Mary sat down and the Chinese girl helped her get her bare feet into these monstrosities. They were much too large for her, but strong adjustable clips kept them on. As she stood up again and took a step forward she nearly overbalanced, the foot she had raised came down with a thud, and she realized that the soles of these horrible shoes must be weighted with lead.

The Countess, meanwhile, had been sorting out the iron-mongery and Mary could see now that it consisted of a rusty set of ancient gyves and manacles. The two women adjusted the leg-irons then fastened the thick handcuffs, that were attached to them by short chains, over her wrists. Standing back they both surveyed her and the Countess said:

137

'I think a No. 2 size mantle would be about right for her.'

'Yes,' agreed Tung-fang Shuo, 'and her feet are a little larger than mine, so she will need size 5 in sandals.' Then she added to Mary: 'Sit down now and wait here until we return. We shall not be long as we have only to undress.'

When they had gone Mary looked at herself in the mirror and found her reflection even more unprepossessing than she had supposed. The shapeless sacking made her look broader and shorter than she appeared normally, and entirely hid her good figure. Her scragged back hair left her face without its attractive frame. Her complexion was still brown, as she had disobeyed Ratnadatta in that one particular, fearing that if she allowed him to see her naturally fair skin, he might suspect that she had also disguised herself in other ways; but she had on no eye-shadow or lipstick, and her mouth now stood out abnormally pale against her bronze-tinted face.

In less than ten minutes the Countess and Tung-fang Shuo rejoined her. Both now wore only transparent mantles, silver sandals and black velvet garters buckled below their left knees. The former, with her lean skinny little body, and loose hanging breasts, Mary thought a repulsive sight for this time she had been given no drugged drink to condition her mind into regarding nudity with detached indifference; yet that very fact enabled her consciously to appreciate that the slender, golden-brown form of the young Chinese was beautifully proportioned and as entrancing to look at as a great work of art.

The Countess said: 'Come now. You will find it difficult to walk in those heavy shoes, but we will help you.'

She was right. The weight of the irons was distributed, and so supportable, but the lead in the shoes made it an effort to lift them from the ground. The two women each took Mary by an arm and between them she staggered along the corridor. When they reached the staircase they made her put her arms round their necks, and so got her down the stairs without the risk of her ricking an ankle.

In the hall Ratnadatta was waiting for them. He, too, had changed into mantle and sandals, so that now his pot-belly stood out undisguised. He led the way round and under the broad staircase. Below it was a pair of big arched doors. Taking a short knob-kerrie from a hook on the wall, he banged with it loudly upon them. From the far side there came a muffled challenge.

'Who seeks entry here?'

'One who repents her past heresies and craves to be accepted into the grace off our Master, Satan; designated by the Creator Lord off this World from its beginning to its end,' cried Ratnadatta in a loud voice.

'Enter penitent, that you may abase yourself before the only true God,' replied the voice, and the doors swung silently open.

Ratnadatta stood aside and motioned to Mary to go forward. The two women let go her arms and Tung-fang Shuo said in a quick whisper, 'Slide your feet. You'll find that easier. It will not take long.'

Mustering her courage, Mary crossed the threshold into the Temple. It was arranged as she had first seen it, with the divans forming short rows on either side of the aisle. The congregation was sitting or lounging upon them but now, instead of their masked faces being turned towards the altar, the twenty-odd pairs of eyes behind the masks were rivetted upon herself.

Through the grille up in the balcony her field of vision had been limited, but she saw now that the sides of the temple were supported by rows of pillars from which rose gothic arches, giving it much more the appearance of a small church than, as she had thought it, a banqueting hall. Then recalling that the Countess had told her that it had once been a convent, she concluded that from a banqueting hall the nuns must have converted it into their chapel. If so, the altar she was approaching must have once been consecrated. The thought that in a few more minutes she would be called on to approve its desecration added to her terror.

The awful effort of moving her lead-weighted feet made her pant for breath and break out in perspiration. But slowly she shuffled forward while, but for the slithering of the shoe soles on the polished floorboards, an utter silence reigned and the many eyes continued to stare at her.

At last she reached the steps in front of the altar. Abaddon was standing behind it, robed as before in heavy black satin. He beckoned her up the steps, then signed to her to kneel down on the top one. When she did so her head came just above the level of the altar top, and as she looked up at him he said in his melodious voice:

'Penitent, the opportunity is offered you to redeem your past. Do you desire to take it?'

'Yes,' she murmured.

139

'Are you prepared to serve Our Lord Satan with your whole mind, body and soul, permitting nothing to deter you from the furtherance of his work?'

'Yes,' she repeated.

'Do you freely undertake to accept without question all orders that may be given to you by those He has placed, or may place, in authority over you?'

'Yes,' she murmured again.

From somewhere behind him he produced a cross about eighteen inches long and made from two thin strips of black wood held together by a single nail. Leaning forward he put it into her hands, and said:

'As proof that you have purged your mind of all false teaching you will now break this and throw the pieces from you, while declaring, "I deny Jesus Christ, the deceiver; and abjure the Christian Faith, holding in contempt all its works.'

A lump formed in Mary's throat. The thought of performing the awful act required of her filled her with terror. If she uttered such an appalling blasphemy surely the wrath of Heaven would fall upon her? All the beliefs she had held when younger surged up into her mind. She had accepted without a shadow of doubt the accounts given her by the nuns at her convent of people who mocked God having been struck dead on the spot. Even if such things did not happen, there could be no escaping the Day of Judgment. The faithful and the backsliders alike would then have to account for their every act. Although she no longer practised her religion she had never ceased to believe that. How could she possibly make herself answerable for having committed such a terrible sin? The thought of it, and the price she must some day pay, would haunt her night and day for the rest of her life.

Yet, what if she refused? She had wantonly placed herself in the hands of these evil people. She was completely at their mercy. They would regard her standing firm in her true beliefs as a defiance of the dark power that they worshipped. To them, it would be like someone in a Christian church standing before the altar and proclaiming his allegiance to the Devil. Their rage at such an insult might cause them to rise up and fall upon her in a frenzy. They might even murder her.

They *would*, from fear that, having refused to serve Satan, if they let her go she would betray their vile secrets. Only by killing her could they be certain of saving themselves, or at least having to abandon this well-concealed meeting-place with all its costly furnishings. They would have nothing to fear from her disappearance; for she was living alone under an assumed name. Her landlady would report in a few days' time to the police that she had gone off leaving her things behind, but that would lead only to her being listed with hundreds of other missing persons. She had cut herself off even from Barney, the one and only person who might have tried to trace her.

Short of a miracle, escape was impossible and, having so long since fallen from a state of grace, how could she hope for one? Either she must pronounce the ultimate blasphemy or die there.

Desperately she sought for some middle course: some plea or trick by which she might postpone the issue. Her mind whirled with visions: of the Saviour, whom she was ordered to deny, upon the Cross; of a picture of Hell she had been shown as a child, in which naked men and women were being thrust by demons with pitchforks into the roaring flames; of a little coloured plaster statue of the Virgin before which she had knelt for many hundred nights when saying her prayers; of the insolently splendid figure of the Great Ram, and his terrifying black imp, as they had stood only a few feet from the spot where she was crouching, no more than a week ago.

These swiftly changing images robbed her of all coherent thought. From the moment Abaddon had spoken the abjuration her mind had been racing with such speed that each fearful idea chased out its predecessor in a flash; but even so the seconds had been ticking by, and she heard the High Priest say in a low voice:

'Come; do as I have directed. Otherwise the Brotherhood will become impatient.'

At that instant yet another mental picture flashed into Mary's brain. It was the pale serene face of the Mother Superior at the Convent she had attended. The old lady's lips and her gentle tones sounded again in Mary's ears, 'Remember, child, the understanding and the mercy of our Lord Jesus is infinite.'

It was the key. He knew that she had come here not for her own gain or advantage, with greed, lust, or a craving to be given power over others, but only in the hope of bringing her husband's murderers to book; and that if it proved possible, she would take steps to wreck this evil community that vilified His name. Nothing she said, in this gateway to Hell, no oath she took to Satan, could be binding provided that in her heart she remained true to the Redeemer.

A new strength suddenly flowed into her. She snapped the wooden cross in half and flung the pieces from her. Then in a hoarse voice she uttered the terrible words.

Abaddon smiled down upon her, and said: 'Stand up and raise your left hand.'

With a clank of the chain that attached her wrist-cuff to her leg-irons, she did so. Leaning forward again he put into her raised hand a life-sized phallus made of solid gold. It was so heavy that she nearly dropped it, but managed to clutch it to her chest.

'Hold it above your head,' he ordered, 'and repeat after me, sentence by sentence, the words I am about to say. "By the symbol of the Creator . . . I swear henceforth to be . . . a faithful servant of His most puissant Arch-Angel . . . the Prince Lucifer . . . whom before departing to perform further wonders . . . He designated as His Regent and Lord of this World . . . As a being now possessed of a human body in this world . . . I swear to give my full allegiance to its lawful Master . . . To worship Him, Our Lord Satan, and no other . . . To despise all man-made religions . . . and to bring contempt upon them whenever that may be done without courting danger . . . To undermine the faith of others . . . in such false religions, wherever possible . . . and bring them to the true faith . . . if after consultation with my superiors they decide that to be desirable . . . I swear to obey without question . . . every order I may receive from my superiors . . . or those who may be placed in authority over me . . . I swear to give my mind, body and soul unreservedly . . . to the furtherance of the designs of Our Lord Satan . . . Finally I swear that as a neophyte . . . and later should I be privileged to be initiated into the Brotherhood of the Ram . . . I will in no circumstances disclose its secrets . . . the places of meeting of its Lodges . . . anything to which I have been a witness while attending their meetings . . . or the identity of any person that I have met at one or more of them. Should I break this my oath . . . may it be decreed that for a hundred incarnations . . . beginning with my next . . . I shall never rise from poverty . . . shall be rejected by all upon whom I may set my affections . . . and die from some agonizing disease." '

At first, as Mary repeated his words phrase by phrase, her voice was a little weak and hesitant, but after a few moments she realized that, having passed the Rubicon by denying Christ,

142

nothing she might say mattered now; so she took the remainder of the oath in firm, clear tones.

When the worst, as she thought, was over, Abaddon said to her: 'Now lie down at full length upon the altar.'

Awkwardly, on account of her lead-weighted feet, she clambered on to it and stretched herself out.

In a loud voice Abaddon cried: 'Brothers and Sisters of the Ram. The penitent has proved worthy of acceptance as a neophyte into our High Order. It is now my happy duty to free her from the bonds of ignorance and superstition.'

With swift, well-practised movements, he knocked off Mary's fetters and unbuckled the heavy shoes, casting them quickly aside. He then gave a gentle pull at her bun and ran his hands through her hair, so that the pins fell out and her dark locks again tumbled about her shoulders. Lastly, with a sharp knife he slit up the sacking shirt and cut the string that held the sacking skirt in place. Ripping the tatters of the ugly garments away he exposed her on the altar naked except for the mask over her face.

'Stand up,' he said, 'and face the congregation so that they may look upon you.'

Mary did as she was bid. It was futile to pretend false shame. She had been prepared at least for this, and she was justly proud of her beautiful body. A murmur of interest and admiration went up from the masked men and women lounging on the divans.

Upon the two nearest, on either side of the aisle, the Countess and Tung-fang Shuo were sitting. The one had folded on her knees a transparent muslin mantle; the other was holding a pair of silver sandals. Both rose, came forward and put upon Mary this livery of the Brotherhood.

As they stepped back, the rest of the congregation suddenly came to its feet and surged forward. Fearful afresh of what might be about to happen to her, Mary stared at the advancing mob with distended eyes and backed swiftly against the altar. But Abaddon had come round it, and said to her:

'You have nothing to fear. It is our custom that the Brotherhood should give ritual welcome to every neophyte, because she is already half-way to becoming a Sister. As High Priest it is my privilege to be the first to do so.' He then put his hands on her shoulders, stooped his head, and kissed her on the lips.

He smelt faintly of lavender water and cigars, so she did not mind in the least. Neither did she when the Countess took his place and gave her a swift peck, or when Tung-fang Shuo, in turn, drew her close and gave her a long, sweetly perfumed kiss on the mouth; but as the Chinese girl released her she was stricken with fearful apprehension. The whole congregation was now thronging round, men and women, old and young; yet there was nothing she could do to evade them.

One after another they greeted her according to their temperaments. Some performed the ritual only as a necessary act, placing their hands lightly on her shoulders or waist, and barely touching her lips with theirs. But others took full advantage of the opportunity offered to them.

The very tall, fair-haired man, whom she had noticed the week before from the gallery, actually lifted her from her feet and held her to him for nearly half a minute, while kissing her until she was breathless. But after him came the huge negress, grinning from ear to ear, to envelop her in a mountain of flesh, so that she had to exercise great control to prevent herself from fighting off the repulsive creature.

Ratnadatta waited until last. As had been the case with several of the others, he took his time about it, and she felt that in accepting his embrace she reached the summit of her ordeal. Her flesh seemed to creep as he put his arms about her, and as his lips opened to kiss her she received the full strength of his sweetish, bad-lobster-smelling breath.

At last it was over. Stepping back, Ratnadatta took her hand and turned her towards the altar behind which Abaddon had again taken up his position. They bowed to him; he returned their bow, then the Indian led her back down the aisle and out through the big double doors of the temple.

Silent, and still trembling, she accompanied him up the stairs. He opened the door of the room in which she had changed and said:

'Put on your own clothes, plees. When you haf dressed come down to the hall. I shall be there waiting for you.'

As she dressed she could not make up her mind if she was glad or sorry that she had not been allowed to stay for longer down in the temple. While suffering her ordeal she had hoped that as the price of it she would be given a chance to mingle with the members of the Brotherhood, enter into conversation with some of them and, perhaps, pick up some pointer bearing on the reason for her having come there. On the other hand, had they let her remain there to take part in their feast and dance, some of the kisses she had received suggested that, although she was as yet only a neophyte, far worse might have befallen her. On balance she decided that, if she could now get away without further unwelcome attentions from Ratnadatta, she would be well out of it.

Down in the hall she found him fully dressed. Without a word he took her out into the cul-de-sac and, with a step so quick that it betrayed impatience, walked her for a quarter of a mile until they reached a waiting taxi. As soon as they were seated in it, he bandaged her eyes, then he said:

'Tonight you haf taken a great step. You behave good; very good. I haf no complaints for you. Not till initiation do you receive baptism and perform service to temple. Also then you will sign pact in your own blood, and will be granted in exchange first stage off power to influence others. But before this you must perform some act decreed as test off your willingness to serve Our Lord Satan intelligently and well.'

He wheezed a little, then went on. 'You must continue attendance at the Tuesdays off Mrs. Wardeel. She ees a stupid woman, but serves good purpose in gathering at her house peoples interested in the occult. Most are harmless fools; but sometimes there comes one like yourself, worthy off advancement and suitable for employment in the great work off Our Lord Satan. I attend always for purpose off recognizing such. It will be there, next week, the week after, I do not know; but when Abaddon tells me to, that I shall inform you off the task allotted to you.'

At Hyde Park Corner he set her down. It seemed to her that a whole night must have passed since she had met him at Sloane Square Tube Station; but to her amazement it was still before eleven. Although she could have sworn that she had been in the Temple for hours, the actual ceremony had lasted only twenty minutes.

On her way home in a bus she still felt dazed and terribly exhausted. Her mind was filled with a medley of recollections of sights, sounds and feelings that she had experienced that evening: the body of the skinny Countess, the huge glittering diamond on the finger of Tung-fang Shuo, Abaddon seated in a lounge suit at his desk, her terror on being ordered to deny Jesus Christ, the weight of those terrible lead-soled shoes, the face of the Mother Superior, the embrace of the very tall fair-haired man, her panic as the congregation crowded round her.

145

Fortunately the bus conductress jogged her memory at the stop she had asked for when taking her ticket. She stumbled off, walked back to her number in Cromwell Road, let herself in, and wearily dragged herself upstairs to her flat.

Going straight to the bathroom she turned on the bath, then tipped some disinfectant into a glass, added water, and taking a gulp began to rinse her mouth. Her impulse to clean it and scrub her face free from the traces left by the score, and more, of mouths that had caressed or slobbered over it brought back into her mind details of the most repulsive kisses to which she had had to submit.

Suddenly she seemed to smell again Ratnadatta's foul breath. her stomach heaved, and she was sick into the basin.

11

Seen in a crystal

MARY'S reaction to the ordeal through which she had passed led to her again contemplating abandoning her self-imposed mission. Although she could not yet resume her old life at Wimbledon, there was nothing to stop her packing her things and leaving Cromwell Road without telling anyone where she was moving, and taking rooms under another name in a different part of London. Or, as she had an ample reserve of money, she could refuse further offers of work as a model and take a few weeks' holiday at the seaside.

The idea of going to Dublin for a while then occurred to her. Soon after Teddy's death she had received a letter of condolence from her young brother. He had said that he was doing quite well in an advertising agency, in which he had found an opening, and was living as a p.g. with a pleasant family. He was her only relative, and the only person she could think of who would at once open to her a new circle of acquaintances, and so solve the question of the loneliness which afflicted her. But, on second thoughts, she felt that a visit to Dublin would revive too sharply her memories of her year of misery there; so the problem of her unhappy isolation remained.

Moreover, by Monday night she was reasoning with herself that after having submitted to Saturday's ceremony it would be absurd to throw away the advantages she might gain from it. To hear the task she was to be set, as a test of her willingness to serve the Devil, should at least give her one more chance of finding

147

out more about the Brotherhood. She might have an opportunity of cultivating her acquaintance with the Countess and Tung-fang Shuo and, if she were allowed to mingle with the rest, perhaps even manage matters so that the very tall fair-haired man, who had obviously been most strongly attracted to her, would make a date to take her out to dinner, After all, she need not carry out the test job given to her, and when the pace looked like getting too hot she could always make a bolt for it to some little seaside place or a village in the country. In consequence, she went again, as Ratnadatta had told her to, on Tuesday evening to Mrs. Wardeel's.

The lecture that night was given by a sprightly, grey-haired American woman, and was on the subject of the doctrine of Theosophy. She started off by enunciating the heart of the creed – that everyone reaches perfection in the end, but must first pass through many incarnations, during which they are subject to the law of 'Karma', and so can increase or decrease the number of lives they must spend on earth in accordance with the efforts they make, or lack of them, to purge themselves from selfishness and all evil tendencies. She then proceeded to describe the Occult Hierarchy.

It consisted, she said, of those who had achieved perfection and it was they who ordered all matters for everyone still passing through lives on earth. Supreme among them was a Trinity formed by the King of this World, the Lord Buddha, and the Mahachohan. The first two represented the Head and Heart of our universe, and the last was like a divine Arm that stretched down to control the practical side of things in this world.

The King and the Buddha each made their influence felt through two representatives, the Manu and the Bodhisattva, the latter being the Protector of all religions. This last office was at present held by The Lord Maitreya, and it was his spirit that had animated the body of Jesus Christ.

Under these Supreme Powers were ranged in order the other members of the Hierarchy, some of whom take pupils, so are known as Masters. Those who particularly concerned themselves with the Theosophical movement were the Master Morya, the Master Koot Hoomi, who were usually referred to as the Master M. and the Master K.H., and the Master the Count, whose special business it was to supervise ceremonial.

It should be the object of all Theosophists to strive to fit

148

themselves to be taken as a pupil by one of these Masters. The two first could be approached only on the astral plane, while in a state of trance, or during what we know as dreams. They were said to live on opposite sides of a narrow gorge at Shigatse in Tibet. But the Master the Count possessed a physical body and was believed to have a castle in Hungary.

The lecturer then went on to speak of the founder of Theosophy, Madame Blavatsky, and those who had succeeded her as enlightened leaders of the Society – Mrs. Annie Besant, C. W. Leadbeater, George Arundale, Cruppumullage Jinarajadasa, James Wedgwood, and several others. All these, she said, had passed several of the Five Initiations, all of which must be passed before a person became liberated from the law of 'Karma'. Madame Blavatsky had achieved this supreme goal and so been permitted to stay for a time with the Master M. in Tibet; while Mrs. Besant and C. W, Leadbeater had both passed the Fourth Initiation, and the latter was said actually to have met the Master the Count in the flesh, when strolling along the Corso in Rome.

She then spoke of the Orders of the Rosy Cross and of the Star in the East, and of the unhappy schisms in the Society which had in turn led to the formal dissolution of both; deplored the differences of opinion between Krishnamurti – who during his boyhood and youth had been accepted by Theosophists as the new great Bringer of Light to the world – and Arundale and Leadbeater, which had saddened Mrs. Besant's last years; and, finally, urged them to refrain from such disputes, which could only bring discredit upon the movement and check the progress along the Upward Path of those who participated in them.

It was not until the lecture had finished that Mary, on glancing round, realized that Barney must have belatedly slipped in; for there he was, sitting in the back row near the door. Her heart began to beat as he caught her glance, but he gave her only a nod and a suggestion of a smile. Then, when the chairs were moved into a circle, instead of coming over to her, he remained helping with them at the far end of the room.

For the second part of that evening's session, Mrs. Wardeel had provided a clairvoyant. She was a fat, blowsy looking woman with dreamy eyes, but not so dreamy by nature as to lack a sense of business. Having taken her seat at a small table with a crystal on it, and another chair on its far side, she announced in a deep voice, 'I'll be pleased to see what I can for those who wish, but owing to numbers I can give each of you only a short session. Just enough to answer, if things prove favourable, one or two questions. But, if any of you would like a private consultation about intimate matters, Mrs. Wardeel will give you my telephone number. My fee for a hour's looking is two guineas.'

All the lights were put out except that of a standard lamp which had been brought in and placed near the table; then she went to work.

Those members of the audience who had questions to ask sat in turn in the chair opposite her and she gave each of them a few minutes. Most of the enquiries were about relatives abroad, the recovery of children or friends from illness or mishaps, journeys it was proposed to take, and law-suits or money matters, but at times her consultants asked only if anything was likely to happen to them soon which would have an important effect on their future.

After a dozen or more people had had their turn, Barney went to the table and put that sort of question to her. The clairvoyant gave him a shrewd look, concentrated on her crystal for a little, then replied, 'I see a fair young lady. Soon now you're going to fall in love with her, but I'm afraid she's going to lead you a fine dance!'

'Have I met her yet? And do I marry her?' Barney enquired.

'Come and see me privately,' replied the sibyl, promptly, 'and I'll tell you more. Next please!'

Mary at once stood up, took his place and asked the same question.

After gazing fixedly down into her crystal for about half a minute, the woman sat back, gave her an uneasy look, and said: 'You're heading for trouble. I'd watch my step, if I were you.'

'What sort of trouble?' enquired Mary.

'You know,' replied the woman darkly. 'Wouldn't do to speak of it here. And if you take a drive into the country with a fair man, you'll have cause to regret it. Next please!'

For a moment Mary had been both startled and frightened; for she had jumped to the conclusion that the clairvoyant's warning must refer to her association with the Brotherhood. But the mention of 'a fair man' set her at ease again, convincing her that the woman was only baiting her hook with the most likely lure to induce a potential customer to spend two guineas on a private consultation.

150

Twenty minutes later the session was over and they all trooped across the hall for the usual refreshments. Ratnadatta paused by Mary to smile a greeting and say to her in a low voice, 'I haf no news for you yet. Next week perhaps. Do not fail to attend here every week; otherwise when time comes I haf the bother to make contact with you where you live.'

He then quickly left her to get hold of the woman wearing valuable jewels, to whom he had spent most of his time talking during the after-session reception the previous week.

As Mary had, two days before, contemplated leaving London, his last words aroused a vague fear in her. They might have simply referred to her flat, the address of which he already had; but they might equally well have implied that wherever she went he had means of finding her. In any case, they clearly indicated that she was no longer free to sever at will her connection with the Brotherhood, and that if she tried to she must expect him to seek her out and, perhaps, inflict some form of punishment on her.

Thrusting that unnerving thought out of her mind, she looked quickly round for Barney. He was near the end of the buffet furthest from her, and engaged in conversation with a small earnest woman who, from an experience of her own, she knew, once started, babbled on like a brook. That he would have liked to break away was evident from the fact that he kept throwing sideways glances at other people, particularly at Ratnadatta, who was only a few feet distant from him.

Mary had accepted a sausage roll from a man who was a regular attendant at Mrs. Wardeel's meetings, and after exchanging a few words with her he moved off with the dish; so she decided that as soon as she had finished it she would both rescue Barney from the bore and gently reproach him for having ignored her. But, before she could put her plate down, she was buttonholed by her admirer, the retired general, who thrust a cup of coffee upon her; and he was such a pleasant old man that she had not the heart to cut him short then push her way across the room to break in on another conversation.

The minutes ticked by without change in the situation until people began to leave. Ratnadatta went out with the richly bejewelled woman and did not return. Barney, who had been listening with only half an ear to reminiscences about a poltergeist, cursed silently, his only reason for having come there having been to get on friendly terms with the Indian.

Quickly, he re-assessed the situation. Through being deprived of the chance of tactfully opening the subject of other occult circles existing which were, perhaps, much more advanced than Mrs. Wardeel's, as a first move in getting Ratnadatta to take him to his, he felt that he had wasted his evening. But not quite, perhaps, as Mary was still there.

He had decided that, lovely as she was to look at, her ill-temper and unpredictability rendered her not worth powder and shot as a woman; but, nevertheless, she had actually been to Ratnadatta's circle, so there was always the chance that she might be in a more amenable mood this evening, and willing to talk about it. Suddenly the boyish smile broke over his round face, he put out his hand to the little babbling brook, seized hers, wrung it heartily and said, 'It's been terribly interesting to hear about your poltergeist; but I must go now. Train to catch. Goodnight.'

Before she quite realized that she had lost her audience, he was across the room and focusing his friendly grin on the retired general. 'Sorry to butt in, Sir; but I promised to see Mrs. Mauriac home, and most people seem to be leaving.'

Mary made no demur until they were in the street, then she said: 'Really! Of all the impudence! First to practically cut me, then stake a claim to me as if I were your . . . your, er . . .'

'Dark lady of the Sonnets,' suggested Barney helpfully.

'No, you fool. I mean, as though there were some sort of understanding between us.'

'Well, there is, isn't there?' he countered, with cheerful assurance. 'I like you and you like me. At least I hope you do. I must admit, though, that I'm a bit jealous of this fair-haired chap who is going to take you for a run in the country.'

'Oh, that was all nonsense.' Mary spoke with confidence, yet she had an uneasy memory of the clairvoyant's face as she had warned her that she was heading for trouble. Could she, after all, have seen in her crystal darkly an aura of evil round her questioner, and – sudden thought – could the 'fair-haired chap' possibly be the very tall Satanist who, on the previous Saturday evening, had lifted her off her feet and kissed her until she was gasping for breath?

'Of course,' Barney agreed. 'The old bag was just throwing out whatever struck her as the most likely draw to induce suckers to spend a couple of quid on a private consultation. As I'm dark, in my case it was a ravishing blonde, and the suggestion that she was going to lead me a dance the subtle twist to intrigue me into wanting to hear just what sort of a dance she might lead me. But as I don't happen to be interested in a blonde, and even if I met one, am too busy just now to run after her, Madame Zero, or whatever she calls herself, was barking up the wrong tree.'

Mary did not reply, but she was thinking, 'You don't realize it, my gay boyo, but you are escorting a blonde home here and now, and with a little luck, it's a pretty dance she is going to lead you!' After a moment, she asked: 'What did you think of the lecture?'

'The first part made sense. Everything these people say about reincarnation is so logical that there seems no answer to their arguments in support of it.'

'Yes, there's something awfully reasonable about regarding the world as a school at which we get a move up, or not, at the opening of each new term as a result of the good or bad marks we have earned the term before. It is much more attractive than the idea of a Day of Judgment on which everyone is tried on their performance in a single life and either carried up to heaven or thrown down to hell, for all eternity.'

'I don't mind paying up for my lapses,' Barney remarked, 'but, like old Omar Khayyám, I feel that when the last Trump sounds we'd be justified in saying to God, "You made me as I am, so what about it?"'

Mary laughed. 'I don't think I'd have the courage to do that; and I really am on the way to becoming a reincarnationist. To have made one's own bed and have to lie on it until one can make a better is the sort of treatment no one could reasonably complain about.'

'True enough; but these Theosophists aren't content to accept the basic teaching, and they've gone right off the rails somewhere. How could that American woman, or anyone else, really know about these big shots who are supposed to ordain all that happens in the world. If one took literally what she said about the two great Masters living on either side of a valley in Tibet, it would conjure up a picture of two elderly crap players throwing the dice, one of whom is an American and the other a Russian. As for the Master the Count, if he ever had any existence outside the wildest imagination, I'll bet that by this time his castle in Hungary has been taken over as a free holiday resort for good little Marxists, and that the Reds put the skids under the old gentleman long ago.'

153

'Of course, you're right.' Mary laughed again. 'And people like Leadbeater and Arundale may have been honest to begin with, but like the ambitious priests of other religions they became corrupted by the power that being leaders of the movement had given them. I haven't the least doubt that they invented all that nonsense about the Hierarchy and their contacts with the Master M. and Koot what's-his-name, just to make their followers treat them as though they were little gods themselves.'

By this time they had arrived in front of the tall old house in which Mary had her flat. As they faced one another, after a moment's hesitation, she said: 'It's not very late. Would you like to come up and share my supper?'

'I'd love to,' he gave her a quick smile, 'if that wouldn't be robbing you too badly.'

'Oh no! That is, if you don't mind something simple, like scrambled eggs?'

'What could be nicer?'

Having been frustrated in his intention of cultivating Ratnadatta, he had decided to ask Mary out to dinner again in the hope that through her he might learn more about the Indian, pending his next chance to get hold of him, which would not be for another week; so her invitation, while it took him by surprise, could not have pleased him better. But as he followed her into the house and upstairs, he felt that it would be wise to keep off the subject for a while, at least; as he thought her such a prickly pear that she might fly into a temper unless he handled her very tactfully.

Mary, meanwhile, was regretting that she could not give him the sort of supper she had prepared the previous week, and wishing that she had tidied up her sitting-room before going out. But she had bought fresh flowers the day before, and the bottle of Hock was still unopened.

While Barney laid the table and opened the wine, she cooked a dish of scrambled eggs, bacon and tomatoes, and as they called to one another during these preparations the very naturalness of this little domestic scene put them more at their ease than they had so far been when together.

Over the meal he got her talking about her work as a model, and of films she had recently seen; so by the time they lit cigarettes with their coffee, her mind was a long way from the supernatural and it came as quite a shock when he asked:

'How did you get on last Saturday?'

His question had been quite casual, but it instantly brought back to her the scene in the Temple. Swiftly averting her eyes, she played for time. 'On Saturday? What do you mean?'

'Why, you told me you were going to meet that chap Ratnadatta again.'

'Er . . . yes; of course.'

He smiled at her. 'Well, how did the party go?'

'Oh, much the same as on the previous Saturday.'

'Just Yoga, and that sort of thing?'

She nodded.

'Look,' he said, 'I'd like to learn a bit about Yoga. Will you take me along to Ratnadatta's place one evening?'

'No. I couldn't do that. I'm not a member and one has to be introduced by somebody who is.'

'I see. Well, anyway, you might let me have the address; then I'll write him a line and ask him if he will introduce me.'

'I can't. I don't know it.' The moment she had spoken she realized that she had made a stupid admission which might lead him to suppose that something less innocent than Yoga went on there, but he only shrugged and remarked:

'Of course, I'd forgotten. He blindfolds you when he takes you there, doesn't he?'

'Oh no.' She quickly retrieved her error. 'I made that up just as I did about the Great Ram and his black imp, and all the other things I told you. The only reason I can't give you the address is that I didn't hear Ratnadatta give it to the taxi-driver either time, and it is in a district that I've never been to before; so all I know is that it's somewhere up in North London.'

Barney knew that she was lying, and it was clear that she did not mean to tell him anything, so he said: 'It doesn't matter. I meant to ask Ratnadatta tonight about his Yoga circle, but I didn't get the chance. I'll have another shot when I see him at Mrs. Wardeel's next week.'

He then tactfully changed the conversation, but her reaction to his questions worried him. As she did not know where the place was to which Ratnadatta took her that meant that he really did blindfold her when taking her there; and he would not do that unless something much more sinister than the innocent practice of Yoga went on at his circle. That being so, she must be playing with fire and might get herself badly burnt. If she would, or could,

155

have let him go with her next time she indulged her curiosity about occult mysteries, that would have been one thing; but for her to continue going on her own to these parties was quite another. In consequence, after they had talked cheerfully again for a further half-hour, and he stood up to go, he said:

'Listen, Margot. You're a queer girl, and a bit of a mystery, living on your own like this with no family and apparently very few friends. But I like you a lot, and I'm worried about you.'

She smiled at him. 'Why should you be? There are lots of girls like me earning a living in London on their own.'

'Not many who are so darn good-looking,' he grinned back. 'But that's beside the point at the moment; and I'll tell you why I'm worried. I was watching your face this evening when that old crystal-gazing bag told you that you were heading for trouble.'

'What, with a fair-haired boy-friend? Don't worry. I'm not a precocious school girl, to be lured to her fate by the offer of a ride in a Jaguar.'

'Of course not. But I mean before she mentioned him. It was when she warned you to watch your step. She rang a bell then; because for a moment you looked as if you were scared to death. You are frightened of something. I'm sure of it. And I've a hunch that Mr. Ratnadatta is the nigger in your wood-pile. He may only be teaching you Yoga exercises at the moment, but you know yourself, or anyhow suspect, that it's leading up to something pretty dangerous. I want you to cut Ratnadatta out. Promise me not to go with him to this place again, there's a good girl.'

She shook her head. 'I'm afraid I can't do that; and, as I've told you, I'm quite capable of looking after myself.'

'Well, cut him out for the time being, then. Come and dine and dance with me again. Let's put on our glad rags on Saturday and go to the Berkeley.'

For a moment Mary hesitated. Ratnadatta had not asked her to meet him on Saturday; he had even implied that it might be some weeks before he took her to the Temple again, so why should she not accept Barney's invitation?

'Very well,' she said, accompanying him to the door of the flat, 'I'd love to; and I'm awfully sorry about our last evening together having been such a flop. As a matter of fact, I'd formed a little plan to make amends.'

'You had nothing to make amends for. That was up to me for having ruined your dress.'

156

'No, it was my fault, and if I'd had any sense I'd have asked you to bring me back here at once so that I could change it; then we could have gone up there again, and still had a couple of hours' dancing. But that never occurred to me, and next day I felt awful about the way I'd treated you. I expected to see you at Mrs. Wardeel's last Tuesday and meant to ask you here to supper as some compensation for having ruined Saturday evening. If you had been there you would have fared much better than you have tonight; Westphalian ham, fresh salmon and all the trimmings.'

'Really?' A delighted grin spread over Barney's face. 'Margot, you *are* a dear. If it wouldn't be taking advantage of your having asked me up to your flat, I'd kiss you. But sometime, perhaps. Anyway, see you Saturday. I'll come down about 7.30 to pick you up; and thanks for this evening. Goodnight.'

With a look of astonishment on her face, Mary stared at his curly hair and broad shoulders as he went down the first flight of stairs. 'Taking advantage' of her! She could hardly believe she had heard aright. Of all the men in the world, Barney Sullivan was the very last she would have expected to let his evident desires be hampered by old-fashioned notions about chivalrous conduct. Could it really be possible that the leopard had changed his spots?

Turning on the lower landing, Barney gave her a cheerful wave, then disappeared from her view. As he descended the rest of the stairs he was thinking. 'She really is a peach, and there can be no doubt about it that she likes me. Saturday should be fun. I wish to God, though, that she wasn't mixed up with that swine Ratnadatta.'

Not being aware that Mary had no appointment with the Indian on Saturday, he went on to congratulate himself on having anyhow stalled her off from going to the circle again for, as he thought, another eleven days; and that, he hoped, would be enough for him to queer Ratnadatta's pitch with her altogether.

Having nothing special to report that week, Barney did not go to the office until Friday, and then only because C.B. had sent for him. The Colonel's reason for doing so was to show him the list of people who paid money into the bank account of the Manual Workers' Benevolent Society. Giving him a copy of the pass-book sheets for the past year, Verney said:

'Sit down and take a gander over that, young feller. Those are the boys and girls who wittingly, or unwittingly, finance some of

157

these unofficial strikes, and probably other Communist activities as well.'

Barney took the wad of sheets and ran his eye down one after another. In several instances there were in-payments of as much as a thousand pounds, and against these the names were nearly all foreign; but the great majority were British and most of them appeared regularly early in every month for amounts ranging from twenty to one hundred pounds. The contributors were men and women in about equal numbers but, apart from the names of a film star, a Conservative M.P., and a big motor-car manufacturer, they meant nothing to him.

Handing the list back, he said: 'I don't get it, Sir. To contribute such big sums, most of these people must be jolly well off. That's not to say that some of them may not be generous enough to give lavishly to all sorts of charities; and presumably, in this case, they have no idea of the use to which their money is being put. But it seems odd that a Tory M.P. should cough up forty pounds a month regularly to a workers' benevolent, and old Benson, who runs Roadswift Motors, has the reputation of a skinflint.'

'I don't get it either,' agreed C.B. 'During the past week we have managed to identify most of the contributors. They are all rich and there are a number of titled people among them. With the assistance of the Treasury we've worked it out that, on average, they are putting into this show about twenty-five per cent of their incomes; and, super-tax being what it is, what in the world can induce them to do that? It doesn't make sense. Neither do the bigger payments. One is from a Dutch bulb-grower, another from an Indian Rajah, a third from an Argentine meat shipper. They were all on visits to this country at the time their payments were made. Why should wealthy foreigners, who are here only temporarily, suddenly donate big sums to help along British working families that have struck it unlucky?'

'Ask me another, Sir. Unless . . .' Barney paused a moment, 'unless they do know what the money is being used for and are fellow travellers. There are rich people who believe that Communism is bound to get the upper hand here in the long run, and this crowd may be paying a form of insurance to be allowed to hang on to the bulk of their fortunes if the worst happened.'

'That's a thought,' Verney conceded. 'But I can't believe it is so. Short of our losing an atomic war, Britain is as safe from

158

having a Communist Government in the foreseeable future as she is from being submerged by another Flood. Awfully few rich people can be so batty as to believe otherwise. In any case, I'm convinced that the majority of the contributors can't know the sort of thuggery they are supporting with their money. There is a Bishop among them, an Admiral and two Generals; all die-hard Tories who'd sooner be cut in pieces than knowingly contribute to Communist funds. I wanted you to look through the list, though, just in case you happened to know anything odd about any of them.'

Barney shook his head. 'As no ranks or titles appear on cheques, and many of them are only surnames with initials, the only name I recognized at first sight, apart from the Tory M.P. and the motor-magnate, was that of Diane Duveen, and I should not have thought a little blonde smack-bot like that would have enough brain to be interested in any serious movement.'

'No, she is a bit out of series. To the majority of them a common denominator applies; they are super-tax payers, middle-aged to elderly, not known to have any affiliations with Labour or to be particularly generous to other charities and, outwardly, at least, respectable. But that doesn't get us anywhere.'

With a shrug of his lean shoulders, Verney put the pass sheets in a drawer, and added: 'Well, that's that; no doubt we'll solve the puzzle in due course. Now tell me what you've been up to?'

'The usual thing, Sir. Attending branch meetings most nights, and getting a bit closer to my Communist buddies in between times. I handed a detailed report in to your P.A. just now. There is nothing in it of special interest; but I've made one bit of progress on what you call my second string.'

'You mean Mrs. Wardeel's set-up and the lovely that you have been interesting yourself in?'

'That's it; Mrs. Mauriac. We had a bit of an upset when I last took her out, two Sundays ago; but I saw her again on Tuesday at Mrs. Wardeel's and we patched it up. In fact, she took me back to her flat afterwards and gave me supper.'

'She did, eh!' C.B. raised a prawn-like eyebrow. 'Then I'll have to ask you for your expense money back.'

Barney grinned. 'No, there was nothing like that. And I couldn't get her to talk. All the same, I'm convinced that her pal, the Indian occultist Ratnadatta, is leading her into something pretty nasty; and I'm more than ever inclined to believe that

Ratnadatta got hold of Teddy Morden and led him up the same street.'

'When we last talked of this you said the Mauriac woman had assured you that Ratnadatta's circle went in only for Yoga. What has happened since to convince you that she was lying?'

'Well, first go off she 'fessed up to Ratnadatta's crowd being a bunch of Satanists and said he had blindfolded her both going to and returning from their hang-out. Then spilling a glass of wine seemed to rattle her, and she abruptly took it all back; swore she had only been pulling my leg. But she had already told me that she was going for the second time to a meeting there with Ratnadatta the following Saturday. Last night I tackled her about it. She tried to sell me the Yoga stuff again, and refused to tell me where the meeting place is. As I had no means of making her, she could have got away with that if she hadn't made a stupid blunder. She said that she couldn't give me the address of the place because it is in a district in which she had never been before, somewhere up in North London.'

'And what do you deduce from that?'

'That she honestly does not know where it is; so she really must have been blindfolded both times when she was taken to it. And Ratnadatta would not have taken the precaution of blindfolding her unless something much more sinister than Yoga goes on there.'

'Come, come! It's too much to expect any woman to know every district well enough to identify a street in which she is set down from a taxi after dark!'

'I agree; but where she bogged it was telling me that the place was in North London.'

'Why shouldn't it be?'

'Because I know that it was not. She was taken to a house off the far end of the King's Road, Chelsea. That S.W.10 district, as you know, is now made up of big blocks of post-war Council flats, mostly built on sites that were left derelict by bombs, and streets of slums that escaped them. This place is down near the river, only a stone's throw from where Cremorne Gardens used to be. At one time I believe they rivalled Vauxhall Gardens as a favourite haunt of eighteenth century boys and girls at which to have their fun.'

'How did you find out that she was taken there?'

'She had told me that she was going to meet Ratnadatta at

Sloane Square Tube at nine-thirty. I parked my car nearby, watched them meet and, when they got into a taxi, followed them.'

Verney gave a thin-lipped smile. 'Good work, partner; good work. And what sort of a place was it that he took her to?'

'An old Georgian mansion, most of which is concealed behind high walls. Sounds a bit improbable in a slum quarter like that; but that's why I mentioned Cremorne Gardens having once been nearby. This place must be a relic from those days. Its entrance can be approached only down a cul-de-sac, and they're darned careful not to attract the attention of the locals to the fact that quite large meetings are held there. In a courtyard in front of the house there were a few cars, but I stooged around for about half-an-hour and nearly all the people who entered the place, including Ratnadatta and Mrs. Mauriac, either paid off their taxis or parked their cars some way off, because they arrived at the place on foot.'

After pulling at his thin-stemmed pipe thoughtfully for a minute, Verney opened a drawer in his desk, took out a folder, threw it across to Barney, and said: 'I'd like you to read that through. It's a report, by our man at the Long-Range Rocket Experimental Station down in Wales, on a scientist there who seems to be going a bit round the bend, and a statement by the egg-head himself. Take it over to the armchair by the window while I get on with some other work. When you've done, let me know what you think of it.'

Barney moved over to the window and spent the next twenty minutes reading through the contents of the folder. To Squadron-Leader Forsby's original report and the two sections of Otto Khune's account of his strange association with his brother, Lothar, a final document dated two days previously had been added.

It was a letter from Forsby in which he said that Otto appeared to be on the verge of a nervous breakdown and had given out to his colleagues, as a reason for his state, that he was suffering from terrible nightmares; so Forsby had installed a tape-recorder in the scientist's bedroom on the chance that it might pick up something if he talked in his sleep.

It had. From the long jumbles of talk that had been recorded, it emerged that Lothar was proposing a clandestine exchange of secret information about the latest rocket fuels, by which, he argued, each of them could gain great prestige as a scientist on producing as his own discovery the other's knowledge. Just as he had in 1950, he was now working on Otto and pressing him to meet him in London on the coming Saturday or, if he could not manage that, on the Saturday that followed, and showing him in his dreams a house to which he should come at midday, with directions how to find it.

When Barney reached that passage, he jumped to his feet and exclaimed: 'C.B.! Sorry, Sir, I mean. The description of the place at which Lothar wants Otto to meet him next weekend . . .'

The buzzer on the Colonel's desk sounded, cutting him short. Verney answered it, then looked back at Barney and nodded.

'That is why I asked you to read the Khune file. I felt pretty certain you'd confirm my impression. It tallies with yours of this Georgian mansion to which Ratnadatta took Mrs. Mauriac.'

12

A tangled skein

O<small>N</small> the previous Tuesday night Mary had gone to
bed in a very happy frame of mind. For the best part of two
hours she had forgotten her loneliness and bitterness and had felt
more like her normally cheerful self than at any time since she
had lost her husband. Barney's anxiety that she should break off
her association with Ratnadatta had obviously been inspired by
genuine concern for her, and to have once more a man eager to
safeguard her well-being was just the tonic she had needed.

Even so, by Wednesday evening she had decided that leopards
did *not* change their spots. There was no mistaking from his
attitude that he would like to start an affair with her, so his wish
to protect her from trouble could as equally well be put down to a
selfish, as an unselfish, motive. Recalling the way in which he had
left her in such a desperate plight five years ago, she felt convinced
that his nature could not have altered, and that he would still use
his gay attractiveness to get what he could out of any pretty
woman, then leave her in the lurch the moment it suited him.

But, she thought, with a suggestion of cynical amusement, it
was he, and not she, who was now playing with fire; for she knew
his form, whereas he still knew nothing about her except what he
had learnt since their meeting just over a fortnight before. Moreover, as a companion he was great fun, and there was no reason
at all for her to hurry the *dénouement* of her plan; so why should
she not enjoy as long as possible the benefits of the present
situation? It would be time enough to tell him that she was the Mary

McCreedy he had put in the family way at the age of eighteen and then deserted when he made the pace too hot for her to keep him on a string any longer. In this mood she began to look forward to Saturday, and when he called for her that evening she greeted him with her loveliest smile.

He had brought his car and, after dropping her at the Berkeley, left it in the garage at the bottom of Hay Hill, then rejoined her. As they had both determined to make the evening a success, it went well from the start. Both of them had healthy appetites, so enjoyed their dinners, and when they danced afterwards, just as had been the case before, they forgot everything else in the pleasure of the movement and rhythm. The time went all too quickly and when the restaurant began to empty he suggested that they should go on to Churchill's. She willingly agreed, so they took a taxi round to Bond Street and spent two more happy hours dancing and talking in the dim rose-shaded light of the night-club.

It was getting on for three in the morning by the time he pulled up in his car with her in Cromwell Road. Having thanked him for a lovely evening before getting out, she said:

'I'm afraid it's too late to ask you in, but here is something you wanted the other evening.' Then she leaned towards him quickly and kissed him.

He put out an arm to catch her to him; but she already had one hand on the door handle, so was able to slip out of his embrace and from the car on to the pavement.

'Hi!' he exclaimed. 'That's only a sample. Don't leave a poor fellow to go thirsting to his bed. Come back, there's a sweet.'

'No,' she laughed, 'that's enough for now,' and turned to run up the steps to the house.

Scrambling out, he hurried after her, and caught her by the arm.

'No! Please Barney. Not in the street,' she said quickly.

'All right,' he agreed reluctantly. 'But what about tomorrow? Today, rather. How about coming for a run in the car and lunching somewhere in the country?'

'If it's a fine day, I'd love to,' she replied at once.

'Splendid!' he grinned. 'I'll pick you up then. Shall we say half-past eleven?'

Getting out her latch-key, she nodded. 'I expect I'll come to about ten; so that should be all right. Goodnight, my dear.'

'Margot, you're a honey! But it's "good-morning", and we're all set now for a happy day together. Happy dreams!'

By mid-morning the weather prospects had worsened and, although it was not actually raining, grey clouds obscured the sky; but they decided to risk the weather and drive down to the Hut, at Wisley.

Just as he felt certain that she had been lying to him about what went on in Ratnadatta's circle, she felt sure that he had lied to her about his being Lord Larne, and that his story of being in England only on a visit from Kenya was a wily stratagem put out in advance, which would provide him with the excuse that he had to return there should he wish to terminate any love affair that looked like becoming troublesome for him. So on their way down into Surrey, she amused herself by asking him, with apparent innocence, a number of awkward questions.

Although unsuspicious of her motive, he was far too old a hand at posing under a false identity to let himself be caught out easily, and by now he had had ample time to get used to thinking of himself, when with her, as a titled visitor from Kenya. About his having a car, he said, he had hired it for his stay; about the length of his visit, that it would depend on how long it took to complete the tie-ups for his travel agency, and that would take another month, at least; about where he was staying, that he was lucky in having many friends who were willing to put him up for a few nights at a time, so he moved around from one to another; about his home in Kenya, that he had a house in one of the better suburbs of Nairobi, but not a very large one as he was not particularly well off; about his parents, that both of them had died while he was still young, which was the truth; and he was able to keep her amused for quite a time by improvising on an imaginary upbringing.

She scored only one hit, and that was when she asked him to tell her where he was staying at the moment, in case she wanted to get in touch with him. In reply he had to give her the address of his flat in Warwick Square, but he said that it had been temporarily lent to him by a friend of his and, as he was a stranger there, any message for him should be sent care of Mr. Sullivan.

Having pushed him into using his own name and, as she saw it, as good as admitting that he had no right to a title, gave her a quiet laugh; but afterwards she wondered a little grimly how many young women he had led up the garden path by the idea that he might make them the Countess of Larne.

They lunched at the Hut hotel and the rain held off until they were half way through the meal, but then for about half-an-hour it came down hard. Barney had been hoping that during the afternoon they would be able to go for a walk in the woods, and find some pleasant spot suitable for improving their relationship from the point it had reached in the early hours of that morning, but as the rain had made mossy banks and fallen tree-trunks too wet to sit on he had, for the time being, to confine his amorous intentions to getting closer to Mary mentally, in a long talk.

They discussed many things and found they had many tastes in common so, by the time they returned to the Hut for tea, a much greater degree of intimacy had been established between them, and he felt that his afternoon had been far from wasted. Unfortunately, however, he was debarred from following it up. That evening he had to attend a subscription concert got up by some of his Communist contacts at which one of their number was to receive a presentation on retirement from office; so he had to excuse himself to Mary for not asking her out to dinner by saying that he had a long-standing date, that he could not break, to dine with friends whom he had entertained when they were on a visit to Kenya.

Throughout the day he had purposely refrained from mentioning Ratnadatta, but he had every intention of doing so before they parted; so he was pleased when, on their way back to London, she raised the subject herself by remarking: 'I take it that you will be going to Mrs. Wardeel's on Tuesday and that I shall see you next there?'

He looked at her in feigned surprise. 'Yes, I'm going. But surely you don't mean to change your mind? You can't let me down like that?'

'Let you down?' she frowned. 'What do you mean?'

'Why, you promised me only last Tuesday that you would keep clear of Ratnadatta—for a while, anyway.'

She hesitated for a second, then took refuge in a prevarication. 'I didn't go out with him last night.'

'No, bless you. But that's all the more reason for avoiding him on Tuesday. You'll escape having to make excuses, then, perhaps being wheedled into promising to go to his circle with him this coming Saturday.'

'I ought to apologize to him for not turning up,' she prevaricated again.

'To hell with that! He's up to no good, and you promised me to have no more to do with him for the time being.'

'By that I thought you meant not going to his circle.'

'I did, as I am sure that doing so is really dangerous for you. But I also think that when you talk to him he exerts a dangerous influence over you. So I really meant for you to keep away from him altogether.'

'He couldn't do me any harm at Mrs. Wardeel's, especially if you are there with me.'

'I don't agree. You've refused to cut him out for good; so even talking to him again might tempt you into attending another of his meetings sooner than you otherwise would.'

As she did not reply, he put out a hand, took hers, and went on: 'Forgive me if I am making a nuisance of myself, my sweet; but I'm becoming terribly fond of you, and I can't bear the thought of your being led into the sort of filthy business that I believe is Ratnadatta's real game. Give me a little time to find out a bit about him. If he turns out to be only an honest practitioner of Yoga, we'll go to his parties together and learn to keep ourselves warm by rhythmic breathing, or whatever they do. But if you won't agree to keep clear of him for a few weeks, you are going to be the cause of my having an awful lot of sleepless nights.'

Mary had been thinking furiously. Ten days ago it would have given her considerable pleasure to picture Barney twisting and turning in his bed, a prey to agonizing thoughts of her being raped by Satanists; but that was so no longer. Her naturally generous nature made her feel that it would be horribly unkind to inflict such torture by imagination on anyone who was striving to protect her. But what would happen if she disobeyed Ratnadatta's order, and failed to appear at Mrs. Wardeel's on Tuesday? Would he descend upon her, demand an explanation and, if he did not consider it satisfactory, ill-wish her? It was a frightening thought. She had herself witnessed examples of the power of the Great Ram. Ratnadatta's, although far less, might still be formidable. But she could say she had been ill and, if he had not actually been overlooking her at the time, how could he be certain that she was lying? The fact that Barney would be there, somewhere in the offing, to stand by her, finally outweighed her fears, and she said:

167

'All right, then. I won't go on Tuesday. But come to supper again afterwards and tell me how the meeting went.'

To that he cheerfully agreed and, a quarter-of-an-hour later, he set her down with a smiling farewell in Cromwell Road.

Before going to the subscription concert, Barney had another date to keep. It was with C.B. at a small hotel in Chelsea to which the Colonel sometimes asked his young men to come if he wished to see them on a Sunday and did not want to go up to the office.

At their last meeting on Friday, after it had emerged that Lothar was pressing Otto to keep an appointment with him at the old house in Cremorne, they had gone very thoroughly into the implications of this unexpected link between the twin of the scientist down in Wales and Ratnadatta's circle.

Up to the point of that discovery, while reading Otto Khune's statement, Barney had been strongly of the impression that the scientist had become the victim of hallucinations; but he had described the old mansion with such unmistakable clearness that, short of the whole document being an apparently pointless fraud, it seemed that a vision of it really must have been conveyed to him by psychic means.

C.B., who knew much more about such matters, had also pointed out that, according to the statement, the twins had been gifted from childhood with supernatural powers, and many times in their lives each had used those powers to inform himself about the situation of the other. Moreover Lothar, in whom the power was evidently greater, having used it with such vicious unscrupulousness to wreck his brother's marriage, obviously had an intensely evil personality; so, his turning out to be a Satanist was not particularly surprising.

The passages in Otto's statement describing his meeting with Lothar in 1950 made it clear that the latter was working for the Russians. The purpose of his visit to London then had been to induce Otto to return to Russia with him; his purpose now was, obviously, to tickle Otto's vanity with the prospect of securing data which would give him new triumphs in his own scientific field, then to trick him in the exchange and make off with the formula of Britain's latest rocket fuel. In any case, there could be little doubt that he was acting as a Communist agent.

The fact that he was both a Communist and a Satanist had raised the interesting question of how far might a tie-up exist between these two supposedly separate forces for evil? It could be that Lothar was using the old mansion in Cremorne from time to time simply as a guest. Satanism, as Verney knew, was world wide, and Black Magic still practised in every country under the sun; so Lothar could have secured an introduction from a Satanic circle to which he belonged abroad to the circle in London. If so, it did not follow that his hosts knew him to be a Soviet agent, or even that he was a Communist, and they themselves might play no part in Communist activities.

But Verney had told Barney that he regarded that as most unlikely. From the beginning he had believed that Teddy Morden had died as the victim of a human sacrifice to Satan. There was no factual evidence that he had ever gone to the mansion in Cremorne but the circumstantial evidence that he had done so was too strong not to be accepted. Not only had the nightmares that had afflicted Morden for several weeks before his death been of a nature to indicate very strongly that he was attending Black Magic cere-monies, but during them he had also several times mentioned an Indian. They knew Morden to have been a regular attendant at Mrs. Wardeel's as, too, was Ratnadatta; and Barney had estab-lished the fact that the Indian was a link between her Theosophist circle and the Satanist circle at Cremorne, so it now seemed as good as certain that Ratnadatta had taken Morden there. But why should the Satanists have murdered him? His mission had had nothing to do with occultism of any kind. It had been the very down-to-earth business of finding out the ramifications of the Communist campaign to sabotage British industry. Yet it must have been something to do with that which had led him to Mrs. Wardeel's and to cultivate Ratnadatta; and, later, the discovery of what Morden was up to that had led to his death.

If that was so, it followed that Lothar was not making use of the house at Cremorne just because he had the entrée to it as a Satanist; it must be because the Satanic circle there was hand-in-glove with the Communists.

To have reached this conclusion was most satisfactory to C.B. and Barney, as they felt that it gave them an excellent chance of killing two evil birds with one stone. But the problem remained of how best to arrange matters so as to get the maximum number of this devilish crew in the bag at one fell swoop.

Apparently Lothar came to the house at Cremorne only on Saturdays, so to raid the place on any other day would leave him at large. It was, too, on Saturday nights that the Satanist circle gathered there, so there was good reason to believe that he came up from some hide-out on that day to be present at their weekly celebration. If, therefore, Special Branch surrounded the place the following evening and raided it about eleven o'clock, they should get him in the net with his associates.

Against such a proceeding there was one snag. The law of England was cumbersome and, owing to its proper concern with protecting the rights of the individual, often made the task of the Security Services extremely difficult. Even should the Satanists be caught naked in the midst of an orgy, whoever owned the place, or was its legal tenant, could be charged only with using it for immoral purposes, and those caught in it with indecent behaviour. Lothar, if it transpired that he was accredited to the Soviet Embassy, might plead diplomatic privilege, and so escape scot-free.

On the other hand, if Otto had called on him there earlier in the day, it would be a very different matter. Once the brothers had actually met, even if Lothar was not caught with British scientific data on him, the tape recordings Forsby had secured, which gave the reason for their meeting, could be used to incriminate them.

In consequence, Verney had decided to have the house at Cremorne watched in case Otto gave way and came to the rendezvous next day. If he did, the place was to be raided that night. If not, they would hold their hands till next Saturday, then repeat the drill.

C.B. had then told Barney that he had to be out of London on other business for the next two nights, so would not be able to let him know what had happened till Sunday, and made an appointment for them to have a drink together that evening.

Barney found his Colonel in a snug little parlour at the back of the hotel and, having been provided with a drink, eagerly enquired what had taken place at Cremorne the previous day.

'No luck, partner,' C.B. replied at once. 'As a matter of fact I had no great expectations anyway. Lothar gave Otto the choice of two Saturdays and it's only natural that anyone under pressure should postpone the issue up till the last moment. It's quite on the cards that he won't give way at all or, if he does come up next Saturday, it will be with the intention of murdering Lothar. But if he doesn't, Lothar won't leave it at that. You can bet on it that rather than go back to Russia empty handed he'll make some

170

other move; and the more desperate he gets, the better chance we'll have of pulling him in red-handed.'

'Was Lothar seen to go to the house?' Barney asked.

Verney shook his head. 'From nine o'clock on in the morning no one resembling him turned into the alley leading to the place; and, as he is Otto's twin, I was able to give Special Branch a pretty good description of him from that I obtained of Otto from Forsby. But, of course, he may have come up from the country on Friday and spent the night there, or perhaps his psychic faculties told him that Otto did not mean to play, so there was no point in his turning up himself.'

'While they were keeping observation did the police pick up anything fresh about the place?'

'Nothing. Apart from deliveries of food, it had the appearance all day of being deserted. Between nine and ten in the evening five cars arrived containing seven people, and a further twenty-one came to it on foot. From about four in the morning they began to leave and by six they had all dispersed. None of them appeared to have been drunk or could have been pulled in for any other reason; and, anyway, I'd given orders that, unless Lothar and Otto had both put in an appearance, nothing was to be done which would prematurely stir up this nest of vipers.'

After thinking for a moment, Barney said: 'It looks to me, Sir, as if Otto is true blue and means to dig his toes in; so how about trying to get him to act as a stool-pigeon? Seeing that he has such good cause to hate Lothar's guts, he might.'

C.B. smiled. 'Good mark to you, young feller, for thinking of it; but I've already cast that one out. In any ordinary case that line would be well worth trying, but in this it would be running too much of a risk. Otto might agree to play but, as Lothar is over-looking him, there is quite a chance that our enemy would tumble to what was going on. Once he realized that we are after him he might skip, and we don't want that. I think that, short of Forsby reporting some quite unexpected move, we'll continue to play it quietly for another week.'

To decrease the possibility of Mary – or Margot, as he knew her – becoming further involved with Ratnadatta, Barney would have liked to see the Satanist headquarters at Cremorne closed down without delay; but he appreciated that to raid it at any time other than when a meeting was being held there would be throwing away an opportunity to break up the circle much more effectively.

For a while they continued to discuss various aspects of the affair, then Barney finished his drink, excused himself, and drove to his rooms in Warwick Square to change out of his country clothes into things more suitable for attending a Communist social.

On the Tuesday Mary made similar preparations to those she had a fortnight before, then waited impatiently, through what seemed one of the longest evenings she had ever spent, for Barney to join her.

At last he arrived, smiling as usual. Within seconds of greeting him she asked anxiously: 'Did Ratnadatta speak to you about me? Was he very angry?'

Barney gave her a shrewd look. 'You *are* frightened of him, aren't you? It makes me all the more glad that I prevented you from seeing him this evening. No; he didn't even mention you, although I managed to get him to myself for five minutes.'

As she led the way into the sitting-room, she enquired: 'How did you get on with him?'

'Not as well as I had hoped. I only prised him away with difficulty from an old trout smothered in rocks, and he was impatient to get back to her. It's pretty clear that he is out to get anyone with some special asset – money, position or beauty – into his net, and in my own case I was banking on my title to act as bait. I think it did to some extent, because he didn't actually turn me down. But I imagine that for the time being he's got his hands full with yourself and the female Croesus. I hinted that I thought the mediums I had seen at Mrs. Wardeel's a bit suspect, and understood that past-masters in Yoga could produce the real thing, then suggested that as he was an Indian he might perhaps know of compatriots living in London who were practitioners of the art.'

'And what did he say?'

'That he did not, as he had never interested himself in Yoga.'

Mary's glance wavered. 'How very strange!'

Barney's smile held no hint of accusation, and he replied: 'Not necessarily. He may not have thought me a good Yoga subject. He did say, though, that he was in touch with occultists who had passed a higher degree of initiation than any I was likely to meet at Mrs. Wardeel's, and that he might, perhaps, some time introduce me to some of them. But he thought that before we talked of the matter further, it would be a good thing if I acquired

172

a better background knowledge of the occult by continuing to attend the lectures at Mrs. W.'s for another month or so.'

'I see; and do you intend to do that?'

'Certainly; if he insists on it. But, as I am pretty good at selling myself, I hope to persuade him to adopt a more forthcoming attitude next week. Let's forget all this now, though, and talk of something else. To be honest, too, I had no time to get a snack before going to the meeting, so I'm absolutely famished.'

The table was already laid. Glad to drop the subject, Mary told him to sit down at it, and hurried into her kitchenette. For a first course, as the weather had turned cold, she had heated up some tomato soup, to which she now added a good dollop of cream. As she did so she thought first how decent it was of Barney to have refrained from tackling her about Ratnadatta's having denied all knowledge of Yoga, and then of the way that the Indian had stalled him off.

She felt very glad that Ratnadatta had, otherwise he might have sounded Barney out over a dinner next Saturday then, perhaps, have taken him on to the Temple and given him a sight from the balcony of what went on there. A fortnight ago, with the idea of leading Barney to believe that she was a bold and sophisticated woman, she had started to tell him about what she had seen herself; only the spilling of the wine had caused her afterwards to insist that she had been fooling, and now she was very glad about that, because her attitude towards him had undergone a subtle change. She knew she would be ashamed if he found out that she really had let Ratnadatta take her to such a party and, instead of breaking with him, still refused to give any promise that she would not go with him to the Temple again.

But soon such thoughts were driven from her mind by Barney's gay, inconsequent chatter, as they tucked in to the good things she had provided for their supper and shared another bottle of the excellent Hock. Afterwards they sat down side by side on the sofa and she felt sure that, as she had kissed him on Saturday, this evening he would display no ultra chivalrous scruples about being in her flat, but soon start making love to her.

She had meant him to from the beginning and now, her original motive temporarily forgotten, she knew that she wanted him to. But, on a typical feminine impulse to postpone the moment a little longer, she lit a cigarette and asked: 'What was the lecture about this evening?'

'The Vedas,' he replied, 'and how Theosophy ties up with the sacred writings of the Hindus. I can't say that it gave me a yen to take up the study of Indian mythology as a hobby, but at least it made more sense than they gave us last week about old Koot Hoomi and the Master the Count. The second part of the show was a bit of a flop, though. They put a large table in the middle of the room and six people and a medium sat round it. Then they set about receiving spirit messages by table rapping. It was a slow and dreary business, and only one came through that was of any interest.'

'And what was that?' she asked.

Turning his head he looked straight into her eyes, and said: 'Some big shot up on the astral plane wanted to know why you hadn't reported for duty.'

Mary jumped to her feet; her mouth fell open, her blue eyes went round with terror, and she cried, 'No, Barney; no! You don't mean it!'

He had got the type of reaction he had played for, but far more strongly than he had expected. Standing up, he exclaimed: 'Hi, steady on! Of course not. I was only fooling.'

'Oh, thank God for that!' she gasped. 'Thank God for that! You gave me a most awful fright.' Next moment her mouth began to tremble and she burst into tears.

Swiftly he gathered her into his arms, and made little comforting noises while for several minutes she sobbed upon his chest. Then, when her sobs eased a little, he said: 'My sweet, I'm terribly sorry that I scared you so badly, but I had to know the truth. You've given yourself away now, and you really must come clean with me. You've got in deeper than I thought, and . . .'

'No . . . really,' she sniffled. 'I haven't seen Ratnadatta recently. I swear I haven't. Not since I promised you I wouldn't.'

'Well, that's some comfort. But tonight he blew wide open your story about Yoga being his game. It's nothing of the kind, and you had started to tell me about it that night at the Hungaria when we spilt the wine. That's the truth, isn't it?'

'Yes,' she murmured tearfully.

He kissed her on the forehead, then said, with a frown: 'You're a darling, Margot, and what puzzles me is how a decent girl like you could even contemplate taking part in such beastliness.'

'I . . . I have a very good reason.'

'Tell me what it is?'

174

'No, please don't ask me.'

'Is it something to do with your past?'

'Yes.'

'All right, then. Don't treat me as though I were a starry-eyed youth who'd never heard the facts of life. At times everyone does things they are ashamed of afterwards. I don't give a damn what you've done.'

'It's nothing I am ashamed of.'

'Then why on earth won't you tell me what it is?'

'I can't. Really I can't. If I did you might insist on trying to help me.'

'All the more reason to go ahead.'

'No. I'm not going to let you run into danger, just because I've been fool enough to bite off more than I can chew.'

'Margot, you must tell me! You've got yourself in the hell of a mess. It's as clear as daylight that you're scared stiff of something. I love you, my dear, and . . .'

She suddenly lifted her face to his and, her eyes still misty with tears, cried, 'Do you mean that?'

For a second Barney was a little taken aback. He enjoyed his life as a bachelor and did not want to put it into her head that he was on the verge of proposing to her; so he replied with a smile, 'Wanting to protect someone is one of the first symptoms, isn't it? If so, I've got it. And I'm determined to free you from the cause of your terror. But I can't fight your battle if you leave me in the dark. That's why you must tell me how you got drawn in to this thing.'

'Well . . . all right, then. I'll give you my reason for leading Ratnadatta on until he took me to his Temple. But nothing more. Nothing. You understand? It was because I hoped it might lead to my being avenged on someone.'

Barney gave her a surprised look. 'Really! I shouldn't have thought you were a vindictive sort of girl. Of course, when a hurt has had lasting consequences, wanting to get one's own back is very natural. Still, what you tell me surprises me all the more because I thought you had become a believer in Reincarnation.'

'I have. But I don't see what that's got to do with it.'

'Then you can't have consciously taken in one of its principal teachings. As I understand it, every evil deed has to be paid for either in this or some future life. There is no escaping that, but payment may be made in one of two ways. Either the injured

175

party exercises his right to return tit for tat or, failing that, Karma takes the form of appearing to have some natural cause – like a brick falling on the head of a chap who at some time in the past had hit someone on the head with a hammer. That someone could have hit him back and, providing the blow was no harder, not received a bad mark. But progress to a higher state can be made only by learning forgiveness, and refusing to take such opportunities. If you are still running around with a tomahawk, you're not going to stand much chance of getting yourself promoted from one of the lower forms in this vale of tears.'

They were still standing in front of the fireplace, he with one arm about her, and she looking down. Now she raised her head, and said: 'I suppose you are right. I heard it all, of course; but, somehow, I failed to apply it to myself.'

'You will, though, won't you?' he urged. 'Please Margot. Give up this idea of seeking revenge.'

Suddenly she began to laugh. She was still wrought up and her laughter held a slightly hysterical note. It had just occurred to her that, although completely ignorant of the fact, Barney was also implying that she should give up her plan for being revenged on him and that, if she did, in some future life as a young girl, someone would put him in the family way.

Taking her by the shoulders, he gave her a quick shake and said, sharply: 'Stop that! This is nothing to laugh about.'

She stopped and shook her head. 'I'm sorry. It was just a thought that crossed my mind. You would laugh, too, if I told you. But no, perhaps you wouldn't; and, anyway, I won't.' Fishing out her handkerchief she blew her nose, and went on more calmly. 'You are quite right, my dear. I must try to forget past wrongs.'

'That's better. Then you'll have no cause for seeing Ratnadatta again, ever. You have no definite date with him, have you?'

'No; er . . . not exactly. He was going to let me know when he would take me to the Temple for my next step towards initiation. But he said that might not be for some time.'

'If he does, you must let me know, and I'll deal with him. But I want your solemn promise that you'll have nothing further to do with him or any other of these Satanists.'

She sighed, then gave him a wan smile. 'Very well. I'll give up the project I'd set my mind on. But . . . but say he comes here and tries to force me into going with him? Like all these people he

176

can call to his aid supernatural power. I'm sure of that. Perhaps I won't be able to resist him.'

Barney thought for a moment, then he said: 'You were brought up as a Catholic, weren't you?'

'Yes.' She sighed again. 'But for a long time past I haven't been a practising one.'

'No matter. I'll bet you've still got a crucifix somewhere about the place.'

She nodded. 'Yes, I would never have parted with it.'

'All right, then. Keep it with you from now on. Carry it in your bag wherever you go. If Ratnadatta comes here, or waylays you in the street, produce it. I know little enough about this sort of thing, but I'm certain that the sight of a crucifix scares the pants off any Satanist. Hold it in front of his face, and tell him to get back to the Devil.'

'Oh Barney, what a comfort to me you are,' she murmured, throwing an arm about his neck. Their mouths met in their first really long, rich kiss. As it ended he picked her up, laid her on the sofa, knelt down beside her, and said:

'You are rewarding me for something I've not yet done. But you must know that I'm crazy about you, and I'd be crazier still if I refused to accept a little payment in advance.'

'It's not payment,' she breathed. 'It's just because I like you. I can't help it.'

Half an hour went by in what seemed to them only a few minutes; then the clock on the mantel-piece chimed twelve. Gently releasing herself from his embrace she said: 'Barney, you must go. By modern standards no one seems to bother much about what goes on up to midnight; but if someone in the house saw you leaving my flat much after that they'd think the worst.'

Reluctantly he stood up, and grinned at her. 'I've never yet wanted less to say "goodnight" to anyone. But needs must, if it's a matter of your reputation.'

'When will I see you again?' she asked.

He thought for a moment, and mentally cursed the fact that on Wednesday, Thursday and Friday evenings he was committed to Branch meetings which it would be neglecting his job to cut. 'I'm afraid not until Saturday. We might go to the Berkeley again. Anyhow I'll call for you, in a black tie, at half-past-seven.'

'Can't we meet before that?'

'I'm sorry, but for the next three evenings I've engagements

177

I can't very well wriggle out of. But what about lunch? Are you free tomorrow?'

'No. I have to take part in a dress show at a big store down in Croydon. And I've another in the West End on Friday, which would put lunch out of the question. But Thursday would be all right.'

He shook his head. 'Stymied again. That's the one day I have to be out of London. I have to run down to Birmingham to interest some travel agents there in trips to Kenya.'

Inwardly she winced. That at such a moment he should have brought up again the Kenya background, which she felt certain was false, as an excuse not to give her lunch, affected her as badly as if he had hit her. She began to wonder how he meant to spend his evenings.

Quite unconscious that this cover for a visit he had arranged to pay to Dagenham, with two Communist officials who were going down to meet local Comrades there, had caused her such distress, Barney prepared to depart. That her 'goodnight' kiss was only lukewarm he put down to her being emotionally exhausted. With a cheerful admonition to keep her chin up and be looking her most beautiful when he called for her on Saturday evening, he left her and tiptoed down the stairs.

On the three evenings that followed he duly played his part at Branch meetings as a disgruntled worker out to seize on any pretext to make trouble. One of the pay-offs that he received from time to time as a result of this bellicose attitude came to him in a pub, while he was drinking there with some of his Communist contacts, just before closing time on the Friday night. Feeling that it was of sufficient importance to call for reporting without delay, he looked in at the office on Saturday morning.

After a short wait, Verney had him shown in, told him to sit down, and said: 'Well, young feller. Saturday's an unusual day for you to call. What's cooking?'

'I'm afraid that the C.G.T. election is going to be rigged, Sir,' he announced with a frown.

The Colonel gave him a sharp glance. 'Got any proof of that?'

'No; it's a tip I was given last night after a meeting in Hammersmith. One of my Red buddies had one over the odds and became confidential. He told me that if I wanted to make a bit of easy money I could do it by laying bets that Tom Ruddy would not top the poll for General Secretary. I played doubtful, but he

178

swore he wouldn't let a pal like me down, and that it was a cert; only I must keep it under my hat and not get people talking by making bigger bets than a pound or two with any one person.'

'That's bad news, but interesting. It confirms a report I had yesterday. Jimmy Sawyer, who is on the same job up in Manchester as you are down here, telephoned me. He said he's sure there is something cooking, because some of the Commies up there are going round giving six to four that Ruddy won't get the job.'

'Perhaps it's just a propaganda stunt, and they think it worth risking some of their funds to impress waverers with their confidence in their own man.'

'Maybe. We can only hope that's all there is behind it.'

'If Ruddy's popularity with the rank and file goes for anything, they'll have to do an awful lot of rigging with the votes to keep him out.'

C.B. laid a finger alongside his big nose. 'That's not the only way they could keep him out, sonny.'

'No, they might stage a convenient "accident".'

'That's what I'm afraid of; so I'm going to get the Special Branch to offer him police protection. The trouble is that he's as tough as they come, and such an independent-minded cuss, that I doubt if he'll accept it. He'll probably take the view that it's preferable to run any risk there may be rather than let his supporters think he no longer has the nerve to face rough meetings without a couple of plain-clothes men tagging round with him.'

At that moment the buzzer on the Colonel's desk sounded. Switching on the inter-com. he said, 'Yes . . . All right; put him through.' Then he picked up the telephone receiver. 'Verney here. Morning, Dick. Have you rung up to let me know that your baby left last night for London?'

After listening for a full minute, he spoke again. 'I see. Damn the man! If he was going to give way at all, why the hell couldn't he do as he was asked and come up here where Special Branch have everything laid on to pinch the two of them? This is going to be very different and damnably difficult to make watertight. If L. gave us the slip and got away across the moors with the formula it would be nearly as bad as O. himself sneaking out of the country and joining the Reds. I don't think we dare risk letting them meet the way they plan to now. On the other hand, if we lay in wait and pulled L. in, unless he had already received the goods from O, we could hold him only temporarily on some

179

minor charge. For all we know, too, he may even have a diplomatic passport and we'd have to let him go right away. In either case, he'd soon be able to agree another rendezvous with O., and if you failed to find out about it we'd be sunk. Hang on a minute. Let me think.'

There was a longish pause, then Verney went on. 'Look, Dick. You know I've every faith in you, but it wouldn't be fair to throw the whole responsibility for a thing like this on your shoulders. I shall come down myself this afternoon. When I've fixed things up this end I'll send you a signal what time to expect me.'

When he had hung up, he turned to Barney and said: 'As you will have guessed, that was Forsby. For the past few nights Lothar has been working on Otto till he's nearly driven him off his rocker. Thursday night's tape recording disclosed that he had given in and agreed to come up and meet Lothar in London today. When Forsby got that yesterday morning, he naturally expected Otto to give notification that he was going on weekend leave. He warned his boys to be ready to tail Otto and got a signal ready to send me the moment Otto left the Station. But Otto didn't leave; he sat tight. Forsby supposed that he had changed his mind and decided to dig his toes in again after all. But that wasn't the case. The explanation emerged from last night's tape recording.'

C.B. knocked his pipe out, and went on. 'Apparently Lothar came through on their psychic wave about four o'clock this morning. He was doing a check up to make sure that Otto did not mean to let him down and, when he found that Otto was still there in Wales, he threatened to put a curse on him that would kill him. Otto protested that he had meant to come but had been prevented at the last moment. When he had gone to the top boy at the Station, Sir Charles Remmington-Rudd, to tell him that he meant to go to London for the week-end, Sir Charles had said he could not let him. A signal had just come in to notify them that an American egg-head was flying down that afternoon to spend a couple of nights at the Station. The Yank is a fuel expert and, as Otto is our star fuel boffin, he had to be there to do the honours.'

'I get it,' Barney put in. 'Otto realized that he dared not ignore his boss's order to stay put, as if he had they would have tumbled to it that there was something fishy about his trip to London. There would have been a hue and cry after him. We should have

180

been alerted to pick him up this end and have him tailed. He saw himself being pinched when he kept his appointment with Lothar and, as he would have had the fuel formula on him, both of them would have been for the high jump.'

'Precisely. That's what he told Lothar. Whether Lothar thought he was lying or not we don't know. Anyway, he made it plain that he was not prepared to wait much longer. He indicated that, since the mountain would not come to him, he meant to go to the mountain. He demanded that Otto should select some lonely spot a few miles outside the Station, which it would be easy for him to find, and that he should meet him there with the formula on Sunday afternoon. Otto gave him as a rendezvous a place called Lone Tree Hill, and described its situation. Lothar said that he would be there sometime between two o'clock and four, and that Otto was to go there dressed in an old raincoat and beret, so that he would be easily recognizable from a distance. He added that, if Otto failed to turn up, or betrayed him afterwards, he would be dead in nine days. And that is that.'

Barney nodded. 'I don't wonder you are worried, Sir. It's going to be a tricky business to draw a cordon round an exposed hill-top without Lothar spotting what you are up to.'

'I know; but I may decide to intervene before they meet. Anyway, it's no good trying to settle on a plan before we've talked the whole thing over with Forsby.'

'We!' Barney echoed.

'Yes. As this business ties up with your Satanist Circle at Cremorne I'm taking you with me. I'm still hoping to be able to pull in and grill both these birds. If I can, something may emerge from what they say that will give you further light on this Indian you are after. The Research Experimental Station is right off the map; but it's got its own airstrip, so we can fly down. I believe they've got some sort of hook-up with Farnborough. I'll have my P.A. find out. Anyway, we'd better have a fairly early lunch and start immediately afterwards. Off you go now. Pack a bag and meet me at the Rag at a quarter to one.'

Barney did not argue. Annoyed as he was at having to cancel his plans for the evening, this was a matter of duty and his Chief had given him an order. He said only, 'Very good, Sir. See you at your Club at twelve-forty-five,' then left the room, went down in the lift, got a taxi and had himself driven to Warwick Square.

Having let himself into his flat he at once tried to telephone

181

Mary, but there was no reply. As she was evidently out and might not return till lunch time, he rang up Constance Spry's, ordered a big bunch of roses to be sent to her by hand, and dictated a card to go with them. When he had finished packing, he wrote her a note saying how disappointed he was that he would not be seeing her over the week-end, but that he expected to be back on Monday and, unless he telephoned her to the contrary, would she please forgive him and go out with him that evening.

As they had agreed that, in the event of any trouble, she should ring him up, and she had not done so, he had no particular cause to be worried about her. On the way up to Pall Mall he posted his letter, then gave his mind to speculating on the strange business that was taking him down to Wales.

The roses were delivered to Mary some ten minutes after she got back from her week-end shopping. As she took them from their cellophane covering she was delighted but, when she read the card that accompanied them, her face fell sadly. It was in a young woman's rounded hand, so obviously not even written by Barney, and it said only, '*Terribly sorry to have to put you off tonight, but have to be out of London on urgent business over week-end. Love, B.*'

She felt it to be the most shocking let down. For a moment she was near bursting into tears; but, swiftly, her self-pity was overcome by angry resentment. Like a fool – like a sentimental ninny – like some little teenager who had hooked her first beau – for the past three and a half days she had been almost counting the moments until she should see Barney again. She knew that he had no right to a title, felt certain that the Kenya story was a myth, and all he said about starting up a travel agency there a pack of lies; yet, even so, she had allowed him to sell himself to her again. Those merry brown eyes, the mop of thick dark curly hair, the spontaneous grin that so frequently lit up his brown, healthy face, had bewitched her into believing that he had become a different person from the man she had known five years before. He had played on her loneliness by giving her the only good times she had known since her husband's death, and played on her fears by insisting that she needed his protection.

Looking back over the days since she had given him supper for the first time in her flat, she thought that she must have been out of her wits to accept without question his glib assertions that for eight out of ten evenings he had had long-standing engagements to dine with old friends. He had even left her on that excuse, after taking her down to Wisley the previous Sunday. To support himself he must have some sort of job, but no normal job entailed a man's having to leave London for the week-end at a moment's notice on a Saturday morning. The explanation was clear. He must have a mistress and quite probably was amusing himself with several other women. No doubt he had had a date with one of them on Sunday evening, and now quite unexpectedly one of them had let him know that morning that she was free to slip off for a week-end in the country with him. He had not changed by an iota, but was still the self-indulgent cynic who took his fun where he could find it and, for any woman who was not with him at the moment, it was a case of 'out of sight, out of mind'.

Angry and miserable, she ate her solitary lunch; but, by the time she finished it, she had decided that it was stupid to spend the rest of the day alternately fuming and moping. She would get out in the fresh air in the afternoon and go to a cinema in the evening.

Putting on her things she went out, walked down to the Earls Court Road, and took a bus to Wimbledon. A blustering wind was blowing which made it less pleasant than when she had last been there, but she strode determinedly across the Common and, after a two-hour walk, ate a hearty tea. By then the wind had dropped and a sunny evening bid fair to usher in good weather for early May, so she did not hurry home and it was getting on for seven o'clock when she got back to the Cromwell Road. Feeling much less depressed after her outing, she pushed open the front door of the house; and there, in the downstairs hall, she found Ratnadatta waiting for her.

183

13

Dead men's shoes

No steps having been taken by Ratnadatta to find out why she had failed to attend the last meeting at Mrs. Wardeel's had lulled Mary into a false sense of security; so suddenly to come upon him there was a most unpleasant shock. Her heart began to hammer wildly. Concealing her agitation as well as she could, she returned his 'Good evening'.

He had come to his feet and, fixing her with his round brown eyes, through the thick-lensed spectacles, he asked: 'Why haf you not come to Mrs. Wardeel's on Tuesday?'

In a voice that sounded firmer than she had expected, she replied: 'I couldn't. I ate something for lunch that day that upset me. It made me quite ill, and by the evening I was running a temperature.'

To her relief he did not appear to have detected that she was lying. Instead, he smiled his toothy smile and said: 'To hear that I am sorry. But I see you haf quite recovered. That ees good, very good; because I haf pleasant news for you. Soon now you are given the test weech ees the second stage towards your initiation.'

Mary strove to control her rising panic. Barney might be a rotten little twister, but he had convinced her that to have anything further to do with Ratnadatta would be asking for real trouble. She must get out of it somehow, give him the soft answer that turneth away wrath, then go into hiding before the date he had evidently come to make with her. Keeping her voice level she asked:

184

'When is it to be?'

'Why, tonight,' he replied in evident surprise that she had not understood that from what he had said. 'I telephone you this morning, I telephone you this afternoon, and both times you haf been out. So I come to fetch you. For this you receive instruction before the meeting. Perhaps we arrive a little early; but for me to go and come back for you in half-an-hour ees no point.'

'I . . . I've been out all day, and I'd like to change my clothes,' she faltered.

'It is unnecessary. You change at the Temple; bath too, if you wish. Come, plees, with me now.'

Desperately she sought in her mind for a way to get rid of him even for ten minutes so that she could make a bolt for it before he returned. But to say that she must go up to her flat before she went out was useless. He would wait for her down there in the hall. Yet she could think of nothing else.

Suddenly she remembered her crucifix. As Barney had suggested, she was carrying it in her handbag. He had been confident that using it would enable her to defy Ratnadatta. She must nerve herself to get it out, hold it in front of the Indian's face and order him to leave the house.

Opening her bag, she fumbled for it; but on looking down, her glance fell on the shoes Ratnadatta was wearing. They were of brown leather and hand-made; but, across the toe-cap of the left one, there was a dark scar that no amount of polishing had been able to remove.

Mary's downcast eyes dilated. For a moment they remained riveted upon the scarred toe-cap with the same fascinated horror that a bird's eyes are held by a snake.

'Come,' said Ratnadatta, a shade impatiently. 'There ees nothing for you to be frightened off. Why do you hesitate?'

Her fingers had found the crucifix but they did not grip it. With a supreme effort, she fought down an impulse to let her mouth open in a scream. She would have known anywhere the shoes that Ratnadatta had on. They had belonged to her dead husband.

Taking a sudden resolution, she withdrew her hand from the crucifix and closed her bag. Then, in a husky voice that belied her words, she said: 'I'm not frightened. It's only that I was not expecting you this evening. Let's get a taxi.'

Shoes had been one of Teddy's few extravagances. It had been

185

his custom to have a pair made for him once a year by Lobb of St. James's Street, and this last pair had been spoiled by an infuriating accident. The second time he had had them on he had been putting a broken kitchen plate in the dustbin; the lid of the bin had dropped back unexpectedly, knocking the pieces of plate from his hand, and the largest had fallen on the toe-cap, making an inch-long gash across the highly glazed leather. She had polished the shoe afterwards a dozen times in the hope of working the scar out, but it remained as a dark streak that there was no disguising, so he had said that he would take the shoe back to Lobb's and have a new toe-cap put on. That had been about a month before his death, and during those last weeks his mind had been so pre-occupied with the work on which he was engaged that he had never done so. And now Ratnadatta was wearing those shoes.

It was the proof of what Mary had long suspected. Teddy *had* met his death at the hands of the Brotherhood of the Ram. More, it showed that Ratnadatta had been personally concerned in his murder. The Indian must have noticed that Teddy had about the same size feet as himself, suddenly coveted the pair of fine, almost new, handmade shoes and exchanged them for his own before Teddy's body had been taken down to the docks.

In another moment Mary would have drawn the crucifix from her bag and defied Ratnadatta, but this sudden revelation caused an immediate change in her mental attitude. Fear of what might happen to her if she involved herself further with the Brotherhood, and an increasing sense of the hopelessness of pitting her wits against such a powerful organization, had determined her to keep her promise to Barney, for his having let her down had no bearing on that; but now, her five weeks of anxious probing had suddenly brought results so definite that she could not possibly ignore them. In less than a minute, she had nerved herself afresh to take up once more her dangerous task. No matter what befell her, she must continue her association with the Satanists and worm her way into their confidence until she obtained the full story of Teddy's murder.

Still in a daze, she accompanied Ratnadatta out into the street and, after waiting a few minutes, they got a passing taxi. Her previous visits to the Temple had been after dark, but they were on their way there much earlier now and it was still daylight; so he turned to her and said:

'To blindfold you this evening would not be good. The taxi-man perhaps see and think something funny. Almost now you are one off us, so no great matter if you know where the Temple ees. Should you fail in test, then I hypnotize you and you forget place to weech you haf been taken. If your failure off test ees not too bad, perhaps you be permitted later to take a second time. But you will not fail. I haf full confidence.'

His words had the effect on Mary of a further shot of a stimulating drug. That she was to be allowed to know the whereabouts of the Temple came as a swift first payment for her renewed resolution to carry on with her dangerous mission. It determined her to face the test boldly and go through with it if she possibly could; so that afterwards there would be no question of depriving her of that valuable knowledge. But her mind was still half engaged on the shoes.

After Verney had broken the news of Teddy's death to her, Inspector Thompson of the Special Branch had called and informed her that he was conducting the official enquiry. She had given him all the help she could by making a long statement and, on two subsequent occasions before she left Wimbledon, he had come to the flat again to ask her further questions. On one of these he had told her that, in due course, Teddy's clothes would be returned to her but for the time being they wished to keep them at the Yard to complete various tests, and she had thought no more of the matter.

Now she realized that, had the clothes been sent back, or shown to her, she would at once have spotted that the shoes taken from Teddy's feet were not his own; whereas the police, having no reason to suppose that a substitution had taken place, must still be ignorant of that fact. It dawned on her then that not only did Ratnadatta's possession of Teddy's shoes indicate that he had been an accomplice in the murder; those that the police held were almost certain to be his and, if so, they constituted most damning evidence against him. They were a rope round his neck, and she now had only to let Colonel Verney know of her discovery for it to lead to the Indian's arrest.

This thought fired a train of new ones. She need not become a Sister of the Ram, after all. By another visit to the Temple she could have hoped only to pick up a hint. No one there would tell her what had actually happened to Teddy until they knew her well enough to trust her fully. To get that far she would have to

187

submit to initiation and attend several more meetings. Even then she might not secure anything approaching such concrete evidence as was provided by this exchange of shoes. A merciful God had taken her will for the deed, sparing her the ordeal of debasing herself and participating in further horrible blasphemies. The job she had set herself to do was as good as done. She need not even go again to the Temple that evening – if only she could manage to get away from Ratnadatta.

Better still – the idea sprang to her mind – have him arrested. As soon as she saw a policeman she would hammer on the taxi window for the driver to stop and shout to the policeman for help. When he came running up she would identify the shoes on Ratnadatta's feet as her husband's, denounce him as a murderer, and have him taken into custody.

The taxi had headed south down Collingham Road and was now running through the Boltons. It was a quiet residential district, but she hoped that she would sight a policeman either as they crossed, or turned into, the busy Fulham Road.

Before they reached it, another thought struck her. What if the policeman refused to believe her? Ratnadatta was no fool. It was certain he would say that she was suffering from delusions and he was taking her to a nursing home, or some such story. Could the policeman refuse to take them to the Station? That seemed unlikely. Yet he might. And, if he did, on that one cast she would have lost everything. She could refuse to re-enter the taxi with Ratnadatta but, before she could get hold of Colonel Verney, the Indian would have got rid of the tell-tale shoes and be calling on the Great Ram to exert his terrible powers against her.

Reluctantly she decided that she dared not risk such a gamble. She must free herself from Ratnadatta in some other way, so that he would have no suspicion that she was anything other than he believed her to be. Then she would go straight to Colonel Verney.

A sudden illness was the thing. A pretended heart attack? No, that would be overdoing it. She had assured Ratnadatta, when he had questioned her about her health on the evening when he had given her dinner, that physically she was as sound as a bell. At the time she had wondered why he had asked, but later realized that he had done so as a precaution against having a young woman on his hands who might collapse from fright at the sight of the black imp. But a faint. She could preface it by saying she

188

felt ill owing to a combination of overwork and banting. The reluctance she had shown to come with him would substantiate that. If she pretended to pass out for long enough, that should do the trick. It could be taken as certain that he had not told the taxi man to drive up to the mansion, and he could not carry her the last quarter of a mile; so he would have no option but to take her home.

By this time they had traversed Park Walk, and were crossing the Kings Road towards the river. As they reached the Chelsea Embankment and turned south-west along it, another thought struck her. She was being taken to the Temple with her eyes unbandaged. If she played her bluff and it succeeded she would lose the chance of finding out where the mansion lay. And she had no idea where Ratnadatta lived. The police should be able to pick him up at Mrs. Wardeel's on the coming Tuesday evening; but, even under intensive questioning, he might refuse to disclose the whereabouts of the Temple and to give any information about his fellow Satanists, some of whom must have been his accomplices in Teddy's murder.

Henry of Navarre, she remembered, had cynically remarked that 'Paris was worth a Mass'. Compressing her lips she decided that to ensure the round-up of the Brotherhood would be compensation enough for almost any degrading act she might be called on to perform as an earnest of her willingness to serve Satan. Ratnadatta had repeatedly assured her that her initiation would not come until later, and he had even said a few minutes back that he expected her business to be through soon after nine. He had not lied to her about last time, so she had no reason to suppose that he was doing so now.

All being well, if Colonel Verney was at home she could be with him by ten o'clock. It should not take him long to get Scotland Yard moving. By eleven, or half-past at the latest, a police cordon could be thrown round the Temple; they would raid the place, catch the Brotherhood of the Ram near-naked in the midst of their Saturday celebrations and, by midnight, have the whole evil crew in the bag.

Mary had barely made up her mind to take anything that might be coming to her during the next hour and a half in order to achieve this master stroke, when the taxi turned away from the river, ran for a few hundred yards up a side-street, and slowed to a stop. Since the night on which she had been received as a

189

neophyte she had realized that the Temple could not be so far away from Sloane Square as North London but, all the same, she was surprised to find that it was actually within ten minutes' drive of Cromwell Road. Having taken her resolve, she made no demur about getting out and, after Ratnadatta had paid off the taxi, walking with him through the mean streets to the entrance to the alley which was now familiar to her.

In the courtyard at its end no cars were yet parked and, now that she saw the front of the mansion for the first time in daylight, she realized more fully how abandoned it appeared. Obviously none of its windows had been opened for many years. Some of the panes of glass were cracked and others missing. In the corners, generations of spiders had spun their webs and, in two places where panes were missing, sparrows had built nests. Behind all the grimy windows were stout wooden shutters that had once been painted white, but were now grey with dirt and mottled where the paint was peeling from them.

As Mary went up the cracked stone steps with Ratnadatta, she was intrigued to see at one side of the front door a small board on which faded capitals announced 'KEMSON'S DEPOSITORY FOR TITLE DEEDS', and underneath in script, '*Antiquarian Society for Estate Research. Meetings Saturdays 9.00 p.m.*' It struck her as a clever cover for the permanently closed windows – as a casual observer would have assumed that behind them were rooms stacked high with dusty files – and for the Satanists who gathered there on Saturday nights since, despite the derelict appearance of the house, people in the immediate neighbourhood must have known that it was occupied and that on certain evenings both cars and pedestrians turned down the cul-de-sac to it.

Next moment, as Ratnadatta rang the bell, her mind was again filled with nervous fears about the test they intended to give her. Barney had said that to play with Black Magic was to play with filth as well as fire, and she knew that he was right. Whatever they asked her to do would, she felt sure, be against her conscience, and it might call for some act so physically disgusting that nausea would render her unable to accomplish it. Now, with a sudden sick feeling of apprehension, she followed Ratnadatta out from behind the blackout curtain into the brightly lit hall. But there she learnt that she was at least to be given a short respite. As one of the negro footmen advanced to take their coats, the Indian waved him aside and said to her:

'We haf some while to wait, and it ees a fine evening. We go to the garden and if not too cold sit there a little.' Then he took her along a passage to the back of the house and out through a door that opened on to a balustraded terrace from which three flights of steps, flanked with lead urns, led down to a lower level.

Not unnaturally, Mary had expected to find the back of the house as derelict as its front, and the garden a tangle of weeds or, at best, a starved lawn with a few struggling trees and shrubs; but, on the contrary, it was as beautiful as any garden in a city could be.

The tall walls enclosed an area of about half an acre and above them could be seen only a few chimney-pots of neighbouring houses. There was no grass, for the garden was laid out in the Italian style with gravel walks, flower beds with box edgings, carved stone seats, fountains, trellissed arbours and many fine pieces of statuary. Down its middle ran a pleached alley; to one side there was a large swimming pool; on the other, an open area of equal size, paved with a mosaic in many colours, in the centre of which stood a stone plinth carrying a head crowned with a wreath.

The swimming pool was still empty and none of the flowers with which the beds were planted yet out; but, even so, on this last day of April, after several hours of sun, this wonderfully sheltered spot was a pleasant place to stroll in. After walking down the alley they came back across the open space and, waving a pudgy hand about it, Ratnadatta said:

'To here on summer evenings, when fine, divans are brought out. It ees a good place, very good, for feast and revel. You will much enjoy.' Then he pointed to the head on the plinth that dominated the mosaic-paved area, and added: 'That ees Our Lord Satan in his aspect off Pan. That he smiles ees symbolic off the happiness he take in our pleasure.'

Mary gave the head one glance, then looked quickly away. It was unquestionably a wonderful work of art, for she could almost have sworn that it was alive; and it was smiling. But the thick, sensual lips, pointed, cynically laughing eyes, and bushy brows beneath the laurel crowned curls from which little horns curved up were those of a satyr, and she had never seen anything inanimate that seemed imbued with so much evil.

They returned to the terrace and sat down at an iron table to which a tray of drinks had been brought out for them by one of the negro footmen. Ratnadatta offered Mary a glass of the dark wine that she had had before, and she accepted without hesitation. Her one glance into the eyes of the sculptured Pan head, which should have been blank but had seemed alive with cruel mirth, had made her feel that she badly needed a drink. Moreover, she could not free her mind from dread that the test she must soon take would require of her some act shameful or obscene and knowing already the subtle properties of the herb-scented wine, she hoped that, as before, it would temporarily blunt her sense of decency.

In an effort to divert her thoughts, she asked Ratnadatta, 'What do you do about the servants here? This garden is beautifully kept, and there are the footmen and, I suppose, others to prepare the food for your feasts. I can hardly imagine you would make them all initiates, yet they must know a lot about what goes on. How do you ensure that they are to be trusted?'

He smiled. 'Do you know what ees called Zombie?'

'I . . . I think so,' she stammered, appalled at the picture the word conjured up for her. 'They are dead people who have been brought to life again, aren't they? I once read a book about the West Indies, and it described how Voodoo witch-doctors took corpses from graves the night after they had been buried, then did something to them which restored enough life to them to work afterwards in the fields as slaves.'

Ratnadatta nodded. 'You are right nearly, but not quite. Such haf not died but been given drug. It makes victim fall into coma and seem dead. Burial ees very soon in hot countries, so it ees not difficult to restore animation after trance off only a few hours. But this drug also destroys many cells of victim's brain. He loses memory, so becomes dumb and no longer knows who he ees; so unable to go home or make trouble. He ees human animal. Fit for work and with understanding enough to obey simple order, but no more.'

'And the servants here are . . .' Mary suppressed a shudder, 'are Zombies?'

'As nearly as making no difference. They are all negro, but haf not been buried. They are given drug to destroy memory, but not so much as to make them animal. In this way they remain capable off more useful service.'

'If they have some intelligence left, I should have thought they would try to escape.'

192

'Oddwhiles one has urge to, but always he betray it by restless manner. He ees then hypnotized by Abaddon and feels impulse no more. But they haf women; negresses for work in kitchen and to clean, who haf been drugged same as men. They haf drink, good food, and the work ees light. Life here for them ees good, very good; and for one to become wishing to see what ees outside so pleasant prison happens very seldom.'

Mary almost found herself subscribing to the idea that these coloured servants were better off where they were than they would have been if free and struggling in some slum for a meagre living. But the thought that they had been robbed of their identities and, no doubt, in many cases separated for ever from their loved ones far outweighed the fact of their material well-being.

It then occurred to her that, if she slipped up, the soul-destroying drug might be administered to her. With a fresh surge of inward terror she recalled Ratnadatta's telling her barely half-an-hour before that should she fail in her test he would hypnotize her into forgetting where the Temple was situated. Supposing she not only failed the test but, during it, gave away the fact that she had come there as a spy? There would then be no question of allowing her to attempt a second test in a week or a fortnight's time. For their own protection they would have to eliminate from her mind every memory of her connection with the Brotherhood.

During her induction as a neophyte she had feared that if she refused to deny Christ they would murder her. They might still do so if she gave herself away. The drug provided an alternative means of silencing her, but one almost as terrible, for the results it would have did not bear contemplating.

She wondered now how she had managed to get so far without putting a foot wrong. Abaddon had read the fears and doubts in her mind but accepted them as not unusual in a young woman. That he and Ratnadatta had not used their psychic powers to probe deeper into her mentality could only be because they had no reason to suspect that she was deceiving them. Fervently she prayed that she might be given the wit and courage to keep up the deception during her coming trial. Reaching out for her glass she swiftly drank the rest of her wine.

Ratnadatta had, for the past few minutes, been telling her more about Zombies, but she had not taken in his words. Now, as he refilled her glass, she made an effort to concentrate on what he was saying. He went on to describe certain Voodoo ceremonies.

Twilight was falling and it was becoming a shade colder, but they sat on there for another quarter of an hour. Then one of the footmen came out on to the terrace. He did not speak but simply bowed to Ratnadatta.

Mary gave the man a sidelong glance. His face looked like a mask and his eyes had a glazed appearance. Now she knew the reason for his complete lack of expression, the idea that he was little more than a walking corpse filled her with horror. But Ratnadatta was saying, 'Come, plees; Abaddon ees ready for us,' so she accompanied him into the house.

The benign-looking High Priest was in his library. As on the previous occasion that Mary had been taken to him there he was wearing a dark grey suit. He came forward to welcome her, led her to a chair and said:

'My child, you are looking more beautiful than ever. You will serve most admirably the purpose I have in mind.'

This reference to her good looks did nothing to lessen Mary's apprehension about what they might mean to do with her, but she managed to smile at him as he went on: 'You will no doubt know that in many ancient Temples there were Priestesses who at times were called on to prophesy. That is the case here; and it is our custom to choose the most beautiful among our Sisters for such work. Tonight, in a little over an hour's time, a prophecy has been promised to a certain person, and it must be made. Unhappily our Sister Catherine de Medici, who was to make it, was suddenly taken ill last night. Among us there are, of course, a number of other lovely women on whom I could have called; but this morning the thought of you, my dear Circe, crossed my mind. It seemed an admirable opportunity to test your worthiness for advancement; so I sent for you to take Catherine's place.'

'Thank you,' Mary replied a little uncertainly. If to play the part of a Priestess was all that was required of her, that was a great relief after the kind of ordeals her imagination had conjured up; but as she was no true Satanist, she thought it unlikely that the Devil would inspire her, so she hurried on. 'But I've never attempted to prophesy. Perhaps I wouldn't be able to, however hard I try.'

Abaddon held up a slim-fingered, beautifully kept hand. 'My child, you have no need to concern yourself on that score. It is I who do the prophesying here. You have only to learn by heart the words I shall give you, and at the right time let them emerge from your lovely mouth.'

194

With a silent sigh of relief, Mary nodded. The plump pink face opposite her smiled and the melodious voice went on. 'We will refer to him who has been promised a prophesy as Mr. X. As poor Catherine is ill, we will tell him that but add that her sense of duty is so strong that she will still prophesy for him, although weak and in bed.'

'Why . . .' Mary began, but he cut her short with a frown.

'It is not for you, child, to question the way in which I think it best to conduct Our Lord Satan's business. You will take her place, be put to bed, and you will pretend extreme weakness. When you speak, your voice must be so low that Mr. X will have to bend right over you to catch your words. You understand?'

'Yes,' Mary now assented at once, although she was greatly puzzled in trying to deduce a reason for this curious and, apparently, unnecessary procedure.

'Now listen carefully.' Abaddon leaned over his desk towards her. 'When Mr. X comes into the room you will be in bed, lying on your back, with the sheets up to your chin, and your eyes closed. He will place his finger tips on your forehead and probably say a few words of greeting. You will not reply, but slowly and in silence count up to two hundred. Should he ask you any question during that time you will make no answer to it. When you have counted two hundred you will flutter your eyes open and whisper the following words.'

Abaddon then gave her some half-dozen sentences which she was to speak at intervals in such a low voice that Mr. X would have to bring his face down close to hers to hear what she said. But there was also a final stage to the prophecy. Before pronouncing the last sentence, she was suddenly to throw the bed clothes right back, sit up, smile at Mr. X, exclaim the words in a much stronger voice and, as she did so, cast her right arm round his neck.

More puzzled than ever, Mary nodded again. Obviously, some sinister deception lay behind the orders she was being given; but she felt that it was 'hers not to reason why', and that if no more than this was required of her to pass her test she would be getting off extremely lightly.

The High Priest now went over the whole proceeding again from start to finish, then he made her repeat twice every word she had to say, and yet a third time run through the whole without any prompting. Apparently satisfied, he looked across at Ratnadatta and said:

'Go, Sásín, fetch Pope Honorius to us.'

Ratnadatta left the room and, a few minutes later, when the door opened again, Mary expected to see him return with another man. Instead, he was accompanied by a tall thin woman of middle age, dressed all in white. Her garments gave her the appearance of a nun, except that she wore her coif far back on her head, so that her ash-blonde hair, parted Madonna style, showed in front. She was not wearing a mask and her features were of striking classical beauty. Abaddon said to Mary:

'Our sister, Pope Honorius, is the High Priestess of this Lodge. She instructs our younger Priestesses in their work, and will give you further coaching in the way you must behave tonight.' To the tall woman he said: 'This is the neophyte, Circe. I trust you agree with me that she is well fitted for our purpose?'

Having seen the newcomer in the distance during her first visit to the Temple Mary had, after a moment, recognized her. She gave Mary a cold appraising glance, then replied:

'You were right, Abaddon. With those eyes, that mouth and such a figure, she could seduce a saint. She should prove very useful to us.'

Her words were spoken with such complete detachment that they constituted a high compliment, but to Mary they spelt only a renewal of anxious foreboding. She wondered if the woman had in mind only making use of her for the Devil's work after she had become an initiate, or if their as yet undisclosed intention was to order her to attempt the seduction of Mr. X that night.

Abaddon turned his pale blue eyes on Mary, gave her a long searching glance, and asked: 'Do you feel confident that you can do that which is required of you? If not, you must say so now. I will excuse you from it, have an experienced Priestess perform the work, and give you some other test. This is an important matter and should you fail in it you will incur my anger. Answer me frankly, and without fear.'

Mary had a good memory, so she was not troubled by qualms that she might forget her lines. If there was no more behind the test than had so far been revealed, it should prove easy of accomplishment, and the alternative to it might be the performance of some act of the kind she had dreaded. In consequence, she replied firmly:

'I shall find no difficulty in doing as you wish, and am grateful to you for this opportunity you have given me to prove that I am worthy of advancement.'

196

Both Abaddon and Ratnadatta nodded their pleased appreciation of her apparent keenness to play the part designed for her;
and even the High Priestess's hard but beautiful mouth curved into
a faint smile, as she said:

'Come with me then, Circe, and I will prepare you for your
first appearance as the mouthpiece of our Master.'

Mary followed her out and accompanied her upstairs to the
second floor. There they entered a sitting-room beyond which
were a bedroom and a bathroom. The whole suite was furnished
in a style seen only in the houses of the very rich or a hotel of the
first rank. Beautiful Aubusson carpets covered the floors, and the
walls were panelled with *toile de jouie*. In the sitting-room the
chairs, settee and escritoire were of *Louis Quinze* satinwood;
two Buhl cabinets containing fine pieces of Sèvres and Dresden
flanked a marble mantelpiece, and in each of the panels hung a
coloured print after Fragonard. The bedroom furniture had a
ground of pale blue on which were painted garlands of flowers,
and all its carved edges were pricked out in gold; the sheets on
the bed were of the finest lawn and, from a coronet supported by
two gilded cupids, drapes of muslin spangled with gold stars
curved down to either side of its head. By contrast the bathroom
was entirely modern, with tiled walls and a large low porcelain
bath, and was equipped with a great variety of sprays, towels,
powders and perfumes.

Mary knew that a small number of people were fortunate enough
to live in such surroundings, but she had never before been in so
luxurious a suite herself; and, as her eyes roved over its delights,
her companion said: 'I can guess what you are thinking, my dear.
"What fun it would be to spend a night here with a lover of your
choice." Well, if you play your part this evening without bungling
it, you shall. We have several other suites similar to this for those
who prefer to take their pleasure in private rather than join in
our Saturnalias. Would you like a bath? There is plenty of time,
and if you have been out all day it will refresh you.'

'Yes, I think I would,' Mary replied.

'Then I will run one for you while you undress. Put all your
things away in the wardrobe. Nothing must be left about to
indicate that you are an ordinary woman. To make her prophecies
more impressive a Priestess should surround herself with mystery.'

When the bath was running, the tall, coldly beautiful woman
came back into the bedroom, and Mary said to her: 'Abaddon

told me that the Brothers and Sisters of the Ram all take the names of wizards and witches who actually lived in the past; so it came as a great surprise to me when he called you by the name of a Pope.'

A faint smile touched the finely chiselled lips of the High Priestess. 'My dear, I fear you are still very ignorant. For many centuries after Christ the Imposter, nearly all the Christian Bishops knew enough of the truth to follow the Old religion in secret, and many Popes served Our Lord Satan well. Pope Leo the Great and Pope Silvester II both enjoyed His special protection, and Pope Honorius was the greatest magician of them all. It was he who wrote *Le Grimoire* which, with the *Clavicule of Solomon*, is the most profound work on the Secret Art ever produced.'

By this time Mary had undressed, and for the next ten minutes she luxuriated in the warm, scented water of the big bath, her enjoyment now only a little marred by thoughts of what the next hour might hold for her. The test she was being given seemed simple enough of accomplishment, and there was nothing about it to disgust or frighten her; yet, all the same, she could not rid herself of an uneasy premonition that it might develop into something much more unpleasant than she had any reason to expect.

As she got out of the bath she was trying to assure herself that her fears were groundless, that by nine o'clock, or half-past at the latest, she would have left this haunt of evil for the last time, be breathing again the clean air of the streets and, soon afterwards, be giving Colonel Verney all the information he needed to swoop upon and arrest Teddy's murderers.

Wrapped in a huge bath-sheet she returned to the bedroom and said to Honorius, 'As I'm to go to bed I must have a nightie. I take it there is one here you can lend me?'

The High Priestess shook her head. 'For this affair you will not wear one. An essential part of Abaddon's design is that when you sit up in bed and put one arm round Mr. X's neck you should be naked.'

Mary blanched. She knew only too well the effect that the sight of her nude body had on men. This was just the sort of thing she had feared. It must be part of their plan that Mr. X should attempt to rape her.

14

In the toils

M ARY had gone into the business with her eyes open. Both Colonel Verney and Barney had not minced matters in telling her the sort of thing she must expect if she became one of a circle of Satanists, and she had frankly intimated to Verney that she would not regard giving herself to a stranger too high a price to pay for a good chance to bring Teddy's murderers to justice. All the same she had hoped, by one means or another, to evade that issue; and luck had been with her. She had that evening secured concrete evidence against Ratnadatta so, even if she had not promised Barney to break with the Satanists, for her to seek to worm her way into their confidence had now become pointless.

Earlier, when she had believed that to become an initiate was the only road to doing so, she had hoped that at least she would be allowed some degree of choice in taking a lover from among the Brotherhood, so that she could select one who would be both physically acceptable and capable of protecting her from unwelcome attentions by the others. When Ratnadatta had told her that she must be prepared to render 'service to the Temple' at her initiation, she had more or less implied that she would not go through with it if the stranger who was to accept her offer of herself proved to be repugnant to her. He had replied that Satan so arranged matters that his votaries always derived pleasure from such ceremonies, and she had accepted that assurance – for what it was worth.

But what was it worth? Or his other assurance that nothing

would be asked of her until her initiation? The Brotherhood of the Ram consisted entirely of men and women given over to evil; to expect any of them to keep a promise was, therefore, to build on sand. She had thought herself clever enough to get away with it; to make this last visit to the Temple so that she could find out where it was situated, and then have it raided that night. She had found out, but she knew now that she had taken the pitcher to the well once too often. It now seemed certain that, willing or unwilling, they meant to give her to one of their number within the next half-hour. And she was trapped.

Glancing sideways at Honorius she asked, 'This man, Mr. X, what is he like?'

'I have never met him,' the Priestess replied. 'But from what I have heard he must be past middle-age and rather a common person. Anyway, not of the type which we should ordinarily admit to the Brotherhood. He is being brought here only so that we can forward Our Lord Satan's work.'

'Am I . . . am I to be left alone with him?'

'Of course.'

'But if he sees me naked in bed, he may . . .'

'I expect he will.' A cold smile again twitched the lips of the tall, fair-haired Honorius. 'He would hardly be human if such a sight did not stir his blood.'

'Then I will prophesy, but I'll not sit up in bed,' Mary declared, firmly. 'I'll not tempt him by letting him see my body.'

'You will do as you have been ordered, my child.' The Priestess's voice was icy, and her fine features more than ever severe. 'Let us have no nonsense about this. Abaddon will be watching your every move. Should you fail him you will find his wrath no light matter. You are as yet not a Sister of the Ram, only a neophyte. He could, at a touch, make all your hair fall out; or might decide to chasten you by giving you for the night as a plaything to the Zombies.'

At these appalling threats, Mary paled and said, hastily: 'I meant only that I'd not expected anything of this kind to happen this evening.'

'Who said it would? You jump too quickly to conclusions. As I have told you, Abaddon will be watching and, should matters look like going further than he wishes, he will intervene.'

Only partially reassured, Mary asked, 'How could he if I am to be left alone with Mr. X?'

Honorius gestured towards the wall on the far side of the bed. 'Look more closely at those two flower paintings. You will see that their frames are not hung but fixed to the wall. Both are painted on two layers of canvas. There is nothing between them and the next room. A person in there can slide back the lower layers of canvas and that leaves several holes among the flowers and foliage of each picture. Through them anyone can see into this room, and from behind one of the pictures Abaddon will be observing how you conduct yourself with Mr. X. When matters have reached the point that he desires he will press a buzzer that sounds in the sitting-room. I shall be waiting there and, on hearing it, come straight in to you.'

These complicated arrangements in connection with Mary's test left her completely out of her depth. Having, while hidden herself, looked down through one of the balcony grills on to proceedings in the Temple, it did not particularly surprise her to learn that in this house of mysteries there should be spy-holes through some of the pictures; or that, having set her a test, Abaddon should wish to see for himself how she carried it out.

What puzzled her so much was the nature of the test. Why should they wish her to play the part of prophetess when Honorius, or some other Sister of the Ram with past experience, must be far better qualified for such a job? Why must she pretend to be ill and prophesy only in a whisper? Why must she throw the bedclothes back and expose herself to Mr. X unless they wanted him to try to seduce or rape her?

Perhaps that was what they did want, then to see how she would react to such a situation. But, if so, why the pretended illness first; for, surely, nothing could be worse calculated to prepare Mr. X's mind for an impulse to make love to her? And why these elaborate arrangements to enable Abaddon to intervene whenever he felt inclined? At what point in the proceedings would he do so?

What was their object in bringing there this elderly man who, by a strange snobbery, they apparently considered not of good enough class to be admitted to the Brotherhood? If her acceptance or rejection of this man on the grounds that he was no maiden's dream was the test, it seemed an extremely stupid one. In her dark days in Dublin she had found that men of middle age were generally much more considerate than younger ones and that, provided a man was decently clean in his habits, once he took off

201

his clothes there was little to indicate, apart from his voice, to what class he belonged.

Anxiously she wondered if they wished her tamely to submit to Mr. X's probable advances, display wit and cunning in stalling him off or, if need be, fight him like a tigress. It seemed to her evident that her passing this strange test depended on her adopting the course they expected of her; but which course that was, she had no means of guessing nor, as it was a test, could she expect to receive any direct guidance. She could only keep herself alert for any hints which might yet come her way and deal with the situation as it developed in the light of them.

Her thoughts were brought back with an unpleasant jolt to the immediate present by Honorius saying, 'Sit down at the dressing table and I will do your hair.'

For the past six weeks Mary had taken considerable pains to ensure that no one should suspect that her hair was dyed, but it grew quickly, and almost daily she had to take precautions against the new golden hair showing as it pushed up from its roots. Even standing close to her, no one would have guessed that she was not born a brunette, but another woman actually combing and parting her hair would almost certainly have become aware that she was actually a blonde, and blondes are not given to dyeing their hair dark brown without some very good reason.

Fearing now that such a discovery would lead to her being asked some very awkward questions, Mary said quickly, 'Please don't bother. I can quite well do it myself.'

For a moment her heart was in her mouth, as she thought it quite possible that Honorius might tell her that the hair of a priestess had to be dressed in some special manner; but to her relief the tall woman, so deceptively clad in nun's garments, replied: 'Very well, then. But part it in the centre as I do mine, then, as there will be no coif to hide it, we can arrange for it to fall to the best advantage framing your face.'

When Mary had brushed and combed her hair, and re-made-up her face, the Priestess dabbed a scent with a strong musk basis behind her ears, where her neck merged into her shoulders, and on her breasts, then told her to get into bed.

As she slid down between the cool lawn sheets, she thought philosophically, 'Since I've made my bed, and have got to lie on it, I could easily have found a worse one. I must try to think of myself as a soldier going into battle. Even if Abaddon does not

202

intervene, it will all be over in an hour and I'll be free of these devilish people for good. And what a kick I'm going to get about midnight as I watch the whole lot of them being bundled into police vans.'

Honorius went for a moment into the sitting-room, then returned carrying a large full glass, which she gave to Mary telling her to drink it up. It was the same rich herb-scented wine that she had drunk while with Ratnadatta on the terrace. The two glasses of it she had had then had quieted her nerves and conditioned her to accept with a certain degree of resignation the fact that she had bitten off more than she had bargained for, and must now go through with it. In two long draughts she drank this third ration of the heady potion and, lying her head back on the pale blue satin pillow, began to view Mr. X's approaching visit as no longer anything to be greatly concerned about, but as a matter which might prove most intriguing.

Abaddon now came quietly into the room. Having looked about him he smiled his appreciation at Honorius and told her to wait in the sitting-room until Mr. X arrived. Then he began to catechize Mary about the prophecy she was to make. Again and again he made her repeat what she was to say until she was word perfect and had got her voice down to the low pitch that he desired. Satisfied about that he then made her rehearse the last phase of the act, in which she was to throw back the bedclothes, sit up and put her right hand at the back of Mr. X's neck.

After she had done it three times and again lay back, he stopped her from pulling the sheets up to her chin, gently touched her breasts and murmured, 'You are a beautiful girl; very beautiful.'

Mary made no reply, but lay there looking up at him.

His long slim fingers moved from her breast up to her cheek. For a moment he stroked it softly. The finger-tips slid down, caressed her chin, then she felt them on her neck. Bending above her he brought his other hand into play, so that the fingers of both stroked her from the ears down to the shoulders, then his two hands became still. They closed round her throat.

Staring up at him she saw his pale blue eyes. They were no longer consciously looking down at her, but faintly glazed.

With sudden awful horror she realized the truth. This High Priest of Evil, who had never shown her anything other than courtesy and kindness, who looked so benign and benevolent, was, in fact, a strangler. It must have been to satiate his lust in

203

safety when the fits came upon him, as a victim of this most terrible of all perversions, that he had become a Satanist.

Her mouth opened to scream. Abaddon's thumbs jabbed downwards, cutting short her cry. His lips curved into a terrible smile and a low maniac chuckle issued from them. His eyes were now quite blank. Throwing up her arms she seized his wrists and strove to break his hold. Violently, she threw herself from side to side, but those slim fingers of his seemed to be made of steel. Her eyes were starting from her head, her lungs seemed about to burst.

Into her wildly agitated brain there came the terrible thought that this must be the end of the road that Ratnadatta had all the time destined for her. He was Abaddon's creature and must be employed by him to lure girls to the Temple so that in this beautiful bed the evil High Priest could strangle them.

Suddenly, through the buzzing in her ears, she heard the voice of Honorius, sharp, imperative, 'Master! Enough! She is needed for Our Lord Satan's work. Later, if you must, but not tonight.'

Ignoring her cry Abaddon, smiling a twisted smile, his now seemingly sightless eyes fixed on Mary's, tightened his grip on her throat. But the High Priestess had evidently had previous experience of his murderous fits, and knew how to deal with them. Her classic features set, like those of an outraged Athené, and her white nun's garments swirling about her, she struck Abaddon with the flat of her hand again and again across the face.

He took his hands from Mary's neck, shook himself, blinked and, after a moment, his eyes regained their normally benevolent expression. Looking down at her again he muttered:

'You . . . you must forgive me. Occasionally I am subject to these little compulsions to . . . to, er, indulge myself, and at the same time send some young woman more swiftly on the way to a new incarnation. But now that I am older I rarely feel so . . . so strongly about the matter as to forget myself with a friend. That I did so in your case you must please regard as a very special tribute to your beauty.'

Honorius having come running in at Mary's half-strangled cry, the pressure on her throat had lasted no more than a minute; but she was still shaking from fright and panting slightly. To Abaddon's courteous apology and horrifying admission, there seemed no adequate reply. She could only pray that never again would she be left alone with him; meanwhile the Priestess wiped away the perspiration that had started out on her forehead and asked her if she would like something to drink to steady her nerves.

She shook her head, and murmured, 'No; I'll be all right in a few minutes.'

Abaddon smiled. 'You are a brave girl as well as a beautiful one. Many would have given way to hysterics and I would have had myself to blame for having rendered you incapable of performing the task that has been set you. Since you are still prepared to carry it out I will reward you later with a special favour.'

Both of them then left her, and went back into the sitting-room. Her relief at knowing that she was not to die there between the soft lawn sheets was only momentary. Fresh fears beset her that, after Mr. X's visit. Abaddon might return and give free reign to his murderous perversion. Yet escape seemed impossible.

Suddenly the thought of the crucifix came into her mind. It was still in her hand-bag and that she had put into the wardrobe with her other things. If she held it up in front of her they might be afraid to attack her. But she could not force her way past them and out into the street still naked. She would first have to dress, and they had left the door of the sitting-room ajar so, if she got out of bed, it was certain that they would hear her. Before she could open the wardrobe and get the crucifix from her bag, they would be upon her. Again she recalled the High Priestess's threats should she prove disobedient. Abaddon might cause all her hair to fall out or, infinitely worse, give her to the Zombies.

She dared not risk that. Perhaps, after all, if she did what was required of her with Mr. X, they would let her go, counting on her apparent willingness to return another night for her initiation. On two previous occasions Ratnadatta had kept his word; why should he not again? If she could only keep her head there was still a chance that she might be out of this gateway to hell soon after nine o'clock and free to bring about its complete destruction.

The frantic twistings of her mind, first this way then that, were brought to an abrupt cessation by the sound of voices in the next room. Although she strained her ears, she could not catch what they were saying. Quickly she pulled the sheets up to her chin and stretched her arms below them down along her sides. She had hardly done so, when the door opened. Then she shut her eyes as she had been directed.

205

Abaddon's melodious tones came to her as he addressed Mr. X. 'I cannot stress too strongly, Sir, that this is no pretended magical hocus-pocus, but a matter of advanced science. Or, it would be more correct to say, a revival of the application of scientific laws known to the ancients. They discovered that young women, while still pure, could be trained to prophesy correctly. But the medical profession still refuses to accept that as a fact; so we are under the necessity of keeping secret our valuable work in this clinic.'

'Yes, I quite understand,' a deep, slightly rough, voice replied. 'It's good of you to let me come here. I must say I congratulate you on your, er . . . prophetess. She's quite a Beauty Queen, isn't she?'

'We have found,' Abaddon returned, smoothly, 'that a definite link exists between beauty coupled with purity and the higher intelligences that exist outside the earthly plane. It is on that account that so few young women can be found who are suitable subjects for training. For the moment this girl is the only one here fully qualified, and it is most regrettable that she should have been taken ill yesterday. But, as Mr. Biernbaum told us that the matter upon which you desired guidance was both urgent and important, I agreed that you should be allowed to consult her.'

'She looks as if she is asleep,' came the other voice. 'Seems a shame to disturb her. Wouldn't it be best to wait until she wakes up?'

'No; she is in a semi-trance, so her state could hardly be better for your purpose. All you need do is to place the finger-tips of your left hand on her forehead and concentrate to the utmost on conveying your thoughts to her.'

Abaddon's voice came more faintly as, while moving away, he added: 'I will leave you now. When you have done, I shall be waiting for you in the next room.'

Mary just caught the sound of his receding footsteps on the soft carpet, then she felt Mr. X's finger-tips on her forehead and heard him say, 'I'm sorry you've been ill, Miss; but they say you're well enough to tell me what my prospects are, and the sort of trouble I ought to look out for. This thing means a lot to me, and I'd be very grateful if you could.'

In accordance with her instructions, Mary silently counted two hundred then she fluttered her eyes open and looked up at Mr. X. He was a well-made, broad shouldered man, and she judged him to be about fifty-five. His hair was short, grey and wiry, his jowls were heavy and his reddish complexion suggested that he was a fairly heavy drinker; but his mouth was good and firm, and his brown eyes looked down into hers with compelling directness.

Keeping her voice very low, she said: 'All will be well, if you act with caution.'

'That's a good start,' he said, a smile spreading over his face. 'But I'd like a few practical details.'

She counted fifty, then spoke again. 'Take no step of importance on Tuesdays. For the next . . .'

'What's that?' He leaned forward over her. 'Speak a bit louder if you can, please. I can hardly hear you.'

Without raising her voice, she repeated the warning about Tuesdays, and went on: 'For the next twelve days eat no meat, drink no alcohol and know no woman, so that greater power to influence others may flow into you.'

'Twelve days,' he muttered. 'Yes, you've hit it. If I get through them I'll be all right. But what's this special danger I've to guard against that Emily Purbess couldn't quite make out?'

Mary counted another hundred, as she had been told, then replied in a whisper. 'Beware of the man with the thick-rimmed glasses. Do not trust him. In secret he is working against you.'

'What; Sir Hamish?' Mr. X burst out. 'You can't mean him! He's spent thousands pushing the boat in the right direction.'

'I see clearly the man who menaces your success,' Mary went on. 'He has thick, dark hair, and dresses untidily. He is still under thirty but has a forceful, abrupt manner.'

'By God, it is Sir Hamish!'

'Be warned by me. I am the vehicle of power beyond your understanding.'

'Yes; yes.' Mr. X appeared greatly agitated. 'I don't get it; but I'll watch out.'

His face was still within a foot of Mary's. Suddenly she threw the bedclothes from her, sat up, smiled at him, quickly put out her right hand, curling it round his neck, and said in a much stronger voice, 'In you the Lion finds a champion against the Bear. Heed my warning and a great future will be yours. Go now, and good fortune be with you.'

For a moment his eyes showed amazement at her unexpected display of vigour. Then they dropped from her face to her body.

207

He drew a deep breath, jerked his head away, stood upright and said, a trifle thickly:

'Get back under the bedclothes.'

She had carried out Abaddon's instructions to the letter and Mr. X's reaction to her prophesy had been just as expected. But how he would react when she exposed herself to him was the question that had been agitating her on and off for the past hour. The display of control with which he coupled his admonition brought her instant relief. Gladly she obeyed him, flopping back and grasping quickly with both hands at the sheets. As she pulled them up to her chin, he asked her in a puzzled voice:

'Why haven't you got a night-dress on? If I hadn't been told that this was a sort of scientific clinic, and you a kind of vestal virgin, I'd think I'd got into a slap-up brothel.'

She made no reply and, as though exhausted by the effort of prophesying, closed her eyes again. After a moment, he went on: 'I suppose when you prophesy you're not properly conscious of your surroundings, and sat up on a sudden impulse?'

As she continued to ignore him, he shrugged and said: 'Well, it's not for me to complain, as you were good enough to see me while ill in bed. Your prophesy was a queer one, but I'll certainly heed the warning and keep away from the man you described to me.'

He was still speaking when she heard footsteps, then Abaddon's voice. 'I trust, Sir, that you are satisfied?'

'Yes,' Mr. X replied. 'She was aware of the date that is important to me, and has told me the quarter from which I can expect trouble. I must say it surprised me, but forewarned is forearmed.'

The voices faded as the two men left the room. Mary opened her eyes and lay still for a few minutes, then Honorius came in to her. The Priestess now had her coif drawn forward hiding her pale gold hair. Evidently she had adjusted it for Mr. X's visit, to give the impression that she was nursing Mary, as from her flowing white robes anyone would have taken her for a nun. Readjusting the coif on the back of her head, she said:

'Abaddon tells me that you played your part excellently. He is very pleased with you.'

With a pale smile, Mary sat up. 'I'm glad about that. I can dress now, then, and get ready to go home.'

'No, not yet.' Honorius checked her with a gesture as she was about to get out of bed. 'Abaddon is seeing our visitor downstairs; but he will be back in a moment and wants to talk to you again.'

Fear leapt into Mary's blue eyes, but the Priestess saw it and quickly sought to dispel her terror by saying: 'There is no need to be alarmed, my dear. He is not often subject to such fits, and you may be certain that he will not be seized by another tonight.'

At that moment Abaddon appeared in the doorway. Quickly Mary lay back and covered herself again up to the chin. Holding the door open for Honorius, he said quietly, 'You may leave us now,' and, when she had walked past him, he closed it behind her.

Her statement had done little to reassure Mary. With his bald head, smiling eyes, smooth cheeks, and dressed in his neat dark grey suit, the High Priest still looked like a benevolent Bishop yet, less than half an hour before, he had calmly admitted to her that he was a strangler. And he was the Master in this den of murderers. His word was law there and Honorius, like the rest of them, was sworn to obey him. He might have told her to still his intended victim's fears and keep her in bed till his return, so that she would be less able to defend herself. Now that she had served her purpose, even if she screamed Honorius might not come to her rescue again, but leave her at the mercy of this elderly maniac.

Mary's heart was beating like a sledge hammer. Perspiration again broke out on her forehead. Her throat had suddenly gone dry and her tongue felt like thick leather in her mouth. As Abaddon moved away from the door, her eyes fixed themselves on his beautiful hands. In another few moments those strong, slender fingers might be choking the life out of her body. Half sitting up, she thrust out an arm as if to fend him off, and gasped:

'Stay where you are! Stay where you are! Don't . . . don't come any nearer!'

His smile became sad, and he said: 'My child, I understand how you must be feeling. Naturally you are afraid that I may give way to another of my little lapses; but you have no need to be.'

As he continued to approach the bed, she did not believe him. Cowering back among the pillows, she repeated hoarsely: 'Don't come any nearer! I'll claw your eyes out if you touch me!'

He halted then and shook his head. 'Calm yourself, I beg. My having so unfortunately, er . . . forgotten myself, must have been a great shock to you. After having your nerve so badly shaken it does you all the more credit that you should have passed your test with flying colours. I come only to tell you of the special favour I intend to grant you as a reward for going through with the task set you in spite of what had gone before.'

209

She continued to regard him with nervous doubt, but his eyes showed no sign of abnormality. With an effort, she stopped the trembling of her hands, and asked in a low voice, 'What is it?'

'That's better,' he nodded. 'Lie back, my child, and relax. I give you my word that I will not lay a finger on you.'

Uneasily, she wriggled down a little, and again covered herself up to the shoulders, as he asked, 'Have you yet decided on your Satanic name? Is it to be Circe, or some other?'

She was about to reply that to her it was a matter of complete indifference, but remembered in time that to him she was a neophyte who, having successfully passed her test, should now be looking forward eagerly to her initiation as a Sister of the Ram. His question suggested that the favour he meant to do her was in connection with it – perhaps the fixing of an early date – and that he was about to tell her of certain things she must do to prepare herself for the ceremony. She was still in their power and, if she was to get out of it in the next half-hour, she must continue to avoid arousing their suspicions by showing delight at her prospect of becoming one of them. Seeking now to please him, she said in a steadier voice:

'I like the name, but you are the Master here. If there is one you prefer for me I will willingly take it.'

He beamed at her. 'I like it too; so Circe let it be. Now, tell me: what do you know of our Satanic festivals?'

'Mr. Ratnadatta told me that your weekly meetings on Saturdays are called Esbats, and that four times a year you hold a Sabat – a great feast at which you sacrifice a ram.'

'That is so; and it is through the blood of the ram that we receive our first degree of power. The central act in an initiation ceremony is the baptism of the neophyte with it. Only so can one become a member of the Brotherhood.'

'I see,' she said, pretending keen interest. 'And as there are only four Sabats a year, that is why a neophyte sometimes has to wait quite a long time before receiving initiation. Mr. Ratnadatta warned me that I should have to be patient.'

'Yes, usually we arrange matters so that three weeks or a month elapse between each stage. You were fortunate that an occasion happened to arise for us to give you your test after only a fortnight.'

Mary was now feeling enough at ease with him again to play her part convincingly. With just a suggestion of peevishness, she

210

murmured, 'And now I suppose it will be the other way. I'll have to wait weeks and weeks before I can enjoy the power that initiation will give me.'

'No, my child.' His smile was seraphic. 'As resident Master of this Lodge, I have authority to ignore normal procedure when I wish, and I intend to treat your case as an exception. That is the way in which I propose to make amends for giving you such a fright.'

'Do you mean that there is a Sabat quite soon, and that you'll let me come to it? If so, that's very kind.'

He looked at her in surprise. 'Do you not know what today is?'

Puzzled, she thought a moment, then replied, 'Yes, it's the 30th April.'

'And Walpurgis Night,' he added quickly, 'the greatest Satanic feast in the whole year.'

Starting up, she stared at him. 'You don't mean . . .'

'I mean that, normally, your initiation would not take place until the end of July. But I am granting you a dispensation which will spare you that long wait and enable you to be received as an initiate tonight.'

'Tonight!' she gasped, her face a picture of dismay.

'Yes. You will be one of five who are to be initiated; two other women and two men. But what has come over you?' he frowned. 'Instead of being delighted, you appear distressed.'

She knew herself to be walking a razor's edge. Desperately she strove to compose her features. Then she faltered: 'It's only . . . only that I've had no chance to prepare myself for it. And I'm tired. Tired out by what I've been through this evening already.'

'You feel so now, perhaps. But it will pass. You have the best part of an hour in which to rest. By then, and after another glass of our Delphic wine, you will feel quite restored and be eager to take your place among us.'

'No! No!' she cried, panic getting the better of her. 'I couldn't face it tonight. Even if I have to wait three months, I'd rather. Let me go home! Let me go home!'

'Now you are being foolish,' he admonished her. 'Of course you are tired and a little overwrought. But tomorrow you would bitterly regret having allowed a temporary weakness to deprive you of this chance to achieve your desires without further delay.'

'I've not the strength to go through with this tonight. I really haven't. I swear I haven't. I'll bungle everything and disgrace you.'

'I am confident that you will not. You took your oaths and made your profession of faith when you were accepted as a neophyte. No further demands of that kind will be made upon you. The ceremony consists only of a little blood being drawn from your arm so that you may sign a pact in it with our Lord Satan, then your baptism with the blood of the sacrificed ram and the tying of the black garter below your knee.'

'But . . .' she stammered '. . . but Ratnadatta told me . . . he said I'd have to serve the Temple.'

'Oh, that!' Abaddon shrugged. 'Yes, you will do so later. But you are not a virgin, so you will both give and receive pleasure by the act. After we have feasted and the dancing begins, you will be filled with desire and eager to make love.'

'Not tonight! Not tonight!' she pleaded. 'I don't feel like feasting and dancing. I'm too tired, I tell you. I want to go home! Please let me go home!'

Suddenly his voice became sharp. 'You silly child! Pull yourself together! Show the same spirit you displayed earlier this evening. I'll not let you rob yourself of the reward I intended for you. I shall leave you now to give orders for your reception with the other four who are to become initiates. As you are the protégé of Sásín – or Ratnadatta, to use his ordinary name – he will come for you when we assemble in the Temple and bring you down to us.'

Before she could plead with him further, he turned on his heel, walked quickly from the room and peevishly slammed the door behind him.

So far Mary had restrained her tears, but now she gave way to them. Her terror of Abaddon had played havoc with her nerves and sapped away her reserves of courage. During these last few minutes, as soon as she had got over her fear that he might again attempt to strangle her, she had once more had high hopes that she would be allowed to dress and leave this devil-ridden mansion. To her utter consternation, they had been shattered. With what seemed the most cruel injustice, the very fact that he had attacked her was now the reason for her being ordered to remain there and face yet another ordeal.

That it would prove one for her was beyond doubt. His glib assurance that the ceremony required no effort might be true;

212

but what of afterwards? He, of course, naturally assumed that, as a voluntary disciple of the Devil, she would willingly perform her 'service to the Temple', and afterwards thoroughly enjoy participating in the wild revels of his Satanic congregation. With tears oozing from the corners of her eyes, she shuddered at the thought and cursed herself anew for her temerity in having let Ratnadatta bring her again to the Temple.

For some five minutes she gave way to despair, then her sobbing eased and she began again to contemplate an attempt to escape. Abaddon had said that she had nearly an hour before her in which she could rest, so presumably she would be left alone during that time. She should, anyway, be able to get dressed without interference. But what then?

A long corridor, two flights of stairs and the hall lay between her and the front door. Could she possibly hope to reach it without being intercepted? And down in the hall there were the two negro footmen. It seemed unlikely that they would have been ordered to keep a look-out for her and stop her if she tried to leave the house; and, as they were semi-Zombies, they might not have the wit to do so on their own initiative.

As against that, the hour of the meeting was approaching and, since tonight was one of the great Satanic festivals, it was certain to be a bumper gathering. Between now and ten o'clock at least thirty people, and perhaps even double that number would be arriving. They would be coming in nearly every minute, so she was certain to run into some of them, and there seemed a big risk that, thinking it strange that anyone should be going out at that hour, they would question her. If so, would she be able to satisfy them without their referring the matter to Abaddon?

From that thought another arose. The numbers arriving would be greater after than before half-past nine, so the sooner she made the attempt, the better chance she would have of avoiding them and getting away. Again she considered the risks involved, recalling Honorius's terrifying threats of what Abaddon might do to her if she had refused to obey his order to expose herself to Mr. X. But, surely, this was quite a different matter? No work for Satan depended on her compliance. She would only be declining a favour he intended to do her. She had already told him in no uncertain terms that she did not feel up to facing initiation that night. If she was caught and stopped she could plead that her nerve had given way and impelled her to flight. As he must consider himself to blame that she should be reduced to such a state, he could hardly decree some awful punishment for her. He might compel her to stay; but he might even relent and let her go.

For another few moments she lay there, a prey to alternate hopes and fears. But time was ticking by and she became increasingly aware that it was a case of now or never. Suddenly resolving to challenge fate, she threw back the bedclothes, got out of bed and walked over to the wardrobe.

As she approached it she caught sight of herself in the long mirror. When she had returned from her walk over Wimbledon Common and encountered Ratnadatta in the hall, she had been wearing the elaborate make-up which she had always used since turning herself into Margot Mauriac. Her recent tears had played havoc with it, and the mascara eye-shadow now ran in streaks down her cheeks. Realizing that if she met anyone in the corridor or on the stairs it was important that she should appear calm and normal, she turned away from the wardrobe and went into the bathroom. There she quickly bathed her eyes and removed the ravages to her face. It was as well that she had done so before starting to dress, otherwise she would have been caught red-handed getting into her clothes; for, as she stepped back into the bedroom, its other door opened, and Honorius came in.

Over her arm she had a star-spangled mantle of transparent veiling; in one hand she carried a pair of silver sandals and a mask and, in the other, a wine-glass half full of yellow liquid. Thankful for her narrow escape, Mary slipped back into bed, while the Priestess draped the mantle across the back of a chair, set down the mask and sandals and came over to her. Holding out the glass to her, she said:

'Abaddon is very distressed about your being so upset. You played your part with Mr. X so well that we quite thought you had recovered from the shock you received before he arrived. But, of course, the effect of shock often does not show till later. Anyway, Abaddon is most anxious that you should thoroughly enjoy our great feast tonight, so he has sent you up this cordial.'

'What is it?' Mary asked, eying the glass with suspicion.

'It is one of our secret preparations, and has wonderful properties. Half-an-hour or so after you have taken it, you will feel marvellously refreshed, right on top of the world, and ready for anything.'

214

Between a quarter-past seven and eight o'clock, Mary had had two glasses of the Delphic wine while with Ratnadatta out on the terrace, and another soon after she got into bed. They had warmed her up and done much to counter her anxieties, giving her at intervals an almost carefree feeling. But Abaddon's attack on her had dissipated their effect, destroying in her entirely the excited expectation which had resigned her mind to accepting the possibility that Mr. X might be tempted to try conclusions with her. Now, she felt sure that the golden liquid contained another and much stronger aphrodisiac, and that was the last thing she wanted at the moment. Shaking her head, she said:

'No thank you. I'd rather not. I've just bathed my face and I feel better already. I shall be quite all right by ten o'clock.'

'Perhaps; but this will make you feel better still. Come, drink it up.'

'No, really,' she protested, 'I don't need it.'

'You must.' Honorius's classical features became stern. 'Abaddon says that while looking at you he discerned a sudden aversion in you to performing service to the Temple tonight. It is understandable that shock should temporarily have robbed you of normal sexual desire, but it is imperative that you should play your part with willingness and vigour. To fail to do so on the night of your initiation would be a flagrant insult to Our Lord Satan.'

'I . . . I shall be all right when the time comes. I promise you I will.'

'You may think that now; but this shock you have had has taken a lot out of you. It is essential that you should fortify yourself, or you will be exhausted long before morning.'

'If I do feel tired, surely I can sit and watch instead of dancing all night.'

A cold smile twitched Honorius's lips. 'My dear, surely you realize how beautiful you are. One of the other women who are to be initiated is middle-aged, and the other, although quite a pretty girl, is not in the same class as yourself. Half the men in the place will be wanting to have their turn with you.'

15

Men without mercy

THE blood drained from Mary's face. For a moment constriction in her throat prevented her uttering. Then she burst out:

'No! You can't mean that! Ratnadatta told me that I must take one stranger. But . . . but not . . . not any men who want me, one after another.'

The Priestess shrugged. 'Sometimes promising converts to the Satanic faith display repugnance at the thought of such a prospect. Ratnadatta is a good psychologist and no doubt he decided that would prove the case with you; so, rather than risk your being lost to us, he decided that, your having expressed your willingness to pay tribute to Our Lord Satan by Temple Service, that was quite sufficient to go on with.'

'Then he deceived me shamefully!' Mary exclaimed in bitter anguish. 'He got me here under false pretences.'

'I daresay he did, but you will not be the first, nor the last, young woman on whom this mild deception has been practised.'

'Mild deception!'

'Yes; mild. If you are willing to let one strange man possess you, why not two or more?'

Tears of rage started to Mary's eyes, and she retorted furiously; 'There is a difference! A vast difference. Ratnadatta said that the man selected would be one that I should find agreeable. Instead, it is proposed to use me as though I were a whore in a brothel.'

216

'You are a fine healthy girl, so will take no harm from it. Abaddon will see to it that you are not overtaxed.'

'What . . . what d'you mean by that?'

'He will make those who want you draw lots with numbers, then call a halt when he decides that you are tired.'

'Have men queue up for me!' Mary gasped. 'I won't! I won't!'

'Nonsense, child. I have had neophytes through my hands before who felt as you do now. Faced with the prospect of taking several lovers instead of one, they make the same protests as you are doing. But, when the time comes, their scruples vanish. After the feast they become eager to be loved and the sight of others throwing off all restraint sets them at their ease.'

'I can't! I couldn't!' Mary cried. 'There are some repulsive men among them to whom I'd never give myself. Never! Never!'

'Never is a long time,' Honorius smiled. 'After a while you will come to set much more store on the pleasure a man can give you than on his features, the shape of his limbs or the colour of his skin. But if you have a prejudice against the ageing or pot-bellied I will tell Abaddon, and he will arrange matters so that only well-formed men embrace you tonight.'

Quivering with fear and fury, Mary retorted; 'No one shall embrace me! I'll not submit to this! Get out of here to hell where you belong! I'm going home!'

With both hands she thrust down the sheets, and drew up a leg to spring out of bed; but Honorius was too quick for her. Ignoring her movement, the Priestess shot out a hand, seized her by the nose and forced her head back. As Mary gasped for breath, Honorius shot the contents of the glass into her open mouth. She choked and swallowed. A little of the liquid ran down her chin, but as her head hit the pillow, nearly all of it went down her throat.

'That's better,' Honorius murmured. 'And now I'm going to send you to sleep for half an hour. You will feel quite a different girl when you wake up.'

'Let me go!' Mary gurgled, endeavouring to spit out the little of the liquid that remained in her mouth, and thrusting her hands up against the Priestess's shoulders.

Honorius did let go of Mary's nose, but dropped the glass, seized both her wrists, broke her hold, and forced her hands down on to her chest.

217

As Mary's breath returned, she panted, 'You bitch! Get off me! Let me go or I'll kill you,' and she began to struggle violently. But the tall Priestess was a powerful woman and had the advantage that she had thrown the upper part of her body on top of Mary and was pressing her down.

In vain Mary jerked up her knees and strove to free herself. She could not wrench her wrists from the firm hold upon them and the weight of the Priestess crushed her against the well-sprung mattress of the bed. Meanwhile, Honorius's face was only a few inches above her own and the big grey eyes in it held hers with a steady gaze.

As Mary stared back the eyes seemed to grow even bigger. Then the Priestess said in a soft voice, 'Sleep. My will is stronger than yours and you must obey me. I order you to sleep.'

Realizing that she was being hypnotized, Mary tried to shut her eyes; but it was too late. She found she could not lower her eyelids, or look away from those great grey orbs that bored down into hers. Honorius's weight was forcing the breath out of her lungs and she knew that her strength was ebbing. The eyes grew larger until the Priestess's face became a blur, then disappeared, leaving only the two huge eyes, now seeming the size of saucers, poised above Mary's face. She could still taste the potion she had been given. It was bitter-sweet, like vermouth, only as strong as a liqueur. Its flavour was the last thing she remembered before she faded into unconsciousness.

When she came to, she was alone. A delightful warmth pervaded her whole body, the feel of the lawn sheets between which she lay seemed like a caress on her bare skin, and she was more conscious than she had been before of the delicious scent that Honorius had put on her in preparation for Mr. X's visit. The drug had stimulated all her senses, and with the lazy sensuousness of a cat she snuggled down in the big bed to doze again for a few minutes.

Gradually, all that had happened came back to her, but she felt no impulse to jump out of bed, hurry into her clothes and attempt to escape. A comforting fatalism now dominated her mind. She had succeeded, or very nearly succeeded, in the task she had set herself. Provided she could continue to remain unsuspected as a spy, in the long run she would get the best of these people who had trapped her. Teddy's shoes linked his murder with Ratnadatta and it didn't much matter that she had failed to bring about his arrest tonight, as she had planned. It would be equally satisfying to witness it tomorrow.

To achieve this she had, after all, to pay the price she had been prepared to pay to start with. In fact, it now transpired to be a much higher price than she had bargained for. But Honorius had been right in contending that it was not beyond her means to pay it. Some of the men she could not have borne, but Honorius had promised to see to it that she was not asked to do so, and the Priestess had been so completely frank about everything that there was no reason to suppose that she had not meant what she said.

And, after all, during a passionate embrace one man was very like another; so would she really mind that, instead of being made love to by one man all through the night, she was to be the partner of several? An episode from her black year in Dublin came back to her. Some young men had come to the club intent on throwing a wild party. When the club closed, two of them had carried her off to a flat belonging to one of them. There they had played strip-tease poker until all three of them had forfeited most of their clothes. Laughing and fooling, one of them had then carried her into the bedroom and put out the light. A few minutes later the other had joined them, and as she had had a lot to drink she hadn't really minded.

The two young men had been friends of Barney's. The thought of him made her wonder what he was doing at that moment. Her immediate guess was that he was at some quiet country hotel in bed with an attractive woman – some easy light-of-love for whom he had so callously let her down. Then she remembered that it was not yet ten o'clock. More probably they were still sitting in the lounge over coffee and liqueurs talking trivialities but mentally savouring in advance the delights of the night to come. He would be smiling into her eyes, entertaining her with some gay nonsense and grinning that devastating grin of his.

What a fool she had been on the point of making herself about him. As though a man with a nature like his could ever really change. Yet he had persuaded her that he had. In her heart she knew that she had forgiven him for the past. If he had asked her to go away with him for the weekend she would have. And she would have told herself that it was to carry out her plan to be avenged on him. Up to the last moment she would have toyed with the idea of telling him the truth about what he had done to her, then leaving him flat. But she wouldn't have done it. Instead,

219

she would have let him make love to her again. She knew that she wouldn't have been able to help herself, because she would have wanted him, and wanted him more than any man she had ever known.

But that was not going to happen now. Once again he had unfurled his true colours. That would give her the strength to resist any future temptation to become his plaything. She was not going to let him break her heart. When he turned up on Monday full of blarney and apparent contrition, she would tell him that she meant to have no more to do with him. He could run his hand through that dark curly hair of his, that looked like a wet poodle's, until he rubbed it off, for all she cared. She was finished with him, and for good. All the same, it was better to stop thinking of him.

Lazily she stretched herself. She wished that she could lie there in the warm scented bed for ever. But not alone. She wanted someone to share it whom she could laugh with and be cuddled by. If only some dark, handsome stranger would walk into the room now, she knew that she would welcome him. Just a pretence of fright and shyness perhaps. But no more. A little persuading, then strong arms round her that she could almost feel as she thought of them; then long luscious kisses and once again the swoon of pleasure that she had for a long while been denied.

Suddenly she wondered if she was oversexed and promiscous by nature. If she could so desire a man, any man, providing he was clean and wholesome, surely she must be? Yet, deep down, she knew that she was not. Although, during the greater part of the four years she had been married to Teddy, their relations had been governed by habit rather than passion, and for the last few months of his life he had become almost impotent as far as she was concerned, she had remained faithful to him. Even thoughts of what other men might be like as lovers had entered her mind only occasionally, and she would never have contemplated for a moment allowing one of them to seduce her. Several of his acquaintances had made exploratory overtures, but she had not even let them kiss her. Those memories reassured her that she was now in a highly abnormal state. The craving that had begun to obsess her was a thing not of the mind, but of the body, and could be due only to the strong aphrodisiac that Honorius had forced her to swallow.

Thinking of Teddy brought to her realization why he had become nearly impotent. To penetrate so far into the secrets of the Brotherhood of the Ram for them to murder him, he must have passed through all the stages that she had and gone still further. The cause of his loss of virility at home must have been due to his participation in these weekly orgies, Evidently he had realized that in doing so lay his only hope of successfully carrying out his mission.

Swift resentment rose in her against Colonel Verney. She felt that he had no right to demand so much from his young men. Then she recalled that the Colonel had known nothing about the Brotherhood, so he was not to blame. It was Teddy's own fetish about duty that had carried him so far. He had always maintained that one should stick at nothing to complete a job.

A little cynically she wondered how he would have liked it if the boot had been on the other foot, and he had happened to find out that she was denying herself to him because she was exhausting her sexual powers in secret debauchery. Would the fact that she was doing so in a most worthy cause have made any difference to him? She felt sure that it would not. He would have believed that she had taken the job as an excuse to return to the promiscuity from which he had rescued her, been mad with rage, accused her of being a born Messelina, and divorced her.

But, there it was. Men were like that. Even the best of them seemed to think that women were different from them and should remain chaste whatever their situation. Since they were not, but subject to the same urges, that was damnably unfair, and men were fools to expect faithfulness unless they gave it.

Anyway, poor Teddy was dead, and whatever she did now could not matter to him. The drug had created a ferment in her, and she knew that even if he had still been alive and in their flat at Wimbledon waiting up for her, it would not have made the least difference. She was impatient now for things to begin, and hoped that they would get through the ceremony of initiation quickly. Her mind whirled with images. She knew it was the effect of the aphrodisiac, but what did that matter? She was ready to play the part assigned to her and would revel in it.

A picture entered her mind of the very tall, fair-haired man who had picked her up off her feet and given her that tremendous kiss when, a fortnight ago, she had been introduced as a neophyte. Would he be there tonight? She hoped he would. If only she could arrange with Abaddon for that fair-haired colossus to be the first in the draw for her. If only he would walk in now. But it need not be him.

221

At that moment the door opened and Ratnadatta came in.

He was dressed in the garb of the Brotherhood: star-spangled mantle, silver sandals and black velvet garter below his left knee, but he had not yet put on his mask. Closing the door behind him, he smiled at her and, raising herself on one elbow, she smiled back.

'Abaddon has told me that he exempt you from normal waiting before you become initiate. This ees very special favour that he makes. For you I am most happy. It ees great delight for me also that tonight you become my sister in the Brotherhood of the Ram.'

'Thank you,' she continued to smile at him. 'But as it was you who found me at Mrs. Wardeel's and introduced me here I really owe it to you. I am most grateful for all you have done for me.'

'It ees pleasure; a great pleasure. And you haf no fears now about the ceremony?'

'No, none. I am anxious for it to begin.'

'It will be soon now. Another quarter off an hour and the Brotherhood will haf assembled in the Temple. Presently you tidy hair, put on mantle and mask and I take you down to them. The ceremony begins at ten o'clock.'

'Will the ceremony be similar to the one you let me see the first time you brought me here?' she asked.

'Yes; but more peoples. It ees our great festival tonight. First all Brothers and Sisters make report off their work for Our Lord Satan. That take an hour perhaps. Next the Great Ram will grant desires and make healings. Then the initiates sign pacts in own blood. At midnight comes sacrifice of Ram and baptism of initiates. After that, great feast and, for you, Service to Temple.'

Mary was thinking to herself, 'So I've another two hours to wait before the really exciting part starts.'

Ratnadatta's rabbit teeth flashed white between his thick lips in a wide smile, and he said, 'I read your thought. It ees you wish early part off ceremony could be over quicker.'

'Well,' she gave a slight shrug, 'I shall naturally be glad when I've got through the formal procedure of being initiated.'

'No! No!' he laughed. 'It is that you haf now become impatient to take your part in revels weech follow.'

'All right, then,' she smiled. 'Why should I not admit it? I never remember feeling so much like enjoying a big party.'

He moved nearer to her, still smiling. 'And offering yourself for

222

Service in Temple, eh? You haf wish that next two hours were already gone, so that straight away you reap joy from rite symbolizing Creation?'

'Of course I feel like that,' she agreed, a shade impatiently. 'It's the result of a terribly strong drug that Honorius made me drink.'

He nodded. 'Yes, I know it. The Golden Liquor of Aphrodite it ees called. It never fails to produce effect. Well, that is why I come early. You perform Service to Temple with me now.'

Up to that moment she had had no suspicion of what he was driving at. For the first time she looked at him not as a mine of information on the Satanic cult, but as a man. Only a few minutes ago she had been wanting desperately to be made love to. And now a would-be lover stood before her. He was dumpy and ill-shapen, but now that did not seem to matter so much; or that she had never before given herself to a coloured man. The skin of his body was lighter than that of his face and, in spite of his little paunch, he looked younger and stronger than when he had his clothes on.

The drug had robbed her of all moral sense. Never had she felt such an urge as now seethed inside her. She had become an animal, a wild thing of the jungle, obsessed with a blind desire to take a mate. Suddenly she shut her eyes, threw herself back, and cried:

'All right then!'

Next moment he had pulled the bedclothes down and sprung into bed beside her. His arm went round her body, his thick lips closed on her mouth.

It was his breath that brought back to her the reality of what was happening. With his kiss she got the full stench of it; the sickly sweet smell of bad lobster. As though her head had suddenly been ducked in icy water, it instantly cleared her brain. She was appalled by the madness that had caused her only a moment before to agree to let him become her lover. How could she have permitted this loathsome creature even to touch her? Jerking her mouth from his, she cried:

'Stop! I didn't mean it!'

Her eyes were open now and she saw the look of surprise that came over his face. Partially releasing her he half sat up, peered down into her face, and exclaimed, 'What ees the matter? I do not understand.'

223

'Get off me! Get off me!' She put her hands up on his chest and pushed at him. At the same moment she caught another whiff of his nauseating breath and turned her face away.

'Ah!' he murmured, enlightenment dawning in his dark, short-sighted eyes. 'It ees my breath that you dislike. It comes from upset stomach. I haf been meaning for some weeks to ask the Great Ram to cure me of this disorder.'

'No! It's you I dislike! All of you!' Her lips trembling, she glared up at him. 'Get away from me! Get away!'

He smiled and shook his head. 'Now you behave foolishly. It ees with me that you must fulfil rite off Temple Service.'

'It's not! I won't!'

'You will. You are my disciple. I haf been the one who brings you here. To be first with you ees my privilege.'

'You're lying! Just as you lied to me about what would be expected of me after my initiation.'

'I make you a little misleading; no more. What difference can it haf for you if it ees now we perform rite together or in few hours time?'

'I'll not perform it with you, ever! Ever!'

'But yes.' He passed his tongue greedily over his lips. 'You shall, and I tell you why. Abaddon will give you order to and you haf taken oath to obey him . . .'

'He won't,' she retorted furiously. 'He'll do nothing of the kind. Honorius promised that I'd not be asked to give myself to anyone I found repulsive.'

His eyes became black with sudden anger. Seizing her by the shoulders, he forced her back and snarled: 'You think yourself better because you haf white skin, eh? Then I teach you lesson. Under skins men and women all the same. You submit to me whether you like or not.'

'You beast! You filthy brute,' she cried and, heaving up her knees, she threw him half off her. But he managed to keep his grip on her shoulders. For a few minutes they wrestled furiously, then he grunted:

'Little fool! Stop struggling! It makes no difference to you in end and make less enjoyment for us both.'

Now half mad with hate and terror, she gave an hysterical laugh. 'Enjoy making love with you! I'd sooner go to bed with a leper! Let go of me, you swine!'

He was in poor condition and his breath was coming fast, but

224

he panted out, 'For insult I pay you later. In Temple we . . . we haf whips for those who get pleasure as sadist. In morning I . . . I give you good whipping. You . . . you go home your white skin red with weals.'

Threats meant nothing to her now. From the exertion of holding her down he had begun to sweat, and the stink of him made her want to retch. Squirming and kicking she strove to force him away from her. She was sobbing for breath and her head was throbbing madly, but with a sudden effort she succeeded in wrenching one arm free. Throwing up her hand she clawed at his face. Her nails missed his eye but scored two furrows down his cheek and blood showed on his dark skin.

Her attack caused him to release his hold. Seizing the opportunity she raised her shoulders and hit him with her clenched fist, this time in the mouth.

Cursing her in Urdu he jerked his head back, thrust her off with one hand and came up on his knees. Wild with elation at the thought that she was getting the better of him, she struck out again. The blow caught him on the side of the chin, knocking him sideways.

Now that he was off balance, she gave a sudden heave. He toppled off her and landed with a bump on the floor. In an instant he had scrambled to his knees, but she had swung her legs round and kicked him with her left foot on the side of the head, sending him sprawling.

Jumping from the bed she stood for a moment gazing wildly round for something to use as a weapon. Had a knife been to hand she would have snatched it up and killed him. Her eyes roved the dressing-table, but the bottles there seemed too small for lethal purposes. Next, her glance lit on the nearest chair. It had spindle legs and was quite light, so she had no doubts about her power to lift and swing it. But it was within a few feet of him. Could she reach and grab its back before he reached out and seized her?

Her momentary hesitation proved her undoing. He was already up on his knees again. As she darted forward he drew back his right arm and hit her with all his strength in the stomach.

With a gasp of agony she doubled up. Coming to his feet he clutched her by the shoulders, swung her round, and threw her backward on to the bed. Every flicker of breath had been driven from her lungs. The pain in her middle was excruciating. Momentarily she was blinded by it so utterly that she was incapable of movement. Now he had her at his mercy. His eyes aflame, blood running down his cheek, slobbering at the mouth, he muttered, 'You white bitch! You white bitch!' and flung himself at her.

Her determination to resist returned, but the blow in the stomach had drained the strength from her limbs. She could struggle only feebly. Tears were running from her eyes and her mind was distraught with anguish. She felt that she would never be clean again; that, for the rest of her life, she would loathe the lovely body she had been given. To go through life with the knowledge that as the result of her own folly she had suffered such degradation was too much. Drug or no drug, how could she ever excuse herself for having invited her husband's murderer to become her lover? There was only one thing for it. As soon as she could get away she must kill herself. The Thames was only a few hundred yards distant. She would go straight to the embankment and throw herself into the river.

While these appalling thoughts flashed through her brain, her wind was coming back. Now she suddenly opened her mouth and snapped viciously with her teeth. They met in his lower lip.

He let out a yelp of pain, threw up his hands and grabbed her by the throat. For a second time that night she knew the foretaste of strangulation. As his thumbs compressed her windpipe, her teeth unclosed, releasing his lip. He jerked his head back and again cursed her in his native tongue.

Her stomach still felt as though it had been kicked by a mule, but the strength was ebbing back into her muscles. She made a new attempt to throw him off, but he had a firmer grip on her than before. With an awful sinking feeling she knew that she was nearly finished. Another few moments and she would be compelled to cease her struggles from complete exhaustion.

While doing his utmost to keep her still, he was looking down into her eyes. Suddenly she realized that he had now decided to hypnotize her into obedience. Recalling how swiftly Honorius had succeeded in rendering her unconscious, she instantly shut her eyes and renewed her efforts to break free. By now her breath had returned to her. Hate, rage, agony, loathing and despair, all combined into one impulse. Opening her mouth she shouted, 'Oh God! Help! Save me! Help!'

This desperate struggle had occupied only a few minutes, and during them she had needed all her breath to fight off her attacker. Even now, as instinct forced the despairing cry from her, she was vaguely aware of its futility; for if anyone did chance to hear it and came in to see what was the matter, being of the Brotherhood they would side with Ratnadatta.

Nevertheless, he attempted to stifle her cries by clamping a hand over her mouth. Snapping her teeth again she bit into the lower part of his middle finger. With an imprecation he dragged his hand away. Hysterical now, she recommenced her screaming. 'Help! Murder! Help! Help! Help!'

With his open hand he slapped her face. Momentarily that silenced her. She moaned and twisted her head from side to side, but there was little else she could do. With a bitterness beyond description, she knew that she was at the end of her tether.

Neither she nor Ratnadatta heard the door open, and both of them were taken by complete surprise when a loud, deep man's voice enquired from close by:

'What the heck is going on here?'

As though a magic wand had been waved, for a moment the struggling couple seemed frozen into complete immobility. Only the rasping of their breath broke the silence of the quiet room. Then Ratnadatta turned his head in the direction from which the voice had come. At the same moment Mary took a quick peep between her lashes. Seeing that he was no longer looking down at her, she slapped a hand on to the side of his face and thrust him violently away. The impulse from her thrust threw him back on to his feet. Letting go of her he swung round to face the newcomer.

Mary sat up and also turned in his direction. Instantly she recognized him as the fair-haired colossus who had picked her up off her feet on the night she had been presented as a neophyte. He stood a good six feet five and was broad with it. She had thought of him as about thirty, but when she had seen him before he had been wearing a mask; now that she had a clear view of his features, she judged him to be in his early forties.

His forehead was broad but not high, his nose a great hook, his mouth a thin hard line, his chin aggressive and deeply cleft in the centre. In striking contrast to his ash-blond hair, his eyes were black and his complexion ruddy. An ethnologist would have graded him at once as a cross between a Scandinavian and a Red Indian. Too overwrought to feel any surprise at the fact, she saw that he was wearing the uniform of an American officer. Actually, it was that of a Colonel in the United States Air Force.

Launching herself forward, she ran past Ratnadatta and fell on

227

her knees in front of the hook-nosed giant. Flinging her arms round his legs, she wailed, 'Oh save me! Help me! Save me from this fiend!'

The deep, slightly husky, voice came again, addressing the Indian.

'Say now, what's all this in aid of?'

'For you it has nothing to do,' Ratnadatta replied angrily. 'Plees to leave this room. It ees private.'

'I wouldn't like to get you wrong,' the Colonel's husky voice was lazy, 'but am I to understand that you're telling me to get out?'

There was a moment's pause, then the reply came: 'I tell you only that this ees private matter. With you nothing to do.'

'Is that so. Well, happen I'm curious. Private or no, I'd like to hear about it.'

'You haf no right . . .' the Indian began, but the American cut him short.

'None of us has any rights, son, 'cept those we take. An' I take plenty. Spill it!'

'I tell you, then. This woman ees neophyte. Tonight she become initiate. She must perform Service to Temple. I give her instruction, but she ees very nervous type and show a little unwilling.'

'He's lying,' Mary sobbed. 'I need no instruction. I'm not nervous. I loath him and he attempted to force me.'

Ignoring her, the big man said to Ratnadatta: 'So that's the game. Trying to beat the gun, eh? You know darn well that lots are drawn for the neophytes, and those who have a yen to try them out have to wait their turn.'

'Do what thou wilt shall be the Whole off the Law,' Ratnadatta quoted in angry protest.

'Yeah, if you can get away with it,' the American sneered. 'And we've an understanding among ourselves that there should be no poaching on the neophytes. They're taboo until their act comes on down in the Temple.'

Almost hysterical with relief, Mary cried, 'I knew it! He was sent only to take me down there. Oh please, please, protect me from him and take me down yourself.'

'I've got to get out of my things yet,' he replied, 'and I'm a bit on the late side as it is. That was lucky for you lady, else, had I gotten here and passed by on my way to change a few minutes earlier, I wouldn't have heard you blowing your top.'

Mary was still on her knees, clinging to his legs and with her face pressed against him. 'Don't leave me!' she pleaded. 'For God's sake don't leave me with him. Take me with you to the room where you're going to change.'

'Stand up so I can have a look at you,' he ordered.

Getting to her feet, she took a step backwards to enable him to get a full view of herself.

His black eyes ran over her body, then fastened on her face. He gave a low whistle. 'You certainly are quite something, aren't you? Why, Lucifer bless us! I believe you're the neophyte who was sworn in only two weeks back.'

She nodded. 'Yes; and when you kissed me you picked me right up off my feet.'

'That's so. I remember. But you had a mask on then. I hadn't seen your face. Reckon I could get five thousand dollars for you in the South American market.' His eyes narrowed a little, and he added, 'Let's see your back view.'

Mary turned round. After studying her for a moment, he muttered, 'Not a blemish. You're just the goods I've been looking for.' Suddenly he gave her a hard slap on the behind, laughed and cried, 'Go get your clothes on.'

She stumbled forward. His statement that she would fetch a high price if white-slaved to South America was the last thing to inspire confidence in him as a rescuer. But he had told her to get dressed. That could only mean that instead of taking her down to the Temple he intended to take her away with him. It was only just on ten o'clock and, once out in the streets of London, opportunities must occur which would enable her to regain her freedom. At the moment the one thing that mattered to her was to get away from the loathsome Ratnadatta. After only a second's hesitation, she ran to the wardrobe, wrenched it open and grabbed up her stockings.

For the past few moments Ratnadatta had stood by in silence, watching them with a sullen scowl. Now, he demanded of the American, 'Tell, plees, what you intend?'

The other laughed again. 'I intend, son, to beat you to it. For the record, you may add that I rate this particular Judy too good to be shared; I'm taking her outer here.'

'You cannot do this. It ees forbidden.'

'Do what thou wilt shall be the Whole of the Law,' the tall Colonel quoted back at him with a sneer.

'But we haf understandings between ourselves. You haf yourself remark that.'

'So what?'

'To do as you say ees to rob this Lodge off one who was made neophyte in it. For that Abaddon make you pay heavy penalty.'

'To hell with Abaddon. I've my own Lodge back in the States, and I'm as big a shot as he is.'

'But tonight ees feast of obligation. To attend is duty to Our Lord Satan. No excuse taken.'

Mary had already wriggled into her belt and thrown her skirt over her head. As she hastily pulled it down, she saw sudden indecision appear on the ruddy hook-nosed face of the American. The appalling thought that he might change his mind and perhaps, after all, leave her in Ratnadatta's clutches had the temporary effect on her of a paralytic stroke. Rigid with apprehension she stood, her hands still on her skirt, her eyes riveted upon him.

Meanwhile Ratnadatta was going on. 'Also all ees arranged for her to become initiate. You take her from here and you deprive the Brotherhood off a new Sister, perhaps very valuable one.'

'She can take her initiation later. Plenty of time for that. It's a bare two weeks since she became a neophyte.'

'All the same, it ees ordered for tonight. Her name will haf been given to the Great Ram. He ees Abaddon's master, your master, master off us all. When he learns that she ees missing he will ask why. Then he haf only to give one thought to know place where you haf taken her. He then put terrible curse upon you.'

The American shook his head. 'You've got that one wrong, son. The Great Ram wouldn't put a black on me just for postponing the initiation of a neophyte. I'd have to do something a mighty sight worse than that before he did me dirt. He needs the sort of help that only I can give him for a project of his own.'

'To haf such strong position ees fortunate for you. But what off feast off obligation?' Ratnadatta persisted. 'For preventing a neophyte's initiation you are excused, perhaps. But not failure to attend yourself. What can this woman give that compensate you for what follow? Why such great hurry? To risk much for something you can get otherways a little later ees height of foolishness.'

It was evident to Mary that the Indian's argument weighed heavily with the Colonel. His ruddy, eagle features were set in a

230

deep frown. For a moment he stood silent, a prey to indecision. Then he said:

'Maybe you've got something there. Now I've happened on this honey, though, I'll share her with no one. Leastways, not till she's gone stale on me. Reckon I'll take her outer here and park her some place, then beat it back in time to be in on the sacrifice.'

Glancing at Mary, he added, sharply, 'What are you waiting for? Get the rest of your things on.'

Seeing himself about to lose his intended victim, Ratnadatta's coffee-coloured face became grey with fury. Losing all control his voice rose in shrill defiance, 'I not let you take her. I not let you. It ees whole Brotherhood off this Lodge you rob for own selfish pleasure. I go tell. I haf them stop you and throw you into street.'

Starting forward, he ran towards the door to the sitting-room. Before he had covered half the distance, the huge American stepped in front of him and swung back a clenched fist the size of a small leg of lamb. It came up with the force of a battering ram, striking the Indian beneath the jaw.

For a second Ratnadatta's feet actually left the carpet. He curved over backwards, came down with a crash and slithered along it to bring up with a bump against the bathroom door. There he remained, a twisted, unmoving figure. Mary wished that she had been capable of giving him that blow herself, but as she stared down at the still, crumpled body she could not help exclaiming:

'My God; you've killed him!'

The colossus smiled. 'Could be. I've known fellers' necks break from being given a little jolt like that. If so, his buddies will find a way of getting rid of the body. But I'd say he's only visiting the astral. He'll be back in about an hour, feeling sorry more than somewhat he didn't behave more civil.'

Quickly Mary pulled her shoes on, then snatched up her coat and bag. Her rescuer took her by the arm. Crossing the sitting-room, they went out into the passage. By this time the Brotherhood had assembled in the Temple, so there was no one about. Side by side they ran down the two flights of stairs. In the hall the two negro footmen were standing, but their lack-lustre eyes remained expressionless, and they made no move to stop the hurrying couple. A moment later they were through the front door and out in the courtyard.

As Mary drew in the cool night air, she thought that nothing had ever felt so good. She had been in the mansion for a little over three hours, but they seemed like three weeks. That morning, when she had believed herself finished with Ratnadatta and been looking forward to enjoying an evening out with Barney, seemed half a life time away.

Her tall companion guided her over to one of the half-dozen cars that were parked in the courtyard. As he thrust her into it she noticed that it was large and powerful. He switched on the lights, started up the engine and turned it into the alleyway. As it emerged at the far end and came out into the street, he muttered:

'Drat this ceremony! Why must it be on the night I've found a honey like you? And what'll I do with you till I can collect you in the morning? Reckon I'd best take you to your home.'

Mary's heart bounded with delight. Ratnadatta's attack on her had dissipated the effects of the aphrodisiac. She no longer wanted any man, and certainly not this hulking American. He too was a Satanist and, apparently, a white-slaver into the bargain. How she could ever have thought of him as a lover she could not now imagine. He might have a fine body, but like the others his mind must be a sink of iniquity. When he had dropped her she would wait for ten minutes in the hall of the house, then go out, get a taxi and drive straight to Colonel Verney's. She should be with him shortly after half past ten. If he was at home he would soon get things moving. If not, she would go on to Scotland Yard. One way or another, by midnight she would pull off the great coup she had visualized earlier. Ratnadatta, Abaddon, Honorius, the whole of this evil murderous crew, would be flung handcuffed into police vans.

'Where d'you live?' asked her companion.

She told him, and he said: 'I'm acquainted with the Cromwell Road, but not sure how best to get to it from here. Can you guide me?'

'Yes,' she breathed, trying to keep the excitement she felt from being noticeable in her voice. 'Take the next turning to the left. That will bring us to the Fulham Road. We cross it and go straight on through the Boltons.'

The car ran smoothly on. As they approached the Fulham Road he said: 'About the morning. You'll not take a run-out powder on me, will you?'

'Of course not!' In order to dispel any doubts he might have, she managed to raise a laugh and, quite unscrupulously, went on to lie to him. 'A fortnight ago I picked you out as just the boy-friend I've always wanted. I bet you are wonderful as a lover. How I wish you hadn't got to go back there, so that it could be tonight.'

Two minutes later they were running along the right side of the oval garden on to which the houses in the Boltons faced. When they reached its far end, instead of steering the car into Gilston Road he swung it round so that it headed back down the other side of the oval.

'Hi!' she exclaimed. 'What are you doing? This isn't the way.'

'Sure it's not,' he grunted. 'But I've been thinking. By sacrificing something more acceptable than a ram, and by delivering you back to Abaddon tomorrow, I could put myself right for cutting tonight's fiesta. And that's the way I've decided to play it.'

'Where . . .' she gasped, all her fears rushing back on her. 'Where are you taking me?'

'Down to the country. I'm stationed near Cambridge, but I don't live in camp. I've hired me a grand little maison with everything that opens and shuts. We'll be there by a half after eleven, and you've hit the jack-pot with your wish. I mean to give you the night of your life.'

233

16

The setting of a trap

O<small>N</small> that same Saturday, all unsuspecting of what fate had in store for Mary, Barney went to his lunch appointment with his Chief at the Army and Navy Club. The hall porter told him that he would find Colonel Verney in the smoking-room so, having parked his bag, he walked quickly up the splendid staircase. As it was a Saturday the big room, with its leather-covered sofas and scores of easy chairs, was almost empty. Verney was sitting at a table near a window with a pink gin and a pint of Pimm's in front of him. He made it a rule never to lunch alone, as he considered that to do so would have been wasting what often turned out to be the most valuable part of the day. On days when he had no appointment to lunch with officers in the Intelligence Departments of the Service Ministries, or senior Civil Servants, he always took one of his own young men to lunch at his Club, because doing so enabled him both to get to know them better and encouraged them to regard him as a friend as well as their master.

'Here's how!' he said, picking up the pink gin as Barney sat down. Barney reached for the Pimm's and grinned. 'What a memory you've got, Sir, to have ordered my favourite tipple.'

'It's just part of the Austin Reed service,' C.B. replied laconically. 'Talking of "service", Farnborough have fixed us up. About twice a week they send an aircraft down to Wales to facilitate the exchange of secret documents, personnel, special parts, and so on. They were sending one first thing tomorrow morning to bring back the American egg-head who is on a visit there. Instead, it is going to fly us down this afternoon and its pilot will remain there overnight. I said we'd be at Farnborough at three-thirty; so we've no need to hurry over lunch.'

While they ate a pleasant meal, they reviewed the extraordinary case of Otto Khune and his twin and, when they got to the cheese, rather gloomily contemplated the risk that would have to be run if Otto were allowed to hand over to Lothar the fuel formula in desolate moorland country at a spot that could be kept under observation only from a distance. But, as they rose from the table, they agreed that it was futile to attempt to assess how great the risk of Lothar getting away would be, until they were on the spot and could make a thorough reconnaissance of the proposed meeting place.

At the entrance to the Club, Verney's car was waiting and he told his chauffeur to drive them down to the Royal Air Force Experimental Establishment at Farnborough. There they were led out to a small six-seater passenger aircraft and, after a short delay for the usual last-minute testing of the engine, took off for Wales. For the greater part of the journey they were flying through cloud, but about five o'clock they could see below them crests in the chain of the Cambrian mountains and soon afterwards began to descend towards a stretch of rugged, desolate coast.

Along it for miles no buildings were to be seen, except those of the Rocket Experimental Station, but those were scattered over a wide area enclosed by a high lattice and barbed-wire topped, fence. The place had little resemblance to an Atomic Station as there were no great buildings housing reactors, and many were temporary structures that had been erected soon after the war when materials were still short.

As C.B. was aware, most of these had now fallen into disuse since. With the development of rockets, another Experimental Station had been established in the Hebrides, much of the personnel had been transferred to it and it was there that the great Inter-Continental Ballistic Missiles were tried out. The experiments here in Wales were now confined to rocket weapons for tactical use, the development of metals having maximum heat resistance in ratio to weight and fuels with maximum power in relation to bulk.

As the landing strip was used only infrequently, its control tower was not kept permanently manned; but Farnborough had notified the Station to expect an arrival, so the staff responsible were on the look-out and, as the aircraft circled out over the sea, her pilot received the all clear signal to come in. Five minutes later, C.B. was being greeted by Forsby and introducing Barney to him.

The landing strip was some distance from the main group of buildings, so the Squadron-Leader had brought his car. In it he drove them past some abandoned hutments, a football ground and a row of hard tennis courts, to a wide quadrangle of well-kept lawn, two sides of which were flanked with modern steel and glass buildings, and a third, facing towards the sea, occupied by one of red brick in the neo-Georgian style. Pointing to it. Forsby said:

'That houses the H.Q., Admin., and the senior Mess; the residential quarters for single types are just behind it. The married quarters are some way away, down by the sea; quite nice little houses, each with a bit of garden.'

At the back of the red brick block there was an avenue with young trees planted on both sides in wide borders of grass, beyond which were two rows of bungalows. Near the end of the avenue an airman, wearing a security-police armlet, was standing. As the car pulled up, he saluted and Forsby said to him:

'Harlow, here are the two gentlemen you are to look after. The tall one is Mr. Smith and the short one Mr. Brown. Their bags are in the boot. They will be coming along for a wash before dinner, so you might unpack for them but, after that, I don't think they will need you till tomorrow morning.'

'Very good, Sir.' Harlow saluted again, and grinned as 'Mr. Smith' and 'Mr. Brown' nodded and smiled at him. When he had got their bags out, Forsby turned the car round and said to his guests:

'Sorry I can't put you up under my own roof, but we always keep a few of these quarters prepared for visitors, and Harlow is a good chap; I'm sure he'll see to it that you are comfortable.' Then he ran the car back about three hundred yards, they all got out and he led the way into his own bungalow.

It had a small hall, but a good big sitting-room which he had furnished with his own things, and a casual glance round it was enough to reveal his main interests. Two fishing rods, a creel and a gaff stood in one corner, and a high proportion of the books in

236

a bookcase at the far end of the room were to do with birds. In the window there stood a gate-legged mahogany dining table which was already laid for dinner and, on the right of the door, a smaller table on which stood the usual selection of drinks. Waving a hand towards it, he asked:

'What will you have?' Then, while helping them to the drinks they chose, he went on, 'In the Mess tonight they are giving a special party for our visiting American. I didn't feel that you would particularly want to be in on that; and, anyhow, it might be better if you didn't meet Khune until you have decided what to do about him. So I've laid on dinner for us here.'

'Couldn't be better, Dick,' Verney nodded. 'We'll be able to natter on without interruption about this pretty kettle of fish with which we've been landed.'

Forsby gave him a far from happy look. 'It's the queerest business I've ever been involved in. I've handled plenty of spies and would-be traitors in my time; but I've never before found myself up against a Black Magician, and I suppose that is what you'd call this man Lothar.'

'You've said it, chum. He's a Black Magician all right,' Verney agreed. 'The way he has used his psychic powers on this wretched brother of his suggested that he might be, and Sullivan here, having discovered that the house in Cremorne where they were going to meet is a Satanic Temple, clinched the matter. The thing that infuriates me is that they didn't meet there at midday today as arranged. We had everything set to pick up Otto quietly as he came out. If Lothar had left the place we could have picked him up too. But Saturday is the night of the week that these degenerates meet to hold their orgies, and today is May Day eve, the biggest Satanic feast in the whole year; so we can be pretty sure that Lothar would have stayed on for that, and that it will be a bumper meeting. I'd been hoping to give them the surprise of their lives and get him and all the rest of the unholy crew in the bag by a Special Branch swoop at midnight.'

'Do you mean to have the swoop carried out anyhow?'

'No. I cancelled it, because there's a chance that if Lothar gives us the slip, he may use the place as a bolt hole. I'm having a round-the-clock watch kept on it, so if he does we'll know, and can go in and get him. His Satanist pals can't possibly be aware that we have tied him up with them; so, if we do pinch him here tomorrow and he uses his psychic powers to tell them that he's in the bag, they won't take alarm. We'll be able to go in and mop them up any Saturday.'

Little Forsby ran a hand over his greying hair. 'I must say I still find communication by psychic means a bit hard to take. I mean, not just odd snatches of telepathy, but when carried on with the same ease as two signallers miles apart could exchange thoughts through their morse buzzers.'

'Like everything else it's largely a matter of practice; that is, of course, given that the people concerned have the right apparatus – psychic sensitivity in this case – to start with. Anyhow, I should have thought the tape recordings that you have taken during the past ten days of Otto's, well – for the lack of a better word – nightmares, would have accustomed you to the idea by now.'

'They have, in a way. But at times, when I play them back, I'm almost inclined to believe that I'm imagining them; that I've taken to drink through having been cooped up for so long between the sea and the mountains, and have got D.T.s, or something! They send shivers down my spine.'

Verney nodded. 'I can well believe it. All the same, I'd like you to run them through for us after dinner.'

'Of course. I was expecting that you would want to hear them. I'm sorry that it should be necessary, and that you should have had to make this trip; but hearing a playover of the recordings may help you to decide how best to tackle the situation.'

'This Lone Tree Hill,' C.B. asked, 'whereabouts is it, and what is it like?'

'It is about four miles to north-eastward of the Station, and quite a well-known landmark in these parts. To reach it one leaves by the main gate and drives for some three miles until reaching a side road, leading north across a bridge that spans a small river. I quite often fish there. Beyond the bridge is moorland with a certain amount of stony outcrop and the ground slopes up fairly steeply. The track does not go up the hill but goes round it to a farm that lies on the far side, a good two-and-a-half miles from the main road. The hill is easy to climb and its top is rounded with just this one big pine on its crest. The tree must be a hundred years old by now, or more, as most of its branches are dead. Beyond it, about two hundred yards down the farther slope, there is a wood, and beyond that another, steeper hill. That's as good a description as I can give you, but I'll take you there tomorrow morning.'

'What is the ground like – the open part from the bridge on? Are there gorse bushes and gullies, or is it just flat heather land?'

'There is a certain amount of gorse, and some gullies. Those and the lumps of outcrop would provide a fair degree of cover, if you are thinking of putting a cordon round it.'

'It's that I have in mind. If I do decide to risk it, how is the personnel situation? How many could you muster?'

'I've a score of R.A.F. police, and, if you were agreeable to my having a quiet word with certain other people, I could probably raise double that number.'

'No; we had better confine this to the police, your assistants and ourselves. That should give us twenty-five or so; enough, if they understand how to handle a rifle. What sort of marksmen are they?'

Forsby shook his head. 'Sorry, C.B., but I wouldn't know. I suppose by admitting that I'm putting up a black, because in theory I should be able to tell you. But you know how things go in peacetime. They are allowed five rounds per annum apiece to bang off on a range and, if they miss the target altogether, what can one do about it? Does your question mean that you would order my boys to fire on Lothar?'

'I would, if Otto had given him the formula and he looked like getting away with it. The thing I have to decide is whether we dare risk even giving him a chance to do so.'

'Better leave that until you've made a recce of the ground for yourself tomorrow morning.' The Squadron-Leader stood up. 'How about a breath of air before dinner? As you are here, it might interest you both to have a look round the Station.'

They agreed, finished their drinks and went out with him. He took them down to the foreshore where, just above springtide level, there were steel and concrete platforms for launching various types of rocket; then to a covered gun-park, lined up in which stood half-a-dozen pieces of artillery, all of experimental types designed either to fire rockets from ground to air targets, or for tactical use with small atomic warheads against ground troops. Towards one end of the curving bay he pointed out the cluster of villas that gave the married quarters the appearance of a small village; then led them in the opposite direction to a much nearer long, low building that was the Station Club. In it there were a dance-hall, cinema, library, lounge, writing-room and bar, provided by the Ministry of Supply with the intention of relieving

239

from boredom, as far as that was possible, the men and women stationed in this lonely spot.

After the best part of an hour's walk, Forsby brought them back to 'Bachelors Avenue' and the bungalow they were to occupy for the night. There they found that Harlow had unpacked their bags and put everything ready for them. When they had freshened themselves up with a wash, they walked down to Forsby's bungalow and drank a glass of good dry Sherry with him while his man set out the grape fruit that was the first course for their dinner.

Over it, owing to Forsby's insistence, Verney talked about the Black Art and gave them an account of a most desperate affair in which, a few years before, he had found himself up against a most powerful Black Magician in the South of France.[1] However, he declared that he really knew very little about the subject, apart from the principles on which it worked; but he assured them that the occasions on which his job had brought him up against Satanic groups had given him ample proof that it did work if operated by a really knowledgeable occultist who was well-versed in its mysteries. He added that, in his opinion, most cases of reported Black Magic were nothing of the kind, but clever trickery skilfully put over by highly intelligent gangs of crooks who, by such measures, got wealthy credulous people who were interested in the occult into their clutches for the purpose of blackmail; but he left them in no doubt that he believed Lothar Khune to be a genuine member of the Devil's fraternity.

When the table had been cleared, Forsby produced the tape recorder and, as they settled down in the easy chairs, he said; 'You will appreciate that for the greater part of each night the tapes recorded nothing. They have been cut to retain only the parts which will play back sound. Much of the stuff you'll find quite unintelligible; at least, I have. But now and then there occur conversations which it is easy to follow. I don't pretend to understand it, but during these nightmares, or whatever they are, Otto Khune speaks with two different voices: his own and, presumably, Lothar's. One can only assume that they carry on a sort of argument, in which Lothar uses Otto's vocal chords to express his views alternately with Otto voicing protests in his own. I should warn you that it will be a pretty long session, as

[1] See *To the Devil – a Daughter*.

240

there is an awful lot about the state the world is in and what could be done to better it.'

'I take it you mean by that,' Verney remarked, 'Lothar producing all the old arguments about how much better it would be for the masses if every country accepted Communism?'

'No,' Forsby replied, and on his face there was a puzzled frown. 'That is what one would expect, but somehow the line he takes does not strike me in that way. He says more than once that he is fed up with the Communists and regards their impetus as burnt out. That may be bluff, of course, with the idea of inclining Otto more readily to do the swap of data on secret fuels with him. But he insists that he wants the results of the work done by Otto's team only to carry out some experiment of his own, which will bring about a new state of things and relieve people on both sides of the Iron Curtain from their fears of being blown to blazes by H-bombs. Anyhow, you can judge for yourself. Here goes.'

He switched on the machine, refilled their glasses with a pleasant Tawny Port, and sat down in his own chair. Then, for the next hour and a half, while he changed the tapes from time to time, they listened, almost without comment. The recordings all began with grunts, shouts, curses and protests, often followed by an unintelligible rigmarole, but then settled down into arguments during which two different voices were clearly perceptible – Otto's in English, as spontaneous and unaccented as though he had spoken no other tongue since his birth; Lothar's, also speaking fluent English, but with a faintly nasal twang. Otto's was almost always angry; Lothar's persuasive and sweetly reasonable, except for occasional outbursts in the later recordings when he resorted to violent threats.

At length the recordings were over, and Forsby mixed his guests and himself whiskies and sodas before they got down to discussing them.

Verney said: 'You are right, Dick, about Lothar giving the impression that he is fed up with Moscow. If one can believe what he says it seems that he hoped the Russians would launch a war against the N.A.T.O. Powers and establish a New Order, more or less on Nazi lines, in Western Europe and later in the United States. But he has come to the conclusion that the Kremlin is not prepared to play it that way and prefers a policy aimed at bringing the democracies to ruin by gradually gaining control of the whole of Asia and Africa and closing all the markets in them to the nations of the West.'

'To me, Lothar sounded like a megalomaniac,' Barney remarked. 'My guess is that personal power is what he is after. He wants to see some sort of drastic upheaval before he is too old to play a part in it.'

'I don't altogether agree,' Forsby countered. 'You may be right to the extent that he no longer sees eye to eye with his Russian masters because he thinks that he'll be dead before their policy of peaceful penetration begins to pay really big dividends; but to me his aim seems to be to bring about a completely new world order. When I was in Spain during the Civil War there, I talked with quite a number of anarchists, and some of the things he says tally with the views they expressed. It's a topsy-turvy sort of doctrine based on the old idea that out of evil cometh good. They want to destroy all forms of government and start again from scratch.'

'He is a destroyer, all right,' said C.B. grimly. 'But I think we must regard all this "good of mankind – brotherhood of nations" stuff as eye-wash. Whatever he may say, there's not much question about his being a Soviet agent.'

'I suppose so,' Forsby agreed, a shade doubtfully. 'Although, in one passage, he did say that having left Russia he did not mean ever to go back there.'

'Come, come, Dick. If he is not a secret agent, what reason could he have for wanting to get hold of this fuel formula? And if he is a secret agent, knowing his background as we do, what country would he be working for other than Russia?'

'It's a hundred to one you're right, Sir,' Barney put in. 'But, as he is a scientist and worked first in the States, then in Germany, then in Russia, there is just a possibility that he's got some box of tricks of his own and wants our fuel to try it out with – a flying saucer, or something.'

'You're off the mark there, young feller. Such formulae are extraordinarily complicated things, and no private person could get one of them made up.'

Forsby shook his head. 'I don't agree with you there, C.B. The ingredients are all procurable from any big manufacturer of chemicals. The only secret is in the combination and proportions. It would be expensive, of course; but I'm pretty sure he could get the job done without being brought to book for having illegal

242

possession of the formula in any of several countries outside the N.A.T.O. group – Sweden, Switzerland or Spain, for example. And if he has the money, there would be nothing to stop him from having built to his own designs some revolutionary type of aircraft as Sullivan suggests.

Verney offered round his case of long cigarettes, took one himself, and said: 'Maybe you're right; but we're wasting our time with these academical speculations. Let's get back to earth. Whatever Lothar's future intentions may be, he is endeavouring to secure a top-secret document, and coming here tomorrow to receive it from his brother. As their arrangements have all been made by telepathic communication, we have not got a scrap of evidence against either of them. The tape recordings would justify our holding Otto in preventative arrest, but what a man says in his nightmares cuts no ice in a court of law, except in support of something much more definite. So unless the document is actually handed over, Lothar will be able to cock a snook at us, walk off, and plan a further attempt to get hold of it which we may not be fortunate enough to find out about. As against that, if we do let Otto hand it over and Lothar manages to get away with it, quite apart from having let down our side, it will be bowler hats for all of us. Now, any suggestions?'

Barney held up his hand. 'Yes, Sir. Otto has had a lousy deal all through. He's resisted Lothar's demands until he has been driven off his chump, and he seems a very decent sort of chap. If you let the show go on you'll have to pinch him as well as Lothar and, whatever we may say afterwards about extenuating circumstances, he'll have committed a treasonable act, so he'll get a prison sentence. That strikes me as damnably unfair.'

'I agree,' Verney nodded, 'and I couldn't be sorrier for the poor devil. But, if we are to get the goods on Lothar, I see no way of letting Otto out. Still, if you've had a brainwave, let's hear it.'

'It is that you should see Otto tomorrow morning, tell him we know what is going on and offer him the chance both to keep in the clear himself and get his own back on his brother. If he agreed to play, instead of taking the real formula to the meeting he would hand over a dud one. If Lothar gets away, there would be no harm done; but, if we catch him, you'll have a clear case to put him away for a good long stretch.'

C.B. shook his head. 'You are forgetting the psychic angle.

Lothar checked up on Otto last night. That's how he learnt that the meeting they had arranged for today was off. He may check up again tonight and again tomorrow, to make certain that Otto isn't slipping and likely to let him down at the last moment. How far he can see into Otto's mind, we don't know. It's not far enough, thank God, to register scientific experiments or he wouldn't need to go to so much trouble to secure a written formula; but he must be highly sensitive to Otto's vibrations. If he sensed a change of mind, suggesting that Otto was helping to lay a trap for him, he would not turn up and, if we miss this chance to catch him, we may never get another.'

'All the same,' said Forsby, 'I agree with Sullivan that we ought to try to think of some way to protect Otto from himself.'

'I only wish we could, Dick. But wait!' C.B. suddenly sat forward and put his first finger alongside his big nose. 'I believe I've got it, boys. Why shouldn't we detain Otto just before he's due to leave the Station, borrow the old raincoat and beret that Otto has been told to use as signs of his identity, dress up in them whichever of the Air Force police we have selected earlier as having a figure most like his, and send this chap to the rendezvous with a dud formula?'

The other two considered his suggestion for a moment, then Forsby objected. 'When Lothar got near enough to see that it was not his brother he would realize that he was walking into a trap and turn and bolt for it. Remember, we couldn't pinch him unless he had actually accepted the document.'

'If he as much as touches it, that, backed up by the fact that he came to the rendezvous agreed on in the recordings, for a felonious purpose, will be all I need to cook his goose; and I believe that, with a little titivating, my idea might be made to work. There must be a path up to the top of the hill. Our phoney Otto could sit with his back to it and his head in his hands, as though feeling frightful at the thought of the treachery he is about to commit. He'd pretend not to hear Lothar approach until he was only a few feet off, then suddenly break into muttered curses and throw the envelope at him.'

'That's it, C.B.!' Barney exclaimed with enthusiasm. 'Sorry, Sir, I mean. If only the Squadron-Leader can produce an Air Force police type with hair the same colour as Otto's, and long enough so that we can trim it to make it look like his and . . .'

He got no further. The electric front-door bell shrilled through the bungalow, cutting him short.

As Forsby got up he shook his head. 'It's pretty wild, C.B. My chaps aren't trained actors, you know. I'm afraid Lothar would smell a rat. Still, all's fair in love and war, and I'd have no scruples in swearing that from a hideout I'd seen him pick up the document. Excuse me a minute while I answer the door and get rid of my caller. I expect it is someone who's been at the dinner then had the idea of taking a nightcap off me.'

On going out to the hall he left the sitting-room door ajar, so when he opened his front door the others heard an agitated voice say, 'Forsby . . . Squadron-Leader . . . I'm in trouble . . . serious trouble. I want to talk to you about it. May I come in?'

'Please do,' came Forsby's reply. After a slight shuffling of feet, the sitting-room door swung back and there stood framed in it a tall, slim, fair-haired man of about forty. He had a fine head, heavy-lidded black eyes, a thin high nose, indrawn lips, a heavy jowl and forceful chin that was cleft in the centre.

At seeing other people there he became rigid, and he did not attempt to conceal his surprise and annoyance. But Forsby, who was behind him, blocking his retreat, said: 'Mr. Khune, I'd like to introduce you to two friends of mine. Both of them are officers of the Security Service.'

Verney and Barney had risen from their chairs. The Colonel said: 'Mr. Khune, I'm very glad to have this opportunity of a talk with you. Anything that you intended to say to Squadron-Leader Forsby you may also say to my colleague and myself; although, actually, I don't think you can tell us much that we don't already know. You may regard it as unethical but there are times when, for the safety of the Realm, we have to adopt unorthodox measures. A copy was taken of the long statement you wrote and we have read it with understanding and deep sympathy. Also, recordings have been taken of your conscious or unconscious nightly – er, arguments, over the past ten days with your brother Lothar. So we know about your proposed meeting with him on Lone Tree Hill tomorrow. It is to prevent your needlessly in-criminating yourself, and to prevent him from securing informa-tion the use of which would be contrary to this country's interests, that we have come down from London.'

After a moment a nervous smile twitched at Otto Khune's thin lips. 'If that is the situation, gentlemen, it looks as if I'm to

245

be saved a lot of talking. And, to be truthful, I was a little afraid that the Squadron-Leader here might not take what I had to say seriously; or, rather, might get the idea that I was well on the way to becoming a candidate for a straight-jacket.'

'No,' Forsby assured him, pulling out a chair. 'We have been worrying about you for quite a time; but not with any thought that we might have to send you to a loony bin. Learning about the strange relationship which exists between you and your brother, and the use he hopes to make of it, have been much nearer driving me in that direction.'

'I'm sorry.' Otto gave another nervous smile. 'But the thought that I can now speak freely about these things is a great relief to me.'

'Whisky and soda?' Forsby asked.

'Thanks,' the scientist replied.

As the Squadron-Leader mixed one he asked, 'When you arrived here just now, what had you in mind to say to me?'

Khune took a gulp of his whisky, and shrugged. 'I meant to tell you what, apparently, you already know.'

'And then?' prompted Verney.

'See if we couldn't devise some means of trapping this villainous brother of mine.'

'Good for you.' C.B.'s thin face showed his pleasure and relief at this offer of co-operation.

Forsby touched the scientist gently on the shoulder, and asked, 'Tell me, Khune, why did you wait until almost the last minute before coming to me like this? You could have saved yourself hours of mental torture if you had confided in me soon after the trouble started.'

Khune put a hand over his blue eyes for a moment, then gave himself a little shake. 'Of course I ought to have. But it meant disclosing the past; telling you about Lothar's visit to London in 1950. He had entered this country illegally and was acting as a Soviet agent then. It was my duty to have reported him to the police at once, but I didn't. I was afraid that if that went on my record I'd be graded at the Ministry as unreliable and transferred to non-secret work. That may not mean very much to you people, but to a scientist like myself, who has spent years on a special type of research, it would have been heart-breaking.'

Verney stretched out his long legs. 'Yes, I understand that; but later, when Lothar began to really plague you, surely . . .'

'It was my battle,' Khune broke in impatiently. 'After what Lothar did to me last time, he hadn't a hope in hell of persuading me to believe that his intentions were anything but evil; and I never even contemplated giving way to him. I'm not a traitor! And you've no right to infer that I am just because I didn't come to Forsby earlier.'

'I didn't infer that.' C.B.'s voice was as quiet as ever. 'But you did give way to him, didn't you? If it hadn't been for the visit of this American you would have met him in London today.'

'Yes, the pressure he was exerting on me was too great. By Thursday night things had reached a point where I knew that I had to do something about it or I'd no longer be responsible for my actions. But I had no intention of taking the formula to London with me. I intended only to see Lothar at a house in Cremorne and have a show-down with him.'

'Why should you have supposed that you would have a better chance of making him agree to leave you alone when face to face than during these arguments you have with him on the astral?'

Khune gave a faint smile. 'Our psychic bond cuts both ways. There are times when I can overlook him and, when his mind is occupied with something else, he doesn't know that I am doing so. He has become a Satanist. I'm convinced of that. I've seen him in a Satanic Temple with a lot of naked women crowding round him. He was seated on a throne dressed in black and wearing a big horned mask; and he had a small black imp standing at his side.'

'Bejasus!' Barney exclaimed. 'Then he is the Great Ram!'

The others looked at him enquiringly. 'You remember, Sir?' He turned towards C.B. 'Ratnadatta's circle is a Lodge of the Brotherhood of the Ram, and Mrs. M. described the Great Ram to me after her first visit to the place. This means that Lothar is the big shot of the whole outfit.'

'That doesn't surprise me,' Khune remarked. 'From his boyhood on he put an immense amount of effort into developing his occult powers, and he has a tremendously strong personality.'

Verney nodded. 'Knowing what we do about him, I'm not surprised either. But please go on with what you were saying. Why did you feel that you would stand a better chance of overcoming him by going up to London?'

'I felt almost certain that the Satanic Temple was in the house

247

at Cremorne, but Lothar had given me a vision only of its out-side; so I couldn't be certain without making a check up. The sight of its front hall would have been enough and, if I'd been right, that would have given me the card I wanted. I could have told Lothar that to rid myself of him I would no longer have to admit to the police that I had been in communication with a Russian agent. I could give them his description, lay an information that he was running a brothel there, and have it raided. I could have said that unless he agreed to let me alone that's what I meant to do; then, instead of being a High Priest with a harem, he would find himself a wanted criminal on the run.'

'To protect his secret, he might quite well have had your throat cut.'

'I had planned to leave a letter addressed to the Commissioner of Police with the hall porter at my Club, before going to see Lothar; and I should have left instructions with the hall porter that, if I had not returned to collect the letter by four o'clock in the afternoon, he was to send it along to Scotland Yard by hand. Even a crew of Satanists would baulk at murdering a man when told that he had left a letter for the police saying that they might.'

'True. And what if the place had turned out not to be the one in which you had seen the Temple?'

'I'd have been no worse off than before. I'd have told him that I'd see him in hell sooner than let him have the formula.'

'Yet last night, when he learned that you were still here, and turned on the heat, you gave way again and agreed to meet him tomorrow. Was that because he threatened to put a curse on you if you didn't?'

'Well, partly.'

'If you meant to turn up without the formula, you must have expected that he would curse you just the same. And, as you have had no chance to check up on the interior of the house in Cremorne, you'd have had nothing with which to threaten him. So what did you expect to gain by agreeing to this meeting?'

Khune hesitated a second, then his blue eyes suddenly blazed, and he burst out, 'The chance to kill him and get away with it. The odds against my being able to do so in London were too heavy. But, when he demanded that I should meet him down here, I felt that he was playing into my hands. Out there on the moor, I could have done the job and buried the body in some gully.

248

In these Welsh hills it would have been ten thousand to one against anyone finding it in my lifetime, and I'd have been free of him for good and all.'

'I see,' Verney nodded. 'Having read your statement it had occurred to me that when you came face to face with him you might be tempted to adopt drastic measures, or even plan them in advance. Would you tell us now why you changed your mind tonight, and decided instead to confide in Forsby?'

The scientist began to twist his long knobbly-knuckled hands together. 'Because a quick death is too good for the swine. He has always loathed discomfort, poor food, ugly clothes, and physical labour. Even more, to be baulked in his ambitions and condemned to a mind-rotting routine, with only common criminals as companions, would be a foretaste of hell for him. I can't get him a long prison sentence; but you can. That is why I'm here instead of thinking out the most painful way to kill him.'

They all recalled the account Khune had given of the break-up of his marriage, and realized how greatly he must have suffered at his brother's hands; yet, even so, the seething hatred with which he spoke left them silent for a minute. Then Verney said:

'It is essential that he should be caught with some document on him that he has received from you, or at least receive such a document within sight of a witness, even if he throws it away afterwards. I take it you are willing to make out a dud formula, go to the rendezvous, and give it to him?'

'Certainly.'

'Good. We shall draw a cordon round the place and, unless we are very unlucky, catch him within a few minutes of his leaving you. I must say, though, I wish you hadn't chosen such an exposed position as this Lone Tree Hill, because it means that, to keep under cover until the meeting has taken place, Forsby's men will have to take up positions a good half mile away.'

Khune shrugged. 'That can't be helped. There are limits to what one can convey on the astral, and it had to be some place that he could easily identify. I had nothing of this kind in mind at the time, but I meant to tell him that up there some bird-watcher might chance to see us through a pair of binoculars; so, before I handed him the paper, it would be best for us to walk down to the wood on the far side of the slope. It was there that I meant to kill him.'

'I'd like you still to carry out that idea as, about fifty yards inside the wood, we could arrange an ambush and he would have much less chance of slipping through our fingers.'

When Khune had agreed, they continued to talk about Lothar for a further quarter of an hour; then it was settled that they should all meet at half past nine next morning and go out to reconnoitre Lone Tree Hill. Forsby accompanied the others out into the avenue and, when they had said good night to Khune outside his bungalow, walked on with the visitors to theirs. As they halted in the doorway, C.B. said:

'Well, Dick, we've had a lucky break. I'm very much happier about this job than when I arrived here this afternoon.'

'So am I.' Forsby nodded. 'In the worst case now, if Lothar does get away, it will be only with a useless bit of paper. All I hope is that he doesn't get wind of what is in the air and fail to turn up.'

'I regard that as much less likely than I did an hour ago. He can't be as sensitive as I feared to what goes on in Otto's mind, otherwise he would have tumbled to it on Thursday night, when Otto agreed to go to London, that he didn't mean to bring the formula with him, and instead had cooked up an idea for doing him dirt.'

'That's true, Sir,' Barney commented. 'All the same, wouldn't it be best to leave Otto behind when we make our reconnaissance tomorrow? If Lothar took it into his head to have a look at him, and saw him with us selecting hideouts from which to trap him, it's a certainty that he'd call his visit off.'

'Good for you, young feller.' Verney turned to the Squadron-Leader. 'Sullivan's right, Dick. We can't be too careful. Slip along to Otto now. Tell him to try to put tomorrow's business out of his mind before he goes to sleep, and that you are going to reinstall the old tape recorder just in case Lothar comes through to him during the night. And that tomorrow we would like him to remain in his bungalow till lunch time.'

On that, they exchanged good nights and Forsby left them. Tired after their long day, they fell asleep within a few minutes of getting into bed and did not wake until Harlow called them with cups of tea and told them he would be bringing them breakfast in half an hour.

At half past nine Forsby came along to them with the most welcome news that Khune had spent his first untroubled night for nearly a fortnight and that the tape on the recorder remained completely blank. They then set out in Forsby's car on their reconnaissance.

Between the Station and Lone Tree Hill there lay a stretch of wooded high ground, so they did not come in sight of the hill until they were within a mile of it; but then they could see that on three sides it was surrounded by open moorland. Turning off the main road, Forsby drove across the bridge and some way along the track that skirted the base of the hill till he reached a path that wound up it. Getting out, they walked the half mile to its summit, had a good look round, then made their way through the knee-deep heath and young bracken down to the wood.

By eleven o'clock they were on the way back to the Station and had made their plan. Verney was to lie in wait in the wood, with six of the police, and the remainder were to be posted at intervals in two semi-circles round the hill behind such boulders and gorse bushes as offered the best cover. As it seemed obvious that Lothar must arrive by car and would approach the hill from the road, that segment of the circle was, to begin with, to be left open. But Forsby and Barney were to keep the bridge under observation from the wooded rise between the hill and the Station. When they saw Lothar cross the bridge they were to drive down the road in Forsby's car, get out and, with his two rods, start fishing in the stream. By that time Lothar should be sideways on to them and half way up the hill, so could hardly fail to see them. This stratagem they hoped would serve the dual purpose of cutting off his retreat to the road and inducing him readily to accept Otto's suggestion that, before he handed over the paper, they should move down the far side of the hill into the wood, and so be out of sight of the fishermen.

At midday they had some sandwiches in Forsby's bungalow and at half past he went to the police quarters to brief his men. The importance of the affair was impressed upon them and the necessity to remain absolutely still in their cover until they heard two blasts of a whistle. They were then to spring up and, if any running figure was in view, make for it, otherwise to remain stationary. Then were they issued with one round blank and four of ball cartridge apiece, but told that they were not to fire upon the wanted man unless he either threatened them with a weapon or, having broken through the cordon, looked like getting away unless he was brought down.

Soon after one o'clock Verney, in a jeep driven by Harlow, collected Khune, who was waiting ready dressed in his old rain-coat and blue beret. A lorry with Forsby on its box transported the rest of the security police, and Barney, driving Forsby's car, brought up the rear of the procession as far as the wooded slope.

By half past one the men were all in position and getting down into their cover. Verney and Forsby took a last look round from the top of the hill, then left Khune there – the one to disappear into the wood, the other to drive back in the lorry and join Barney. Harlow followed in the jeep and reversed it under the trees so that, should Lothar succeed in getting back to his car, he could be pursued by road without a moment's delay.

As is so often the case in early May, the weather was pleasant and warm enough to have spent this Sunday afternoon dozing among the ling on the moor, but from two o'clock onwards over twenty very wakeful pairs of eyes kept watch on either the road or the hill-top. Between a quarter past two and a quarter to three, four car-loads carrying families of picnickers passed from the Station on their way inland towards the foothills of the rugged mountains that formed the skyline in the distance, but the majority of the Station's personnel preferred to laze at home, tend their gardens, or spend their afternoon on the beach. No car approached from the other direction.

By three o'clock all those concerned were beginning to feel the strain of watching; by half past, Verney was beginning to fear that Lothar did not, after all, mean to keep the appointment he had made for between two o'clock and four. By four o'clock he had resigned himself to disappointment, but he decided to give Lothar another half hour. That half hour dragged interminably, yet even after it he held his hand for a further five minutes before blowing his whistle.

As soon as Forsby saw movement on the hillside, he ordered up the lorry. The security police were collected and the Squadron-Leader, with Barney beside him, picked up Verney and Khune. As they got into his car, he said resignedly, 'Well, it's not the first time that I've had that sort of wait for nothing, and I don't suppose it will be the last. Lothar must have smelt a rat.'

'You've said it, partner,' agreed C.B.

'I wonder what his next move will be,' Barney hazarded.

'God alone knows!' For once Verney's voice was a shade

petulant. 'Anyhow, there's no point now in our remaining here. We'll get back to London as soon as possible.'

'It will take some while to get your aircraft ready,' Forsby told him, 'and you had only sandwiches for lunch, so to fill in time I propose to give you a good solid tea at the Club.'

'Thanks, Dick. I must say it would be welcome.'

When they turned into Bachelors Avenue the little Squadron-Leader again broke the gloomy silence. 'I'm going to get out here. Sullivan can take over the wheel again and Khune will show him the quickest way to the Club. Meanwhile I'll get on the blower, locate your pilot, and tell him you want to get off. Then I'll have Harlow pack your bags and I'll bring them along to the Club in about half an hour's time. You'll act as host to our friends until I can join you, won't you, Khune?'

'Of course. It will be a pleasure,' replied the scientist.

The change over was made and Barney drove off round the Headquarters building. As they came out alongside the quadrangle of lawn in front of it, Khune said:

'It will be an hour at least before they have found your pilot and got your aircraft ready. It always is. Would it interest you to spend ten minutes having a look at my laboratory, and seeing the sort of stuff my swine of a brother is so keen to get his hands on?'

'Yes, I'd like to,' Verney replied. 'Although it may be only a jelly to look at, the thought of the way it can propel tons of metal at thousands of miles an hour through the air is fascinating.'

Khune directed Barney to drive the car round to the back of one of the big steel and glass blocks, and at an entrance to it that had above the doorway, in bold lettering, 'A FIVE', they all got out.

As it was a Sunday the door was shut, but Khune pressed a bell-push and after a few minutes it was opened by a portly elderly man, in a dark blue uniform. He gave Khune one look, then his eyes grew round and he exclaimed:

'Lord alive, Sir! Did you have a crash?'

'Crash! What d'you mean?' Khune frowned.

'Why, for the moment I thought you was a ghost. Can't be more than an hour and a half since you left for Scotland.'

'Scotland?'

'Yes, Sir. You came here round half past two. Special order, you said. Needed urgent for our place in the 'Ebrides. I got hold of Tommy Carden and we loaded twenty drums out of the store on to a runabout. He drove you with it out to the airstrip and

253

when he got back he told me you meant to deliver it yourself and had gone off with it in a plane. Leastways, that's what I thought he said.'

Verney, Khune and Barney stared at the man dumbfounded. The same awful thought was in all their minds. Lothar had never intended to keep the appointment on Lone Tree Hill. He had made it only to get Otto out of the Station for the afternoon. He had arrived there in an aeroplane and impersonated his brother. He had not got the formula, but he had done far better. He had made off with twenty drums of the fuel all ready for use.

17

Unhappy return

VERNEY was quick to realize that unless he intervened at once, Otto might say something that would start all sorts of undesirable rumours running round the Station, so he glanced at his watch and said:

'I really think we ought to postpone our visit to your laboratory, Mr. Khune, until after we have been along to the airstrip. Perhaps we'll have time to see it later.'

Khune gave him a blank stare for a moment, then took the hint, muttered something to the doorkeeper about 'change of plans' and turned back to the car. They all got in it and, as soon as the engine was running, he exclaimed:

'It must have been Lothar! How utterly damnable! Yet there's no other explanation.'

'None, I'm afraid,' C.B. agreed grimly. 'I didn't want you to start cross-questioning that chap, because the fewer people to get wind of it that something's wrong, the better. He was quite definite though, and he can hardly have been dreaming. We'll know for certain as soon as we get to the airstrip. Is it usual to send the stuff up to Scotland in an aircraft?'

'Yes. It's not only quicker, but safer, than rail, and if some of it went astray. . . .' Khune broke off short, and ended with a groan.

'It looks as if twenty drums of it has! Is that the normal quantity in a consignment?'

'No. Usually we send eighty to a hundred drums at a time.'

'Lothar was clever then, in not opening his mouth too wide.

255

The doorkeeper must assume that you know your own stock, and he might have thought it fishy if Lothar, whom he took to be you, had asked for a greater number than there happened to be available. I take it, too, that quite a small part of what he's got would be sufficient for him to have the stuff analysed, and after that there would be no limit to the quantity that could be made up?'

'The analysis would take time, and they might not get the formula exactly; but near enough. And the Russians have many clever chemists, so they might even improve on it.'

'How often do you send consignments up to Scotland?'

'As required; but, on average, about once every three weeks. We send larger consignments now to Australia for the I.C.B.M. range there, but less frequently.'

By this time they were approaching the air strip. The aircraft that had taken the American up to Farnborough that morning, and since returned to collect C.B. and Barney, stood at one end of it; but evidently Forsby had not yet succeeded in getting hold of the pilot, as there was no sign of life. Neither was there any sign of life near the two hangars, in the control tower or at the building that housed the small ground staff. Barney drove up to the latter and they got out.

The building contained only an office and off-duty room on the ground floor and a dormitory for half-a-dozen men above. Verney hurried into the office, found it deserted, then crossed the passage and strode into the room opposite. An R.A.F. Corporal was lounging there with his feet up, reading a Sunday paper. Verney addressed him sharply.

'I am a colleague of Squadron-Leader Forsby's. Are you the duty N.C.O.?'

'Yes, Sir.' The corporal replied, coming quickly to his feet and switching off the radio.

'I understand that about half past two an aircraft came in and took off about half an hour later.'

'That's right, Sir,' the man confirmed their worst fears. 'Quite unexpected it was. Usually we are warned in advance and given the E.T.A. in ample time for whichever of us is on duty to get hold of the others and man the control tower. But with good weather, like it is today, and the strip clear that isn't really necessary. All the same, it's against regulations, and I was a bit took aback.'

'What did you do?'

'I walked over, Sir, and had a word with the pilot. He said that he had come down from our I.C.B.M. Station in the Hebrides to pick up some stuff that was wanted urgent, and he couldn't understand why they had failed to send us a signal about him.'

'What did you do then?'

'I told him he'd better watch out for the aircraft from Farnborough that was due in about half past four, but he said he'd have taken off long before that; so I came back here.'

'Didn't you report this unscheduled landing?'

'I did, Sir, to Flying Officer Leathers, when he and others came along to see the Farnborough arrival in.'

'And what did he say?'

'He entered it in the log, and said he'd send the Hebrides Station a rocket for having failed to warn us that they were sending this aircraft down.'

'Then you let two hours elapse before you reported it?'

The corporal's face became a little sullen. 'Well, it isn't the first time that someone's forgot to send a routine signal, Sir. Anyhow, I didn't think it was anything to get excited about, and neither did my officer when I told him.'

'All right! All right! Describe the pilot to me.'

'He was a tallish chap, age about thirty. Clean shaven, and I think his eyes were brown. He was wearing pilot's kit, not uniform.'

'How many people had he with him?'

'Only one man, Sir. He'd left the aircraft by the time I reached her and, being Sunday, with no one about, he'd walked over to the hangars to get the runabout out for himself. He drove it off towards the laboratory block, to fetch the stuff they'd come for, I suppose.' The corporal turned towards Khune, and added, 'I didn't see him close to, but he was about your build, Sir; dressed like you too, in a mack and a beret.'

'What make was the aircraft,' Verney asked.

'I'm afraid I didn't notice, Sir. She was a two-engined job and I'd say she'd carry up to a ton of cargo.'

'Did you take her number?'

'No, Sir.' The corporal bridled again. 'This isn't like a civil airport, you know, with aircraft coming in from all sorts of places all the time.'

'Hell!' muttered C.B. and, turning, he strode across the passage to the office. He was just about to pick up the telephone when it rang. The corporal, who had followed, murmured, 'Excuse me, Sir,' reached a hand past him, and answered it. After a minute he said:

'It's Squadron-Leader Forsby, saying to have the tower manned to clear the Farnborough plane in three-quarters of an hour.'

C.B. took the receiver from him. 'Dick. This is Verney. There's been a spot of trouble. Instead of going to the Club, drop everything and come here. Yes, at once, please.' Hanging up, he said to the corporal:

'There's no need to get your team together yet. The Farnborough plane won't be leaving till later. I expect the pilot is on his way here though. Go outside and, when he turns up, tell him there has been a postponement.' Then, to Khune, he added, 'Would you be good enough to wait for us across the passage.'

Directly the two men had left the room, he rang the exchange and asked for a priority call to the Air Ministry. While it was being put through he remarked with a frown to Barney: 'As it's Sunday the place will be practically empty and none of our people available. We can only hope that the Duty Group Captain is a live wire.'

The Group Captain proved willing but far from hopeful about tracing Lothar's plane. He too remarked upon its being Sunday, which meant that, in addition to normal traffic, hundreds of trainers and aircraft from Flying Clubs all over the country would be up, so that with such an inadequate description to go on, the chances of the plane being identified were extremely slender. But he said he would send out an emergency signal to all airports to hold any twin-engined transport aircraft that came down to refuel, pending special clearance.

C.B. then got on to Special Branch and asked for a warrant to be taken out for Lothar's arrest, and for a check up that a night and day watch was being kept on the house at Cremorne, in case he returned to it.

While he was still on the telephone, Forsby joined them and Barney told him in a low voice what had happened. When he realized how completely they had been fooled, he shut his eyes and began to curse under his breath. Verney hung up and turned to him.

'This is a bad business, Dick, and I'm afraid I can't congratulate you on your security arrangements for your airstrip.'

'Yes, it's I who am to blame, Sir.' Forsby's tone had at once become formal. 'Normally one of my men is present at every aircraft arrival and departure, to check the passes of the crew as they come off or reboard the plane. The thought that an unauthorized aircraft might come in without warning, land, and get away with it, never occurred to me.'

'In a place of this importance, I think it should have.'

'I'll resign, of course, Sir.'

Verney gave him a gentle pat on the arm. 'You'll do nothing of the kind, old friend. This afternoon we've all been taken for a ride. If anyone is responsible, it is myself, as I came down here to take charge. Now, as an airman, tell me – what is the chance of our bird getting out of the country with his loot?'

The Squadron-Leader glanced at his watch. 'It's now twenty minutes to six, so he must have been gone the best part of three hours. From the description of the aircraft it doesn't sound as though he has anyway near a full load, so he should have had plenty of petrol. Anyway, by now he could have refuelled at some small landing-ground near the East coast and be well out over the North Sea.'

'I feared as much. Still, we might get a break even in Belgium or Holland through the Air Ministry tie-up with N.A.T.O. Anyway, there is no more we can do for the moment, so I'm in favour of accepting that late tea you offered us.'

Having collected Khune, they drove round to the Club and, owing to the hour, settled for drinks instead of tea. Taking their drinks into a corner, they held a gloomy inquest. As a result of it they reached the conclusion that Lothar had probably taken Otto's excuse for not coming up to London – that an American boffin was coming down – to be a lie; so, from Friday night, he had given up hope of persuading him to co-operate and switched to threatening him with a death curse unless he left the Station for a few hours to keep a rendezvous, thus leaving the field free for his double to move about the Station during that time, without fear of coming face to face with him, and to make off with a quantity of the fuel instead of its formula.

It was Barney who produced the idea that, owing to Otto's psychic link with Lothar, the former might be able to secure some clue to the latter's whereabouts. Otto who, since the discovery of the way they had been tricked, had hardly spoken, brightened at once, and said:

'That certainly is a possibility. Anyhow, I will do my utmost;

but, for such an attempt, I must have solitude and silence, so I had better go back to my quarters.'

Forsby looked across at C.B. 'I ought to be moving, too. I've the unpleasant task in front of me of reporting this business to the Chief, and I don't want to leave it much longer, as he usually asks a few people along to drinks on Sunday evenings. Do you still wish to set off to London as soon as possible, or would you prefer to dine here first?'

'Dine and sleep, I think,' Verney replied. 'I told the Air Ministry to report back here if they manage to trace Lothar's plane; and now Mr. Khune is going to have a cut at that too from the psychic angle. If either succeeded while Sullivan and I were on our way back to London, we'd lose hours of precious time in getting after him; so we will stay put for the night. We'll all go along to Sir Charles now, and I'll break the news to him for you.'

'That's damned decent of you, C.B. The old boy is bound to take it pretty badly – the actual theft, I mean – and what he'll say when told about the psychic angle, I can't imagine. If I tried to explain that part of it to him without support, he would probably think that I ought to be certified.'

They finished their drinks, returned to the car, dropped Khune at his bungalow, then drove to the Headquarters block, in which the Director of the Station had a flat overlooking the quadrangle. Forsby sent up his name and a few minutes later a man-servant showed them into a pleasant sitting-room.

Sir Charles Remmington-Rudd was a portly man in the middle fifties. He was nearly bald and had heavy sagging jowls, but an alert manner and a friendly smile. When Forsby had introduced his companions, C.B. reported the bare facts.

The eminent scientist said nothing for a moment, then he shook his head. 'This is a very serious matter. Sit down please, gentlemen, and give me full particulars.'

'Thank you, Sir.' Verney took a chair. 'It is an extraordinary story and, I'm afraid, a long one. May I ask to begin with whether you believe in psychic phenomena?'

Sir Charles raised his eyebrows. 'I can answer that only if you give me a precise definition of the meaning to yourself of the term you have used. However, it may help you if I say that science now admits the existence of certain faculties in the human mind which cannot be accounted for by normal processes. Before you go further, though, you say the story is a long one, and I am expecting

260

a few friends in for drinks quite shortly. I take it everything possible is being done to trace these stolen drums of our special fuel?'

'Everything, Sir.'

'Very well, then.' Sir Charles stood up. 'It is now too late to put my friends off, but I can put off a couple who were to dine with me. If I can be of no immediate help this long story of yours will keep for an hour or two, so I suggest that the three of you should return at eight o'clock and tell it to me over dinner.'

They thanked him and took their leave, then repaired to Forsby's bungalow, where they again mulled over the shattering event of the day without getting any further. After a wash and brush up, they dined with Sir Charles, who at first found it difficult to believe what they were saying; but Forsby had brought along a copy of Otto's statement and, after the scientist had read it, he had to agree that the psychic bond between the twins must be accepted.

At half past ten they looked in on Otto. He had tried for an hour before dinner to get into touch with Lothar, then dined in the Mess and, since, tried again, but on both occasions without success. Forsby set the tape recorder in the hope that it might pick up a conversation between the twins during the night, then they all turned in.

On Monday morning the tape proved blank, but Otto reported that he had woken at about half past six after a vivid dream. In it he had seen Lothar getting into an aircraft, standing near which were a number of men in uniform, and he felt sure that these were Americans. He also had a feeling that the place was one of the air bases occupied by United States Forces in Eastern England.

Verney at once rang through to the Air Ministry and asked the senior officer in the Security Department there to take the matter up with his American opposite number and ask for exhaustive enquiries to be made.

This first earnest that Otto might succeed in helping them to trace his brother decided C.B. to take him to London, so that if he had further visions he could give full particulars of them with a minimum of delay. While the aircraft was being got ready to fly them back to Farnborough, Otto arranged with his number two to carry on with the experiments on which he was engaged, then Forsby ran the three of them along to the airstrip.

At Farnborough, Verney's car was waiting to meet them. On

the way into central London they stopped at the little hotel in Chelsea and arrangements were made for Otto to stay there, then C.B. dropped Barney in Warwick Square and went on to his office.

In spite of his preoccupations over the week-end, Barney had several times thought of Mary, and he feared that she might have taken rather badly his having had to let her down on Saturday night. So the first thing he did on getting into his flat, was to ring her number. As it was just on lunch-time he hoped to catch her in but there was no reply, so he assumed that she was probably out for the day on one of her modelling jobs.

In the evening he considered buying more roses to take to her, but decided that might give the impression that he had been enjoying himself over the week-end and now had a guilty conscience; so he arrived in the Cromwell Road at half past seven empty handed but armed with an elaborate story of a millionaire who had suddenly become interested in his Kenya travel project and had insisted on carrying him off to the country on Saturday to discuss putting money into it.

To his disappointment and annoyance, his ring at the front door of Mary's flat brought no response, so evidently she was still out. Hoping that something had detained her, he hung about for nearly an hour, but she did not put in an appearance; so he was forced to the conclusion that she was so annoyed with him that she had decided to ignore the invitation he had posted to her before setting off for Wales, and had already gone out for the evening either alone, or with someone else.

Consoling himself as best he could with the thought that having been up early that morning an 'early bed' would be welcome, he ate a solitary dinner at a little restaurant in Gloucester Road and returned to Warwick Square. But it was quite a time before he got off to sleep as thinking of Mary made him realize how much he had been looking forward to seeing her again and how much, in the past fortnight, she had, almost imperceptibly, come to mean to him.

Next morning he rang her number at eight o'clock and, as there was no reply, repeated the call at half past, but still without result. It might be, he thought, that she had had to go out early to catch a train for a model show that she had been booked for somewhere outside London. On the other hand, he knew that she had very few acquaintances, so probably guessed that it was him ringing up and, still suffering from the sulks, had deliberately refrained from answering the telephone. Taking this last to be the most likely assumption, he decided to leave her for thirty-six hours to stew in her own juice.

Before he set about the routine jobs that he had in mind to do that day, he looked in at the office. There he learnt from C.B. that all attempts to trace Lothar had so far failed. The enquiry set on foot by United States Air Force H.Q. had drawn a blank, and Otto's efforts to locate his brother via the astral plane had, so far, produced only a strong impression that he had crossed a sea and was now somewhere on the Continent. Interpol had been asked to help, but with the thousands of aircraft that criss-crossed Europe daily, there was small hope that they would be able to identify the airfield on which a plane, of which they had only a very sketchy description, had come down some twenty-four hours earlier.

That evening another meeting was due to be held by the Communist-dominated branch, down at Hammersmith, of a Union to which Barney belonged; so just before seven he clocked in at the rather dreary little hall that was used on such occasions. There ensued a long wrangle, carried over from the previous meeting, during which the leaders urged the men to refuse to work overtime until a new claim for higher wages was settled. A few older men stood up to say that it seemed wrong to them to put a break on production before the employers had actually refused to grant the new rates of pay, but they were accused by the Reds of being mouthpieces of the bosses, and shouted down. The go-slow motion was passed and about nine o'clock the meeting broke up. The little fraternity of Communists who had control of the branch made for the pub they frequented, and Barney with them.

After they had had a few rounds of drinks, the leery little man who had tipped Barney off to lay wagers that Tom Ruddy would not be elected as the new Secretary-General of the C.G.T. drew him aside and asked him if he had made good use of the tip.

'I stand to win about ten quid,' Barney told him with a grin.

'You bloody fool!' the little man snorted, and spat in the cuspidor. 'You ought to have made yerself fifty. But you've missed the blinking boat now. That is for taking on any more suckers. News'll be out tomorrow morning. Mr. bloody Ruddy's standing down.'

263

'Are you certain?' Barney asked, concealing his dismay under an expression of surprised cheerfulness.

'Course I am,' came the prompt reply. 'He's thrown his hand in. I can't tell you why. Don't know meself. But I had it straight from the horse's mouth that the Comrades meant to put a fast one over him.'

At closing time the groups broke up and, as was his custom on such occasions, Barney set out by a circuitous route back to the Tube Station. On his way he thought of Mary again and his resolution of the morning – to make no further attempt to get into touch with her for the next thirty-six hours. Reconsidered, it seemed to him that he was probably cutting off his nose to spite his face and that, as he was so anxious to make it up with her, the more evidence he gave of his eagerness to do so, the more likely she was to relent. In consequence, instead of taking the Underground to Victoria, he got out at Gloucester Road and walked along to the tall old house in which Mary had her little flat.

On his way there, as it was nearly half past ten, he was expecting to find her in; but she was not. Since it was a Tuesday, it occurred to him that, although she had promised him not to, she might have gone to the weekly meeting at Mrs. Wardeel's. If so, she should soon be back; if not, the odds seemed to be that she had gone to a cinema, in which case also she would soon be home. He decided to wait for her, but feeling that in his 'worker's' clothes he might be taken for a suspicious character if found lurking on her landing by one of the other tenants, he went out into the street and took up a position on the other side of the road.

There had been many occasions when Barney's work had necessitated his waiting outside a block of flats or offices for hours at a stretch; so the undertaking was not new to him and he thought himself lucky that the night was fine. Now and then he changed his position, taking a short stroll but never going beyond clear sight of the house, for to do so would have been to risk her arriving just at the moment when he had ceased to watch; then he might wait on till dawn, accuse her next day of having stayed out all night, and later find that she could show proof that he was entirely mistaken.

Eleven o'clock came, half past, and a quarter to twelve, without Mary appearing. By then he had decided that she must have gone out to dinner with a man and the thought annoyed him considerably. Although she had given him to understand that she had no family, the fact that she appeared to have no friends at all had often puzzled him. Even if she had not been living for a long time in London, it seemed strange that any young widow with her attractions should not have acquired at least one man friend. That she had not, thus leaving him a free field, he had come to accept; so, now he believed that someone had entered it against him, he felt a quite unjustified resentment.

Animated by more than a suspicion of jealousy, he decided to continue his watch, so that when his rival brought Mary home he might have a sight of him. Between midnight and one the volume of passing traffic down London's long main western artery fell steeply, the buses ceased, while private cars and taxis, from having been a steady stream, were reduced to a trickle. By half past one Barney began to think of throwing his hand in. It was an hour since he had run out of cigarettes, and Mary's failure to return suggested that she had not only gone out to dinner or a show, but also gone on to supper somewhere.

He had been telling himself that if she was out with a man it was probably some middle-aged director or important customer of one of the fashion houses for which she modelled, and that she had accepted an invitation to dine rather than give offence; but, if so, she should have been home by this time. The idea that she was more probably dancing with some young, attractive man now became insistent in his mind, and the memory of her firm young body against his own when they had danced together added fuel to his jealous imaginings.

Two o'clock came, and with it the conviction that Mary and her new beau must have gone on to a night club, which meant that she might not now be home for another couple of hours. More put out than he had been for a long time, Barney hailed a taxi that was crawling westward and had himself driven to Warwick Square.

While he undressed, he had a whisky and soda and some biscuits; then, as he got into bed, he tried to put Mary out of his mind. It was no good, but his thoughts did take another direction. Perhaps that evening she had gone out with a chap, yet it seemed strange that she had also been out the night before and out, apparently, on the several occasions when he had tried to ring her up. The explanation might be that she had suddenly decided to take a holiday.

265

Yet if that were so, why, before leaving London, had she not let him know? The note he had written on Saturday morning must have reached her by first post on Monday. Surely, even if she was furious with him, she would have let him know it by writing a few angry lines in reply, which he should have received that morning? Could she possibly have met with an accident over the week-end and be in hospital? Or, unlikely as it seemed after the way she had broken down at their last meeting, and sworn to have no more to do with the Satanists, had Ratnadatta, after all, again got hold of her?

At that disturbing thought Barney switched on the light again and set his alarm-clock for six o'clock, determined now to go really fully into the question first thing in the morning.

Soon after seven he was back in Cromwell Road. As there were a dozen tenants in the old house, its front door was always left on the latch from first thing in the morning up till eleven at night; so he walked straight in and upstairs. His ring at Mary's door remained unanswered. Hoping that she was still in bed, and perhaps sleeping very soundly after her late night out, he waited for a few minutes then rang again, this time insistently. Taking his finger from the bell he listened but no sound of movement came from within the flat, so he then felt certain that she could not be there.

In anticipation of such a possibility, he had brought with him a small implement, the efficient use of which he had been taught when training for his job. With it, in less than a minute he had the door open without damaging the lock. The first thing his eye lit on, face upwards on the mat, was the letter he had posted to Mary on Saturday morning. Evidently the caretaker, or somebody, brought up the tenants' mail and pushed it through their letter-boxes. Anyhow, the fact that it was still there showed that Mary had not been in her flat during the past two days.

Closing the door behind him, he took a quick look into each of the four rooms of the flat. The bathroom and tiny kitchen were clean and in good order; the bed had been made up and on the sitting-room table stood a vase holding a dozen long-stemmed roses. In the wastepaper basket he found the four pieces of a card, confirming that they were the roses he had ordered from Constance Spry's for Mary and, from the way in which the card had been ripped across, an indication of her anger on realizing the reason for his sending them to her.

Taken together, the roses, the letter on the mat, and the unslept-

266

in bed added up to Mary's having gone out sometime between Saturday afternoon and Sunday evening and not returned. With the hope of coming upon some clue to where she had gone, he began a systematic search of the premises. In the circumstances he felt no scruples about doing so and, as his duties made it necessary for him to carry out such searches fairly frequently, he did the job swiftly and thoroughly but with an automatic care which resulted in everything he disturbed being left exactly as he had found it.

The only room to yield any information of interest was the bedroom. The cupboards and drawers were full of Mary's clothes. On checking through the major items he found everything there in which he had seen her, with the exception of a grey coat and skirt. It could be assumed that she had been wearing those when she went out, so had last left the flat in daytime. Up on a high shelf there were a hat box and a beauty box, and under the bed he came upon three suitcases. Two of them bore the initials M.M. and the third E.T.M. The latter Barney guessed to have belonged to the deceased Monsieur Mauriac and he wondered for a moment what E. stood for in the name of Mary's ex-French-customs-officer husband – Emile, perhaps, or Edouard.

Anyway, the presence of the clothes and luggage made it clear that Mary had not gone off for a holiday; or even, as was confirmed by the finding of her sponge-bag and washing kit in the bathroom, deliberately for a night. Now really worried about what had become of her, Barney relocked the front door of the flat and hurried down to the basement.

Down there in the gloomy depths, as Mary had told him, lived a not particularly likeable couple named Coggins. The landlord had put them in charge of the building and, theoretically, they were supposed to perform any reasonable small services that the tenants required but actually they would not lift a finger without being tipped. The man went out to work but could be bribed to carry up heavy luggage on his return. The wife took in parcels, cleaned for some of the tenants and did small commissions in the way of shopping for those whose jobs prevented them from doing their own regularly.

Barney found Mrs. Coggins sorting out some washing, which had been drying in the backyard on the previous day. Her thick brows lifted at the sight of a stranger, and she enquired: 'What do you want, walking into my scullery like this, young man?'

267

With his most disarming smile, he replied, 'I'm a friend of Mrs. Mauriac's and I'm worried about her. She is not in her flat, and I have reason to suppose that she has not been home for the past three nights. Can you give me any idea what has happened to her?'

'Tenants' business is none of my business,' said the blowsy woman, with a suggestion of malicious pleasure. 'And if she'd wanted you to know where she was goin' off to, she would have told you, wouldn't she?'

Barney had had plenty of experience of dealing with Mrs. Coggins' type. He spoke again, with an edge on his voice. 'Mrs. Mauriac's disappearance may turn out to be a very serious matter. Either you will answer my questions truthfully, promptly and politely, or I shall bring the police in to question you for me.'

'Lor!' exclaimed Mrs. Coggins, immediately both overawed and stimulated by a new interest. 'She hasn't been murdered, has she?'

'I sincerely trust not. Tell me; when did you see her last?'

'Saturday, around one o'clock. Some flowers came in a big box from a florist, and I took 'em up to 'er. All them stairs. I tell you them stairs'll be the death of me. But she gave me a bob for me trouble, as I knew she would.'

'And you've no idea what happened to her after that?'

'No. Leastwise, not for certain. But there was the coloured gentleman what came enquiring for her about six o'clock.'

'What's that?' Barney snapped.

Mrs. Coggins shrugged and, sensing the possibility of getting under Barney's skin, replied with a superior smile. 'I wouldn't have thought one like her would have taken up with a coloured man; but there's never any telling, is there? Some people say as how they are more manly in a manner of speakin' than white fellers, and a lot of girls prefer their fellers to be that way. Of course. . . .'

'I am not interested in your speculations,' Barney cut her short. 'What was this coloured man like, and did she see him?'

'Well, he weren't a coloured man in the proper sense. Not a real nigger with curly hair an all; just coffee. Some sort of Indian I suppose, and very well spoken. It's expected that tenants' visitors shall go up and ring the bells of those they want. But this man rang again and again for me. I went up prepared to give whoever it was a piece of my mind, but he told me he'd rung Mrs. Mauriac's bell again and again and couldn't get no reply, and could I tell him when she would be coming in. Of course I told him I'd no idea; then he asked my permission to wait there in the front hall till she came in. To that I said, "You can please yerself, there's no law against it". Then when I come up about an hour later with a bottle of whisky for the gentleman in the second floor back that we call "the Colonel", the coloured gent was no longer there. So maybe she'd come in and gone straight out again with him.'

'Thank you.' Barney turned on his heel, ran quickly up the basement stairs and went out into the street. He had no doubt whatever that the 'coloured gentleman' was Ratnadatta; but what could possibly have induced Margot – as he thought of her – to go out with him? Surely just pique at his, Barney's, having let her down could not account for her reversing her decision to have nothing more to do with the Indian? And if, from annoyance and boredom, she had allowed herself to be persuaded, why had she not returned to her flat since? Perhaps he had hypnotized her and was now detaining her against her will in the mansion at Cremorne? In any case, it seemed certain that Ratnadatta having come to Cromwell Road on Saturday evening, it was he who was responsible for her disappearance; and its implications were now extremely alarming.

Barney's immediate impulse was to go to Cremorne, but a moment's thought was enough to check it. Bulldog Drummond tactics were all very well in fiction, but for him to break in and attempt to tackle on his own the permanent staff that must live in the house could result only in disaster. He must restrain his impatience, make a report, secure a search warrant and have Special Branch raid the place officially. But it had taken him barely half an hour to search Mary's flat, so it was still not yet eight o'clock and C.B. would not be in his office until half past nine.

Now a prey to acute anxiety, Barney strode along to the Earls Court Road, went into a Lyons and killed time as best he could by having breakfast there. Well before half past nine he arrived at the office and posted himself in the hall ready to waylay C.B.

Verney arrived punctually, nodded 'good morning' to him and made for the lift. Barney returned his greeting and said hurriedly, 'Can I come up with you, Sir? There is a matter I want to see you about urgently.'

'Sorry,' C.B. shook his head. 'I think I know what it is, but I can't see you yet. I must go through my mail, and Thompson of

Special Branch is coming over at a quarter to ten. When I've seen him I hope we'll know more about it. Go to your room and I'll ring through for you as soon as I am free.

Wondering how the Colonel could possibly have got to know of Margot's disappearance. Barney went up to the room which, when he was working in the office, he shared with two other young men. At five past ten Verney's P.A. summoned him, and he went up to the big office on the top floor.

On his entering the room the Colonel waved him to a chair, and said: 'This is a perfectly damnable business, and there's nothing we can do about it. Thompson got the truth out of Tom Ruddy last night, but he flatly refuses to prosecute.'

'Tom Ruddy?' Barney echoed, momentarily taken aback.

'No, Father Christmas!' retorted C.B., with an irritable impatience quite unusual in him. 'Or am I wrong in supposing that you came here this morning to report to me that he has withdrawn his name as a candidate for Secretary-General of the C.G.T.?'

'Yes; no, I mean,' faltered Barney, suddenly recalled to the duty entailed by his major mission. 'I picked up a pretty definite rumour to that effect in Hammersmith last night, and of course intended to report it.'

'Very well then. This ties up with your second string; so sit down and I'll tell you about it. I heard that Ruddy had thrown his hand in yesterday afternoon, so I asked Inspector Thompson to go to see him and try to find out why. Of course, it's none of our business officially, but I felt certain there must be something fishy about it, and that if Ruddy could be persuaded to accept police help we might be able to restore the situation. At first he was very reluctant to talk but, after Thompson had given him his word that no action of any kind which might involve him should be taken, he got the story.'

C.B. stuffed some tobacco down into his pipe, and went on. 'One wouldn't have thought that a man like Ruddy would be a superstitious fool; but he is. Apparently his old mum used to tell fortunes pretty accurately, so he has been a believer in that sort of thing all his life. About a year ago someone introduced him to a crystal-gazer named Emily Purbess, a middle-aged and apparently respectable body. He has consulted Mrs. P. several times in the past six months and she's given him guidance that he says has paid off well on various problems connected with his election campaign. About ten days ago she warned him that there was trouble ahead;

someone he relied on was going to double-cross him, and if he didn't watch out that would wreck his chances. But she couldn't tell him who or what to watch out for.

'Naturally that got him worried, so she suggested that he should consult someone who had greater occult powers than herself and gave him the address of a man named Biernbaum, who is in practice in the West End as a psycho-analyst. Biernbaum gave Ruddy a lot of gupp about seeing into the future really being a science which was understood by the ancients and is only now being rediscovered, and how it had recently been proved that they were right to use pure young girls as priestesses in the temples because nubile virgins were the best vehicles for conveying the voices of unseen powers; then he said that, for a fee, he could take Ruddy to a house in which a young woman who had been trained to prophesy invariably produced the goods. Ruddy agreed to cough up five pounds and was told to report at Biernbaum's consulting room again on Saturday evening.'

'Saturday evening,' Barney repeated. 'That's the night the Satanists meet. Did this chap Biernbaum take him along to the house in Cremorne?'

C.B. nodded. 'You've hit it, partner. At least I'm pretty certain that is where they went. Biernbaum must have put Ruddy under a light hypnosis because after they got into a taxi he doesn't remember the streets through which they passed, or those by which they returned about an hour later; but his description of the approach to the place, and of its outside, tallies. He says the inside was like that of a nobleman's mansion, as seen on the films, but he was received by an elderly bald-headed doctor, who runs the place, and a fine looking woman who was dressed as a nurse. They told him that their most gifted girl had been taken ill but, as the appointment had been made, she had agreed all the same to prophesy for him. Then they took him up to a luxurious bedroom where a lovely girl was lying in bed with her eyes shut and the sheets up to her chin.'

Barney grinned suddenly. 'This sounds more fun than getting a blowsy old woman to peer into a crystal. Did the lovely prove a good oracle?'

'Yes, she prophesied all right. In fact, so plausibly that she shook poor Ruddy to his buttoned boots. She described the chap who was supposed to be going to do him dirt, and unmistakably she was seeing young Sir Hamish McFadden.'

271

'The chap whose father left him about ten million pounds worth of shipping, and is now regarded as quite a big shot among the Socialist intelligentsia?'

'That's right. But even if he is ass enough to believe in their old fashioned theories, he at least has the sense to realize the Communist danger, and he has been spending quite a lot of money lately to finance the campaigns of honest Trade Unionists like Ruddy, who want to oust the Reds. Ruddy was going down to lunch with him at his place in Kent last Sunday, to fix the final details about I.T.V. appearances, leaflets, and other anti-Communist propaganda for which Sir Hamish is footing the bill. But the prophecy decided Ruddy to call his visit off.'

'So that's how they worked it.' Barney made a grimace. 'I suppose by Monday Ruddy and Sir Hamish had quarrelled violently and, after the break, Ruddy felt that, without the financial support he had been promised, he no longer stood a chance?'

'Good Lord, no! With, or without Sir Hamish, Ruddy could still romp home. He has thrown his hand in on personal grounds: on account of his family. The lovely oracle predicted for him, despite everything, a smashing victory. She even got so enthusiastic about it that, although she was as naked as when her mother bore her, she suddenly sat up in bed and threw an arm round his neck. It was at that moment that from some camouflaged point of vantage someone took a photograph of them.'

'Blackmail!' exclaimed Barney.

'That's it. On Monday a man who was a complete stranger to Ruddy brought him a copy, gave it to him and said: 'We thought you might like to have this as a souvenir. We have plenty more and either you lay off standing for Secretary-General, or your wife gets one tomorrow.'

'What swine these people are!'

'Of course. Communists are of two kinds only. Gadarene Swine whose wits have been taken from them so that they rush headlong down the slope to their own destruction, and ordinary voracious swine who, if you were standing in their sty, had a heart-attack and fell among them, would instantly set upon and devour you – just as did the pigs in T. F. Powys' novel, *"Mr. Tasker's Gods"*.'

'I know, Sir. But this sort of thing really is frightful. Did poor old Ruddy cave in right away?'

'I gather so. He told Thompson that he had been happily

272

married for twenty-four years and counted his wife his greatest blessing; but she was not the sort of woman who would even tolerate his dancing twice in an evening with the good-looking wife of another chap at a Trade Union social and that once she had made his life a misery for a couple of months because she had found out that, while she was on holiday at the seaside with the children, he had taken a pretty typist to a movie. He said that the sight of the photograph would be a terrible shock to her. He felt sure that her principles would prove stronger than her affections: that, filled with righteous indignation, she would leave him, taking their two unmarried daughters with her, and that no political success he might achieve could compensate a man of his age for the loss of his family.'

'Couldn't he explain?' Barney asked. 'Surely if his wife loves him, and he told the truth, she would believe him?'

'Put yourself in his shoes, or hers.' C.B. gave a short hard laugh and tossed across the desk a photograph. 'Take a look at that. Thompson asked Ruddy to let him have the loan of it so that Scotland Yard could try to identify the woman, and Ruddy said he was glad to get it out of the house, provided it was destroyed afterwards. Can you see yourself endeavouring to persuade a middle-aged, narrow-minded and distrustful wife that you had gone to the bedroom of this naked lady for no other reason than the hope that she would predict for you the winner of the Derby?'

Barney had picked up the photograph and was staring at it as though his eyes might pop out of their sockets. It showed the stalwart grey-haired Tom Ruddy leaning forward on the far side of a richly furnished bed. Sitting up in the bed, nude to the thighs, an inviting smile on her lips, an encouraging hand on Ruddy's shoulder, was the beautiful prophetess. Almost choking with mixed emotions, he stammered:

'But . . . damn it . . . this is Margot Mauriac! How . . . how could she have lent herself to this sort of thing? How could she?'

Verney raised his prawn-like eyebrows. 'Really! Is she, now? Perhaps I ought to have guessed, but somehow I didn't. Her real name isn't Mauriac, though; it's Mary Morden.'

18

'When rogues fall out . . .'

WHAT!' exclaimed Barney, dropping the photographs. 'Teddy Morden's widow! Bejasus! Well, that explains a lot of things. The last time I saw her she confessed to me that her reason for wanting to become a Satanist was to have it in her power to be avenged on somebody. I understand that now. She must have believed, just as I did, that a link existed somewhere between Mrs. Wardeel's set-up and Morden's murder, decided that Ratnadatta was the link and that it was his crew of Satanists that had done Morden in; then made up her mind to become one herself as the only way of getting evidence against his killers.'

'That's right; or, at all events, it's the line she said she intended to follow when she came to see me before starting on the job.'

'Hang it all, Sir! Since you knew that she and I were working along the same lines, why didn't you tell me about her?'

C.B. shrugged. 'In our work it often pays better to let two people carry on an investigation unknown to one another. Otherwise, if one gets on the wrong track and tells the other, both may follow it, with the result that both of them waste a lot of time. That is why I said nothing to you about Mrs. Morden when she told me what she meant to do.'

'But later, Sir. My reports made it clear that both of us were on the right track. If only . . .'

'No; you are off the mark there. When you told me that an attractive young woman had begun to attend Mrs. Wardeel's evenings a little before yourself, and of her having persuaded

Ratnadatta to take her along to his Satanic circle, it did occur to me that she might be Mary Morden. If you remember, I questioned you very closely about her, but the description you gave me of Mrs. Mauriac was so totally unlike that of the Mrs. Morden I knew that I concluded they must be different women.' Picking up the photograph, C.B. went on, 'I told her that she would be wise to disguise herself, but I didn't credit her with being able to do the job so thoroughly. In this, her hair, eyebrows and mouth are entirely changed from when I last saw her. In fact, it wasn't until I began to study the photograph carefully that I recognized her.'

'I see. She hasn't been reporting to you in person, then, but in writing.'

'She hasn't been reporting to me at all. She offered her services but I told her that I couldn't possibly take her on officially.'

Barney's brown eyes smouldered. 'D'you mean that you let her go into this filthy business on her own, without either guidance or protection?'

'I did my best to argue her out of her idea, but she refused to be put off. I told her then that it would be better for her not to communicate with this office or myself unless she secured definite evidence which might give us a case against her husband's murderers because, if they learned that she had any connection with us, she might be murdered herself. But all this happened over seven weeks ago and, to tell the truth, I'd forgotten all about her till Thompson produced this photograph this morning.'

'Forgotten all about her!' Barney repeated angrily. 'Good God, Sir; I'd never have thought it of you. To let a lovely girl like her, with no experience of the game, go butting her head into a nest of the vilest crooks imaginable and never even give her a thought. . . .'

'Steady on; steady on!' Verney cut in, but his voice remained as low and even as ever. 'Don't let your sense of chivalry run away with you; and try for a moment to appreciate what it means to occupy this chair. I gave you a key role in an important mission, but you are only one of a score of my people who are engaged on it. I have to receive all their reports as well as yours. And that is only one of my jobs. I have to supervise the watch that is maintained in every port in the kingdom against undesirables entering it; I'm responsible for security in all secret Scientific Establishments; I am having at least fifty potential spies or saboteurs either hunted or kept under observation. Even that is no more than

275

half of it. I have to attend conferences at half-a-dozen Ministries and quite frequently others that take me abroad. This afternoon, for example, I shall be flying to Bonn at the invitation of my opposite number there, for a two-day visit to compare our methods with those in use by the West German Security Services. So your suggestion that I can find the time to keep a private eye upon any young woman who elects, against my advice, to play at being an amateur detective is really rather foolish.'

'I'm sorry, Sir. I'm afraid I hadn't thought of it like that, but . . .'

'That's all right, Barney. But if you are to go up the ladder here, as you show good promise of doing, you must train yourself to keep a sense of proportion. If it is any comfort to you, I did tell Mary Morden that should she find herself in danger she was to let me know, and I would at once come to her assistance.'

'But she is in danger. That's what I've been wanting to tell you. Of course, I should have told you what I'd heard about Ruddy when I saw you but, to be honest, I'd temporarily forgotten all about him. I came here this morning to tell you about Margot – Mary, I mean. She has been kidnapped by these fiends.'

'Kidnapped? How d'you know?'

'I was to have taken her out on Saturday evening, but I had to put her off because of our going down to Wales. As soon as we got back on Monday I tried to get in touch with her, but couldn't. I tried again several times yesterday, but it was no go; so I kept watch outside the house she lives in last night, hoping to catch her when she came in. By two a.m. she was still not back, so first thing this morning I did an illegal entry job on her flat.'

'You'd have been in a fine mess if you had been caught.'

'No. We know through Otto that Lothar is the Great Ram. Margot – Mary, I mean – has actually seen the Great Ram; which is more than we have. She told me so; even though she went back on it afterwards. My case would have been that I was searching for evidence of a connection between her and a wanted criminal that might lead us to him; and you would have told the police to lay off me.'

C.B. gave a grim little smile. 'Good line that. One up to you. I expect I should have hauled you out anyhow, but don't count on that as *carte blanche* to ride rough-shod over the law in future. Well, what did you find?'

'That she had been absent from Sunday, if not longer, and her clothes and luggage still being there showed that she had not gone off on a holiday. I went downstairs and questioned the woman who acts for the landlord. She had not seen Margot – damn it, Mary – since midday Saturday, and on Saturday evening Ratnadatta called, asked for Mary and, on learning that she was out, said he would wait in the downstairs hall till she returned. When she did come back, he must have hypnotized her or used some threat to make her go off with him. Anyhow, it's certain that he is at the bottom of her disappearance.'

'But she hasn't disappeared, much less been kidnapped.' Verney declared. 'We know from Ruddy that this photograph was taken on Saturday night, and his description of the house to which Biernbaum took him tallies with the one at Cremorne. It is a fair bet, too, that if Ratnadatta collected her an hour or two earlier that is where he would have taken her. So we have a double check on where she went to and no evidence whatever to suggest that she did not go there willingly.'

Barney frowned. 'Even if she did, it's impossible to believe that she played the part that she is reported to have willingly. She must have been coerced.'

'I'm afraid I can't agree about that.' Verney tapped the photograph. 'Take another look at her. Far from appearing to be acting under coercion, she is all smiles. Ruddy says he was left alone with her for several minutes. If she had not been a willing agent, she would have found some way of tipping him off that her prophecy act was a fraud.'

'You forget, Sir, that, as they were photographed without Ruddy's knowledge, they were being watched the whole time. She must have known that and did not dare to alter the lines she had been given to say from fear of what they might do to her afterwards.'

'You've got the wrong angle on this, Sullivan. You don't seem to have yet caught up with the fact that we are talking not about Margot Mauriac but about Mary Morden, and the two are poles apart. The woman you have been seeing a lot of has presented herself to you as a nice respectable girl, fascinated by the occult to a degree that for the sake of a little excitement she was prepared to play with fire. Having taken a liking to her and believing yourself to know better than she did the risks she would be running, you have naturally done your utmost to prevent her from getting herself badly burned, and now you are afraid that she has landed herself right in the middle of the fire. But the real

277

woman is the widow of Teddy Morden and, although warned by me, she went into this thing with her eyes open. By getting herself accepted into the Satanic circle she has done far better than I ever expected; and we must not hold it against her that she led poor Ruddy up the garden path. Obviously they picked her for the job because she is very good-looking, but the fact that they asked her to play prophetess shows that they trust her; and, since she did it so well, they will now trust her even further. There is no question whatever of her having been kidnapped or coerced. On the contrary, every move she made has been deliberate and, with a little luck now, she is going to step right out of the fire, bringing the chestnuts with her.'

'Maybe you are right about Saturday night,' Barney admitted, reluctantly, 'but that doesn't account for her continued absence from her flat. If she had meant to stay away several nights she would have taken a suitcase and some clothes.'

'Not necessarily. At that place in Cremorne I don't doubt they have all sorts of exotic raiments to dress themselves up in.'

'That does not explain her not having taken her toilet things,' Barney argued. 'No woman would go off to stay anywhere without her own tooth brush, scent, powder and that sort of thing. I'll bet every cent I've got that she intended to return home in the early hours of Sunday morning. But having got her there they wouldn't let her, and they are holding her there against her will.'

C.B. shrugged. 'Then I think you would lose your money. If she is still there all the odds are that they asked her to stay on and she agreed to because she thought it would prove worth her while. But, say that you are right and that she is no longer a free agent, what do you expect me to do about it?'

'Why, have the place raided, of course. We have ample grounds on which to apply for a search warrant. Have the place raided and get her out.'

'Nothing doing, young feller.' Verney shook his head. 'There is still a chance that Lothar might return there, although I'm afraid now that is unlikely.'

'Does that mean that you have had news of him?' Barney asked quickly.

'Well, hardly news. Otto has been doing his utmost to get a line on him. He seems to be able to look down on him without much difficulty, but to locate him is a very different matter. All Otto is certain about is that Lothar is somewhere among high

278

mountains that have snow on their tops. At times he actually goes up one of them to a great cave in its side. Otto says there is a cable railway up to the cave, and that he can feel it vibrating when Lothar goes up there. Of course, all this may be Otto's imagination playing him tricks, but if he is right it sounds as though Lothar was in Switzerland or Norway, or perhaps even the Caucasus. Anyhow, these visions give some grounds for supposing that he has left this country and, as he has got the fuel that he came for, there seems no reason why he should return.'

'Then why not raid the house at Cremorne tonight?'

'Be your age, Sullivan. Lothar or no Lothar, to bag this nest of Satanists with Communist affiliations will be a fine feather in the cap of the department, and for having unearthed it most of the credit will go to you. But Thompson tells me that his men who have been keeping the place under observation report that hardly anyone goes in or out of it during the week. To raid it while it is nine-tenths empty would be a crazy thing to do. We must wait now until all these boys and girls have gathered there for their Saturday orgy; that's the time to pounce.'

'But, damn it all!' Barney protested 'Think what may happen to Margot – oh hell, Mary – in the meantime. She must have gone there in ordinary outdoor clothes. If she is a free agent there would be nothing to stop her leaving the place for an hour or two whenever she felt like it. Her flat in Cromwell Road can't be more than a mile away; so she would have walked to it at least once to collect some of her things. But she hasn't; therefore, they must be keeping her a prisoner.'

'There may be some other explanation. Anyhow, just on the chance that you are right, I can't afford to lose the bulk of our bag by having the place raided before Saturday.'

'I am right. I know I'm right. And you must raid the place, C.B.' Barney argued desperately. 'This girl has put up a wonderful show. She has displayed magnificent courage; but now she is in the soup. You can't just leave her there. And some of these swine must live in the place. Just think what they may be doing to her.'

'If I am thinking of the same thing as you are, she'll come to no harm from it. She probably won't even mind very much.'

'What the hell d'you mean?'

C.B. sighed. 'I'm sorry to have to disillusion you but, to set your mind at rest, it is best that you should know the truth. Before her marriage, Mary Morden was a prostitute.'

279

Barney rose slowly to his feet. The blood had suffused his cheeks and his eyes had become unnaturally bright. Suddenly he blurted out, 'I don't believe it! You're lying! You're lying for some purpose of your own.'

'Sit down!' Verney's voice, for once, was sharp. 'I am not in the habit of lying to the members of my staff. Perhaps the word prostitute was a little strong; but I used it deliberately in order to bring you back to a truer sense of values. If I remember rightly, she said she was a cabaret girl. Anyhow, she told me herself that she had come up the hard way and had had to throw her morals overboard in order to earn a living. And that, within the meaning of the act, is prostitution. She told me this in reply to my telling her that the Satanist creed was the glorification of sex, and that she would not stand a dog's chance of getting anywhere with her investigation unless she was prepared to go to bed with at least one man, and probably more, whom she would have no reason whatever to like. She said that she had done that before and was ready to do it again, if that would give her a chance to nail her husband's murderers. So, you see, you have no need to harrow yourself with visions of her being held down and raped.'

For a long minute Barney remained silent, then he said: 'I suppose you are right. But what you've just told me came as a bit of a shock, and it is going to take me a little time to get used to the idea of her being so very different from what I thought her.' Then he stood up, and added, 'Well, I'd better be going, Sir, and get down to some work.'

'That's the spirit,' C.B. nodded. 'I shall be back on Friday night. Come in on Saturday at midday and I'll let you know about the final arrangements for the raid. I'll have you sworn as a temporary Special Constable so that you can take part in it.'

'Thank you, Sir; but I'd rather not. From now on I'd prefer to stick to my major mission of narking on the Reds, and keep out of this other business.'

'I'm afraid that is not possible. You'll be needed to identify Ratnadatta, and to substantiate certain portions of the statement we shall take from Mary Morden. As far as she is concerned, I think you should look at it that she is doing no more and no less than what quite a number of other brave women did during the war – putting a good face on some rather unpleasant experiences as the price of outwitting the enemy, gaining his confidence and bringing home the goods. It is important, too, that we should

280

endeavour to get hold of the negative and all the copies of that photograph of her and Ruddy; and, if they can be found, you would be the most suitable person to take charge of them at once; so I think you had better go in with the police.'

A ghost of Barney's old grin momentarily lit up his face. 'Yes, I can well imagine a bawdy-minded copper trying to slip one in his pocket if he got the chance. I'll do as you wish, then, and make getting hold of the photographs my special task.'

When Barney had left him, C.B. thoughtfully refilled his pipe. He felt far from happy at having given away Mary Morden's past, but he had seen no other means of dealing with the situation that had arisen. Personally he had no doubts at all that Mary had gone willingly to the house in Cremorne on Saturday night, and that she had remained there because she believed that doing so would give her the chance she had been seeking to win the confidence of the Satanists; therefore the only danger she was in was that she might give herself away, and that was no greater risk than she had run when making her earlier visits to the place.

But Barney, not knowing the true facts about Mary, had naturally viewed the situation very differently, and the acute anxiety he had displayed on her account had made it evident that he was in love with her. It was that which had shown C.B. the red light. Knowing that Barney was not only brave and resourceful but, under the skin, a wild Irishman, there had emerged the possibility that he might take the law into his own hands and attempt, unassisted, Mary's rescue.

Such an attempt Verney regarded as not only unnecessary but both liable to upset Mary's campaign and almost certainly doomed to failure; above all, the last thing he wanted was for the Satanists to be prematurely alarmed by a one-man raid, as that would mean losing the bulk of the bag. Therefore, the only way to make certain of preventing Barney from ruining the whole *coup* had been to tell him that, even if for the next few days Mary had to submit to being treated as though she was an inmate of a brothel, her early life had conditioned her to come through that mentally unharmed, and that she had actually expected that she might have to lend herself with apparent willingness to such treatment.

Barney meanwhile, having gone down in the lift, was walking, without thinking where he was going, along the street, desperately

281

trying to reconcile his feelings for Margot with what he had just learnt about Mary.

During his long abortive watch for her in Cromwell Road the previous night, the belief that she was out dancing with some other man had brought home to him the fact that he really was in love with her; and, since his discovery that morning that she had been carried off by Ratnadatta, the thought of what she might be going through as a prisoner of the Satanists had made him aware that he loved her desperately. But now? Could one possibly love a girl who had been a prostitute?

To do so was against all a man's natural instincts. If one really loved a girl one wanted her for keeps. That meant marriage, and through the generations male mentality had been fashioned to demand that the future mother of a man's children should be chaste. Basically that was his own view, but he recognized that standards of morality had grown far more lax since women had claimed equal rights with men in almost every sphere of life and, like most men of his age, he would have been quite ready to ignore the past if, on asking a girl to marry him, she had confessed to having already had a lover, or even several, providing they had been genuine love affairs and she had not made herself cheap. But for a girl to sell her body for money to anyone who cared to buy it, to go to bed night after night with a succession of different men, most of whom she did not even know by name, was a totally different matter. The thought of Mary's having led such a life made him squirm, and he could not bring himself to believe that she had really ever done so.

There then came into his mind the first night that he had taken her to dinner at the Hungaria and how, in the taxi afterwards, when he had tried to kiss her, she had accused him of treating her like a tart. Her then seemingly unreasonable outburst was now explained, and with bitter cynicism he recalled the saying that there was 'no prude so great as a reformed whore'. Yet she had been far from prudish on that last evening when they had been up in her flat together and, as they lay embraced upon the sofa for a while, she had returned his caresses with a fervour equal to his own.

Even so, C.B.'s horrible revelation did provide the basis for the intense sympathy she had shown for girls whom men paid to make use of without a thought of what might happen to them afterwards should they get in the family way, and it now caused

282

Barney to wonder if such a misfortune had ever befallen her. It was certainly a possibility and, if so, as from the secret report on Morden's death he knew that Teddy had been married for four years, she must have been very young at the time, anyway not more than nineteen.

Visualizing her at that age in such straits wrung his heart with pity, and he recalled C.B.'s remarking that she had 'come up the hard way'. In an intelligent woman, given a reasonable amount of money, present appearances were nothing to go by, and her natural alertness of mind would have enabled her to make the best of any education she had been given. But perhaps she had been brought up in a slum and driven on to the streets by a drunken father before she was old enough to stand up for herself.

But no, that did not fit in with her having been a cabaret girl, and C.B. had made it clear that she had been not actually a professional prostitute, but a glamour-girl who needed a bit of extra money. That implied that she had not exposed herself to such depths of degradation but, theoretically at least, was guilty of a greater degree of moral turpitude; and Barney could not make up his mind if that made matters better or worse.

As far as the present was concerned, he had to acknowledge the justice of C.B.'s defence of her. 'Coming up the hard way' implied that she had derived little enjoyment from her youthful promiscuity; so it was fair to assume that anything of a similar nature that she might have let herself in for with a crew of depraved Satanists would mean for her a highly disagreeable experience. Yet she did not stand to better herself from it in any way. She had gone into the ring prepared to face this punishment in a gallant fight against evil and for no other reason.

For that, who could blame her? He certainly had no right to do so. They had met on the 5th April, barely a month ago, and the *affaire* on which they had tentatively entered had not developed into anything worthy of the name until the previous week. There had not yet been a hint on either side that she might soon consent to become his mistress, much less that they should become engaged; so she was perfectly free to dispose of herself as she saw fit and he had not the faintest grounds for thinking of her as being unfaithful to him.

After blindly walking the streets for over an hour he pulled himself together and decided that he must get her out of his mind by throwing himself headlong into his routine work. On Saturday he must take part in the raid. He would see her then, and would have to do so on several occasions afterwards while the papers concerning the prosecutions arising out of the raid were prepared. At such times he would endeavour to mask the mixed emotions it was certain she would arouse in him by a display of cheerful friendliness; but he would excuse himself on the plea of urgent work from making any further private dates with her. Then as soon as the case was over, he would no longer have to see her at all, so the sooner he practised forgetting her, the better.

But he could not forget her. For the rest of that day, and on the Thursday and Friday, and for the best part of the nights in between, she was never out of his mind for more than a few moments. At times he thought of her as a cold, callous, young harlot, slipping out of bed to pick the pockets of half-drunken men who had fallen asleep beside her; at others, as the innocent victim of some hulking brute who bullied her unmercifully and lived upon her immoral earnings. In his waking dreams there were times when he saw her with the Satanists, her mouth dripping from spilled red wine and her eyes brilliant from the aphrodisiacs they would have given her, revelling with wanton delight in their debaucheries; at others, waging a losing battle to hide her disgust and terror as they forced her to join them in unmentionable obscenities.

And through it all he knew he loved her. More than anything in the world he now wanted to gaze into her deep blue eyes again, to hear her laugh, to watch her, carrying herself so erectly, as she walked with her firm springy step, to hear her voice with its faint familiar touch of Irish brogue, to hold her in his arms.

All this he could do, and more; providing only that she had not given herself away, so was still safe when the raid took place on Saturday. There was nothing to stop him resuming his *affaire* with her, and on an even better footing, as he would then be free to use Verney's name as a link between them. Explanations would follow, and there would no longer be any necessity for them to deceive one another. She liked him; judging from their last meeting, more than liked him. With her past there could be no question of her having moral scruples. He would only have to go all out for her to make her his mistress.

But what then? He knew in his bones that this was different from his other *affaires*; not just a delightful pastime that could be entered on lightly and dropped with equal casualness. She had got

284

under his skin, into his blood, captured his mind. If once he lived with her he would want to be with her always. How long would she be content to go on like that? A time would inevitably come when he would either have to marry or lose her.

Well, why shouldn't he marry her? If Verney had said nothing of her past he might have done so; and, unless she had told him of it herself, the odds were that he would never have known anything about it. But the awful thing was that he did know. It was only on very rare occasions that the thought of his ancestors crossed his mind, but at this point in his tortured deliberations he saw them rising up out of their graves and screaming at him, 'You cannot! You cannot! You cannot make an ex-prostitute a Countess of Larne!'

At midday on Saturday, looking tired and ill, he reported at the office. Verney told him that he had seen Otto that morning, and the scientist was convinced that Lothar had now returned to England. For a moment Barney feared that might mean a postponement of the raid; but C.B. said he meant to go through with it for two reasons. If Lothar was in England it was quite on the cards that he would attend the Saturday orgy in Cremorne and, unless the place was raided, should he use a really clever disguise in going to, and coming away, from it the police might not spot him and so the chance of catching him would be lost. Secondly, even if they did not get him in the bag, by raiding the place they might secure papers which would inform them of other hideouts of his in England, in one of which he might be laid by the heels in the early hours of the morning.

Inspector Thompson arrived a few minutes later. All the arrangements for the raid were then completed and afterwards Barney, knowing that he would be up most of the night, returned to Warwick Square with the intention of making a light lunch and spending the afternoon dozing on his bed.

For half an hour he lay there, turning restlessly from side to side, once more a prey to the harassing speculations that had repeated themselves over and over again in his mind during the past three days. It then occurred to him that since early on Wednesday morning he had not been down to Cromwell Road; so there was just a possibility that Mary might have returned there. He knew it to be a forlorn hope but, to while away an hour or so of the time still to go before the raid, any action was better than lying there doing nothing. Slipping off the bed he put on his tie, coat, shoes and a light mackintosh and went out to find a taxi.

As usual during the day-time, the front door of the house in Cromwell Road was on the latch, so he walked straight in and upstairs. Using his little instrument he again picked the lock of the door to Mary's flat. The sight of his unopened letter still lying face upwards on the mat told him at once that she had not been back there. Closing the door behind him he spent some minutes in having another look round. The rooms were just as he had left them, except that the roses had used up nearly all their water and were now drooping.

The sight of them brought the thought to his mind that, if all went well, she should be back there that night. Knowing that for her the past week, at best, must have been one of intense strain from fear of being caught out and, at worst, one of physical inflictions coupled with mental anguish, he felt that she deserved something better to come home to than half-dead roses and stale food in her larder. To attend to the matter was the only decent thing to do; so he went downstairs in search of Mrs. Coggins.

He found her in her basement sitting-room, knitting a jumper while she watched T.V. When he appeared in the doorway she turned and gave him a peevish look, but made no move to switch off the blaring voice coming from the instrument. Above the din he shouted to her:

'Mrs. Mauriac is coming home tonight. She sent me the key of her flat and asked me to get a few stores in for her. Could you oblige me by lending me a shopping basket?'

Reluctantly Mrs. Coggins came to her feet and shouted back, 'I was wondering wot'd become of 'er. She's bin gone a week now and, after your talk on Wednesday of bringin' in the police, I was thinking I'd soon better go to them myself.'

'I was worrying unnecessarily,' Barney told her. 'Mrs. Mauriac met with an accident while out with some friends and they took her to their home. That's why she didn't return last Saturday night; and, as she has been in bed ever since, she didn't need to send for any of her clothes. Now, how about lending me something to shop with?'

Grumbling about not having 'bin let know', Mrs. Coggins produced a large string bag and with it Barney proceeded to the Earl's Court Road. At a delicatessen store he bought a cold chicken, bacon, eggs, cheese and various other items, then he

286

collected bread, milk, butter and fruit, and ended his round at a florists, from which he emerged with an armful of flowers.

Returning to Mary's flat he threw away the food that had gone off, replaced it with his purchases, then arranged in both the sitting-room and bedroom the spring flowers he had bought. When he had finished, he made himself a cup of tea and, while he drank it, thought of the surprise and pleasure which his efforts would give Mary on her return.

That thought, however, gave rise to another which had not before occurred to him. She would know that it was he who had made these preparations for her home-coming, and that would be bound to confirm her belief that he was in love with her. He was; there was no doubt about that; but, if he meant to break the afaire off, doing as he had was certainly not the way to set about it. He would have to see her home. He could not decently avoid doing so, and when she saw the flowers it was certain that she would kiss him for them He could make some excuse not to come in, but he knew that he would want to, if only to see her just once more in these surrounding where they had had those few happy hours together

Besides, he might have to come up. She might need help to climb all those stairs. If his worst fears were realized, shock, beatings and exhaustion had by now reduced her to a nervous wreck. Now he had made certain that she had not been back to her flat for a whole week, he felt more than ever convinced that C.B. was wrong in his contention that she had stayed on with the Satanists only because that would give her the chance to secure the evidence she was seeking. Had that been the case and she was still on friendly terms with them, what objection could they have had to her leaving the place for a few hours to collect the sort of personal belongings no woman likes to be without? The fact that she had not done so could only mean that they had demanded of her more than she was prepared to give willingly, so had resorted to force and then decided to keep her there until they had no more use for her.

At this already familiar mental picture of Mary naked, weeping, beaten and abused, he was once more possessed by a frenzy of distress and helpless anger; and to those feelings was now added a great surge of compassion. He knew that he must not only get her out of that hell and bring her back to her flat, but must comfort and cherish her until she had got over her ghastly experience and was really well again. Would he then be able to break with her? He didn't know. He doubted it. But the future must take care of itself.

The afternoon was now well advanced so, having relocked the door to the flat, he left the house, took the Underground from Earl's Court to Victoria and so made his way back to Warwick Square. There he freshened himself up with a bath and, not knowing when he would get another chance to eat anything, sat down in his dressing gown to a scratch meal of sardines, cake and a whisky and soda. Then he put on an old suit, slipped into his pocket a small automatic that he had a licence to carry, and went out to collect his car from its garage.

On reaching Cremorne he drove slowly round the streets adjacent to the old mansion until he found a place only a few hundred yards from it where, outside a small warehouse, he could park his car without causing an obstruction. Getting out, he strolled along to the 'World's End', at which he had a rendezvous with Inspector Thompson. Five minutes later the Inspector joined him in the saloon bar. They greeted one another as though casual acquaintances who had met by chance, asked after each other's wives, talked for awhile about the Derby, tossed up to decide which of them should pay for their drinks, then left together.

Unhurriedly they made a tour of the area. The entrance to the cul-de-sac was being kept under observation by plain-clothes pickets on the look out for Lothar, but as yet no other police had taken up their positions. From eight o'clock a number of plain-clothes men would enter the area independently, so that they could be summoned at once should the meeting for some reason break up unexpectedly early; but the bulk of the raiding force would arrive in vans only a few minutes before zero hour. The same vans would later be used to remove the prisoners. As far as was known the only exit from the mansion was by way of the cul-de-sac; but in case there were others through some of the small houses that backed on to the garden, all these were to be cordoned off.

Thompson suggested that Barney should accompany him when he led the way in at midnight, and Barney said he would like to. He then told the Inspector that he intended to waylay one of the Satanists on his way to the meeting and take him off to put some special questions to him. The picket keeping watch on the entrance to the cul-de-sac were informed of this, so that, if they saw a fight start, they should not intervene; then Barney took up a position not far from them, and Inspector Thompson left him.

For a long time now Barney had had an itch to give Ratnadatta a thorough beating up, and he had every reason to suppose that soon now he would be able to gratify it. In fact, his sole reason for coming down to Cremorne several hours before the raid was due to take place was to make sure of catching the Indian on his way to the meeting. It was still only just after eight o'clock and, from the watch kept on the place the previous Saturday, it was known that the majority of the Satanists did not arrive till about half past nine; but a few individuals, two couples and a car had entered the cul-de-sac at intervals, a good while earlier.

Much the same occurred on this occasion and, as darkness gradually closed down, from his point of vantage on the opposite side of the road Barney saw several people give a furtive look round then swiftly turn into the alley leading to the mansion. It was about ten minutes to nine when he caught sight of Ratnadatta coming along the street.

The paunchy Indian seemed to be walking jauntily with his head held cockily high, but as he passed under a light standard Barney saw that the angle of his chin was due to his wearing what appeared to be a stiff, high, white collar. When he was within ten yards of the entrance to the cul-de-sac, Barney crossed the road and followed him into it. Another half-dozen paces and they had been swallowed up in the darkness of the alley. Swiftly closing the gap, Barney tapped him on the shoulder and opened a little act he had thought up by saying, with a laugh, 'Caught you, Mr. Ratnadatta!'

The Indian halted, swung round and asked nervously; 'Who are you? What do you mean by that?'

'I'm Lord Larne,' said Barney in a friendly voice. 'You remember me. We met two or three times at Mrs. Wardeel's. I won't keep you a minute, but I want a word with you.'

'This ees not a good time. It ees not convenient.'

'It is for me.' Barney gave the guffaw of a fool. 'You might not think it, but I'm a bit of an amateur detective. Sorry to trouble you, and all that, but having traced you here I want to know what goes on in the big house down at the end of this alley.'

'That ees not your business,' declared Ratnadatta angrily. 'You haf no right to ask. Leave me. . . .'

'No right at all,' Barney agreed cheerfully. 'But I'm itching with curiosity, so unless you tell, I'm going in with you.' He produced his pistol and showed it to Ratnadatta. 'See, I've got my rod, so no one's going to stop me. Stop me and buy one, eh? Ha! Ha!'

The Indian took a quick step back, but Barney suddenly grabbed him by the arm, and went on, 'My car is just round the corner. Let's go and sit in it and have a quiet cigarette while you tell me. I won't keep you more than a few minutes. Come on.'

As Barney had hoped, Ratnadatta, supposing him to be no more than a nosey young idiot who, as a member of the privileged classes, perhaps enjoyed some degree of protection for such lawless frolics, decided that it would be better to humour him than to risk a scene on the doorstep of the mansion which would draw attention to it.

The avoidance of a scene had also been Barney's object in adopting his role of an inquisitive buffoon. While they walked along to his car, he could almost hear the Indian's brain ticking as it hastily endeavoured to formulate a plausible, non-criminal, but intriguingly mystic reason for the meeting he had been about to attend. But he was given no opportunity to produce it. No sooner were they both in the car than Barney, having achieved his object, switched on the ignition, let in the clutch and drove off.

'Hi!' exclaimed Ratnadatta. 'What do you do? Where are you taking me?'

'For a ride,' replied Barney. 'To a place where we can talk without interruption. We'll be there in less than ten minutes.'

'Stop!' cried the Indian. 'I do not wish to go! Plees, you let me get out.'

'No, sweetheart. Alive or dead, you are coming with me.'

'You are mad!'

'Yes, I am. With you. So you had better shut up. I showed you my gun. I'd welcome an excuse to put a bullet into your guts.'

Completely bewildered by this unforeseen encounter, and now extremely frightened, Ratnadatta, breathing heavily, fell silent. The car had already reached the embankment and was heading towards Battersea Bridge. They crossed it and ran swiftly through the streets on the south side of the river to Barnes Common. Driving across it along a track that led past the cemetery, Barney pulled up in a deserted spot and said tersely, 'Get out.'

'You are mad,' Ratnadatta said again as, quaking with fear,

290

he eased himself out on to the grass. 'Plees, Lord Larne, I do you no harm. Why haf you bring me to this place?'

Barney jumped from the car and came quickly round its bonnet. Grabbing Ratnadatta by the lapel of his coat, he cried in a harsh voice that no longer had the least suggestion of the detective-crazy idiot in it: 'I've brought you here because I mean to beat hell out of you. I know all about your Satanic Temple and the way you act as a tout for it.'

'No! No!' Ratnadatta gasped. 'It ees not true! White Magic! We practise White Magic only. Also I invite only those peoples weech ask to come.'

'You filthy, lecherous, lying swine! You lured Mrs. Mauriac there a week ago. Don't dare to deny it. What did you do to her, eh?'

'Nothing! Not me! I take oath.'

'You're lying!' Barney raised his fist. 'Tell me the truth or I'll smash your ugly face in.'

'Plees! No! No!' wheezed the Indian. 'My neck. I have been struck great blow. It rick my neck. You strike again and it ees too much. Perhaps you kill me, then you hang.'

'So that's why you are wearing that bandage. But don't think a ricked neck is going to protect you from me. I know plenty of ways to make you squirm without killing you.' As Barney spoke he struck the Indian a sharp blow on the muscle of the upper arm with the hard edge of his palm.

Ratnadatta let out a yelp, and Barney went on, 'Now, you are going to tell me the truth or I'll pulp every muscle in your body. Mrs. Mauriac has been absent from her flat for a week. She left it with you, and you took her to that hell-dive where you hold your orgies. I want to know whereabouts in it you are keeping her. You are going to describe the inside of the place to me, so that when I get into it I can go straight to her.'

'She go with me there on Saturday. Yes, I admit. But she haf left it again same night.'

'Stop lying!' Barney struck him a second blow on the muscle.

'I tell no lie!' the Indian gulped. 'This ees truth! I swear so! I take oath! She ees taken away by another member off the Brotherhood.'

'Why? Who was he? Tell me his name!'

'He ees an American. A Colonel off their Air Force.'

'I don't believe you!'

'It ees true. Listen plees, listen.' Ratnadatta began to ring his hands and burst into a spate of words. 'I giff you good reason why I not lie. This ees same man who struck me great blow. For four days I am in hospital. Then I come out. I wish to put curse upon him for what he haf done to me. To do that I must find out about him. His real name and where he live. I make opportunity to get quick look at secret records. In list off visiting Brothers against name for magics Twisting Snake, I find name Colonel Henrik George Washington, United States Air Force, Fulgoham, Cambs. Post Office tell me Cambs. mean Cambridgeshire. Yesterday I go there and make much enquiries. It ees a big camp with many great aeroplanes, buildings, huts and all; but this Colonel does not live there. He has private house not far off, near Six Miles Bottoms, weech is called the Cedars. I go there. It ees good size, pretty house, in little park. Now I haf seen I can make bad magic for him there. This is truth; all truth. A friend I am not man to betray; but for this Colonel I haf great hate.'

Barney had to admit to himself that the chapter and verse produced by the Indian in support of his story made it highly plausible. But, to test it further, he said: 'I'm not letting you go back to the Temple tonight and I have means of getting into it myself. If I go in and find that you have been holding Mrs. Mauriac as a prisoner there after all, I'll keep you locked in a cellar till you die of thirst, then throw your body in the river. Now you know what to expect if you have been lying; do you still stick to your story?'

'Yes, my Lord; I stick,' Ratnadatta replied without hesitation. 'In the Temple she ees not. She was there for two, three hours, no more; then the American haf taken her away.'

'To this house of his in Cambridgeshire?'

'Yes. It ees there that he live, and he had big car.'

'It doesn't follow that he took her down there.'

'No; but plees, it ees very best bet. At London hotel she ees perhaps not willing to stay with him. Perhaps she make ugly scene and lands him in bad trouble.'

'He took her away by force, then?'

After a moment's hesitation, Ratnadatta replied, 'On Saturday night it was arrange for her to become initiate. To one part of ceremony she make objection. The American haf eye for her all along. She see that and he ees big man, very big; so she ask him to take her home. That ees against rules off Brotherhood. There

292

ees a fight and he carry her off. But he ees not what you call Knight Errant. He do this because he want her for himself.'

'So it was a case of rogues falling out?' A lump had risen in Barney's throat. It was all he could do to prevent himself from smashing his fist into the Satanist's face, as he went on, 'You quarrelled about who should have her, and the American got the best of it. Bejasus! I've a mind to kill you here and now.'

'No, my Lord, no!' the Indian whined, shrinking back. 'I only obey order off Master off our Lodge to prevent her being taken away. We should haf discuss matter more, agree to postponement off initiation; perhaps decide that she ees not suitable after all to become Sister off us. But she refuse to listen, she show great temper, then row starts. Perhaps too she thinks the American fine man, and would haf been willing to go with him anyway. That I do not know. But believe me plees, that he has her in his house in Cambs. was her fault. Yes, indeed, she bring that on own self.'

'You seem quite convinced that she is still there.'

Ratnadatta shrugged. 'How can I say? But you haf tell me that she has not returned to her flat. So all points that she ees still with him.'

After a moment's consideration Barney decided that the odds were all upon the Indian's being right. He was obviously lying in his own defence about the part he had played on the previous Saturday night but, if he had cooked up this story about the American Colonel with the object of sending his captor off to Cambridgeshire on a wild-goose chase, he would have said that the day before he had actually seen Mary at the house called the Cedars. In this case the very fact that he would not swear to her being there made his account more likely to be trustworthy. From the afternoon onward Barney had been thinking of little else than the moment when he could bring Mary safely back to her flat. If she was no longer at the house in Cremorne, as far as he was concerned the raid on it could only prove a bitter disappointment. To bank on Ratnadatta's having told the truth now seemed the better bet. Grabbing the trembling Indian by the arm, he said:

'All right; get back into the car.'

Ratnadatta, holding his head rigid, wriggled in and, as Barney slammed the door on his side, asked anxiously, 'Plees, my Lord; what do you mean to do with me?'

'You'll see,' came the terse reply; and no further word was

spoken until, ten minutes later, they pulled up outside Fulham Police Station.

Ordering the Indian to get out, Barney marched him into the Station, produced his official pass, showed it to the Duty Sergeant and said: 'I am charging this man with kidnapping a Mrs. Margot Mauriac at or about six p.m. on Saturday last, 30th April.'

'It ees not true,' quavered Ratnadatta, his face now a dirty shade of grey. 'This man, he ees mad. He carries a pistol and haf threaten me with it.'

The Sergeant ignored him, and wrote out the charge. Looking the wretched Satanist full in the face, Barney went on, 'You may add, Sergeant, that the name Margot Mauriac was an alias for Mary Morden.'

Instantly Ratnadatta realized the terrible implication that lay behind that disclosure. His mouth dropped open, his eyes grew wide with horrified despair. Barney then administered the *coup de grâce*.

'I hope that soon we shall be able to prefer a further charge against this man of participation in the murder of the lady's husband.' At that, Ratnadatta gave a loud groan, put a hand over his eyes and, his knees buckling, slid to the floor in a dead faint.

While two constables picked him up and carried him away to a cell, Barney completed the formalities. He then asked the Sergeant to telephone a message to Special Branch for immediate relay by wireless to Inspector Thompson. It was simply to the effect that he would not, after all, be participating in the raid, so the Inspector must take over the job of doing his utmost to secure the incriminating photographs.

Immediately he was back in his car he got out his maps and soon located Fulgoham as a village near the southern end of the county and about five miles east-south-east of Cambridge. It was barely fifty miles from the centre of London and only just over half an hour had elapsed since he had waylaid Ratnadatta in the cul-de-sac. He reckoned that if he stepped on it, he should get to Fulgoham well before eleven o'clock.

At this hour the roads, apart from those in west-central London, were fairly free of traffic, so he decided it would be quicker to go by way of Kensington and Cricklewood until he struck the North Circular Road beyond Golders Green. There he turned north-east and made good going along the broad by-pass till he reached the

Great Cambridge Road which took him to within a few miles of his destination.

In Fulgoham village there were still a number of American Servicemen about, mostly with girls whom they had picked up in Cambridge and brought out for the evening on motor cycles or in small cars. After enquiring of several men for Colonel Washington's house, Barney found a Top Sergeant who was able to give him definite directions to it. The Cedars lay two miles further on along the road to Six Mile Bottom. It was on the right side of the road and a white-painted, five barred gate stood at the entrance of a drive leading to it.

Barney heaved a sigh of relief. The fact that Colonel Washington was known in Fulgoham and that he lived at the Cedars on the road to Six Mile Bottom was the first confirmation he had had that Ratnadatta had not been lying; at all events as far as the Colonel was concerned. It now remained to see if he was right in his belief that Mary had been taken to the house and was still there.

Fifty yards past the gate, Barney ran his car on to the grass verge, pulled up and got out. Fully aware that he was now about to enter on a desperate venture, he made certain that his pistol was in working order, then walked to the gate, opened it, slipped through and shut it softly behind him.

The drive was only about a hundred yards long, and there was sufficient moonlight for him to see the house at the end of it. Ratnadatta had thought it pretty, but it was in fact an Edwardian monstrosity of jumbled roofs and half-timbered stucco.

Stepping on to the grass beside the drive, and taking such cover as he could from groups of shrubs, he cautiously made his way forward. Chinks of light showed between the drawn curtains in some of the downstairs windows; so when he was within twenty yards of the house he began to skirt round it. At the back, from what he guessed to be the kitchen windows, chinks of light were also showing.

This indication that the inmates of the place were all still awake made him decide that he must postpone breaking in until later; but for hours past his mind had been obsessed with the thought of freeing Mary so, having made his way right round the house, he could not resist the temptation to creep up to a big bow window on the right of the front door, and see if he could get a glimpse of the room on the off-chance that she was in it.

The gravel crunched faintly under his feet as he tiptoed across the drive, but he felt confident that the sound would be drowned by that of a radio which came from the room towards which he was stealthily making his way. He reached the bay window and spent some minutes trying to get a view of the room, but all he could see through the chinks were strips of carpet and the legs of a chair. Greatly disappointed and still wondering if Mary was in the room, he backed away towards the front porch.

Suddenly a dark shape leapt from it. Footfalls grated harshly twice on the gravel behind him. His hand went to his automatic but, before he could swing round or draw it, he was struck on the back of the head. Stars and circles whirled before his eyes, his knees gave way and he fell to the ground unconscious.

19

The night of her life

MARY'S first conscious thought on waking on the previous Sunday morning had been that she was in a strange bed. The feel of the sheets, warm but slightly slippery, told her that. She opened her eyes and caught her breath. They were black satin. For a moment she gazed across them at the side of the room she was facing. In its centre there was a bay window with drawn curtains, but bright light filtering between them showed it to be broad day outside. An ornate dressing-table made of pale grey wood stood in the embrasure; its stool and two chairs which were also within her view matched it, showing that it formed part of an expensive modern suite.

Her heart began to beat more rapidly. Cautiously she turned over, feeling certain already of what she would see. There, on the pillow next to hers was a man's head. The hair on it was crew-cut and so fair as to be almost white. The face was turned towards her but inclined downwards, its lower part concealed by the top of the folded sheet. Under the hair-line there was a good forehead – broad rather than high–two thick, fair eyebrows and, between them, a great hooked nose. Her bedfellow was fast asleep and breathing so gently that she had to listen to catch the sound.

Chaotic memories of the previous night's events were now tumbling about in her mind: Abaddon, with his strangler's fit upon him, gripping her by the throat; Ratnadatta wearing her murdered husband's shoes; Pope Honorius forcing her to swallow the aphrodisiac; the middle-aged grey-haired man for whom she had been made to play the role of prophetess; Ratnadatta again, and her desperate struggle with him; her boundless relief when she found herself outside the temple in the cool night air, and believed that the American was going to take her home. But he hadn't. Instead he had suddenly decided to compound with his infernal master for not attending the Walpurgis Eve Sabbat by performing some special sacrifice on his own. Then he had said that he would give her the night of her life. Well, in a sense, he had.

As he had headed the car back and turned north-west along the Fulham Road, she knew that after the act which she had so rashly just put on – of appearing disappointed that he meant only to run her home then return to the Temple – she could not possibly revoke on that and suddenly declare that she felt too tired for love-making. She knew instinctively too that, even if she had attempted to make him change his mind, now he had decided to take her down to the country nothing she could say would stop him.

There had remained only the possibility of catching her rescuer off his guard and making her escape. But of succeeding in that, her chances were far less good than they had been when she had thought of getting away from Ratnadatta earlier that evening. Then it had been daylight and she could have seen any policeman they were going to pass a hundred yards before they reached him; now it was dark. Then they had been in a taxi so, had she decided on desperate measures, she could have called on the driver for aid; now she was in a private car, alone with her captor. One thing only could favour an attempt by her to get away from him. That was the car's being held up by the lights at a main cross-road for some minutes. Even if she failed to get the door open and scramble out before he grabbed her and pulled her back, if she shouted for help while the car was still stationary, someone might have come to her assistance.

But at this hour there was little traffic and the American drove skilfully and fast. At both Knightsbridge and Hyde Park Corner the lights favoured him; without once having had to pull up they turned north and ran smoothly through the Park. At Marble Arch she had had her chance. If she had been her normal self she would have taken it; but the succession of crises she had been through that evening had left her still half dazed and mentally exhausted.

298

As the car slid to a standstill, he whisked out his cigarette case and a lighter. Holding them out to her he told her to help herself and light a cigarette for him. It was then that her mental reactions, having slowed down, betrayed her. Instead of ignoring him and making her bid for freedom, she automatically took the case and lighter. With both hands occupied she was rendered temporarily as helpless as if she had been handcuffed. For a moment she thought of throwing the things back at him or dropping them; but, before she could nerve herself to take the plunge, the traffic lights turned orange.

She lit a cigarette for him but did not take one for herself. While the car sped up the Edgware Road she lay back and shut her eyes. Tears welled from their corners as she upbraided herself for her lack of resolution. She knew by then that she was beaten; that she was no longer capable of making the violent effort necessary to give her even a chance of getting away. She tried to console herself with the thought that, in spite of all she had gone through that evening, she had been incredibly lucky. She had escaped being strangled by Abaddon, being raped by Ratnadatta, and being made a prize in a lottery for a number of other men after her initiation as a Sister of the Ram. Perhaps her luck would still hold and some unforeseen occurrence prevent the American from having his way with her. If not, he was, anyway, only one man and a fine, clean-limbed, fiercely handsome specimen of manhood at that. Mental fatigue dulled her concern about what might happen to her when they reached their destination, and she resigned herself to the belief that she had now become the plaything of Fate.

He, meanwhile, thought she had fallen asleep; so he refrained from talking to her. And, in fact, before they were clear of the suburbs of London, nature did take charge. Fears, hopes, memories, all became submerged under the urgent demand of her brain for rest and for the next hour she slept soundly, untroubled by even the suggestion of a dream.

When he woke her the car was stationary before the porch of a house. It had been raining and she smelt the fresh scent of the wet on grass and conifers. As she got out she glimpsed a stretch of lawn and a big cedar caught in the headlights of the car. He had already rung the bell. After a few minutes lights went on, there came the sound of bolts being drawn back, and the door was opened by a big negro in a dressing-gown. He murmured apologetically:

299

'I wern't expectin' you back, boss.'

'No matter, Jim,' his master replied. 'Rout out Iziah and tell him to take the car round to the garage. Then you can both get back to bed. We'll look after ourselves.'

In the lighted hall Mary had a chance to get a really good look at the man into whose power she had now fallen. Although she was a little above the average height for a woman, her head came up only to his shoulder. His face had a reddish tan, his eyes were black as sloes and, as he grinned down at her, he exposed a mouthful of strong, ivory-white teeth.

'Honey, your sleep's done you good,' he told her. 'You're looking fine now, just fine. All you need is an underdone steak and a carafe of red wine to make you feel like the Queen of Sheba. But you'll have to make do for tonight with what we can find in the Frigidaire. Come along now, this way to the cookhouse.'

He led her down a passage to a twenty-foot square kitchen, with a scullery and larder, both of ample size, beyond it. They were equipped with every modern device that could help to provide good food and easy service: a huge deep freeze, a giant fridge, a double-width automatically-controlled cooker, a double sink, dish-washer, mix and whip, and numerous other gadgets. Waving a ten-inch long hand round, her host said:

'This place was quaint before I moved in. All of thirty years out of date. But I soon fixed it. What are dollars for 'cept to make life different from dressing in a bearskin and living in a cave. I put things right in no time, and shipped over a team of house-trained coloured boys to look after me.'

Throwing open one door of the fridge he went on: 'Now, what'll you have: jellied eels, smoked salmon, cold fried fish Yiddish style, prawns in aspic, Russian salad, stuffed tomatoes? And in the larder there'll be a raft of other things: cold meat, onion pie, gherkins, pickled walnuts and lots else.'

They selected several dishes and put them on the kitchen table. He showed Mary where the plates and cutlery were kept, so that she could lay up two places, then took from the other side of the fridge a bottle of champagne and two of stout, by mixing which in a big jug he made up two quarts of Chancellor Bismarck's favourite tipple, usually known as Black Velvet.

Mary had had no dinner, so as soon as they sat down she suddenly felt hungry. He encouraged her to eat and drink, and himself ate with obvious enjoyment a supper that three normal-

300

sized men would have found more than enough if shared between them. In less than half an hour, the jug that held the Black Velvet was empty.

Meanwhile, between great mouthfuls of food, and often while still chewing noisily, he talked and laughed, as gaily as a schoolboy at an end-of-term dormitory feast. There was nothing about him to remind Mary that he was a Satanist. Temporarily she entirely forgot that and, infected by his enormous zest for life, found herself talking and laughing with him.

When they had finished eating, she instinctively suggested that they should wash up; but he roared with laughter and said, 'My! so you're a good squaw too! Guess you've got everything. But you don't have to bother, honey. No ma'm, not in my menage. What do I hire my team of boys for?'

Stooping suddenly he threw a great arm round her, low down under her behind, and pitched her, as though she had weighed no more than a child, over his right shoulder. With his left hand he switched off and on the several lights as he carried her upstairs, singing cheerfully meanwhile a couple of verses of that favourite American bawdy song, 'Frankie and Johnny were lovers'.

When he had set her down in the bedroom with the olive-wood furniture, she had made no attempt to get away. Such an attempt would, in any case, have been utterly futile; but her sound sleep on the run down from London had had the effect of forming a psychological barrier in her mind between all that had happened earlier that night and the present. She no longer felt any fear, the good food and Black Velvet had recruited her strength, and either the potency of the latter or the delayed effects of the aphrodisiacs she had been given earlier expunged from her mind the awareness that the wickedly handsome man who towered above her was a Satanist and, perhaps, a murderer.

Twelve hours later, as she lay in the big bed, now completely sober and again the prey of anxious speculation about her future, she thought of that; but she had to admit that she could not plead as an excuse to herself that she had been raped. That he would have raped her had she resisted she had no doubt at all; but she had not resisted. On the contrary, at his first kiss she had suddenly let herself go and, apart from intervals when he had twice gone downstairs to fetch up champagne and a cold duck that they had eaten in their fingers, she had spent half the night meeting his seemingly insatiable passion.

301

She felt now that she ought to be ashamed of herself. Not for having enjoyed, after several months' abstinence, having again slept with a man, but because he was the sort of man he was. Although she had been prepared to submit, if need be, to the embrace of some Satanist during an initiation ceremony, she had expected that to be swiftly over. That, too, could have been excused as necessary to the furtherance of her plan to ferret out the secrets of the Brotherhood. But the way she had spent the night had brought her no nearer to doing that than she had been the previous evening.

At that moment her companion woke, gave her a slow smile, then suddenly thrust a huge arm beneath her and pulled her towards him.

'No!' she gasped. 'No! Please! I'm feeling awful. Please let me sleep a little longer.'

Her protest was useless. He only laughed and cried, 'Lots of time for sleep later, honey. It's Sunday. We'll stay put here all day.'

She tried to thrust him off but, as his black eyes bored down into her blue ones, her will became as weak as water. With a sigh of mingled self-reproach and resignation, she let herself respond to his kiss.

When he released her he lit a cigarette, took a few puffs at it, then jumped out of bed. Striding to the door he threw it open and, a bronzed olympian figure, marched out on to the landing. From it he bellowed, 'Jim! Buster! Breakfast! And make it plenty. I could eat a horse. Get moving!'

The sounds of running feet and cheerful cries came from below in response. Swinging back into the room, he slammed the door behind him, pointed to another and said: 'Go help yourself to a wash if you want, honey. Them coons know I don't stand for being kept waiting. The chow'll be here soon as the stove can fry the eggs.'

Eggs he had said and eggs he meant. Eight of them, flanked by a plentiful supply of bacon and sausages, arrived still sizzling on a big hot-dish. Beside it, on the travelling table that had been wheeled in while she was in the bathroom, were a great aluminium drum of steaming coffee, a jug of cream, toast, marmalade, butter and fruit. The sight and smell of them suddenly made her feel ravenously hungry; so she did justice to the ample helpings he gave her while he demolished the greater part of what remained.

302

She had already noticed that facing the end of the bed there was an outsized television set. When they had finished eating he pushed the wheeled tray out on to the landing and turned on the set. They were just in time for the one o'clock news. Nothing of startling importance had occurred so the alarms and excursions reported were mainly developments of matters that had already occupied headlines. As Mary listened to further particulars of an air-liner disaster that had happened the day before, she could hardly believe that she was not dreaming.

To her, yesterday seemed weeks ago; yet it was barely twenty-four hours since she had received Barney's roses and been so furious with him for letting her down. She wondered what he would say if he could see her now, and felt certain that the sight of her, propped up against the pillows with the arm of her big companion cast casually round her shoulders, would send him into a frenzy of jealous rage. So she wished that he could see her. It would serve 'his lordship' right for having gambled on her liking him enough to accept any excuse he might cook up as cover for his having gone off for the week-end with some other woman – as she was fully convinced he had.

For a few minutes she tried to guess what the other woman was like but, having not a vestige of information to go on, she soon realized the absurdity of attempting to do so. Mentally shrugging it off, she thought with sudden vicious satisfaction, 'Anyway, whatever her colouring and vital statistics, I bet she hasn't as much physical attraction as this super-man who has got hold of me'.

Next moment she was appalled at her own thought. The man beside her was a criminal. As a professed Satanist he must have committed all sorts of abominations and evil deeds. He had even implied, while surveying her and about to rescue her from Ratnadatta, that he was a white-slaver. She was, at the moment, in the position of a white-slave to him. To have mentally admitted that she had allowed herself to be attracted to such a man now seemed a terrible degradation. It was the sort of sin against the higher nature which could be wiped out only by taking the veil. She began to wonder miserably if she would ever again be able to look a decent man in the face.

But the giant on whose shoulder her head was resting was anything but miserable. With the breakfast, on the lower shelf of the wheeled table, the Sunday papers had been brought up. He

303

had switched off the T.V. and was reading them. Now and then he read extracts aloud to her with either humorous or salacious comment. Presently he came to an article on the British Government's attitude towards Communist China and began to sneer at the British as a dirty lot of double-crossers who would have gone down the drain long ago had it not been for the innocent belief of the Americans that there was something like old brandy about them in that, however much they might cost, they paid for keeping.

Mary, being full-blooded Irish, shared the political schizophrenia which is characteristic of a great part of that people. She had been brought up to believe that the British were the root of all evil but that the Empire as a whole, to the building of which the Irish had made such a great contribution, was a thing that, if need be, one should lay down one's life for; and woe betide any foreigner who had the impudence to belittle either its past achievements or present power to find the best answer to difficult situations which were constantly arising all over the world.

She knew little about international politics but enough to tell him that, if Churchill had had his way, and Roosevelt not been a gullible fool, Stalin would never have been allowed to get his claws on Central Europe; so the massacre of the Hungarians and the enslavement of millions of Czechs, Poles and Rumanians lay at America's door. And that if only their sanctimonious moron, Dulles, had not prevented the British from putting in a 'stitch in time' at Suez, hundreds of honest, intelligent Arabs would not since have been murdered and the whole of the Middle East fallen under Soviet influence.

Amazed and intrigued by her vehemence he entered into a man to man argument with her and, although she spoke more from instinct than from knowledge, he found it impossible to reason soundly against her reiterated assertion that the 'proof of the pudding was in the eating' and that he had only to look at the shrinkage of the territories free from Communist domination, since the United States had assumed world leadership, to realize what a mess his countrymen had made of things. On the other hand, she could not honestly deny his charge that, when Britain had had the leadership of affairs between the wars, she had done little better, and that her refusal to back the French, when they wanted forcibly to resist the re-entry of the Germans into the Rhineland, had been the key error from which had sprung

304

Hitler's confidence that he could tear up Treaties with impunity, and so led to the Second World War.

This acrimonious discussion occupied them until three o'clock then, by mutual consent, they broke it off and, turning over, went to sleep again. Soon after five they roused up and went into the bathroom. He had a shower while she had a bath and when she had finished, instead of getting back into bed, she began to put her clothes on. Suddenly realizing what she was doing, he exclaimed: 'Hi, what's the big idea?'

Endeavouring to make her voice sound indifferent, she replied:

'You said last night that today you meant to take me back to the Temple, and there's not much of the day left; so I thought we would be starting soon now.'

Actually the last thing she wanted was ever to enter the Temple again, but knowing that the Sabbats took place only on Saturdays she was hoping to persuade him that there was no point in his delivering her there so, instead, he should drop her at her own flat; or, if that failed, once they were back in London she would find a better chance than she had the night before to get free of him.

'You sound as though you want to go back,' he flung at her with a frown.

'No,' she lied hastily. 'Of course not. But I thought you had made yourself liable to some sort of penalty for having carried me off, and that the longer you kept me the heavier it would be.'

His frown deepened into a scowl. 'Yeah. I'll have to pay a forfeit; but not for having snatched you. The Great Ram is quite a buddy of mine, so I can square that one with him. It's cutting the Walpurgis Eve party that's put me in the red.'

'If you hadn't been so impatient . . .' she began.

'I know. I know. Sure, I could have parked you at your flat and picked you up this morning. But patience isn't in my make-up. If it had been I'd not have got halfway up to where I am now.'

She shrugged. 'Well, you've had what you wanted as far as I'm concerned. I hope it's been worth it.'

'And how!' His scowl gave place to a sudden grin. 'Sure; sure. But mighty few of the best-looking dolls have anything inside their heads. And you've got everything, honey. I'm a man who likes to get fresh angles on things, and if the angles come from someone who's got the right kind of curves as well, what more could a guy want? I want to see a lot more of you yet; so how about staying on here with me for a while?'

At that her hopes of being through with him in a few hours' time sank to zero. But she dared not show it. Although his latest idea had been couched in the form of an invitation, she knew that he would not allow her to refuse it, and that her only chance of getting away now lay in not letting him suspect that she wanted to. It meant that she would have to spend at least one more night with him, but it seemed certain that tomorrow he would have to leave the house to attend to his duties, which would then give her a good chance to escape. Summoning up a smile, she said:

'Yes, I'd love to do that. I'm sure we'll find lots to talk about.'

'Fine oh!' He gave her a resounding slap on the bottom. 'Would you like to eat up here or downstairs?'

'Let's go downstairs, and you can show me the rest of the house.'

Half an hour later he was mixing Vodka Martinis for them in a sitting-room below the big bedroom. Like the other rooms it had been furnished expensively, but without taste. In the bay window stood another big television set, a separate radio and a walnut gramophone cabinet for long-playing records. As he handed her a drink she said:

'You know, I don't even know your name!'

'Among the blessed of our Lord Satan, I'm known as "Twisting Snake",' he replied with a grin. 'But in these parts it's Colonel Henrik G. Washington of the U.S.A.A.F.; though, among themselves, my boys call me "that big bastard Wash".'

She could not help laughing and, lifting her glass, said: 'Well, I much prefer that to Twisting Snake; so here's to you Wash!'

He sunk his first cocktail at a gulp. 'That's to your blue eyes, Circe. I recall that's the name you took as a neophyte. But what'll I tell Jim and the others to call you while you're my house-guest here?'

'Mrs. Mauriac; Margot Mauriac. Tell me, why did you choose such an ugly Satanic name as Twisting Snake?'

'The original was an ancestor of mine. Maybe you've guessed that I've got Red Indian blood, and that old medicine-man was the greatest ever wizard of the Five Nations!'

Mary nodded. 'Yes, I can imagine you looking magnificent in a feathered head-dress and all the trimmings. Where did your very fair hair come from, though?'

'I'm a thorough-bred half-caste,' he told her, 'born in an Indian reservation of a squaw. My father was some kind of a crook. Leastways, he was hiding up in the forest when my Ma came on

306

him. She was only about fifteen, but that didn't worry him any. I was the result. I guess she fell for him though, as she took food to him in secret for around a month, and insisted on calling me Henrik, which was the only name she knew him by. One day he took a runout powder on her and was never seen again. He must have been some sort of Nordic, and he'd talked to her of a big island where he'd been a fisherman before he hit the States, so maybe he was an Icelander; but that I'll never know for certain.'

'It's a big achievement for a little boy, brought up as you must have been in an Indian reservation, to have become a Colonel in the United States Air Force.'

'Yeah. It weren't easy; but I made it. I owe that mainly to my Grandaddy. He was the medicine-man of the tribe. I'll bet he beat hell out of my Ma when he knew the games she had been up to in the forest; because, of course, no brave would take her as his squaw after she'd had a child that way, and she must have been worth quite a few head of cattle to him. But he brought me up. Taught me all he knew, and by the time I was fourteen I was a better medicine-man than he was.

'Nominally all the redfolks are Christians these days; but that's only lip-service to gip free blankets and baccy out of the padres. They know what's best for them and still practise the old religion on the side – totem rites, palavas at the full of the moon, and the rest. My Grandaddy could kill or cure plenty and he wanted me to follow him as Our Lord Satan's top priest in the reservation. But he was old and ailing so he had to give me the red feather of initiation much earlier than he would else have done. I earnt it though. Makes me sweat now to recall some of the ordeals I went through. All the same, I took to making magic like a heron takes to diving for the fish.'

As he paused, Mary asked: 'And did you succeed your grandfather?'

'Not me. Leastways, only for a few weeks. Taking dimes off our poor folk for curing cattle, or causing some old joker to turn up his toes a bit sooner than nature meant him to, was too narrow an alley for me to be happy playing ball in for long. One night I lit out with a travelling circus, and I never went back.'

'At sixteen I was already as big as most men ever come, and still growing. Add to that I met few people I couldn't hypnotize into doing what I wanted. I'd brought Grandaddy's ceremonial feathers with me and I made the circus boss let me put on an act of my own. It was lassooing, bow and arrow, and throwing the tomahawk. I got a programme girl to stand in for me to shoot and throw round. Poor kid, she was so scared she near died of fright every time before we went on. She needn't have feared. Once she had her back to the target I could hold her there with my eyes, as rigid as an iron bar, and long as she didn't move she was in no danger. But she hadn't enough of what it takes to keep me for long with her under a blanket. I decided to team up with the Gipsy Lee of the outfit and move into her caravan. She was near twice my age but she had "it" all right, all right. Trouble was she had a husband. Sid was his name. So I carved a little wooden doll and scratched SID on it. Then I talked magic talk to it all night long and took it out in the morning and buried it. Within a week Sid caught a cold and started coughing. That was before the days of penicillin. In a fortnight pneumonia had taken him, and I was in the caravan teaching his woman the quick way to forget him.'

At the mention of the doll, Mary had guessed what was coming, so she had time to glance away and repress a shudder at this confession of cold-blooded murder. Now happily launched on his life-story, the hook-nosed giant went on.

'Come the fall, the circus went into its winter quarters at Detroit. Gipsy, as was her custom, took a room for telling fortunes. She was mighty good at it. Could have done far better for herself that way all year round, but she had real gipsy blood in her and preferred a roving life. What I knew of magic put me wise to it that she was pulling in power from some source outside herself. One night I got out of her the how and why. She was an initiate of a Satanic Lodge there in the city. I made her take me along. That's how I became a Brother of the Ram.'

He poured Mary another cocktail, and resumed. 'It was by way of a guy I happened on in that Lodge that I got my first real break. He ran a big brothel. Seeing I was strong as a young bull, he asked me if I'd like to take a hand breaking in new girls. Most of those that get to the houses know what to expect; but there's some that don't, and make trouble. They have to have their heels rounded off, and it's strong men's work to do that. After I'd been at this dame busting game for a while it hit me that I was a sucker to do it for another guy when I might be doing it for myself.'

'Gipsy was making enough to keep me, but I felt it would be good to have some extra dough to throw around; and setting up

308

as a knife-thrower in a booth wouldn't have paid the sort of dividends I had in mind. Within three months I had a string of five girls working the streets for me. From then on I never looked back. I made Gipsy cut out the fortune-telling and set her up as the Madame in a place of our own. By the time I was nineteen I'd gone into the export business, and was shipping as many as eight judys a month down to S.A. The Feds were always after us, of course, but Gipsy had only to look at a girl to judge if she was too hot to handle, and as a seer myself I always got wise to it in advance if danger threatened our organization. Time war broke out I had tie-ups with all the big operators in the States and was one of the biggest shots in the racket.'

Revolting as his disclosures were, Mary had to simulate interest, so she said: 'No wonder you have lots of money. But this doesn't explain how you became a Colonel in the United States Air Force.'

'It was the yen to fly, honey,' he smiled, 'and ambition. From the time I was a kid in the reservation, I'd thought nothing could thrill like being a bird-man. The war was my chance. I'd a partner who's half Puerto-Rican and half Jew. I told him to carry on and he knows that if he bilked me for ten cents I'd have him die in a fit. I flew out to California where no one knew me, and joined up. As a pilot I proved a natural, as I knew I would. Soon as they let me go into battle I became an ace overnight. They gave me a commission and decorations. Maybe you noticed them on my tunic. Everything from the Purple Heart to the Legion of Merit – the whole works.'

'And that decided you to stay in after the war?'

'That, and ambition. The old set-up is still working. Must be hundreds of judys back in the States earning me a dollar or two every night; but dollars isn't everything. I wanted to go places and meet people as a guy who is somebody apart from what he can spend. As Colonel Henrik G. Washington, I am that.'

He then told her of some of his experiences during the war, and of how he had at times used his occult powers to restore the morale of other pilots who, after many missions, had nearly reached breaking point; and also that he devoted a percentage of his income to helping the widows of ex-comrades who had been killed while serving with him. He mentioned this last matter as casually as he had spoken of breaking down the resistance of unfortunate girls who had been trapped into brothels, and Mary found it quite beyond her to reconcile such opposite traits in one personality.

The negro Jim, dressed in a spotless white housecoat, duly announced dinner and waited on them while they ate an excellent meal. Afterwards 'Wash' entertained Mary for two hours with long-playing records, mostly pieces by serious composers of whom she had never heard, and it was obvious to her that he knew very much more about music than she did. They then went up to bed.

On the Monday morning they were called at six and by half past seven Wash, now again a truly martial figure, was ready to be driven to his office. He had told Mary that there was no point in her getting up until she felt like it; so she had drifted off to sleep again. But before leaving he shook her into wakefulness and said:

'Look, honey; make yourself at home in the house, but don't go outside it. My General's not a bad scout about giving leave to London or Paris, so his officers can blow steam off, but he's a stickler for them setting a good example while in the area; so I don't want it to get around that I've got a dame here as a house-guest.'

As soon as he had gone she set about planning her escape. It looked as if he had no suspicion that she might wish to, but of that she could not be certain, and it was possible that he had told his coloured boys to keep an eye on her. Anyway, they might think it strange and stop her, or telephone to him, if she got up at once and walked out of the house. Anxious as she was to get away, she decided that her chances would be better if she remained there during the morning while the boys were doing their routine jobs, then try to slip away unseen early in the afternoon as soon as they had settled down for their easy.

At eleven o'clock she got up, and when she was dressed went downstairs to the sitting-room, where she put on a record. It had been playing for only a few minutes when Jim appeared accompanied by an older, fatter negro, in a white apron and chef's cap, who introduced himself as Buster. Both gave her friendly grins; the one asked her what she would like to drink and the other what she would have for lunch. Having asked for their suggestions, she made her choice and they left her to go about their work.

At the unexpectedly early hour of half past twelve, Jim came in to tell her that lunch was ready. She remembered then that Americans both started and finished their day's work earlier than

the British; so Wash might be expected back in m'
A little nervous now that she might be leaving hers
a margin to get clear away, she got through th
then went back to the sitting-room and, leaving its
waited there listening impatiently until all sound of mo
should have ceased.

By half past one, the house had fallen completely silent. Tiptoeing across the hall, she let herself out of the front door. As she
walked down the drive, she did not dare to look back for fear
that one of the boys was watching her from a window. He might
take such a gesture as an indication that by going out she was
disobeying his master's orders. Every moment she expected to
hear the sound of running footsteps coming after her but only her
own crunched faintly on the gravel.

When she reached the road, she glanced quickly from side to
side. In the distance to her left there were low hills and below
them, about two miles away, the roofs of some big aircraft
hangars. To her right there was flatter country and the road ran
along one side of a long shallow valley into which three aircraft
were gliding. The hangars obviously formed part of the U.S. Air
Force base, so turning her back on them she set off at a swift
pace in the opposite direction.

She still had her handbag and in it ample money to get to
London; but as soon as she came to a village she meant to telephone to Colonel Verney. There was no reason whatever to
suppose that during the past forty-eight hours Ratnadatta had
disposed of those incriminating shoes, and if he could be caught
with them still in his possession she would have won her fight
against at least one of Teddy's murderers. She would tell the
Colonel too about the house in Cremorne, so that he might rope
in the whole Satanic crew and, perhaps, find evidence there against
others of them. But what about Wash?

The thought of the genial but evil giant presented her with an
unexpected problem. Her sense of justice compelled her to admit
that she had no personal cause for complaint against him. He had
not taken her by force. Even his carrying her off from London
had been largely due to her own folly in overplaying her hand
with him. He obviously believed that she had been perfectly
willing to stay with him and was thoroughly enjoying herself.
More, he had both rescued her from Ratnadatta and saved her
from initiation.

To that it had to be added that he was not a Satanist in the same sense as the others. He had not thrown off the tenets of a decent upbringing and all moral scruples to join a Lodge in order to acquire wealth or satiate his lust in wild orgies. He had been brought up from his childhood to worship the Devil, to practise magic and follow a creed, the only dictum of which was, 'Do what thou wilt shall be the Whole of the Law.' It was evident that he had never regarded the world as anything but a jungle in which the strongest and most determined were fully justified in living well at the expense of weaker animals. That his mind had developed from infancy completely lacking all moral sense must be taken at least as some mitigation of his having shown no trace of scruple in bull-dozing his way to affluence by criminal means.

But what a calendar of crimes lay at his door. Murder, rape, and the unlimited terrorization of innumerable people. His house, his coloured servants, the *de luxe* equipment of his kitchen, his gramophone records and champagne, were all still being paid for from the earnings of scores of unhappy women in the United States, and the shipping of scores of others, still more greatly to be pitied, to a living hell in the brothels of South America. As Mary thought of the misery she had suffered herself during her black year in Dublin, her blood boiled, and she knew that she must not even consider giving such a man an hour's warning, but do her utmost to ensure that, like the others, he was arrested with the least possible delay.

While these thoughts had been agitating her mind she had walked nearly two miles, but there was still no sign of a village. Another half mile of open road lay before her with hedges and fields on either side, except in one place a few hundred yards distant where, among a few fruit trees, she could see a cottage.

Suddenly she heard the blare of a klaxon horn in her rear. Looking back, she saw a large car hurtling towards her at seventy miles an hour. Another minute and, as she jumped to the side of the road, she caught a glimpse of the driver. He was the hook-nosed giant that, two minutes before, she had been planning to have arrested. With a screech of tyres suddenly braked, the car pulled up fifty feet beyond her.

20

Wanted! A human victim for sacrifice

M ARY had a moment only in which to make up her
mind. Two courses were open to her. She could jump the ditch,
scramble through the hedge and run for it across the fields, or stay
where she was and accept capture. To do the former was to pro-
claim that she had deliberately set out to escape, whereas if she
did not take to her heels she might still bluff it out.

Had he pulled up behind her she might have reached the cottage
before he could catch her, but to do so from where she stood she
would have to pass him. She could still get to it by making a
detour through the hedge and round to its back, by way of the
field, but, if she did succeed in outrunning him to it, there might
not be anyone there to whom she could appeal for help. Realizing
the small start she would have and the huge stride that his long
legs would give him, with bitter reluctance she decided to stay
where she was.

In a succession of violent swerves he backed the car until it
came level with her, then demanded: 'Where in heck d'you think
you're going?'

'To the village,' she replied, concealing her anger and disappointment with a nervous smile.

'For why?' His black eyes were glittering and his voice terse.

Defensively she retorted, 'What do you think? To buy a few
things, of course. It's all very well for you; you've everything you
want in the house. But I haven't even a toothbrush of my own,
or make-up things; except for the powder compact and lipstick

313

in my bag. If I'm to stay with you I don't mean to be reduced to looking like a drab.'

'You've gotta tongue. You should have used it, and I'd have had them gotten for you. I said you were to stay put, didn't I?'

'You've no need to worry. I specially chose the quietest hour of the day when no one was about. Except for two labourers in a field I haven't seen a soul.'

'You would have, if you'd made the village. A quarter of an hour back I had a hunch you'd quit the maison; so I did a quick overlook and saw you beating it along the road. Get in.'

There was no alternative; so she got in and in stony silence he drove her back to the house. Following her in he waved a great hand towards the stairs and said: 'Get on up to the *Schlafzimmer*.'

Now pale with apprehension as she wondered what he meant to do with her, she went up to the bedroom. Two minutes later he joined her there carrying a largish square box covered with imitation leather. Setting it down on a chair he scowled at her and snapped, 'Get your clothes off.'

With mounting terror she obeyed; then, trembling a little as she stood in front of him, she began to stutter further excuses.

Ignoring them he suddenly shot out a hand. At the level of his own shoulder his outspread fingers ploughed through her hair. Suddenly they closed, so that the hair they grasped became a thick fistful. With a violent gesture he flung her sideways. She staggered and would have fallen but he wrenched her back. At the tug on her hair she let out a scream of pain. Grabbing at his wrist she strove to free herself but his grip was fast. Still holding her by the hair he flung her first to one side then the other, let her fall to her knees then jerked her upright, let her fall again then dragged her screaming half across the room and back.

Releasing her and stepping away, he said: 'Treatment number one for judys who disobey orders in the red-light dives. Way up on beatings. Doesn't mark 'em and spoil their appearance for the customers. There's treatments two and three. Best not go walking again, honey. Get into bed and stay there. I'll be seeing you.'

As he turned on his heel and left her, she collapsed on the bed. The hair on her forehead was wet with sweat and the top of her head one terrible ache where for several moments her scalp had had to take the weight of her whole body. After a while, still sobbing, she crept between the sheets and lay there in abject misery for what seemed an endless time.

314

Actually it was about two hours, then the door opened and he came in again. Putting down a big parcel he had with him, he leant over her and said abruptly, 'Sit up.'

'You brute!' she flared, cowering further away from him under the bedclothes.

'Sit up,' he repeated. 'I'll not hurt you this time.'

Doubting him, but not daring to refuse, she levered herself up into a sitting position. Her head was still aching intolerably where the hair had been almost torn from it, but when she instinctively put up her hands to defend herself, he took them both and pushed them down to her sides.

'Not a move, now,' he ordered. Then, while muttering some gibberish under his breath, with the index finger of his left hand he made the sign of the reversed swastika on the top of her head. As though by magic – and, indeed, it was by magic – the pain eased then faded away completely.

'Thanks,' she sighed, her eyes wide with wonder. 'Oh, thank you! But why did you have to be so brutal?'

'Teach you not to try to run out on me.'

'I wasn't,' she lied.

'Can that! I know you were. I picked it up from your vibrations. What's been eating you? You get plenty kick out of being my squaw, don't you?'

Knowing she must humour him, she raised a smile. 'Yes, of course, lots. You are a wonderful lover.'

'Then why the yen to quit?'

Swiftly she searched her mind for some reason that would sound plausible, yet not offend or make him angry. After a moment inspiration came to her, and she hedged. 'I didn't want to really. It was not until I was walking along the road that the idea suddenly came into my head. You see, I'd been looking forward tremendously to my initiation and on Saturday night, but for you, I'd have been made a Sister of the Ram. Don't think I'm not grateful to you for having saved me from that beast Ratnadatta. I am. But I do want to be initiated and I can't be until I'm back in London. I felt sure you wouldn't be willing to let me go; so I was toying with the idea of going while I had the chance. That was the thought wave of mine that you must have picked up.'

'Well, now,' he smiled, 'so that's how it was. Why in heck didn't you say so then, instead of giving me all that gup about wanting to buy beauty-parlour goods?'

315

'But I did want to. That's all I started out to do.'

Turning away, he picked up the parcel, threw it on the bed and said: 'Take a look at that lot. Dames I've had here as house-guests before have known they were coming and brought their own muck. I oughta have realized you were shy of all the aids.'

Evidently he must have gone into Cambridge as the parcel contained a variety of the most expensive creams, lotions, powders, shampoos and scents, which could never have come from a village shop. As she thanked him for this generous present he said: 'I don't go for nightwear, either for myself or dames, but you'll want undies, nylons, mules and frocks. Just jot down the old vital statistics for me tomorrow and you can have all you wish.'

She thanked him again and while she was still examining the packets and bottles he went on thoughtfully, ''Bout your initiation. You don't have to go to London for that. I run a Lodge for some of my airforce boys down here. It's only if happen I'm in London on leave, or for top ceremonies, that I check in with old Abaddon's crowd. Most Saturdays I do High Priest for my own set-up. And I've this forfeit on my neck. That entails a sacrifice. Seeing you're so set on losing no time in becoming a Sister, I guess I'll make my blood offering come Saturday and initiate you myself.'

Her heart sank at his words, and sank still further as he added in a slightly reluctant tone, 'It'll mean loaning you for a while to some of my boys, but there's no avoiding that. Still, wouldn't be right for me to stand in your way of becoming a full-blown witch. I'll get a pay-off afterwards, though. You'll be qualified to act as my assistant in some private magics I've a mind to undertake. Two members of the cult always get better results than one.'

Avoiding his eyes she continued to finger the bottles, miserably conscious that she had again overplayed her hand, and so now had fresh cause for dread. She could only pray that before Saturday some unforeseen occurrence would enable her to escape the threatened ordeal.

The evening and night they passed together differed very little from that which had preceded it but, in the morning when they were called, before going into the bathroom he pressed a switch at the side of the square black box he had brought up to the bedroom the previous afternoon. Mary was still dozing when his voice issued from the box. Harshly it commanded: 'Get your clothes off!'

316

Sitting up she stared at it. She had heard of, but never seen, a tape recorder. As she listened she realized that that was what the box must be and that it was now playing back the sounds it had registered in the room while she had been receiving punishment for her attempt to escape. She heard again her own terrible screams and pleas for mercy, then his voice again, followed by her moans and sobs as she had collapsed upon the bed. The sounds brought flooding back to her the memory of the agony she had suffered, and she shuddered afresh.

When he returned from his shower, he grinned at her and said: 'Just a reminder, honey. Don't try anything you wouldn't like me to know about while I'm on the job today.'

'I won't,' she assured him quickly. 'I've no wish to leave here. I'm enjoying every moment of it.'

'Some moments,' he agreed, his grin becoming a little twisted. 'But yesterday evening I had a feeling that you'd something on your mind. A looker like you couldn't have been running solo before I snatched you. Maybe it's that you've a boy-friend in London that you're getting boiled up to be back with. Guess I'd better fix you proper, so you won't land yourself in no more pain and grief.'

Coming over to her he took her face between his two great hands. His eyes held her like magnets for a minute, then they seemed to grow very large and she heard him say: 'Repeat after me, "I'll not put a foot outside this house except with that big bastard Wash".'

Steeling herself to appear willing, she said the words not once but, at his order, three times; then he released her.

Later in the day she resolved to test the strength of the spell he had put upon her. Having waited until Jim was out of the way she went to a door at the far end of the hall that led to the garden. Opening it she looked out across a lawn to a group of trees; then she told herself that she was going to walk over to them. But she could not. The hypnotic suggestion that he had implanted in her mind held her fast. Strive as she would she could not lift a foot to step out over the door sill.

In the hall there was a telephone and it had extensions in both the sitting-room and the bedroom. She had already thought of trying to get through by one of them to Colonel Verney, and now she considered that possibility again. She actually got as far as lifting the receiver in the sitting-room, but as the dialling tone

317

sounded quickly put it down again. Since her absent captor had so swiftly and accurately become aware of her intentions the previous afternoon it seemed certain that his highly developed psychic sense would again warn him that she was about to betray him. She was no longer capable of even leaving the house. If he returned imbued with the belief that she had been endeavouring to bring about his arrest it was quite on the cards that he might kill her. The risk was too great to take.

She then searched the room for a book in the hope that it would take her mind off her wretched situation, but apparently the telephone directory was the only book in the house. Too depressed even to listen to the radio, for the remainder of the afternoon she abandoned herself to miserable forebodings about the next stages of this seemingly bottomless pit of afflictions into which, by her own actions, she had plunged herself.

Her gargantuan host returned much later than he had the day before, and the reason for his lateness was apparent when he had Iziah – a third coloured boy who did the rough work and serviced his car – bring in a great pile of cardboard boxes. They contained at least a hundred pounds' worth of lingerie and as Mary inspected it, being human, she could not help feeling temporarily cheered up.

Confronted with this sort of thing she found it impossible to hate Wash wholeheartedly, and felt more than ever that, as he attracted her physically, she must endeavour to put all other thoughts about him out of her mind, and play up to him in the hope that when she had spent a few more nights with him he might relax his restriction on her leaving the house, or tire of her and send her back to London.

It was next day, Wednesday, that in the evening they talked for quite a while about the H-bomb and the chances of a Third World War. The subject arose through her having asked him what type of planes he had at his Station and his telling her that he commanded a squadron of giant bombers that could carry enough nuclear explosive in one mission to blow the whole of Moscow off the map.

'Should it ever have to be, let's hope they don't blow us off the map first,' she commented.

'No fear of that,' he asserted. 'Leastways, not unless some guy on their side goes crackers.'

'If you're right about that we've little need to fear an atomic war at all, then.'

318

'I wouldn't say that. Time may come when Uncle Sam decides to pull a fast one.'

She stared at him in amazement. 'Surely you don't mean that America would ever attack Russia without warning?'

'Could be,' he shrugged. 'Got to be realistic. Take a look at the world situation. For years past now the Soviet's been beating us to it all along the line. Uncle Sam's policy of shelling out dollars to sitters on the fence has got him nowhere. Blacks, browns, yellows take our money with one hand and aircraft, tanks and guns from the Kremlin with the other. Meantime Soviet agents and their buddies in these Afro-Asian countries riddle their administrations like maggots in a cheese. Whenever it suits, the boys in Moscow pull a string and one of these little nations blows up. The Great Panjandorum and the feudal types, who've been playing along with the West so as to keep their hooks on their bank rolls, are bumped; and there's another chunk of territory in the Communists' bag. The ring's closing all the time, and as it closes the West is losing markets. The Kremlin can put the black on the countries its nominees control to buy Russian. Add to that Soviet production being on the up-and-up, and their labour only what they've a mind to pay it, they'll soon be pricing us out of Europe and Latin America. And there's one thing folk back home won't stand for. That's a reduction of their living standard. What's the answer. Ask yourself?'

Mary shook her head. 'I don't believe any United States Government would ever launch a world war without provocation.'

'Provocation huh! They'll have plenty. The Kremlin hands it out every day. And democratic Governments aren't free agents. The White House is under pressure from our industrial tycoons all the time. As unemployment mounts they'll be able to turn the screw. If it comes to war or the bread line they'll have the ordinary folk behind them. The Russians will find that they've played at brinkmanship once too often and the big shots in the Pentagon will be told to press the button. That's how it might go, and sooner than you think.'

Owing to the circumstances in which Wash had come upon Mary he had from the beginning accepted her as a Satanist, and she had, ever since, been careful to maintain that illusion in his mind; so for the past three days during all their talks they had treated every subject from that point of view. Speaking from that angle now she said:

319

'If either side launched a surprise attack I should have thought it much more likely to be the Russians. We know that the old religion is making use of Communism, because it aims to destroy the Governments and false religions of the West. Isn't it quite a possibility that the Brothers of the Ram in Moscow might influence the men in the Kremlin into going to war with the idea of putting an end to the Christian heresy for good?'

He smiled at her. You've got it all wrong, honey. There's Communism and Communism. The sort that's outside the Iron Curtain is the genuine old Marxist goods, and useful to us. But not the Soviet brand. The boys in the Kremlin threw true Communism down the drain years ago. Take a look at what's been happening there. No more free love but a big build-up for family life. Go to church if you want to. Cut down the drink, or else. A new bourgeois society with all the old taboos. The guys at the top aren't going to risk the good time they're having for the sake of going crusading in Europe. They're reckoning on getting the whole works without. I've told you how, honey. Giving the impression that the Cold War is over and they really want to be friends, taking over wherever we stop paying out, industrial sabotage and using sweated labour to undersell us. I'm telling you, unless Uncle Sam blots Russia first it'll be the only country worth living in ten years hence.'

'We are always told here that the American people are scared stiff at the idea of an atomic war. And so are we for that matter. Anyhow, it would end in the whole world going up in flames; so however bad unemployment in the States becomes, I can't see them urging their Government to let them commit suicide.'

'They wouldn't do that. Not consciously. The danger is things could get so bad there'd be a threat of revolution. Rather than face that the Government might plunk for taking the big gamble. All I'm telling you is that economics might push the U.S. into pulling the trigger, whereas the Soviets are getting more prosperous all the time. They're as scared of starting anything as we are, and they've more to lose. They've only to go on playing it the way they are to get Europe's cities, ports and industries as going concerns. They'd be plumb crazy to reduce them to heaps of ruins.'

'Then why is it that all these conferences about doing away with nuclear weapons have never got further than nibbling at the problem of preventing an atomic war? If what you say is right surely the Russians should be only too anxious for both sides to scrap everything, then they would have a free field to go on with their peaceful penetration without any risk of the United States suddenly banging off at them?'

'Sure, sure, honey; and they are. They've offered again and again to go the whole way; but they're not such *Dummkopfs* as to agree to half measures. And the West digs its toes in at the idea of packing up the great deterrent altogether, because the Soviets hold the bigger stick where conventional forces are concerned. That's the deadlock, and the Russians would put out the biggest ever red carpet for anyone who would break it for them.'

'It seems an impasse out of which there is no way.'

'Oh, there is a way. I could do it myself if I wanted.'

'You can't mean that,' Mary said with a smile, feeling certain that he was either pulling her leg or making an absurd boast to impress her. 'How could you possibly change the views of all the leading statesmen of the Western Powers?'

'By dropping just one egg in Europe. Vague ideas are one thing; seeing is another. Headlines, radio, eye-witness reports, T.V., documentaries on the flicks. All the horror of an H-bomb bang brought fresh from the scene right into every home in the N.A.T.O. countries. Just think of the pressure there'd be on their Governments. Millions of women blowing their tops, voters of all shades shouting "It mustn't happen here", demonstrations, strikes, threats to Cabinet Ministers. And as I was telling you a while back, democratic Governments aren't free agents. They'd have no option. None at all. They'd be pushed into making a pact with the Soviets to scrap all nuclear weapons and make no more.'

'Really, Wash!' Mary protested. 'It's you who are off the mark this time. Apart from doing such a terrible thing as dropping a bomb out of the blue that would kill or maim countless innocent people, can't you see that in whichever N.A.T.O. country it fell everyone would immediately assume that the Russians had opened hostilities. Within minutes your squadron and everything else we've got would be on the way to Russia; and in no time the Russians would be fighting back. Such an act could only precipitate a general blow-up.'

He gave her an amused look. 'I didn't say drop it in a N.A.T.O. country, honey. I said Europe, and there's still neutrals. Say we put one down in Switzerland, both sides would hold their hands. They'd sit tight, batting their heads who done it, and why.

Meantime, the camera boys would be having a red-letter day; pictures and films would be getting around and the demonstrations starting.'

'I see. Yes; I suppose you're right. But think of the poor Swiss. As far as they are concerned it would be cold-blooded mass murder.'

'Seeing they stayed at home in both world wars they're about due for a token blood letting,' he replied callously. 'Besides, if the egg were dropped among those mountains its effects would be localized. A small town or two, some villages, a few thousand yodellers and tourists would take the rap; but that'd be no price at all to pay if it deprived the East and the West of the power to blow one another to pieces.'

'Looked at that way,' Mary admitted after a moment, 'perhaps there would be a case for martyring several thousand people. After all, hundreds of thousands were massacred by the Nazis with no benefit to anyone. Perhaps if one could definitely save all the great cities of Europe and America, and the millions and millions of people who live in them from a terrible death, it would be justifiable. All the same, to kill men, women and children en-masse like that would be an awful thing to do.

'I've no inhibitions about killing,' he asserted cheerfully. 'And remember, if the two big boys do get to pulling their guns there'll be mighty little left in the world that'll be worth having. Those of us who aren't disintegrated instanter or scheduled to stagger around for a few days, without teeth and our hair dropped out, will be left pretty near where you Anglo-Saxons started. For a generation or two maybe worse; anyway, for a time it's certain to be as simple as dog eat dog.'

Mary sighed. 'What a gloomy picture! And it doesn't seem that your imaginative idea for preventing an atomic war would lead in the long run to a situation that was much better. It would simply open the gate for the Russians to walk in.'

'Sure, but wouldn't that be better than death or going back to nature?'

'I'm not certain that it would.'

'It certainly would for ninety per cent of the folk who make up the population of the Western Powers. The other ten would be for the high jump or Siberia, but that's their funeral.'

'As an Air Force Colonel you'd be among them.'

'Not me, honey. As a servant of the Lord of this World I've

322

an international ticket to the easy life in any country. That would go for you too. The Brothers of the Ram would see to it that little Sister Circe didn't lack for potatoes.'

She gave him a smile. 'Well, if it ever looks like happening, that will be nice to know. You seem to have forgotten one thing, though. This career you're so keen on would be finished; that is, unless you could get yourself taken on in the Soviet Air Force.'

'My career's finished anyhow, I'm on my way out now.' He spoke with such sudden bitterness that she momentarily felt a touch of sympathy for him, and said:

'I'm sorry, Wash. But why? I understood from what you told me that only the very best men were given command of these squadrons of big bombers that are right in the front line and all ready to go.'

'That's so, honey.'

'Then why shouldn't you become a General? Have you blotted your copybook in some way?'

'No, there's not a thing against me on the record. It's just that war-plane flying is finished. The rocket guys are taking over, and fast. They're making no more big bombers, or fighters; the types in service now are the last. In a year or two my beauties will go in the ash can, and I'll be out on my ear.'

'You will still have lots of money.'

'Yeah. But dollars aren't everything. I've ambition; and though I'll have to start again, some way yet I mean to make myself a big shot.'

The following afternoon when he got back from the base there was a letter waiting for him. For some time after he had read it he remained plunged deep in thought, then he said to her:

'You'll recall how I was nattering last night about the U.S.A.A.F. putting me on the pension list come a year or two's time. I've been throwing out lines for a future, and one of them's matured sooner than I thought. From Saturday I'll have to take some leave, on that account.'

Mary hid her sudden elation. It looked from what he said as if in another forty-eight hours she might be freed by him and, even greater blessing, escape the initiation which she so much dreaded. Endeavouring to appear disappointed, she said:

'In that case you won't be able to make me a full witch on Saturday night.'

He gave her a reassuring smile. 'Don't fret yourself, honey.

I don't mean to miss out on the Esbbat. I got to hold that so as to pull down more power to myself for the new deal I'm set on making. Besides, there's the forfeit I've got to ante up for cutting loose on Walpurgis Eve.'

Concealing the blow her hopes had sustained, she asked:

'What form does it take?'

'Human blood,' he replied, and went on with a callousness that appalled her, 'Back in the States there are plenty of coloured folks who'll trade a piccaninny for fifty bucks, and the Lodges in the South sends them up on mail order. But here snatching kids is apt to mean trouble. It'll have to be one of the floosies who hang around the camp. There are scores of them, and I'll rope one in tomorrow night.'

Mary had gone dead white. After a moment she said in a low voice:

'Would you . . . would you please mix me a drink; a . . . a stiff one.'

'Sure, honey.' Levering himself up to his enormous height from the armchair in which he had been lounging, he stepped over to the cocktail cabinet. 'Idea of human sacrifice still gives you the willies, eh?'

'I . . . I'm not used to it yet. Not . . . not being an initiate I've never seen one. But aren't you afraid that the police might trace the girl?'

'That's about as likely as me peddling peanuts on the moon. There's thousands of young dolls go missing in Britain every year. Most of them just quit home because they're fed with handing in their pay packets to their mommas, or because they've got hot pants for some married man. Mighty few of them are ever traced, and if some get in bad with a guy who gives them a passport for the golden shore there's no one to start a hue and cry after him. These teenage harpies who claw the dough outta my boys' wallets aren't local girls either. Leastways, precious few of them. They're East-end bitches down from London; so if there's one less come Sunday morning who's to worry?'

Taking the Bourbon on the Rocks that he handed her, Mary gulped some of it, drew a deep breath, and asked, 'Do the Brotherhood often offer up human sacrifice?'

'There's no fixed rule. One time it's same as now, an adept having to put himself in the clear after a lapse; another it's to celebrate the induction of a new High Priest. Times are when it's

324

done with some special intention—maybe a Brother or Sister wanting a relative to make a quick exit, so they can get their hands on some lolly, or skip a divorce. Then once in a while some Lodge finds its secrets are being betrayed. Soon as the traitor is caught out there's an atonement ceremony in which he or she is the victim. That was the case with the last human whose blood I saw offered up.'

Mary's heart stopped for a second. A sudden paralysis seemed to run through all her limbs. With a great effort she raised the glass and took another quick drink. The strong spirit, hardly yet diluted at all by the ice cubes, seemed to burn in her chest, but it again sent her circulation racing, and enabled her to get out the question, 'How long ago was that?'

'Bit over two months. This guy was a police-spy. Someone tumbled to it that he was taking photographs of the Temple with a mini-camera. Under some pretext old Abaddon gave him deep hypnosis and dredged him clean, then sent him off to collect all the notes he had taken. There was enough dynamite in them to have blown the whole Lodge sky high. Seems he was only waiting for info' about when the Great Ram meant to officiate there again to fix for the place to be raided. Leastways, that's the story as Abaddon gave it to me. I was only in on the ritual killing.'

Wash was mixing himself a Vodka Martini and had his back to Mary, so while he was talking he did not see the horror in her eyes. She knew that he must be speaking of Teddy. The date tallied so it could be no one else. When she had least expected it she had reached the end of her self-imposed quest. It was possible that Ratnadatta might only have played the jackal, and made off with the victim's shoes, but she was now hearing about his murder from a man who had actually witnessed it. She heard her voice, as if coming from a great distance, say, 'What did they do to him?'

'Oh, there's a special drill for dealing with initiates who become apostates. Assumption is they've gone back to the Christian heresy; so we give 'em the treatment same as J.C. got for getting up against Our Lord Satan in Palestine. Only difference is we have to cut their throats so the blood'll run, and for convenience sake we crucify them upside down.'

Mary set down her glass, lurched to her feet and, with a strangled sob, ran from the room.

Half an hour later she returned to find him working at his

desk. Looking up, he said casually, 'Bit strong meat for you, eh, honey? But you asked for it, and that was just as well. If you're going to be a good witch you've got to get acquainted with what goes on, and be prepared to stand in at any sort of ceremony. Play the radio now if you want, but set it on a musical programme. I can't abide canned voices while I'm working.'

In due course he bulldozed his way through the usual abundant evening meal, washing it down with copious draughts of cider laced with calvados, which seemed to have no effect upon him. Ghastly pictures flickering about in Mary's mind robbed her of all appetite, but she made a game pretence of eating; and his mind was obviously on other things, as he made no comment.

Afterwards, he returned to work and she put on some gramophone records. About ten o'clock he broke off to mix himself a long drink, and said: 'You get up to bed any time you feel that way, honey. If I'm to take leave from Saturday I've a whole heap of things need clearing up, so I'll be at it here for hours yet.'

Gladly she accepted the suggestion and cried herself to sleep. She woke when he came up but to her immense relief he did not disturb her, and soon after he had settled down she drifted off again.

Next morning her mind was more than ever harassed by fears, half-formed plans and nervous speculations. Somehow, while she had the chance, she must get from him a full account of Teddy's murder, so that details about those who had taken part in it could be made to stick.

Then, what of her future? How could she find some means of escaping this loathsome initiation ceremony? And what did he intend to do with her after Saturday? Presumably he would take her to London with him; but did he mean to let her go when they got there? She had not dared to ask him. At least if it was his intention to retain her as his mistress during his leave, she would stand a better chance of escaping from him after they had left the house.

Last, but by no means least, there was this new development of the human sacrifice he intended to make. The victim was to be chosen by chance from the scores of vicious little sluts who battened like lice on the well-paid American servicemen. But however unprincipled and depraved she might be she had a right to her life. How could this unknown be saved from the awful end that menaced her?

326

21

Death of a woman unknown

WHILE Wash had his shower and dressed, Mary continued to lie between the black satin sheets, but unconscious of their subtle caress as she cudgelled her wits to think of an answer to the nerve-shattering problems which faced her. In due course he went off to his duties and she lay there for another hour, but now that she was tied to the house by invisible bonds she could think of no way in which she could either help herself or prevent Wash from carrying out his ghastly plan to ensnare some wretched girl and offer her up as a sacrifice.

At length she got up, and it was while she was dressing that her glance happened to fall on the square box containing the machine with which Wash had taken a record of her screams when torturing her on the Monday afternoon. He had made no use of this ingenious toy since, and it was still where he had set it down on a chair that was half concealed by the side of the big olivewood wardrobe.

Lifting its lid she experimented cautiously with its switches, again playing back the first part of that horrifying scene, then recording and playing back a few bars of a tune that she hummed softly while standing beside it; and she found that it was quite easy to work.

The idea had come to her that if she could get Wash talking again about Teddy's murder within sound range of the machine while it was working, it would record his own guilt and perhaps that of others. If she could succeed in that, with luck she would find a chance to remove the spool of tape and take it with her when they left for London. Even if she had to leave it in the house, once she had got free of him she might still be able to return and retrieve it later. Having adjusted the tape to 'ready' she put the machine under her side of the big bed, so that she had only to reach a hand down to the switch to set it in motion.

All the same, so racked was she by thoughts of the horrors that Wash was planning to carry out that, after lunch that day she made another attempt to escape. It had occurred to her that if she bandaged her eyes that might enable her to pass the invisible barrier. Going to the door at the back of the house that led to the garden, she opened it, lowered the edge of a thick silk scarf that she had draped over her head, and willed herself to walk forward.

It was no good. She could lift each of her feet from the ground, but she positively could not thrust either of them out over the doorstep. Perhaps foolishly, but in desperation, she conceived the idea that since she could not walk out she might be able to crawl out. Removing the scarf she went down on her hands and knees. But her strivings in that position proved equally futile. To add to her distress and also fill her with confusion, while she was still crouching on the mat a voice behind her said:

'You bin lost something, missy?'

Jerking round her head she saw that Jim had come up unheard behind her and was regarding her with a puzzled grin.

'Yes,' she replied, seizing on the excuse to explain being there on her knees; 'a little pearl button off my blouse.'

For some minutes they both hunted for the button, but of course without result. Then she told Jim that it didn't matter, and retired defeated to the sitting-room.

Wash returned at his usual hour, but at once sat down to his desk and almost ignored her until after dinner. Then he told her that he was going out and might not be back until very late, so she should not wait up for him.

Although, with a slightly sinking feeling, she already guessed, she asked him where he was going, and he said: 'I'll be stooging around in my car till I come on a judy that's padding the hoof on her lonesome with no one in sight. Then, after we've had a short session in the bushes, I'll offer her a lift home. Time I got her in the car she'll have as good as had it. I'll put her in a deep sleep, bring her back here, lock her in the cellar and keep her there on ice till tomorrow night.'

There was nothing Mary could say or do which would have deflected him from his intention; so, maintaining the rôle to which she was all the time forcing herself, she begged him not to be later than he could help, and waved him away on his grim mission.

He got back at about two o'clock in the morning and, flicking all the lights on in the bedroom, strode into it in a furious temper. Mary, blinking and still half asleep, roused herself to listen to the account he gave of his venture and pretend sympathy with him over the ill-luck which had brought it to ruin.

Apparently, without being observed by anyone, he had picked up a girl who had been drinking and necking with some of his airmen. He had driven her a short distance to a wood and a little way into it, as before taking her back to the house he had wanted to make certain that she would suit his purpose. When picking her up he had realized that she had had a skinful of whiskey and when they got out of the car she had been unsteady on her feet, but not too tight to make sense.

The talk he had had with her had satisfied him that she could not have suited him better. She was a North-country girl who had run away to London and had worked the streets round the Elephant and Castle for a few months. Then, tempted by stories of the big money to be made in the neighbourhood of the American bases, she had come to Cambridge. But she had not been in the district long and the previous week her landlady had thrown her out for taking a man up to her room. Since then she had been sharing a caravan with an out-of-work that she had met in a pub, who was glad enough to give her sleeping space for a share of her earnings. From this it was clear that, like many more of her kind, if she was never seen again not a soul in the world was going to ask what had become of her.

As they got up from the bank on which they had been sitting, she said she must leave him for a minute, and went off deeper in among the trees. Two minutes later he heard a cry, then silence. A dozen yards away he found her. The drink she had taken had caused her to stumble and fall while on her way back to him. She had hit her temple on a tree stump and was stone dead.

He realized at once that if he left her body there it would be found, and it was possible that another couple necking in the darkness, or perhaps a poacher, had seen them together. Both his car and himself, owing to his unusual height, might easily lead to his being identified. The only way to make sure of not being connected with her death was to dispose of her body. Putting it in the car, he had driven some miles to a ruined Abbey in which his Lodge held its meetings. There was a deep well there down which he had intended to throw it after having offered her up as a sacrifice; to his fury her unexpected death compelled him to do so twenty-four hours earlier. And by the time he had done that it was too late for him to have any hope of finding a substitute.

Harrowed as Mary was by this awful story, it at least aroused in her new hope that a merciful Providence intended sparing her the black hour with which she was threatened on the following night; and she said: 'As you won't be able to make a sacrifice I suppose my initiation will have to be put off.'

'Yeah,' he grunted, 'I'll have to hold the Esbbat just the same; but you'll remain here. I'll pick you up afterwards. Now for some shut-eye. Praise be, I've not got to show up at my office tomorrow morning, so I told Jim earlier to bring us up breakfast at eight o'clock.'

Immensely relieved, and much comforted by the thought that by Sunday she would be back in London, Mary drifted off to sleep.

While they were breakfasting in the morning she put into operation her plan for getting him to incriminate himself on the tape recorder. Having put a hand down beside the bed while he was not looking, and switched it on, she said:

'I behaved very stupidly yesterday when you were telling me about human sacrifices. If I'm to be a really good witch I ought to prepare myself to witness such ceremonies. I'd like you to tell me exactly what takes place.'

Sleep had restored Wash to his normal good humour, so he gave a chuckle and replied, 'Good for you, honey. It'll be a pleasure to put you wise.' Then with the same air of detachment he might have used had he been a doctor describing a series of surgical operations, he went on.

'You'll have heard of Black Masses. Well, all human sacrifices take that form; only difference being that a genuine Black Mass in Christian countries has to be performed by an unfrocked priest. I don't reckon that adds up to much, though. There's ritual killings by the Mau Mau, and plenty other Africans, by Chinese, Indians, Patagonians, and all sorts. All of them offer up the blood to Our Lord Satan, and that's what counts. The drill varies, though, according to the type of victim that's being offered up. When it's a kid, then a woman stretches herself out starko on the altar. If I'd been able to snatch one in these parts I'd have used you for that rôle.'

Mary had finished her breakfast and was lying back in bed, so she was able to shut her eyes and conceal her shudder as he continued placidly:

'The High Priest intones the incantation, and states the intention. That's the event the sacrifice is ante-d up to bring about: maybe for someone's death, to get a verdict in a law case, or get elected to some post that means power or a lot of dough. Then the kid is laid on the woman, its throat is slit, and all and sundry take a drop of the blood with the middle finger of their left hand. When it's a dame that's to take the rap, she's bound and laid on the altar. The High Priest says his piece, then cuts her throat.'

Mary felt that she could bear to hear no more, but in blissful ignorance of her feelings he proceeded. 'If it's to be curtains for a Brother or Sister who's double-crossed the Brotherhood it's like I told you yesterday. Assumption is they've relapsed to Christian; so they're given the treatment head down – hung from an inverted cross.'

Glancing down at her he noticed how pale she was and said: 'Bit much for you, honey? Sorry about that, but you asked for it, and you've got to know about these things sometime.'

Steeling herself to go through with her plan, she muttered, 'Yes . . . Yes . . . of course I have. Go on, tell me about that police-spy that you saw sacrificed two months ago. Give me the details. I can take it.'

He told her then how Teddy had been murdered. It had been only Wash's second visit to the Temple at Cremorne; so he had played no part in it but had been one of about a score of on-lookers. Ratnadatta and three Brothers whose Satanic names were Roger Bacon, Albertus Magnus and Gilles de Rais had trussed the victim up. Abaddon had cut his throat and Pope Honorius had caught the blood in a chalice.

At the price of searing her mind with nightmare pictures that she would never be able to forget, Mary had got what she wanted. For a few minutes she felt so sick that she dared not move, then she slid her hand down, switched off the tape recorder, and said:

'Thanks, Wash. I'll know now what to expect, and be better

331

able to stand up to it. I can't help shuddering, though, at the thought of anyone suffering such a terrible death.'

To her surprise he volunteered her a crumb of consolation.

'Oh, it's not all that bad as a way to die. This guy was brought out from under deep hypnosis no more than ten minutes before he was dead meat. What's that against a medico wising you up to it that you've got incurable cancer, or being tortured till your heart gives out, way the Japs played it on some of our boys they captured in the Pacific war?'

When he had dressed and gone downstairs she switched on the machine again and in a low voice spoke into it. With the possibility now in mind that she might not be able to deliver it herself, but might come across someone she could trust to post it, or leave it with, she gave her name and such particulars as she could about Wash's activities, together with a brief account of how she had become associated with him. She added that anyone into whose possession the spool came should send it to Colonel Verney, care of the Special Branch, New Scotland Yard. Then, with trembling fingers, she cut off the used portion of the tape, concealed the little roll it made in a small box that had held a bottle of nail varnish, put it in her handbag, and replaced the machine on the chair where it had been left from Monday to Friday.

It was as well she did, for later in the day Wash went up to fetch it to be packed with numerous other things he was taking on leave with him. When he said he was going up for it she almost fainted with terror. It seemed certain that he would look inside the box, notice that part of the tape had been cut off, and with his highly developed psychic sense guess what it had been used for. If that happened she knew that he would kill her – that there would after all be a human sacrifice that night, and she would be the victim.

With her heart in her mouth she waited for his return. He seemed to be away for an eternity. At last he reappeared. She could hardly believe it when she saw that his great hook-nosed face was as tranquil as ever and, after he had bellowed for Jim, saw him hand the machine unopened over to the coloured boy.

He had said nothing to her about where he meant them to stay while in London or why, instead of waiting until the Sunday, he intended to drive up there after the Esbbat, which meant that they would arrive there in the early hours of the morning. And she had not liked to ask him about his plans, from fear that he

332

might suspect her intention of trying to get away from him. She could only assume that he was anxious to lose not an hour in opening his business negotiations, and that perhaps the people concerned were also Satanists who had a house to which he meant to take her. All she knew for certain was that he had paid his boys a fortnight's wages; so presumably that was the period of leave he had obtained from his General.

In the afternoon, while she was doing her own packing in a big suitcase with which he had provided her, he went off to the airfield for an hour, then on his return he came upstairs and said:

'We'll be awake a good part of the night, so I've ordered additional chow for having with our coffee round five o'clock. After, we'll catch a few hours' shut-eye. Then come eleven we'll eat again. At half-after I've a guest arriving who'll be going with me to the Esbbat. The Lodge I run here is no big show like Cremorne – just a coven of thirteen so as initiates on the Station can keep their hand in. Soon as I've done the ritual I can quit; so I'll be back here to pick you up round half-after-one. And you'll be ready on the dot. I'm working to a time schedule; so if you've left anything upstairs that'll be just too bad. You'll leave without it.'

The rest of the day went in accordance with these arrangements, up till eleven o'clock. They were in the big lounge waiting for Jim to announce that their supper was ready. Suddenly the door to the hall was thrown open and, instead of Jim, Iziah thrust his head in. A little breathlessly, his white eyeballs rolling in his black face, he blurted out,

'I'se copt a snooper, boss. I were goin' out to the garage to check on all bein' dandy with the automobile, when I spots him. He were paddin' around peepin' in the winders. Fortunate, I had my gumshoes on. I sneaked up on him and give him the K.O. from behind. He were packing a rod, too, boss; but I'se took it off him. Jim and Buster got him in the kitchen. What'll you want we do with him?'

'Good work, Iziah, good work,' smiled his master. 'Bring the bum in, so I can run my eye over him.'

Two minutes later all three coloured boys hustled in a short broad tousled figure, still only partly conscious, as was evident from the fact that his chin was on his chest and his head of short dark curls stuck forward rolling slightly. Yet the moment he appeared in the doorway Mary realized that it was Barney.

For his having been caught while surreptitiously reconnoitring the house there could be only one explanation. Somehow he had learned that she had been carried off to it and had come there to rescue her. During the past week she had thought many harsh thoughts about him. This wiped them all out in an instant. But he had bungled it. That was no fault of his. How could anyone foresee that a garage hand would suddenly emerge from a house at eleven o'clock at night to make sure that a car was in perfect running order? Nevertheless, he had been caught. And Colonel Hendrik G. Washington was not the sort of man who would take lightly being spied upon. Certain of his activities were definitely of such a kind that he would go to any lengths to prevent their discovery.

Mary felt certain that the giant American would not hand Barney over to the police. It was much more likely that he would have the boys give him a terrible beating, then throw him out – more likely still that Wash would not rest content until he learned what had led Barney to act the spy, and use torture on him to find out.

Frantically she searched her mind for some way to save Barney from the results of his ill-starred attempt to come to her help. Suddenly a possible though dangerous line occurred to her. If it did not come off, if Barney failed to pick up her lead, or made a mess of things while trying to follow it up, they would both pay a price that she did not allow herself to contemplate. But there was no other way of attempting to explain his presence. Swallowing hard, she forced a smile and exclaimed,

'What in the world are you doing here?' Then, swinging round on Wash, she cried with a laugh, 'This is a boy-friend of mine; and I've got it. As I've been missing from my flat for a week he must have become worried about me. How lovely! Learning that you'd carried me off he must have come here to play the Knight Errant and rescue me.'

The big American frowned. 'How come he learned it was me who took you from – from you know where – and that I'd brought you this place?'

'From Ratnadatta, of course,' she replied quickly. 'Our visitor is a neophyte. He was attending Mrs. Wardeel's evenings at the same time as myself. That blow you hit Ratnadatta couldn't have broken his neck, and I expect he was only too glad of a chance to . . .'

'Couldn't be,' Wash cut in. 'Ratnadatta doesn't know my real name or where I am stationed.'

Barney was still groggy, but his wits were coming back to him and he had taken in every word Mary had said. Seizing the life-line she had thrown him, he said, a trifle thickly,

'Oh yes he does. And Margot's right. Your blow didn't kill him; but he's got a bandage as thick as a board round his neck. I didn't know how to get hold of him till tonight; but I was with him not much over an hour and a half ago. He's got it in for you. He ferreted out particulars about you from the secret list, and came down here yesterday himself to make a recce. Of course he hadn't got the guts to come in and have a crack at you, but he jumped at giving me the chance to do it for him.'

With a nod of thanks to the boys, their master told them to release their prisoner and get back to the kitchen. Standing up, he towered over Barney, and said with a wide smile, 'Well, you've made it, buddy. Now you are here I'm invitin' you to take a crack at me.'

'No.' Barney declined the honour with a slightly sheepish grin. 'But as Margot went off without leaving any sort of message you can't blame me for having been anxious about her.'

'I've nothing against that, son,' Wash threw out generously. 'Even if you have been wasting your time; shows your good taste. As you're a neophyte you'll no doubt have chosen your Satanic name. Mine's Twisting Snake; what's yours?'

That was a facer. Barney had no idea how to reply, but Mary had had more time to become knowledgeable about the history of the Black Art, so she swiftly stepped into the breach and said to Wash, 'I'm sorry; I ought to have introduced him. He is taking the name of Doctor Dee.'

'After the ace-high Elizabethan wizard, eh?' The American held out his huge hand. 'Glad to be acquainted, Doc.! Put it there. You've driven quite a way already tonight. Right now we were about to sit down to supper. Reckon you'd better join us and stoke up a little 'fore you hit the trail back.'

Feeling that to accept was the natural, and therefore least dangerous, line to take, Barney, who, apart from a headache, had now fully recovered, replied, 'Thanks, that's very kind of you. I'd like to.'

'You're welcome,' said his host, and led the way through the door at the far end of the room, which gave directly on to the smaller dining-room, where Jim was waiting for the signal to serve supper.

Mary was aghast at Barney's having accepted. That they had avoided disaster even for so short a time seemed to her a miracle. Silently she cursed him for a fool for not having said that he meant to stay the night in Cambridge, apologize for his intrusion and get out while the going was good. She thanked her stars now that she had not said that he was an initiate. If she had, knowing next to nothing of the Satanic cult he could never have got by. As a neophyte he would not be expected to know more than the rudiments, but she feared that he would never be able to sustain even that rôle for half an hour in conversation with such a penetrating mind as Wash possessed.

Being very far from a fool, Barney was fully conscious of that danger. In consequence, as soon as they were seated he quickly got off the subject of the occult and led his host into a discussion about the respective prospects of the Republicans and the Democrats in the forthcoming elections in the United States.

The topic served for ten minutes, and the gulf between the British and American methods of democratic government served for another ten; but then Wash asked Barney who had sponsored him as a neophyte and when. Barney replied to the first question, 'Ratnadatta', which was safe enough, but he had to take a chance on the second and, having swiftly worked back the dates to a suitable Saturday, said: 'The 9th of March.'

That was the night that Ratnadatta had given Mary dinner, then taken her on for her first visit to the Temple. And that night the giant American had been there. He said he felt sure he had, but had no recollection of a neophyte resembling Barney having been introduced. He admitted that his memory might have let him down about the date, but that such lapses did not often occur with him. Then he asked Barney if it had been Abaddon or the Great Ram who had cut the penitent's clothing off from him.

For Mary and Barney it was a case of being saved by the gong, for at that very minute Jim came in to tell his master that the visitor he was expecting had arrived and had been shown into the sitting-room.

Without waiting for an answer to the question he had just asked, Wash came quickly to his feet and said: 'Both of you may chalk this up as one of your lucky nights. The Great Ram is here, and I'll make you known to him. Quit eating now and come with me.'

Obediently they left the remains of the *foie gras* and toast with which they had been finishing their supper, and followed him back into the sitting-room.

Standing in front of the fireplace was a tallish slim figure. On the only previous occasion when Mary had seen the Great Ram he had been wearing his big curly-horned mask, but she recognized his cruel, beautifully curved mouth and strong, deeply dimpled chin. Owing to his extraordinary resemblance to Otto, Barney, who had never seen him before, recognized him as Lothar.

Wash took a couple of strides forward and said: 'Exalted One, it's great to have you with us. I've two neophytes here, Circe and Doctor Dee. They'd be mighty pleased to have your blessing.'

Mary and Barney were standing side by side. She touched his hand with hers, praying that he would have the sense to follow her lead; then she went down on one knee, and taking the slim, strong left hand that the Great Ram extended to her, she kissed the splendid blood-red ruby of the ring that he wore on it.

Barney had given one quick look at the man's eyes. He knew then that he was in the presence of something which he could not contend against; so, dropping on one knee, he followed Mary's example.

As they touched the stone in the ring with their lips it felt as cold as an ice cube and, when they rose to stand before the Great Ram, both of them were conscious of a chill that emanated from him which gave them the sort of sensation they would have had from standing in front of an open deep freeze. As he looked at them his glance, too, was icy. Without addressing a word to them, he glanced at Wash and said: 'I wish to speak to you alone.'

The American signed to the other two to return to the dining-room. Gladly they did so. As the door closed behind them Mary's urge to thank Barney for having made an attempt to rescue her was overridden by an instinctive feeling that his life hung by a thread; that even if a second were wasted he might lose it. Without an instant's hesitation she pointed to the curtains drawn across a window and said:

'You were crazy to come here! Get out! That way! That way! But one moment, take this with you.' Diving her hand into her bag she drew out the little nail varnish carton containing the precious recording tape, and thrust it at him.

Automatically he took it, pushed it into the pocket of his jacket, and in a puzzled voice replied, 'But I came to get you! Go on! You go first. I'll follow.'

'No, no!' She shook her head. 'I'm in no danger, but you are. He suspects you. If we had sat here at supper another minute he'd have caught you out.'

'I'm not going without you,' he retorted doggedly.

Only too willingly she would have made a break for it with him, but she knew that she could not. She knew without further experiment that she was still under the hypnotic command of her kidnapper, and that during his pleasure she was definitely chained to the house.

'I can't,' she said. 'It is not possible. I've got to stay.'

His brown eyes suddenly hardened. 'There's no question of you're having got to. You mean you want to.'

'No, no!' She cried in extreme agitation. 'It's not that. But I'm more or less safe here; and you are not. For God's sake stop arguing and go!'

'You are the mistress of this American, aren't you?' He shot at her.

'Of course I am,' she snapped back. 'Does he look like a village curate or an inmate of an old folk's home?'

'I guessed as much during supper, when he kept on calling you "honey",' Barney declared bitterly.

'Oh, God help me!' Mary wailed. 'What does it matter! Open that window. Get out and run for it while you still have the chance.'

'And leave you here, eh?' For what now seemed weeks to Barney his mind had been obsessed with the one idea of getting her out of the clutches of the Satanists, at whose hands he had imagined her to be suffering every kind of distress and degradation. No matter what she might have done in the past, it was the woman he had come to know and love during the past two months that counted. And now he had come upon her as beautiful as ever, untroubled by fears and displaying a cheerful affection for this giant American Colonel. Her frank admission that she had become the man's mistress was the last straw. Final disillusion caused his eyes to go black with anger and he added furiously,

'All right then! Stay here if you want to! Stay and wallow with that great hog! Once a whore always a whore; and now I know why you became one.'

Mary's eyes went as round as marbles; her mouth fell open; she gave a gasp. 'What . . . what the hell d'you mean?'

'What I say,' he snapped. 'Your name's not Margot but Mary. I know all about you and the life you led before you married.'

When he said 'all' she thought he meant all. Never in her wildest dreams had she visualized a dénouement like this. She had believed that she knew all about his past while he knew nothing of hers. But now the cat *was* out of the bag. Hands on hips, her blue eyes shooting sparks, she let him have it.

'All right! I was a whore! And who made me one? Who put me in the family way and left me in the lurch? Who went gaily off to America leaving the poor kid that I was to borrow the money for the illegal; so that for months afterwards I had to sell myself to pay it back? Who took little Mary McCreedy's virginity and left her at six in the morning with the fine words, "See you again soon, sweetheart", then without a thought that he might have got her into trouble, or a word of good-bye, took himself off to the United States? Who but that great Irish gentleman, Mister Barney Sullivan. The dirty rotten lecherous cad who now, to lead girls easier up the garden path, pretends to have property in Kenya and has the nerve to tell them he is a lord.'

Barney's eyes had gone as round as Mary's before she started to storm at him. From the moment he had come face to face with her on Mrs. Wardeel's doorstep he had had a vague feeling that they had met somewhere before. But in five years she had altered from an unsophisticated slip of a girl to a fine self-possessed woman, and her hair being dark instead of fair had accentuated the difference. It was over a week now since she had had a chance to treat it with the dye she used, and as he stared at her he saw that, although she still had the appearance of a brunette, the quarter-of-an-inch of hair nearest to her scalp was golden.

Stunned by this revelation that she was the little cabaret girl who long ago in Dublin had exercised a fascination over him for a few weeks before he had come into his title and left Ireland for good, he was temporarily at a loss for words. Before he could collect himself the door opened. The huge American stood framed in it. He was smiling at them, and said:

'Young feller, this is your lucky day. It is the prerogative of our Exalted Master, the Great Ram, that he can make initiates any-when, by using one drop of his own sacred blood. That eliminates the necessity for a sacrifice, and he's consented to admit you two

339

to the Brotherhood tonight. Come on now. We've no time to lose. It's well past half-after eleven. We must be on our way to the Esbbat.'

Still dazed by the explosion of their personal relations, yet unable to exchange another word upon them, Mary and Barney followed the hook-nosed giant out into the hall. The front door was open. The Great Ram was already seated at the wheel of a large car outside it. Wash told Barney to get in beside him.

Barney hesitated only a second. The man at the wheel was Lothar. All else apart, it was his duty, now he had so unexpectedly got on to him, to stick with him, and let C.B. know their whereabouts at the first possible opportunity.

Wash's car was drawn up in front of Lothar's. Iziah was standing by it. Jim had picked up the suitcase containing Mary's things, which had been standing ready in the hall. Carrying it out, he added it to the pile of luggage already in the back of the car. Having helped Mary on with her coat, Wash took her by the arm. Her mind was in such a turmoil that she did not even think of the invisible barrier which had for days prevented her leaving the house. His leading her out automatically nullified it. He opened the door of the car and she got in beside him. The engine purred and the big car slid away down the drive. As it turned into the road he said:

'I'm still all of a dither, honey. It was a mighty fine break the Great Ram coming here tonight. You've been had for a sucker. The Exalted One's got a no-good brother. He overlooks him from time to time. Last week-end, some place down in Wales, he saw this guy Doctor Dee in cahoots with his brother and a bunch of R.A.F. security boys. The Doc is another police-spy. But it pans out good. We sold him the story about your both being initiated. You're going to be initiated alright; but he's to be the sacrifice that'll both pay my forfeit and provide the blood to baptize you.'

22

In the ruined abbey

For a moment Mary's heart stopped beating. Her mind reeled as it grasped the appalling situation which had so suddenly developed.

Now for the hundredth time she cursed her folly in not having let sleeping dogs lie. The early stages of her investigation had held for her only a spice of danger sufficient to intrigue, and her first successes with Ratnadatta had strengthened her resolution to ignore the warnings she had been given – until Barney had extracted a promise from her that she would have nothing more to do with the Satanists. But by then, through having become a neophyte, she had already forged a fatal link with them, and the sight of Teddy's shoes on Ratnadatta's feet had proved her undoing.

From that night, as a result of her own actions, she had become the plaything of Evil and exposed to one peril after another. That she had, after all, succeeded in securing concrete evidence against her husband's murderers was now small comfort. If these fiends with whom she had consorted dealt with Barney as they had with Teddy his death would lie at her door.

As her heart suddenly began to beat again she drew a sharp, rasping breath.

'Surprised you, eh, honey?' Wash commented grimly. 'Surprised me too, seein' you claimed to be well acquainted with this Doctor Dee. Tell what you know of him.'

His tone implied no suspicion of her, only curiosity; but she knew that she must exercise the greatest caution about every word she said. In a low voice she murmured,

'There's not much I can tell you. I believed him to be one of us and it's a nasty shock to hear that he's not.'

'Give, honey, give.' Wash's voice had suddenly become impatient. 'He's your boy friend, and came to these parts set on trying to snatch you off me. Fellers don't go that far unless they and the dame are pretty close to one another.'

Mary's mind was still a whirl of misery, but she managed to co-ordinate her thoughts sufficiently to reply. 'He is in love with me, of course; but he's never been my boy friend in the sense you mean. I met him only a few weeks ago at Mrs. Wardeel's. She is a woman who holds evenings for dabblers in the occult. Ratnadatta always goes to them to pick up anyone there who looks a likely convert to the True Faith. He was introduced to me as Lord Larne and . . .'

'Lord Larne,' Wash interrupted. 'He must have plenty gall to have taken a title for his front.'

Instantly Mary covered up for Barney by asserting, 'It wasn't a front. He is Lord Larne. No one's ever questioned that. Anyway, after some of the meetings he walked home with me. Then he asked me out to dine and dance, and twice I've given him supper at my flat. He was an amusing companion and we had the common interest that we both hoped to become initiates. We had started an *affaire*, and if things hadn't gone as they did the night you carried me off I expect that in due course he and I would have become lovers. His having come after me here shows only that he must have fallen harder for me than I thought.'

'So that's your side of it. Maybe, though, it's not hot pants that brought him here. Seeing he's a cop it's on the cards that he's been stringing you along for what he could get out of you, and followed your trail on a hunch that you'd give him the dope about what goes on in these parts.'

'Perhaps,' Mary admitted; and for a moment her misery was rendered even more intense by the thought that possibly that might be the truth. She had hardly yet had time to assimilate the idea that Barney was some sort of detective. If he was, that explained many things. On the assumption that he was a playboy whose time was his own, she had bitterly resented what she had believed to be his lies about his Kenya travel agency arrangements interfering with their meetings; but that, she realized now, could have been cover for periods when he had to perform certain duties. It also excused his taking a title as a pseudonym, as doing

342

so would have made him more readily acceptable at Mrs. Wardeel's. It even made it probable that he had not deliberately let her down the previous week-end to go off with some other woman. As against that there did seem to be a possibility that from the very beginning he had been making use of her only because she had got in with Ratnadatta before he had, and had succeeded in penetrating the Satanic circle at Cremorne.

After only the briefest consideration Mary thrust that last idea aside. Had there been any foundation for it Barney would have urged her to go through with her initiation, then pumped her about what had taken place. As it was he had used his utmost endeavours to persuade her to have no more to do with the Satanists. So if he was a detective he had put her safety before his duty as an investigator. At this thought, in spite of the harsh words with which they had parted, her heart both warmed towards him and was wrung afresh with terrible visions of what lay in store for him.

Virtually a prisoner as she was, she could think of no way in which she could save him or help him to escape, until Wash remarked, 'There's times when you British can be mighty sly. Who'd have thought that for special missions Scotland Yard would have kept on its pay-roll a real live Lord?'

Seizing the opening given her, Mary said quickly, 'I can't believe they do. There's a mistake somewhere. There must be. This fellow is Lord Larne all right. If he had been a fake someone at Mrs. Wardeel's would have been certain to have found him out and exposed him. He is an Irish Earl and only on a visit to England. He has estates in Kenya and has lived there most of his life, so he can't possibly be a member of the British Police Force. The Great Ram must have mistaken him for someone else.'

Wash gave an ugly laugh. 'The Great Ram doesn't make mistakes, honey. Could be you're right about his coming from Kenya. If so, his tie-up with the police here is only temporary. But if the Great Ram says he's a spy, a spy he is. Had we the time we'd put him under hypnosis and get details about his assignment. As things are tonight we're working on too tight a schedule. Just have to bump him and get on with our own business.'

'You can't!' Mary cried in protest. 'You can't. Not without giving him some form of trial. At least you must give him a chance to show that this is all a terrible mistake.'

'Having liked the guy it's natural you should see things that

343

way.' Wash put his big hand on her knee and gave it a friendly squeeze. 'I guess, too, maybe you'd been countin' on him making you his Duchess or something; so him turning out a rat is a bad break for you. Still, none of us can expect the little old ivories to roll as we want all the time, and now you're my squaw I'll see you lack for nothing. At this point, though, I'll warn. When your Lord Larne is about to get his, no throwing a scene. The Great Ram wouldn't take that kindly, and it might make things mighty awkward for us both.'

For a few minutes Mary remained silent while the car sped on through the dark night, then she asked, 'Where are we going?'

'To the ruined Abbey I was telling you of last night. Place where I dumped the body of that floosie down the well.'

Mary shuddered. 'To . . . to hold a Sabbat in such a place must be very different from holding one in the Temple at Cremorne.'

'They've one thing in common: altars once used for Christian rites. That's a must in Christian countries. Leastways, they give ten times the potency to the conjurations of a priest of Our Lord Satan.'

'I see. But after the ceremony? Surely it's too cold and uncomfortable for anyone to enjoy feasting, and that sort of thing, in an old ruin?'

He laughed. 'You'll not find it cold, honey. To alter temperature within a radius of a hundred yards is a simple magic. I create a fog belt round the ruin as a precaution against passing casuals seeing our lights from the road and getting a mind to snoop. Then I call off the rain – if need be – and ante-up the heat inside the magic circle to a degree that's pleasant.'

Having witnessed the Great Ram perform more astonishing miracles, Mary accepted without question Wash's claim to control local weather conditions by magic, but she said, 'All the same, unless you can turn slabs of stone into divans, and the hard ground into a carpet, there can't be much fun in holding an orgy there.'

'We don't; not in the ruin. I've rented a house not far off that's got all the etceteras. Once a month we adjourn there after the ceremony. There's no women initiates in this little Lodge I've founded for my boys. I get out from Cambridge a picked bunch of dolls for them to hit it up with. The dolls are not wise to what goes on beforehand in the Abbey. They're just invited to a party where there'll be prizes for the hottest momma, and paid off in the morning.'

344

'Shall we be going there to-night?'

'No. We've only to do the rituals, perform the sacrifice and initiate you; then we beat it just as fast as we can.'

'Does that mean that I'll have to . . . to do my Temple Service in the ruin?'

'Yeah. You'll have to take it on the altar stone, honey. And for once in my life I'll be jealous. You've sure got under my skin. I'll just hate the others even eyeing you on the stone, let alone what'll follow.'

'I . . . Wash; listen!' she burst out. 'I'm going to hate it, too, now I know you feel like that about me. And as long as you do I'd be content to remain a neophyte. You can give me everything I want without my becoming a witch. Let's postpone my initiation. You can drop me somewhere before we get to the Abbey and I'll wait on the roadside until you are through with your rituals and can pick me up again.'

With her pulses racing she waited breathlessly for his reply. If he agreed, not only would she escape the dreaded ordeal of initiation but, infinitely more important, she would have a chance to get to a telephone and bring the police on the scene before they could murder Barney.

'That's mighty handsome of you, honey,' he said softly. 'You must care quite a lot about old Wash to offer to forgo this chance to acquire power, so as to spare him the sight of you playing the part of a push-over. I'd give a packet to be able to take you up on your offer.'

'But you can! Why shouldn't you?'

He shook his head. 'No dice, honey. I could have if the Great Ram wasn't in on this party. But he is; and he's offered to initiate you himself. That's one hell of an honour. To turn it down just isn't possible; and the initiation wouldn't make sense unless you do your stuff in the Creation rite. If you tried to stall now he'd maybe think it was because you couldn't take our giving Doctor Dee the works, and meant to apostasize. Then he'd send out a curse that would blast you where you stood.'

With a sigh Mary lay back and closed her eyes. Her brief hope had been dashed and it now seemed that nothing short of a miracle could save Barney's life. Silently but fervently she began to pray to the Holy Virgin to intercede for him.

Barney's thoughts, meanwhile, were almost equally chaotic. Being completely unaware of the peril which threatened to bring

345

his existence to an abrupt termination in the very near future, the idea of trying to get away from his sinister companion never entered his mind; it was filled with a jumble of speculations which shuttled swiftly to and fro between the man beside him and Mary.

To him it seemed a marvellous piece of luck that while seeking for Mary down here in the country he should have stumbled on Lothar. Although an Irishman, Barney had the quality of an English bulldog and, having made contact with the Satanist whom his chief was so anxious to lay by the heels, nothing could have induced him to let go. To him it was now only a question of how best to secure Lothar's arrest. Yet he found it exceedingly difficult to concentrate on the problem because Mary's enraged face and furious denunciation of him persistently rose up in his mind.

The revelation that she was the Mary McCreedy of his salad days had left him temporarily stunned. He could not think now how he had failed to recognize her; she had made it clear enough that she had recognized him. But why had she not revealed the fact, and given him a chance to explain?

He wondered then, a shade uneasily, what explanation he could have given, except that on coming into his title his uncle had insisted on his changing his whole way of life. But evidently she believed that he had invented his title, and that was hardly surprising in view of the lies he had told her about his having spent most of his life in Kenya. That could be put right, but how much was he really to blame for the miseries she had suffered after he had left Dublin?

Thrusting the question aside, he switched his mind back to Lothar. Evidently the Satanist did not suspect either Mary or himself, as he had offered to initiate them. What form would the initiation take? Something pretty vile without a doubt. Spitting on the Cross, oaths of fidelity to the Devil, and a sexual 'free for all' to finish up with, seemed the probable programme. At the last item his thoughts switched back to Mary.

Was she really as hardboiled as she now appeared? Apparently she had been thoroughly enjoying herself here for the past week with the great hulking American. Perhaps, then, she would not mind giving herself to several different men during the course of a midnight orgy. Mentally he groaned at the thought.

In his fury he had stormed at her, 'Once a whore always a whore!' but was that really true? Not necessarily; and certainly

346

not in her case. He knew now that she had been forced into prostitution, and it was clear from her having married Teddy Morden that she had escaped from it as soon as she had the chance. The fact that she was now living with the American could not be held against her. It needed only a second thought to appreciate that she was doing so as a stage in her campaign to get evidence against Teddy's murderers. If that was so she was going to hate taking part in an orgy as much as he did the thought of her doing so.

Lothar had not addressed a word to him. With regal unconcern for the fact that he had a passenger the Great Ram remained deep in his own thoughts, driving the powerful car with ease and skill so that it maintained an almost unvarying distance of some fifty yards from the rear lights of the other car.

Barney shot Lothar a sidelong glance. He was wondering now if by some means he could prevent the Satanist from getting to the Esbbat, and so save Mary from the ordeal of initiation. The only possibility seemed to be to wait until the car slowed down, then turn and strike him senseless by a sudden blow behind the ear. But as long as they were moving at more than twenty miles an hour that would be much too dangerous. Barney realized that before he could grab the wheel the car would be off the road. If it turned over or crashed into a tree he might be seriously injured, and so have robbed himself of the chance to capture Lothar. Yet if he waited until the car slowed down on approaching their destination, it was certain that the car in front would already have pulled up. The big American would be getting out and would be bound to see the result of an attack on Lothar. He would come dashing to the rescue long before the stunned Satanist could be pulled out of the car and dragged off into the bushes. These considerations swiftly decided Barney against making such an attempt unless they lost touch with the car ahead or for some unforeseen reason Lothar had to reduce their pace to something near a crawl.

Again his thoughts went back to Mary. He now remembered her clearly as a lovely golden-haired slip of a girl who had been the pick of the dance-hostesses in the restaurant where she worked, but he had only vague memories of the single night they had spent together. He had had a big win that day on a horse called 'Cherry Pie' and, as usual when his luck was in, splashed a good part of the proceeds in standing champagne to all and sundry; so he had been pretty tight himself by the time he had persuaded her to let him take her to an hotel. He recalled his disappointment at finding her frigid and later his annoyance at her not having told him to begin with that she was a virgin, but apart from that his mind was a blank.

He knew himself well enough to be sure that he had not abused her or treated her unkindly, and no doubt on leaving he had promised to see her soon again. After all, it was usual to say something of that kind to a girl after having spent the night with her, whether one meant it or not. In this case he probably had meant it, and all the odds were that he would have, had not his whole life taken a different turn a few days later.

But if he had, it would not have been to assure himself that he had not put her in the family way. The idea that he might have had not even occurred to him. His lighthearted amours with other cabaret girls had led him to believe that they all knew how to look after themselves or, in the event of an accident, take early steps to remedy it. If Mary had let things slide that was her fault, and he could not be blamed.

Yet, on further thought, he had to admit to himself that fundamentally he was responsible, because he had tempted her with money. She had not been like the other girls who had cheerfully accepted his advances on a business basis. She had more than once refused him, declaring that she 'did not do that sort of thing'. Then, on the night of his big win she had been very depressed, and he had got out of her the reason. Her brother was in trouble and she was too hard up to help him out.

He had not supposed for one moment that she was a virgin, but a girl who normally would not give herself for money, as many of her companions did; so he had seized the opportunity of her needing money and bid her twenty pounds, reasoning that the offer of so large a sum might do the trick – and it had.

Only later, had he been more sober, could he have appreciated the mental struggle she must have been through before giving way to the temptation to have that fat wad of pound notes in her handbag next morning; and only now could he begin to appreciate something of the misery with which she had ultimately had to pay for them.

The thought of her at seventeen, or eighteen at the most, concealing her harrowing secret for many weeks, until only an illegal operation could free her from it, wrung his heart. And then

348

the way she had had to earn the money to pay for it. What she must have been through did not bear thinking about. He might count himself innocent of intent to harm her, but he had, and the wonder was that she had survived it to become the charming and courageous woman he had met at Mrs. Wardeel's.

That, he realized, was the real Mary; and now that he knew the whole truth concerning her the doubts he had had during the past week about allowing himself to go on loving her were entirely dissipated. The dangerous and distasteful rôle she was playing at present was that of a Crusader against Evil, wielding a woman's weapons. The life of ill-fame she had led in Dublin had been forced upon her, and by his act as an irresponsible young rake. If she would let him he would do his utmost to make up to her for that. The moment they were free to be together again he would beg her forgiveness for the abuse he had heaped on her that night, and tell her how desperately he loved her.

But when *would* they be free to be together again? Once more he glanced at Lothar's aloof, hatchet-like profile and silently cursed him for having turned up at the Cedars. Had he not done so the present situation would never have arisen. Instead of Mary being on her way to play a part in some revolting ceremony she would still be at the Cedars; he could have left, driven into Cambridge, collected the police, bagged the American and then driven her back to London.

Suddenly he began to wonder why Lothar had turned up at the Cedars when he had. Surely the Great Ram had not come all the way from the Continent, or even from London, simply to preside at a meeting of a little local coven and, at that, a meeting that was only an Esbbat, not even a Sabbat, let alone one of the great Satanic feasts of the year to which the covens of several countries would have been summoned. What devilry was he up to, then, in a remote village like Fulgoham?

Perhaps the fact that his host was a Colonel in the United States Air Force gave the clue? Yes, something to do with the great American air base in the nearby valley must be the answer. Down in Wales he had succeeded in making off with a considerable quantity of the special rocket fuel. What could he be after here?

For some minutes Barney's mind roved over possibilities. Surely he was not planning to get away with one of the giant aircraft? What could he do with it if he succeeded? Besides, it would need a trained crew to fly it. But an H bomb perhaps? No, that did not make sense either, if Forsby was right in his belief that Lothar wanted to try out some private experiment of his own; because bombs were dropped from aircraft so did not need rocket fuel to launch them. But Forsby might be wrong. As C.B. had always maintained, Lothar could still be working for the Soviets. If so, such secret devices for waging war as he obtained for them need not tie up. And an American H bomb, if he could get one out of the country, would be an invaluable prize to hand over to the Russians.

Barney got no further in his speculations. The car ahead had turned off the road on to a rough track. They followed and bumped along at a slower pace for about half a mile. The leading car pulled up in the shadow of a group of trees, and from them several figures emerged to meet it. Barney had already abandoned as too risky any idea of trying shock tactics against Lothar, but he felt now that whatever happened, even if Mary got into difficulties, it was his imperative duty to play up to the Satanist and stick to him like glue.

As the leading car bumped its way to a halt Mary was nerving herself to wait until Barney got out of the one behind, then shout to him, 'Run, run for your life! They've found you out and mean to kill you.' But Wash must have read the way in which her mind was working, for he said to her,

'You're all het up about Doctor Dee, aren't you, honey. I'd let you out of seeing him given his medicine if I could, but I just daren't. Not with the Great Ram around. And don't you try to give the Doc the tip-off that he's in danger. He couldn't get away, nohow. Before he'd gotten a dozen yards the Great Ram would halt him. Yeah, as surely as I could lasso a steer, but just by a thought wave. And any little game of that kind would end in curtains for you too.'

As he finished speaking he took a black satin mask from a pocket in the car, handed it to her and added, 'Put this on, and stay where you are till I come and fetch you.' Then he got out and strode over to join the group of figures that had come out from the trees.

For a moment hope surged up in her again. If they all went off together she meant to jump out and run for it, trusting to get away under cover of the darkness. If she succeeded there would at least be a chance of her finding a house from which she could telephone and secure help before Barney was murdered.

But the figures moved swiftly forward and met Wash while he was still within ten yards of the car. She could see now that there were five or six of them, and that they were all wearing monk-like robes with cowls that hid their features. The group remained where it had met Wash, talking with him, and with a sinking heart she knew that they were much too near for her to slip away without their seeing and catching her.

Meanwhile Lothar and Barney had got out of the other car; the latter with very mixed feelings, for he was now both intensely curious about the ceremony that was to take place, yet greatly concerned and anxious about Mary.

Going round to the boot Lothar unlocked it, then opened a large square leather case from which he took out and put on the ram's head-piece with the big curling horns, and a robe of black silk embroidered in gold with the signs of the Zodiac. Signing to Barney to accompany him, he then walked towards the group of cowled figures.

As he approached they all made a deep obeisance. A few words were exchanged after which, with the exception of Wash, the whole party moved off along a path that led in among the trees. Wash came back to the car, said to Mary, 'I'll be with you in a moment, honey,' then went round to the boot.

Two minutes later he reappeared, having put on over his uniform a robe of white satin, decorated with black twisting snakes, and wearing on his head a silver circlet from which reared up in front a striking cobra of the same metal with flashing red rubies for eyes. He opened the car door and Mary got out. Under the mask her face was chalk white, and she was trembling. He put his great hand under her arm to steady her and they followed the others along the path through the trees.

After a hundred yards or so the trees ended and beyond them there reared up against the dark night sky irregular patches of deeper blackness made by still-standing portions of the walls of the ruined Abbey. Between two of them a faint light glowed, which was just sufficient to show up the tangle of weeds and low bushes that had grown up among the ancient stones. Wash guided Mary through the gap and they entered the main body of the Abbey church. She saw then that the light came from the only part of the ruin that remained something more than piles of crumbling masonry overgrown with ivy. This was a still partially intact side chapel, and set up in it were thirteen tall black candles.

By their light she saw that above the far end of the chapel a jagged fragment of roof still hung suspended between two pillars with Norman capitals. Beneath it lay the altar, an oblong block of stone, broken at one end and raised on two worn steps. Below the steps to the left there was a three-foot high sarcophagus upon the lid of which lay the carved stone figures of a Crusader and his wife, but the images were so worn by time and exposure as to be hardly distinguishable from one another. On the opposite side was a blank wall with one small arched window in it through which the branch of a tree was growing.

As Mary stumbled forward, still half supported by Wash, she caught the stench of sulphur from the candles. Between them the mysterious figures moved, temporarily obscuring one or other of the candle flames as they took their places for the ceremony. Wash gave her a little shake and said in a low, sharp voice:

'Pep up now! For Pete's sake don't show yellow before the big shot. He'll give you a treatment else. Maybe cause all your hair to fall out as a penalty for not glorying in Our Lord Satan's work. We'll be through and on our way in an hour. Till then you gotta act as though you was one hundred per cent the eager neophyte.'

Her last hope of warning Barney had gone. The moment of his death was approaching with terrible rapidity. At the thought of the hideous scene that she would be forced to witness in a matter of minutes, she was on the verge of fainting. But quite suddenly her trembling ceased, the muscles of her limbs tautened, and she felt able to hold her head erect again. Instinctively she knew that this was due not to any change in her own mentality, but because the giant beside her was pouring some of his strength into her.

By then they had reached the wide open entrance to the chapel. The Great Ram was now standing to the right of the altar. Barney was standing, as he had been directed, facing and about six feet away from it. The twelve robed and cowled men who made up Wash's coven had formed two lines lower down the chapel and facing inwards. The two furthest from the altar were holding one a saxophone, the other an accordion. Wash led Mary up to the right of the altar, and signed to her to stand with her back to the Crusader's tomb. He then bowed to the Great Ram, stepped to the front of the altar, faced the congregation, and said,

'Brothers of the Ram. You are all wise to it that to-night we

352

have a very special assignment to carry out for the furtherance of Our Lord Satan's work. To bless and guide our efforts His Mightiness the Great Ram has come among us. To him Prince Lucifer has delegated the greatest power in His realm the Earth. To have him with us, folks, is an outstanding honour. Presently he'll grant you 'most anything you ask, and far more than I could do, as a sorta blank cheque against any risks you may run of meeting trouble later. But first he's graciously agreed to initiate two neophytes: warlock Doctor Dee, and witch Circe. Now we'll make a start with the usual drill. Give me fog music.'

The men with the saxophone and the accordion began to play. The notes they drew from their instruments were unlike anything that Mary had ever heard before. It was a strange tuneless wailing that had something sad about it but without rhythm or form. While this cacophony of sound continued Wash remained motionless in front of the altar, his eyes cast down, his face rigid with concentration.

Within a few moments the spell began to work. A deeper gloom shrouded the irregular piles of ruins outside the chapel, wisps of white mist drifted across its open end, and soon these thickened until they formed a solid impenetrable curtain.

Wash released his breath in a long loud sigh, then ordered, 'Give me music to turn on the heat.'

The players broke off and, after a moment, started a quite different arrangement of sounds. Again they were tuneless and apparently uncoordinated, but the movement was quicker and gayer. Again Wash stood unmoving as he concentrated on creating a change in the temperature. The May night was not cold, but on the previous day heavy rain had saturated the weeds and bushes that formed a miniature jungle between the ivy-covered mounds of the ancient ruin, leaving it dank and chill. Now, with surprising swiftness, the faint mist that had permeated the interior of the little chapel disappeared, and its atmosphere became as warm as that of a garden on a sunny day in June.

Mary was hardly conscious of these changes. Grateful for the support of the Crusader's tomb she stood partly leaning back against it, her eyes riveted on Barney. Still not remotely suspicious of the horrible death that had been planned for him, he was standing in an easy attitude facing Wash, but now and then giving a covert glance about him.

Once he smiled at Mary, but she was too distraught to respond;

so he assumed that she was still furious with him, and he did not look in her direction again. Had she not been masked the agonized expression on her face as she stared at him might at least have conveyed a hint that for some reason she was apprehensive on his account; but after the way they had blackguarded one another at the Cedars, he could only suppose that until he could have a quiet talk with her alone there was no hope of healing the breach between them.

Wash bowed to Lothar, then they changed places so that the former now stood on the right of the altar and the latter in front of it. As they moved, Mary instinctively turned her gaze from Barney to them. Both made imposing figures. Wash, with the Cleopatra style diadem and rearing cobra set upon his thick near-white hair, his great hook nose, and huge body draped in the white satin robe decorated with the entwined black snakes, resembled some fabulous Aztec Emperor. Yet, for all his height and massive bulk, he did not steal the picture from Lothar. Slim, erect, his deeply cleft chin jutting out, and his cruel, beautifully modelled mouth hard set beneath the great horned mask that now concealed the upper part of his face, the Great Ram positively radiated power. It seemed to pulsate from him in waves that could be felt, and without question he was the dominant personality in the assembly. Suddenly, in his harsh, slightly nasal voice, he spoke.

'My children! As your High Priest Twisting Snake has told you, we have a great work to perform for Our Lord Satan to-night. To some of you it may appear to involve risk of arrest and imprisonment. Have no fears. Prince Lucifer always looks after his own. Ways will be found to protect you, or more than compensate you later for any temporary unpleasantness you may have to undergo.'

He paused for a moment, the tip of his tongue passed slowly over his red lips, then he went on. 'Before we set out on our important mission, I shall grant all your reasonable requests. Later I intend to perform a ceremony of initiation. The neophyte Circe is to be received among us as a Sister. She is of unusual beauty; so no doubt most of you will wish to perform with her the Sacred Rite of Creation when she offers herself for Temple Service.'

As he paused again Mary choked back a sob of dread and Barney, the blood now drained from his face, clenched his fists until his nails dug deep into his palms. Surrounded, as he was, by

354

fourteen strong men, he knew that he had not the faintest chance of saving her from this devastating physical assault. He could only pray that he would by some means be spared from witnessing it, and might be granted the small satisfaction within the next twelve hours of bringing about the arrest of the whole unholy crew so that justice might be done upon them.

Again the Great Ram's cold, sneering voice broke the deadly silence that reigned in the little chapel. 'As you all know, for the ceremony of initiation blood is required. Normally it is the blood obtained from a sacrifice. To that there is only one alternative. By a special dispensation Our Lord Satan has granted me the power to use one drop of blood from my own veins for this purpose. But to-night I shall not need to open one of my veins. There is a traitor among us! A spy!'

Suddenly his left hand shot out and he pointed at Barney. 'There he stands! Seize him! I decree that here and now he shall serve as a sacrifice.'

It was evident that Wash had warned the group of men who had met him under the trees to be prepared for this denunciation. The very instant that Lothar's accusing finger stabbed the air, as though at a signal the two cowled figures nearest Barney leapt towards him. He had no time to turn, let alone run. The attack was so sudden that he had hardly raised his arms to defend himself before they were seized. Next moment he was struggling between the two men and making desperate efforts to free himself from them.

Now that the dreaded crisis was actually upon her Mary was utterly distraught. To the last she had hoped for the miracle for which she had been praying so frantically – some benighted stranger stumbling on the scene and causing a diversion, a fall of the remainder of the chapel roof, a sudden heart attack that would lay the Great Ram low, lightning directed at his evil heart, a thunderbolt, an angel with a flaming sword – but no intervention, human or divine, had occurred to prevent the Satanists carrying through their terrible purpose.

Bitterly she upbraided herself for not having shouted a warning to Barney as he walked past the car in which Wash had left her, or as she had come through the ruin to the chapel. That she had not was partly due to fears for herself aroused by Wash's threats of what the Great Ram might do to her. But only partly. It was more that at no point had it seemed possible to her that he could have

355

got away. Yet he was strong, resourceful and swift of foot; so he might have. And now it was too late.

Tears welled from her eyes and ran down her cheeks beneath the mask. Her hands were damp, her hair matted on her forehead. The struggle in the middle of the temple had as yet only lasted a few moments, but there could be no question about how it would end. Even if Barney could wrench his arms from the grip of the two men who held them, there were ten others between him and the open end of the chapel. Within a matter of minutes it was certain that he would be overcome. Then they would rig up some form of crucifix, tie him to it upside down and cut his throat – just as the Satanists at Cremorne had cut Teddy's.

She could shut her eyes but that would not prevent her seeing with her mind all that was happening step by hideous step. And the awful sound of his cries as they butchered him would ring in her ears to torture her to the end of her days.

A wave of faintness swept over her. She swayed slightly and her knees began to give. Instinctively she thrust her hands behind her to keep herself from falling by supporting herself on the Crusader's tomb. One of them descended on her handbag. She had carried it from the car under her arm then put it down there behind her.

In an instant she had grasped the bag and once more stood erect. With frantic fingers she tore it open and plunged her right hand into it. Ever since she had left the Temple at Cremorne with Wash the crucifix had remained in it, but in a side pocket and forgotten by her.

To produce it, she knew, would mean a hideous death for herself. But by its power she might save Barney. His bitter angry words 'Once a whore always a whore' came back to her. From the moment of the abrupt interruption of their furious quarrel she had felt certain that even if they both got away from the Satanists he would henceforth always despise her. Yet she loved him. She knew now that he was the only man in her life that she had ever really loved or ever would love. Had some other man been in his present extremity, however great her urge to help him, fear for herself would have restrained her. She would have stood by until mounting anguish proved too much for her and she fainted. But it was Barney who was to die. No matter what happened she must play, in an attempt to save him, this last card that the Powers of Good had thrust into her hand.

These thoughts coursed through her brain with the speed of

356

lightning. The Great Ram was still standing at the foot of the altar steps, side face on to her and no more than six feet away. Pulling the crucifix from the bag she threw it with all her force at his face.

It hit him on the chin. As it struck him there came a blinding flash. He uttered a piercing shriek and fell backwards against the altar. His great ram's head mask was knocked off and rolled across the floor. For an instant the chapel and the ruins outside it were as bright as though lit by brilliant sunshine. Next second all other sounds were drowned in a crash of thunder. The floor of the chapel rocked, a part of the roof fell in. The flames of the black candles flickered wildly then went out, plunging the whole scene in darkness.

For several minutes pandemonium reigned. Shouts and curses rent the air mingled with the sounds of groans and trampling feet. Then the beam of an electric torch stabbed the blackness. Another and another appeared, until five beams were sweeping to and fro, revealing the wild disorder into which the Satanists had been thrown.

Lothar, apparently still dazed, was hunched on the altar steps nursing his burnt chin in his hands. Wash was bending over him. Two of the congregation were cowering in a corner; another, having been kneed in the groin by Barney, lay writhing in the middle of the chapel floor. Barney, to Mary's unutterable relief, had disappeared. Three more of the Satanists were missing, having either gone in pursuit of him or, being overcome by panic, fled into the night.

Mary needed no telling that she would have to pay for her success, and she made no resistance when two of the hooded men ran up to her, seized her by the arms, and hustled her forward towards the Great Ram. For a moment he stared up at her with lack-lustre eyes, then comprehension and hate dawned in them.

Extending a hand to Wash he said thickly, 'Help me up.' Then when Wash had got him to his feet he went on, his words still laboured but pregnant with menace. 'Give me a moment. I must think. I will not kill her. Death is too good; too easy. I must think – think of a curse. A curse to bring her living death. I have it. I'll destroy her mind; turn her into a Zombie. No; no, I won't. Here they would put her into an asylum and idiots can be quite happy when given enough food and the barest comfort. I'll mar her beauty – teeth, eyes, hair – and cause her lingering agony from the gradual rotting of her bones.'

357

Mary faced him, her eyes distended, her mouth suddenly gone dry from horror. She had expected death, but no sentence so terrible as this. Yet she knew that even if she flung herself at his feet and grovelled there, she could expect no mercy from him.

There was a moment of dead silence. Even the lesser Satanists who had crowded round were awed by the thought of a once beautiful woman, toothless, hairless, pur-blind, dragging herself about while her bones were being slowly and painfully eaten away by a curse that would take the form of third degree syphilis.

The silence was broken by Wash, who said in a harsh voice, 'She's asked for everything that's coming to her, Master. But in this place we're all washed up now. That accursed crucifix is laying somewhere around. None of us dare touch it and the vibrations it gives off would stymie any magic attempted here.'

'You are wrong.' The Great Ram spoke tonelessly but with authority, 'When it . . . it came in contact with me it burnt itself out. There is now no more power vested in it than in any other pieces of wood and ivory. Have the candles re-lit so that I may put my curse upon this woman.'

Several of the Satanists made a move to obey, but Wash called sharply, 'Hold it, folks; I've first a word to say.' Then he turned back to Lothar. 'To-night, Chief, we've work to do: Our Lord Satan's work, and a top-ranking mission at that. You don't need me to tell you that laying curses drains power from even the strongest of us, and within an hour you may need all yours to pull us out should we come up against some snags. Leave this crazy bitch to me. I'll deal with her later.'

'No, I mean to curse her here and now,' Lothar replied doggedly. 'I am no little High Priest but the Great Ram; and under Prince Lucifer my power is inexhaustible.'

'Sure, sure; no question about that.' Wash's tone was soothing but suddenly it changed to a sharper note. 'When you're yourself. But at this point you're not. You're as groggy as a brand-new battle-shock case. I've seen plenty and I know. So temporarily I'm taking charge here, and we're all quitting this place right now.'

Amazement dawned in the Great Ram's heavy-lidded blue eyes, then anger, and he exclaimed, 'How dare you! No one gives orders in my presence.'

'Maybe it's unusual; but it's just that I mean to do.'

'Defy me at your peril. Remember there is always a to-morrow. At my leisure I could break you as easily as I could a reed.'

358

'I know it, Exalted One, and I'm not such a fool as to defy you. But I want you to give me my way. To get it I'll make a bargain with you.'

'I do not make bargains with my inferiors.'

'If you don't make this one we'll all go up in smoke, for having mucked the deal between us – you for playing unreasonable in refusing to delay your curse, me for having dug my toes in on that account.'

Wash reached out an enormous hand, clutched a handful of Mary's hair, jerked her head roughly from side to side, and went on. 'This woman is mine. For as long as I want her she's to remain intact: hair, sight, hearing, toenails and all that goes on inside her. When I'm through with her you can lay your curse, but not before. You'll either agree to that or to-night's assignment is off. I'll walk out on you.'

Still sweating with fear, Mary waited for the Great Ram's reaction. Had he not been so shaken she felt certain that his hard, imperious, overbearing nature would have forced him to reject any compromise; but temporarily he had become like some great capital ship that had suffered a devastating air attack in which bombs had put all her barbetts out of action, so that she was heaving half awash in the sea, and capable now of using only the fire power of her minor armament.

After a moment of excruciating suspense his answer came. With a sneer he said, 'The chains of the body must still be heavy on you to play such high stakes for any woman. But this is no time for us to quarrel. Let it be as you wish. Providing she does not escape the penalty for her sacrilegious act, a few weeks or months are of little importance. Anticipation of what is in store for her may even prove a refinement of her punishment. But you must inform me when you have tired of her.'

'I'll do that,' Wash agreed. Then, raising his voice, he turned to the others. 'Get moving, now! Two of you give a hand to the Master, here. The rest of you beat it back to the transport. And make it snappy. When you hit the base you know what to do.'

The fog still hung thick outside the chapel. It was that which had enabled Barney to get clean away. Wash did not delay to practise a magic which would have dispersed it, as the men of his coven were all so familiar with the ruins of the Abbey and the wood beyond that with their torches they could quite well find their way through them.

359

Except for the two who had come forward to support Lothar, they hurried off and were swiftly swallowed up in the greyish darkness. The Great Ram refused the aid of the two men who remained, but accepted their guidance and, with one of them carrying his head-dress, while the other shone a torch, they set off along the now trampled path through the sea of weeds that carpeted the ground between the mounds of stone. Wash, grasping Mary firmly by the arm, brought up the rear.

On reaching the far side of the wood they emerged abruptly from the belt of fog just in time to see three cars, which had been hidden among the trees, carry away the other members of the Brotherhood, all of whom had removed the monks' robes that had concealed their uniforms. Wash ordered the two men who were escorting the Great Ram to take his robe and put it with his mask in the boot of his car, then follow with it. Lothar himself he installed in the front passenger seat of his own car, while Mary squeezed herself into the back among the pile of luggage. Having put his head-dress and robe into the boot, Wash came round to the driver's seat and a minute later they were bumping their way back along the track to the road.

The drive lasted for some fifteen minutes during which, for the first time in what seemed many hours, but actually was little more than one, Mary breathed freely again. She had saved her dear Barney and had herself been spared the gruelling infliction of initiation. Lothar's threat to reduce her to a ghoulish physical wreck remained. But Wash had saved her from that, at least for the time being; and she had an optimistic feeling that, now he had so clearly shown that he had fallen in love with her, somehow he would manage to ensure that she escaped the Great Ram's vengeance.

She had heard Wash tell his men to return to the base, but had not realized that they too were on their way there until the car slowed down and, at a loud challenge, drew up. A sentry and a military policeman came forward. Wash gave the countersign, the two men saluted and the great wire gates were opened. They drove through them and on for a quarter of a mile between clusters of buildings, to pull up beside a hangar that faced on to the airfield. The three of them got out and Wash led them into it.

Inside there stood a small passenger aircraft that several men were preparing for flight. Its engines began to tick over and the hangar doors were opened. For a few moments they stood beside it. The luggage was brought in from the car and carried up the movable staircase into it. Lothar turned to Wash and asked,

'Has the thing I've come for been loaded into her yet?'

Wash nodded. 'My boys saw to that this afternoon. It's in a big case and stowed in the tail. Go up and satisfy yourself it's there if you wish.'

Without a word Lothar left them, walked up the steps and disappeared into the aircraft. That gave Mary the first chance she had had to thank Wash, without risk of being overheard, for saving her from being cursed. In a spate of words she began to do so.

Angrily he cut her short. 'You sure must have been round the bend to do what you did. And later there'll be no side-stepping for you from paying for it. All you've got to thank me for is a reprieve. Best make your mind up to get all you can outa life while your health is left to you.'

A junior officer came up, saluted and reported, 'All set to get moving, Sir.'

Wash acknowledged the salute and, as the officer turned away, led Mary towards the boarding steps. In sudden apprehension she exclaimed, 'Are we going too? I saw your luggage going up but I haven't got my wits back yet. I didn't realize . . .'

'Yeah, we're going too. Your suitcase is on board.' He thrust her before him up the steep steps.

'But where?' she cried with rising panic, as he forced her on in front of him. 'Where are you taking me?'

'To Russia,' he answered tersely, 'and we're not coming back.'

23

The terrible deduction

W HEN Barney had been seized in the chapel he had instinctively fought back, but the odds assembled there against him were so overwhelming that he knew his struggles to be hopeless. With the Great Ram's denunciation ringing in his ears he knew, too, that his life was not worth a quarter-of-an-hour's purchase.

Then, as he was facing the altar while swaying wildly between his two antagonists, he had seen Mary throw the crucifix. The blinding flash, thunderous crash and heaving of the floor that followed had stricken all the Satanists with instant terror. The one holding on to Barney's left arm let go. Swinging round he had kneed in the groin the other man who was clinging to him, and wrenched his right arm free. The rest of them, by stepping forward, could have barred his path to the open end of the chapel; but it had been plunged into darkness and they had been thrown into a panic. He cannoned into one and brushed by another; next moment he was out in the body of the Abbey and running for his life.

It was a nightmare dash, for out there fog combined with the darkness to prevent his seeing where he was going. Several times he ran slap into sections of wall and twice tripped to fall at full length among the weeds and brambles. Yet it was that spell-induced fog that saved him from determined pursuit and recapture.

After four or five minutes of staggering blindly about, he got clear of the ruin and could vaguely make out the trunks of big

362

trees as he ran on now dodging between them. Another five minutes and both the wood and the fog-belt ended. He had no idea of the direction he had taken but there was no sign of a track or the cars in which the Satanists had arrived, and as far as he could see ahead of him lay only a ploughed field.

Pulling up on the edge of it, he stood gasping for breath and striving to collect his thoughts. He owed his life to Mary; he had no doubt about that. But what about her? Unless she too had got away in the darkness and confusion they would inflict a terrible vengeance on her. She was no fool; she must have known the sort of penalty she would have to pay for throwing a crucifix in the Great Ram's face. That meant that, despite the bitter abuse she had hurled at him not much over an hour ago, deep down she must love him. Courageous men and women will take great risks to rescue children, and often complete strangers, from fire or drowning, but they do not voluntarily invite a terrible death for themselves in order to save the life of someone they hate. And after what had passed between them there could be no halfway house. If she did not hate him, then she loved him. At the thought that she must almost certainly still be in the clutches of the Satanists, he groaned aloud.

As his breathing eased a little, he swung round to plunge back into the wood. But he had taken only a few steps before he pulled up. The ruined Abbey must be anything between a quarter and half a mile away. In the fog and darkness nothing but a fluke could lead him back to it direct, and he might wander about in the wood for an hour or more without finding it.

Besides, when he did, what was he going to do? His gun had been taken from him by one of the American's coloured boys. He had intended to ask for it back after supper; but Lothar's arrival had precipitated a series of events which had denied him the chance to do so. Even if Lothar had been rendered *hors de combat* by the blaze as the crucifix hit his face, there was still the giant American and the dozen men who made up his coven. Barney was far from being a coward and he had the greatest difficulty in resisting the urge to make an immediate attempt to rescue Mary; but he knew that on his own he could not possibly succeed.

He groaned again, leant against a tree and, covering his face with his hands, endeavoured to make up his mind about the best course to take. To bring the police on the scene was the

363

obvious answer; but how could that be done most quickly? After a moment he decided that the best bet would be to get hold of one of the Satanists' cars and drive in to Cambridge. Even if he could have found a house with a telephone fairly quickly, it might prove difficult to convince the police that he really needed the help of at least a dozen of them, and urgently; whereas if he went to a police station he had only to show his official pass to secure immediate assistance.

At a run he set off along the edge of the trees, but he had completely lost his bearings and actually was on the far side of the wood from the track along which the cars had come to it. After he had been running for several minutes, the wood ended in a right angle. Turning the corner he ran on, only to find that this side of the wood seemed longer than that on which he had come out; but having covered some distance along it he struck a path. To the right it led into the fog-shrouded wood, to the left to a cottage some hundred yards away, of which against the paler sky he could just make out the chimney and the roof line.

Realizing now that he must have come out on the opposite side of the wood from the cars, and might yet have to run a long way to reach them, he decided to find out if the cottage had a telephone. Two minutes later he was hammering loudly on its door, and shouting, 'Wake up there! Wake up!'

In response to his shouts a tousled head was thrust out of an upper window. Without waiting to be questioned or abused he cried, 'I'm a policeman. This is urgent. It's a matter of murder. Have you a telephone?'

'No, I haven't,' angrily replied the man at the window; then, as the reason for his having been aroused from his sleep sunk in, he added, 'Sorry I can't help. But there's one at the vicarage. Turn left and straight up the road. It's just past the church; you can't miss it.'

With a murmur of thanks Barney, still panting, dashed down the garden path to the lane on which the cottage faced, and up the road. After another gruelling run, now gasping for breath and sweating profusely, he reached the vicarage. The same tactics there led, after a few moments, to the front door being opened by a tall, middle-aged man in a dressing-gown, who said he was the vicar.

Using 'murder' again as the best means of getting swift action, Barney was led to the telephone and induced the desk-sergeant at the Cambridge police headquarters to put him through to the night-duty Inspector. To have mentioned Black Magic might have aroused scepticism; so Barney gave the code name by which his office was known to the police, and said that he was on the trail of a wanted enemy agent who was a known killer. Even so he had the greatest difficulty in persuading the Inspector to send more than one police car and also come out himself with a strong force of constables.

The vicar, his eyes on stalks as he listened, supplied the name of his village, which lay just over the crest of the hill; but this produced a new snag, as it was well across the county border, in the north-western corner of Essex. All Barney's persuasive powers were needed to induce the Inspector to cut red tape and enter another county but, by promising to take the responsibility if there was any trouble, he succeeded.

At Barney's request the vicar produced a map of the district. From it he quickly memorized the way to get back on to the other road from which the track led to the ruined Abbey; then he gratefully accepted the vicar's offer of a whisky and soda.

Twenty minutes later the Inspector arrived with three car-loads of police. Barney was waiting for them on the doorstep. Hastily thanking the vicar he showed the Inspector his special identity card, told him the direction to take and got into the back of his car. While they drove the better part of two miles along roads that went round the wood, he gave the Inspector the bare facts of the situation, then they bumped up the track to the place where the Satanists had left their cars.

The cars were no longer there but the sight of their fresh tracks, thrown up in the headlights of the police cars, dissipated the Inspector's suspicions that Barney was suffering from overstrain and had brought him out on a wild-goose chase. The wood was still dank and eerily silent, apart from the constant dripping from the trees; but the fog had cleared a little and they made their way as quickly as they could towards the Abbey.

As they approached it, Barney's fear that they would find Mary there, but dead and mutilated, was so great that his throat contracted till he thought he was going to choke; and when they came in sight of the chapel, as the police shone their torches into it, he had to make a great effort in order to force himself to keep his eyes in that direction.

No twisted body lay sprawled there, but his fears were hardly lessened until he had run forward and looked at the altar. Upon it there was no trace of newly-spilled blood. Only then was he able to hope that by some means Mary had succeeded in escaping the Great Ram's vengeance, temporarily at least. But, owing to her position in the chapel at the time she had wrecked the proceedings, he thought it most unlikely that she had got away; and he knew that as a result of her act every moment that she remained in the hands of the Satanists her life must be in danger.

In consequence, before the police had had a chance to do more than take a first look at the big black candles, he hurried them back to the cars and gave the Inspector directions on how to reach the Cedars. Another quarter of an hour sped by while the cars made their dash back into Cambridgeshire. They screamed their way through Fulgoham village then, as they reached the place where Barney had parked his own car some two hours earlier, he had them flagged down to a halt.

They all got out and the Inspector gave swift directions to his men to surround the house so that nobody could get away from it. He allowed five minutes for the men to take up their positions, then he and Barney walked up to the front door. Their ringing, after some minutes, brought Jim down to it. Barney said,

'You remember me. Your friend Iziah got the wrong idea and slugged me, but later I had supper with the Colonel. I've come back to talk to him again.'

Jim's eyes grew round. 'But he's not here, Boss. He left with you. He's gone off on leave, an' we're not looking to see him back for a fortnight. Didn't he tell you?'

Barney's hopes of catching the American and rescuing Mary were dashed, but he asked quickly, 'Where has he gone?'

'I wouldn't know, Boss,' came the obviously truthful reply. 'The Colonel don't go tell us boys how he's planning to spend his time.'

'All right,' Barney snapped. 'Perhaps I can find out by running over the house.'

The Inspector drew him aside and whispered, 'We haven't got a search warrant.'

'To hell with that!' retorted Barney. 'Stay outside if you like. I'm going in.' Fixing the coloured boy with a basilisk stare, he said to him, 'Go and get my gun. You'll find me in the sitting-room.'

Seeing that Barney was accompanied by a police inspector and that other policemen were standing about in the offing, Jim

366

offered no opposition. Marching inside, Barney went straight to the telephone and got through to his office. He told the night-duty officer to ring the Chief and inform him that Sullivan had contacted Lothar Khune at a house near Fulgoham, in Cambridgeshire, in company with Mrs. Morden and an American Air Force Colonel named Henrick G. Washington, but had lost them and now had reason to believe that the trio were on their way to London.

He then helped himself to a whisky and soda and rang the bell. Jim appeared holding the little automatic. Barney took it, slipped it in his pocket and spent five minutes firing questions at him. But none of Jim's replies threw any light on whither his master might be bound. Barney sent for the other two boys, but his questions to them proved equally unrewarding.

He then spent half an hour going over the house. The sight of the black satin sheets on the bed in the principal bedroom aroused in him mingled feelings of nausea and homicidal jealousy, but he steeled himself to go through the drawers and cupboards. Neither there, in the sitting-room, nor anywhere else in the house did he discover any evidence which would have connected Colonel Washington with Satanist activities, and clearly his coloured servants regarded him as a quick-tempered, but generous, cheerful and entirely normal master.

Rejoining the Inspector, who all this time had been glumly waiting outside, Barney arranged for him to have the house kept under observation, on the off-chance that Lothar, or the Colonel, might return to it; then he collected his own car and accompanied the police cars back to Cambridge. On their arrival in the city the Inspector knocked up an hotel for Barney and, feeling that there was nothing more that he could do for the time being, he took a room in it.

By then it was close on three in the morning, and he had had a twenty-hour day, the last eight hours of which had been filled with constant strain and endeavour. Yet, tired as he was, he did not manage to get to sleep for over an hour after he had got into bed, because he was still so agitated about what might be happening to Mary.

He had left a call for seven o'clock. By a little after eight he was on his way to London, and well before ten he was in the office of C.B.'s P.A., declaring that he must see the Chief urgently as soon as he arrived.

'He's already here,' the P.A. replied with a slightly sour grimace. 'He has been here half the night, and wrecked my Sunday by calling me up at eight o'clock to report for duty. But he is expecting you, so you can go right in.'

C.B. was seated at his desk, but for once there were no papers upon it; apart from a used coffee cup it was empty. As Barney entered Verney turned his head and asked quickly, 'Any news of the Great Ram?'

'News?' Barney repeated. 'Not since I telephoned. I was hoping that the police had picked him up.'

'No, you were wrong about his being on his way to London. I had Scotland Yard lay on everything they'd got, but to no purpose. My bet is now that he has again left England by air.'

'What makes you think that, Sir?' Barney asked with nervous sharpness.

Verney gave a wry grin. 'If you've got a flask on you, you'd better take a pull from it. About one o'clock this morning your new pal, Colonel Henrick G. Washington, left his base in an aircraft. With him he took a little souvenir. Can you guess what it was?'

'Not . . . ' Barney's eyes widened, '. . . not an H bomb?'

'You've hit it, chum; or near as makes no difference. Actually it was one of the latest pattern U.S. nuclear warheads.'

'And Lothar went with him?'

'Everything points to that.'

'But Mary! Mary!' Barney's voice was an anguished cry. 'What have they done with her?'

C.B. spread out his long hands. 'I can guess how you must be feeling, and I'd give a lot to be able to tell you that she is safe and well. As things are I think that you can take it that she is still alive. They went straight from the Abbey to the air base; so if they had killed her it is pretty certain that by now someone would have found her body. Unless she got away and is wandering, temporarily out of her mind, that leaves only one alternative. It is that they took her with them.'

Suddenly sitting down Barney began to hammer his clenched fists together. 'Oh God!' he moaned. 'Oh God, this is too ghastly! If only I'd gone direct to the air base. Earlier I was speculating on what Lothar was up to down there, and it occurred to me that he was probably planning to snatch some major secret from the Americans. But later, well, later . . .'

368

'Easy on, young feller, easy on. You'd had a packet yourself, and I'll not hold it against you that your thoughts were on the girl.'

'But if I'd gone to the air base I might have wrecked their plan, bagged Lothar, and rescued Mary.'

'No; you couldn't have done that. You were lost, you had no transport, and after you got away from the ruined Abbey over half an hour elapsed before you were able to communicate with the police. Even if you had directed them straight on to the air base, by the time they arrived and had explained matters to the Security people there it would have been too late. Colonel Washington's aircraft would already have taken off.'

Barney looked up in surprise. 'When I telephoned the office, I gave only the bare facts about my having got on to Lothar. I said nothing about the Abbey and the hellish business that took place there. How did you know . . .'

Smiling slightly, C.B. replied. 'Otto had a vision, and knocked me up in the middle of the night. I've since had a long report from the Cambridge police, and another from the U.S. Security people. Between them I've managed to form a pretty good picture of what happened. But of course there are gaps in it; and I'd like you now to give me a detailed account of your activities from the time you left Inspector Thompson after having a drink with him at The World's End.'

With an effort Barney dragged his thoughts away from Mary and for ten minutes made, in jerky staccato sentences, his report about his encounter with Ratnadatta and all that had followed.

When he had done, C.B. said, 'That clears up quite a lot of points. Now I'll give you my side of it. A little before two o'clock the Office called me and relayed your message. When I learned that you had actually contacted Lothar and believed him to be on his way to London I naturally went all out to get him. I not only alerted Special Branch, but got the Chief Constables of all the Home Counties out of bed to lay on networks in case he made for some hideout on the East or South coasts. After half an hour I'd done all I could so, having told the Office to call me if they got him, I put out the light and went to sleep again.

'About an hour later my step-son roused me out. Otto had woken him by hammering on the front door. I had Otto in and this is what he had to say. Round about midnight he was awakened by a violent blow on the chin. He says it was as though a flaming torch had been thrust into his face. Instantly he became identified with Lothar and, I suppose one can say, inside his mind.'

'He saw as clearly as though in strong sunshine, a chapel in the ruined Abbey to which you had been taken, and you struggling in the grip of two hooded men. He was aware that Mary Morden was there and that it was she who had inflicted this grievous injury upon him. Although within seconds everything went black, he knew that you had got away, but at the moment his mind was obsessed with his desire to be revenged on Mary. Some of the Satanists produced torches and he rallied his strength to put a terrible curse upon her. But Colonel Washington intervened and threatened to rat on him unless he postponed taking any action against her.'

'So that's what happened.' Barney let out a swift sigh. His relief for Mary was faintly tinged with jealousy at the thought that it was the American instead of himself who had succeeded in protecting her; but he added quickly, 'And what then? Did they go straight to the air base?'

'I gather so. Otto's chin was paining him severely; so he got out of bed and bathed it. As the injury was a form of burn, that made matters worse rather than better, and for a time he lost touch with the situation. He says that when he picked it up again he seemed to be poised above a dark wood that was filled with fog; but he could see through the fog. He saw Lothar and the others making their way to several cars on the edge of the wood, then get into them and drive off. He saw you, too, on the other side of the wood, stumbling about in it, and obviously lost.'

'Then, instead of getting on the telephone to me at once, the fool swallowed five or six aspirins to dull his pain, and got back into bed again. As he lay there he picked up Lothar in a car with Colonel Washington and Mary Morden. The car was approaching the air base, but soon after they had entered it the aspirins began to work and he dozed off. About three o'clock he woke, thought over his vision and decided that he ought not to wait until the morning to tell me about it; so he got up, dressed and came round to Dovehouse Street.

'As soon as I had heard Otto's story I felt sure that you were on the wrong scent about their being on their way to London. What is more, in view of the last *coup* Lothar pulled off, the idea that he had been taken into a United States air base by an Air Force Colonel who was another Satanist properly put the wind up me.

I telephoned a warning to the base and asked that Colonel Washington and anyone with him should be put under preventive arrest. Then I hurried into my clothes, came up to the Office and gave the whole story over the scrambler line to H.Q. Strategic Air Command at Lakenheath in Suffolk.

'Half an hour later they came back to me to say that we'd missed the boat. Apparently Washington is a real rough diamond, but he was an ace flyer in the war, and stayed on in the Air Force afterwards only because he is mad-keen on flying. He has stacks of money and in addition to living like a prince in this house, the Cedars, outside the base with a team of imported coloured boys to look after him, he has his own private six-seater aircraft that he flies himself whenever he goes on leave to the Continent. He had applied for leave in the regular way and been given a fortnight. His 'plane is fitted with equipment for night flying; so no one thought it particularly strange that he should elect to take off at one in the morning. His service record is a brilliant one and there has never been the slightest hint of anything against him on security grounds.

'They knew nothing of anyone who might be Lothar, and the night duty-officer who was reporting to me obviously thought that I'd been sold a cock-and-bull story. No doubt that was partly because I had suggested in the first place that Washington was probably about to fly one of their super-bombers off to Russia; and it transpired that he hadn't. I told this sceptical type to order a check-up on all secret equipment at the base to see if anything was missing; and that he had better get his Chief out of bed to take over from him, or he might regret it. After that, to fill in time I got on to Thompson to enquire how the raid on that place at Cremorne had gone off.'

Barney suddenly looked up. 'Bejesus! My mind has been so taken up with Mary and Lothar that I've never given it a thought. How did it go, Sir?'

'Ace high. We bagged the lot with their pants down. Thompson said that when they went in it was like a scene from the *Folies Bergère*, and that he hadn't seen so many nudes since his uncle took him on a trip to Paris when he was a youngster. They were bundled up in a blanket apiece and taken off to Cannon Row. There were about thirty of them and some dozen coloured people, men and women, but they were only staff, and all appeared to be slightly loopy.'

371

'Have you got the names of the Satanists yet?'

'Not the lot. When I rang up the Special Branch boys were still grilling them. But among them there is one cop that the Yard are particularly pleased about. He is a saintly-looking old gentleman named Bingley. His speciality is luring little girls into back-lots and strangling them. After his last murder the police had a clear case against him but before they could arrest him he disappeared. That was five years ago, and evidently he has been lying low very comfortably in the house at Cremorne ever since.'

'How about Ratnadatta?'

'Oh, he's been sent up from Fulham, to join the rest of the bunch.'

'Do you think the police will succeed in getting enough evidence to prove that some of them murdered Teddy Morden?'

Verney shook his head. 'I rather doubt it. Our best hope of that is that one of them will turn Queen's Evidence. But these people are not ordinary crooks. Such previous experience as I've had with Satanists has shown that generally they are so terrified of their Infernal Master, and of other members of their Fraternity who have escaped the net, that they prefer to face any legal punishment for obscene behaviour, and so on, rather than risk what might come to them if they spilled the beans about anything the police have failed to find out for themselves. But, of course, Special Branch are searching the place from attic to cellar, so there is a chance that they may come upon some incriminating documents.'

'How about the photos of Tom Ruddy and Mary?'

'Thompson got those and several dozen others of a similar nature; and the negatives. The Ruddy job was no isolated case. It is clear that they have been running a regular blackmail racket, either to get money out of people or force them into doing the Devil's work. Now that we've busted the racket, with luck we may be able to persuade some of the victims to prosecute.'

'They might,' Barney agreed, 'seeing that in such cases the victim is protected from having his name made public; and if they did we'd be able to get some of these Satanist swine much longer sentences than any they would receive for moral turpitude. But what about the air base, Sir? You must have heard something further?'

'Of course. About seven o'clock Colonel Richter rang up. He is the U.S. top security man, and by then they knew they'd had it.

372

The base had made their check and reported a nuclear war-head missing. Richter sounded nearly as explosive as if he were an atomic war-head himself. He was just leaving to drive there to conduct a personal enquiry, and he promised to telephone me again as soon as he had got from his people the facts about Washington's departure. It is to hear from him I am waiting now.'

'May I wait here, too, Sir,' Barney asked.

'Certainly. I'll send for some more coffee. I expect you could do with a cup. As it is Sunday I have no appointments and I've already asked my No. 2 to attend to any special business, other than this, that might turn up. This thing is too big for either of us to take our mind off it until we are quite certain that there is no hope of retrieving the situation.'

Barney's face brightened. 'You think there might be, then?'

C.B. laid a finger alongside his big nose in a familiar gesture. 'From Cambridgeshire to Moscow is all of fifteen hundred miles. He couldn't fly that far in an ordinary aircraft without coming down somewhere on the way to refuel. As soon as Otto told me about his vision I saw the red light and I didn't wait for the Americans to do any checking. I got straight through to the Security Chief at N.A.T.O., and passed on to him Otto's description of Colonel Washington. I said I thought he had got away with a big bomber, but it might be a smaller aircraft, in which case he would have to come down to refuel and could easily be recognized on account of his unusual height and features. In any case, all stations were to be alerted to watch for any unscheduled aircraft crossing Europe in the direction of the Iron Curtain, and if spotted fighters were to be sent up to intercept and force it down.'

'You're certainly jolly quick off the mark, Sir.' Barney said with a note of admiration.

The older man shrugged. 'But not quick enough in this case, I'm afraid. If only Otto had come round to me at once we would have caught them for certain; but it was four o'clock before I could get cracking, and they had been in the air for three hours by then. If they were in anything that had the speed of an average airliner, they would have needed only another half hour's flying to cross the Iron Curtain. And once over it, of course, they would be in the clear; they could refuel without risk and fly on to Moscow. Still, there is just a chance that they had to come down this side of the Curtain and, if so, they may be being held pending

373

a check up on them. If they are, we should hear pretty soon; or Richter may have done so already, as this is really a U.S. responsibility and he too will have been in touch with N.A.T.O.'

They had their coffee and some sandwiches and, to keep Barney from sitting brooding about Mary, C.B. made him give a much more detailed account of his doings the previous night. At eleven o'clock, as Colonel Richter had not come through, Verney 'phoned the Fulgoham air base and learnt that the Colonel was on his way up to London. At half past he was announced over the buzzer, and C.B. had him shown in at once.

The American Security Chief was short, tubby and round-faced, but there was nothing soft about him. His mouth was a hard line and his brown eyes, half veiled by heavy lids, were shrewd and calculating, yet he was not without a sense of humour. With a wry twist of his rat-trap mouth he declared that he would not waste time letting off steam. He had already done that by leaving a score of people down at the air base under close arrest for negligence; but he doubted if there was any case against most of them, as they had broken no regulation by allowing their Commanding Officer to fly off at any hour he liked in his own aircraft.

The aircraft had been a twin-engined six-seater. Recently it had had extra fuel tanks fitted and with these had a comfortable range of seven hundred miles. It had taken off on a north-easterly course and automatic radar plots showed that it had continued on that course out over the North Sea for at least a hundred miles. If the course was held that meant that the aircraft should, at about five o'clock in the morning, have been over Southern Norway. The questioning of Colonel Washington's officers had brought out the fact that he had told several of them that he intended to spend his leave fishing in Norway. Richter therefore suggested the possibility that Washington was innocent and that someone else had stolen the atomic war-head earlier in the day; or perhaps several days ago.'

Verney promptly shot down that theory by making Barney give an account of Washington's association with Lothar, and stating that within his own knowledge Lothar had only a week earlier stolen a quantity of secret rocket fuel from the Experimental Station in Wales.

Richter blinked a little at Barney's description of the Black Magic ceremony from which he had narrowly escaped with his life; but he knew that such circles existed and, as a man answering

Lothar's description had entered the air base with Washington, he agreed that the association left no doubt that it was they who had made off with the war-head.

Anxiously Barney asked, 'Was there a girl with them? A good-looking dark-haired young woman of about twenty-three?'

'Yep,' the Colonel replied. 'She was sitting in the back of the car. Washington told the gate guard that his two passengers were accompanying him on his leave. According to regulations they should have been signed in and given temporary passes, but seeing they were with the C.O., and he was in a hurry, the guard skipped that formality. He is sitting in the cooler now, wishing he hadn't. Both passengers were later seen to board Colonel Washington's aircraft.'

That killed Barney's last hope that Mary might have got away and was somewhere in hiding. Instead she was still a prisoner of the two Satanists and perhaps by now behind the Iron Curtain. To hide his sick misery, he turned away to the big window that looked out over London's roof-tops.

'The course from Cambridgeshire to Moscow is North by East,' C.B. remarked, 'so, after flying about half-way to Norway, Washington would have had only to alter course to due East to be heading for his real destination. But he'd have to fly over Denmark, and she is a member of N.A.T.O. I had a hope that the 'plane might be picked up before it got through, and forced down.'

Richter shook his head. 'No dice, friend. His seven hundred mile range would have enabled him to get over the Iron Curtain before he had to come down to refuel. Still, I would have thought our observation posts would have had some record of an unscheduled aircraft flying over. But they haven't. I was on to N.A.T.O. H.Q. before I left Fulgoham and from round four o'clock on they had alerted every station from the Northern tip of Denmark down to Frankfurt, and they've registered nothing crossing the line that might have been our man.'

Barney turned back from the window and said to his Chief, 'I know it has always been your opinion, Sir, that Lothar is a Soviet agent; but Squadron-Leader Forsby takes a different view. He thinks that Lothar has broken with the Russians and has become just a scientist with cranky views, who is anxious to try out some private experiment. And Otto, you will recall, did report last week seeing him up in a cave among snow-covered mountains. If Forsby is right it seems possible that it really was to

375

some secret hide-out in Norway that Washington has flown Lothar.'

'Maybe you're right, young feller,' Verney admitted. 'I only hope to God you are. That would account for his aircraft never having flown through the radio check, as the Norway stations were considered too far North to be worth alerting. Anyway, Otto intended to do an all-out concentration this morning on trying to locate his brother; so let's go down and find out if he has anything fresh to tell us.'

Five minutes later the three of them were in Verney's car on their way to Chelsea. Barney sat with the chauffeur and the other two in the back; so during the run C.B. was able to give Richter an idea of the strange bond that linked the Khune twins, and enabled them to contact each other on the psychic plane. While listening, the American eyed him somewhat dubiously but, in view of what he had already been told of the Satanic background to the whole business, he remarked: 'Well, there are stranger things . . . and so on, as it says in Hamlet; so it's not for me to question your beliefs about this business.'

At the small hotel at which C.B. had secured accommodation for Otto, Verney told his friend the landlord that he wanted to have a quiet talk with his guest; so the landlord placed his private sitting-room at their disposal, and a few minutes later Otto came down to it.

After he had been introduced to Colonel Richter, and been told that they still had no definite information concerning Lothar's whereabouts, he said, 'He has not gone into Russia. I'm sure of that. He is back in the mountain hide-out where I saw him last week. I saw him there again this morning about nine o'clock, just after I woke up. And it can't be in the Caucasus because he wouldn't have had time to fly that far. He could hardly have got so far as Dalmatia, either; so it must be either in Norway or the Alps. It is a cave, high up above snow level. There is a cable railway up to the broad platform at its entrance, and inside the cave a number of lean-to's have been made and furnished as bedrooms and living quarters. I saw him there as clearly as I see you; and with him were the hook-nosed giant in American uniform and a pretty dark-haired woman.'

'Was she . . .' Barney gulped, 'was she looking all right? '

'Well, she was a bit dishevelled and pale. No doubt she was tired from the journey. But otherwise she looked quite normal.'

376

By this time it was close on one o'clock; so C.B. asked the landlord to serve lunch for them in the private room in order that they could continue their talk without being overheard. It was not the first time Verney had made such a request, and the landlord willingly agreed.

After they had had a round of drinks they all felt better, and over the good meal that followed they were able to discuss the affair with relative calmness. But they got no further. When they had finished their meal C.B. told Barney that as no action could be taken for the moment, and he looked all in, he was to go home and to bed, so as to catch up on his loss of sleep. The others agreed to keep in touch in case of any fresh development, and before they separated it was agreed that they should all meet at Verney's office at nine o'clock the following morning.

On the Monday C.B. arrived at his office a little early to find that Otto was already there waiting for him. Without any preamble the scientist announced, 'They are in Switzerland; I'm sure of it.'

Verney's long face lit up. 'I supposed that they had come down near this mountain hide-out of Lothar's only to refuel from it, and that by this time they would have flown on to Russia. If you are right we may get them yet. But what makes you so certain that they are in Switzerland?'

'I couldn't swear to that, but I've spent several holidays in Switzerland and now I've been able to see more of the locality I'm convinced that it can be in no other country. Yesterday, in the evening, I got through to Lothar again, He was with the big American and they were standing on the rock platform outside the cave looking down into the valley, and all the features in it were of the kind I have seen in scores of Swiss valleys.'

C.B. picked up a ruler from his desk and stepped over to a big map of Europe that hung on the wall behind his chair. Stuck in it there were many pins with different coloured heads, the significance of which were known only to him and the senior members of his staff. Using the ruler as a rough measure, he said:

'Could be. From Cambridge to the southern tip of Norway or the frontier of Switzerland is just about the same distance – roughly five hundred miles. This aircraft had a fuel range of seven hundred, so he could have headed north-east for a hundred miles then swing right round to south south-west and gone in over Belgium with still enough fuel to carry him well into Switzerland. As only the radar screen that covers the Iron Curtain countries was alerted, he would have outflanked that, too. Have you any idea what they are up to in this cave?'

'I hadn't last night; but I have now.' Otto's face suddenly became grim. 'I woke about seven and succeeded in getting another look round the cave. I found that it is really a big curved tunnel. Its other entrance is from another broad outjutting shelf that cannot be seen from the valley below because it is hidden by a spur of the mountain. On it Lothar has a rocket, a mass of gear and . . .'

'A rocket!'

'Yes. As he has any amount of money he would have had no difficulty in getting a rocket shell and parts made to his specification, and he could assemble them himself. But, of course, it wouldn't have been any use to him unless he could get proper fuel and a war-head; so those he had to steal. Anyhow, on the far shelf outside the cave a twenty-five-foot rocket is lying, the drums containing my fuel are in a stack nearby, and for a launching pad he could not have a better base than the solid rock.'

'Good God, man!' C.B. exclaimed, aghast. 'D'you mean that he is intending to launch it?'

'There doesn't seem much doubt about that. At seven o'clock he, Colonel Washington, and a thick-set dark man were all hard at work round a forge, adapting the casing of the war-head from the bomb to serve as a cone for the rocket.'

At that minute Colonel Richter was shown in. When Verney told him the alarming news his rat-trap mouth worked silently for a few moments, then he said, 'Well, we've got something to be thankful for. Neither the fuel nor the H-bomb head have reached the Russians; and it doesn't look as though they are likely to.'

'But . . .' Verney began.

'I know, Colonel; I know,' the American cut in. 'Instead of having been left standing by an enemy agent, we have a madman on our hands. And the sort of party he may start with that war-head is no laughing matter. Still, with luck we might locate and grab him before he has a chance to set it off. If not it's going to be just too bad for quite a lot of Swiss.'

'I can't offer any concrete proof that this place is in Switzerland,' Otto said a shade hesitantly, 'although I've the strongest possible feeling that it is. But saying I'm right, there must be hundreds of valleys similar to the one I saw in my vision, and I've no means of directing you to it.'

378

'Only a small percentage of them would have cable railways,' replied Richter quickly. 'But what I don't get is why this crank should want to launch a rocket. And why do it in Switzerland? What does he expect to gain by killing a lot of Swiss? Mad he may be, but there must be some object that his crazy brain is aiming to achieve.'

'Because he launches it from Switzerland it doesn't follow that the war-head will explode there,' remarked C.B. Then he turned to Otto and asked, 'Can you give us any idea how far the fuel he's got would carry his rocket?'

After thinking for a moment the scientist said, 'I can give only an answer that may be widely out. So much depends on the weight of his rocket but, if it conforms to normal standards, I'd say that with my new fuel he could send a rocket of that size anything from four to eight hundred miles.'

Richter's heavily-lidded eyes opened wide, and he exclaimed, 'Snakes alive! Then if he has the know-how to direct it accurately he might put it down on Paris, London or Berlin.'

'He has the know-how all right,' Otto replied glumly. 'He has been a top-line rocket scientist from the Peenemünde days, and that is sixteen years ago. But he won't put it on Berlin. My family is of German extraction, and Lothar has always had a passion for the Fatherland.'

The door opened and Barney came in. He made a quick apology to his Chief for being late, explaining that a learner-driver had run into his taxi, so held him up while a policeman was taking notes. Then he said excitedly,

'I've got something here, Sir, that may prove important. Mrs. Morden thrust it on me just before we left the Cedars on Saturday night. Owing to all that happened afterwards I forgot about it, and yesterday afternoon I was so dead beat that I simply threw my clothes on the floor and flopped into bed. This morning when I picked them up I came across it in my pocket. It's a spool of recorder tape.'

Verney took the small nail-varnish carton and shook out the spool; then he switched on the inter-com. and asked for a tape-recorder machine to be sent up. Five minutes later the tape was inserted in the machine and being played back.

An American voice said harshly, 'Get your clothes off,' then Mary's voice came, panic-stricken and pleading that she really had not meant to run away. Next second her piercing screams

379

rang through the room, followed by a ghastly sobbing, then silence.

Beads of sweat had broken out on Barney's face. Fiercely he exclaimed, 'The swine! The swine! Then she did try to escape from him but he caught her. Oh, the swine! What did he do to her!'

'Shut up,' snapped C.B., for Mary's voice was coming from the machine again, but now it was quite normal. She was saying, 'I behaved very stupidly yesterday when you were telling me about human sacrifice. If I am to be a really good witch I ought to prepare myself to witness such ceremonies...'

There followed her conversation with Wash which had culminated in his describing to her exactly how her husband had been murdered. Then there came another short silence.

'By jove, she's got us the goods!' Even C.B. could not suppress the excitement in his voice. 'What courage! Just think what she must have gone through without giving in; and the skill she showed in leading him into the trap. She deserves a decoration.'

Mary's voice came again, but this time so low that it was hardly more than a whisper. She said, 'This is Mary Morden with a message for Colonel Verney, care of Special Branch, Scotland Yard. Mary Morden for Colonel Verney. Anyone who comes into possession of this spool should take it at once to the nearest police station. You will have heard my screams. I was being tortured by a Colonel Washington of the U.S. Air Force in a house called the Cedars near Fulgoham. It was he, too, whom you heard give particulars of the murder of my husband. Colonel Washington brought me here last Saturday night from a Satanist Temple at Cremorne...'

While they listened with bated breath Mary went on to relate how she had gone to the Temple because she had recognized her dead husband's shoes on Ratnadatta's feet. After describing them she again spoke of Wash, giving a brief outline of his personality and background. Then she said,

'If Colonel Washington's confession to having witnessed the murder of my husband is not sufficient to arrest him on, some pretext for removing him from his command should be found at once; because he may endanger peace. He says his flying career may soon be brought to an end by the introduction of rockets, and I believe he is planning to start a new career by going over to the Russians. He says that Russia will never attack the U.S., but

380

the U.S. may be driven by economic reasons to attack Russia. He thinks that given peace Russia will be able to wreck the commerce of the West and so dominate the world in ten years time. Therefore she would lay down the red carpet for anyone who could bring about the abolition of all nuclear weapons. A way to do this would be to drop an H bomb on Switzerland. Neither side would take action while trying to find out who dropped the bomb. Meanwhile, eyewitness reports of the horrors caused would lead to the democratic Governments of the West being forced by their people to agree a pact with the Soviet Government to scrap all nuclear weapons. The Russians could then go ahead without fear with their programme of underselling the West in the world's markets and conquest by peaceful penetration. Colonel Washington could fly one of his big aircraft out at any time, drop an H bomb on Switzerland, and fly on to reap a great reward in Russia. It is imperative that he should be deprived of the power to do so. Mary Morden for Colonel Verney, care of Scotland Yard.'

Dramatically the whispering ceased and the tape came to an end. For a moment the four men standing round the machine remained white-faced and silent. Then C.B. looked across at Otto and said,

'You were right. They are in Switzerland. But why, instead of taking one of his bombers and dropping the bomb, did Washington take only the war-head for use with the rocket?'

'Because in the Satanic hierarchy Lothar is his boss, and Lothar wanted it that way,' replied the scientist.

'But why?' Verney asked again.

'Only one answer to that,' snapped Richter. 'Lothar doesn't mean the big bang to take place in Switzerland. He has just kidded Washington along about that. He means to launch his rocket so that it hits some place else; and that could start a world war.'

'No,' C.B. shook his head. 'Forewarned is forearmed. He's got only one war-head. God knows that's bad enough. But as the Russians won't have launched it they will believe one of ours has gone off through some ghastly accident; so they won't follow it up with others. We must send out a signal to all concerned that we are expecting a maniac to launch one, and that the Russians have no hand in it, so there is to be no retaliation.'

'You are assuming that he will aim it on London or Paris,' said Otto quickly.

'Of course. He is a Communist, or at all events he worked willingly for the Russians for years.'

'He worked for the Russians, but he was never a Communist. He is a dyed-in-the-wool Nazi. Over and above that, though, he is a Satanist. His aim is to disrupt all stable forms of government; to create a state of world anarchy, so that it becomes every man for himself, and in a new era of complete lawlessness and disorder the Devil will come into his own again.'

'Well, what do you deduce from that?' asked Richter sharply.

'That if his rocket had the range to do it he would try to land it on New York; because it is the United States that he hates with a positive fanaticism. As it is he'll probably put it down on the other side of the Iron Curtain, hoping that the Russians will retaliate and blow most of the American cities off the map.'

'Maybe you've got something there,' the American admitted. 'I doubt though if Moscow would fall for that. He could aim it at Prague or Budapest, but I don't see the Russians entering on an all-out war because one of their satellites has been blitzed. They'll not risk their own cities being laid in ruins. It would be a different story if he could put it down in Moscow, but Moscow is thirteen hundred miles from Switzerland; so praised be the Lord, he can't.'

'One moment,' Barney cut in, addressing Otto. 'Have you any idea how high above sea level this cave is where Lothar has his rocket?'

'From what I know of the Alps it would be anything between eight and ten thousand feet.'

'Well, the atmosphere must be much more rarefied at that height. Isn't that going to decrease the resistance to the rocket on its take-off and greatly increase its range?'

Otto stared at him appalled. 'You're right!' he muttered. 'You're right! It could double it. It could give him the thirteen hundred miles he'd need to land it on Moscow.'

'God help us all, that's it then!' Verney smashed his fist down on his desk. 'Even if we warn the Russians in advance they'll never believe that we didn't launch the rocket. Within minutes of its landing they'll retaliate on America and Britain with everything they've got. At any moment now the world may go up in flames.'

382

24

In the Cave

MARY sat hunched in the aircraft. In front of her Wash's huge shoulders blocked out the greater part of the dimly lit instrument panel. Faintly she could hear him humming to himself and, now that he was in his favourite element – the air – he seemed completely happy and relaxed. Behind her Lothar was sitting. She had caught only a glimpse of him as Wash had hurried her into the 'plane, but she was terribly conscious of his nearness to her and could actually feel on her spine the chill that emanated from him.

Wash's abrupt disclosure that he was taking her with him to Russia had shattered her completely. More, even, than the Great Ram's threat to put a curse upon her. About a curse there was something nebulous. For some inexplicable reason it might not mature; given unshakeable faith in one's own powers of resistance it could be made to rebound on its initiator or, if one could find a priest of sufficient saintliness one could get it lifted. But to be carried off to a distant country from which there was very little chance of ever getting back was a down-to-earth matter; and it was actually happening to her.

The lights of the air base had already disappeared and the 'plane was climbing steeply. In a matter of minutes now they would have left England behind and be flying through the dark night out over the North Sea. Dully her mind sought to probe the future. It would be utterly different from anything she had ever known. Never again would she see any of the friends she had made while married to Teddy, or live again in the pleasant little flat at Wimbledon on which she had lavished so much care. Her only link with the past – the only person she would know who could even speak her own language – would be Wash; and although he had the power to arouse her physically she felt no faintest spark of love for him. On the contrary, knowing the cruel and evil nature that lay below his casual cheerfulness, she hated him more bitterly every time she recalled, with shame, her own weakness in having let herself respond to his passion.

And when he had tired of her, what then? He had shown very clearly that when he wanted a thing he would stop at nothing to get it – and get it quickly. Rather than wait twenty-four hours he had made himself liable to an onerous penalty by carrying her off to the country instead of attending the Walpurgis Eve ceremony. Since, he had developed such an obsession for her that, only an hour ago, he had taken the appalling risk of defying the Great Ram rather than have her spoiled for him as a mistress. But such fierce obsessions never lasted. Within a few weeks, or months at most, any man who had made a habit all his life of sleeping with one pretty girl after another would tire of his new plaything. Mary had no doubt at all that his desire for her would cease as swiftly as it had begun; and that overnight he would throw her out for some fresh charmer. Where would he throw her? Presumably to the Great Ram to be cursed – unless with his revenues from the United States cut off he found himself in need of money. If that happened the chances were that he would postpone letting the Great Ram know that he had done with her, and first sell her into a Russian brothel.

Once again she bemoaned her folly in having let herself become caught in this terrible web through having recognized Teddy's shoes on Ratnadatta's feet. If only she had kept her promise to Barney! Well, at least she had saved him from paying with his life for her stupidity. She wondered if while struggling with his captors he realized that it was she who had enabled him to break free, and thought it unlikely. If that was so he would not even feel that he owed her anything. Neither could he have any idea how desperately she loved him. When he did give her a casual thought in the months ahead it would only be as Wash's mistress, and a born whore who, having delighted in the licentious rights practised by Satanists, had willingly left the country with her great brute of a lover.

The tears coursed silently down her cheeks until at length she drifted off to sleep.

She was woken by the aircraft beginning to bump. It was in cloud, but she could sense that it was descending, and shortly afterwards it broke clear so that on looking down she could see the extraordinary panorama that lay spread below them. They were flying over what seemed an endless vista of deep valleys and snow-capped mountains. The sun was still low and on their left, so that it lit only one side of each peak, and the valleys, in sharp contrast to the blinding whiteness of the snow-clad heights, were still irregular chasms of night-shrouded blackness.

As they came lower the bumping became much worse, so Wash took the aircraft up again to just below cloud level. Even there it was far from comfortable, and every few moments the 'plane dropped like a stone from fifty to a hundred feet. Several times now Wash changed course, and in one case circled right round a giant peak. Then he evidently got his bearings and in a series of shallow dives brought the 'plane right down until it was flying between two ranges of mountains. Turning where they opened out he came back, now perilously skirting great jutting crags. But he was a superb pilot and still seemed perfectly relaxed as he lay back with his long legs stretched out, his great hands firmly on the controls.

It was lighter now. Mary could see the dark woods on the lower slopes, and the green of fields in the bottom of the valley. They passed over a cluster of dwellings, came lower, gently now, and in another minute were running low over a long stretch of meadow. But Wash did not land. In a steep climb he took the 'plane out of the far end of the valley, circled and came in again, still more slowly. The 'plane bumped once, twice, then ran on smoothly for several hundred yards, until he braked it to a halt in front of an open hangar.

A short, swarthy man with a shock of dark wiry hair ran out from it, followed by two Chinese one of whom was carrying a ladder. Wash stretched a long arm back and undid the clamps of the aircraft's door. The ladder was put against it and, pushing past Mary, the Great Ram stepped out. Seizing his hand, the swarthy man kissed his ring, greeted him in some foreign language and helped him down the last few rungs.

When he had left the aircraft Mary found her voice. She was staring in surprise at the Chinese, and said to Wash, 'Where are we? Surely there are no great mountains like these in Russia. Have you brought us down in . . . no, it couldn't possibly be Tibet; we haven't been in the air long enough.'

He laughed. 'This is Switzerland. We're stopping off here for a day or so on our way to Moscow; that's all.' As he spoke he ducked his head and thrust his great body through the doorway. Springing down, he turned at the foot of the ladder, held out his arms, and told her to jump.

Lothar was speaking to the swarthy man. When he had done, he turned to Wash and said, 'This is our brother Mirkoss. He is an Hungarian and a very clever engineer. He also speaks fluent Chinese, but he does not understand English. I have told him that you and your woman will be staying with us until the great work is completed, and that his men are to unload the crate with the greatest care. He will bring it and the luggage along later in the box car. We three will go on ahead.'

Mirkoss and Wash exchanged grins, then the latter, with Mary beside him, followed Lothar across the field to a narrow road running alongside a rock-strewn stream that foamed and hurtled along the valley bottom. On the road a car was waiting with another Chinese at its wheel. Lothar got in beside him, the other two got into the back, and it set off up the valley.

The road was steep and winding; soon it became no more than a rough track. It was bitterly cold and with a shiver Mary drew her coat more closely about her. They climbed for about two miles then, round a sudden bend, the track ended at what looked like a big barn with a chalet roof. From it steel cables looped upward from a succession of tall steel pylons set in the mountain-side, to end far above the snow line at what looked like a small black hole.

They left the car and went into the chalet, which Mary now saw was an engine-house, with an opening at one end near which stood the cabin of the cable railway. The cabin was divided by a partition, the front section having benches to seat four passengers; the rear section was empty and evidently for carrying up stores. A fourth Chinese came out from a room at the back of the chalet and started the engine up, the others got into the cabin. There was a grinding sound as it ran the few yards along its landing rails, then, as it swung out into the open, silence.

The cabin moved steadily at a moderate pace but the ascent took nearly a quarter-of-an-hour. First they passed over rough

386

grassy slopes, then a deep belt of dark fir trees, the branches of those in the higher part of which were powdered with snow. Beyond them the mountain was much steeper and, except where here and there grey rocks broke through, a convoluted sheet of dazzling white.

The sun had now risen above the chain of mountains opposite, so that only a part of the valley was left in deep shadow and Mary, who was seated facing it, found the scene one of almost terrifying grandeur. She had never before been up a mountain and would have enjoyed the experience had her mind not been distracted by thoughts of the grim company she was in.

Suddenly there came a clatter of steel on steel, and she looked round in alarm, but was reassured on seeing that they had reached the top. The cabin ground to a halt on a broad flat shelf of rock.

She now saw that the black spot she had seen from below was in fact the entrance to a cave at least twenty feet in height. It was lit by a row of electric bulbs spaced out along its ceiling, and along one side of it ran a range of low-roofed shallow wooden sheds; but it curved away into the mountain so she could not see its end.

As they got out, a blast of icy wind, carrying a flurry of snow, struck her with such force that she could hardly stand against it; but Wash took her by the arm and hurried her into the cave. Ten feet inside it they were sheltered from the wind and it was comparatively warm there, although she never discovered whether it contained some normal heating installation or conditions in it were made bearable by the Great Ram's Satanic powers.

He led the way down it and they passed the open doorway of a lean-to made from stout planks in which a Chinese cook was busy at a stove. The next shed along was a small dining-room. It was not even deep enough to have a bench along the far side of the table, which was formed by a flap projecting from the wall, but it was long enough to seat six people in a row on the near side and at its far end had shelves on which were a number of bottles. Their host pointed to the shelves and said:

'No doubt you would like something to warm you up. Food will be brought to you presently, but I shall not join you. I have learnt to do without such things for long intervals. You will also need sleep. But you will not sleep together. While you are here I forbid it; because it would arouse vibrations on the animal plane which could disturb the transcendental links that I have created.'

For Mary this last ordinance was a crumb of comfort, and Wash took it philosophically, remarking to her as Lothar left them, 'Me, I'm all for remaining just a simple Mage. What's the fun in becoming an Ipsissimus when it means that most all the time you're on an astral plane so high you've no use for your body. But don't fret, honey, we'll not be stuck here more than thirty-six hours. Come Tuesday night at latest we'll be in little 'ole Moscow, and by then we'll have gotten a fine edge on our appetites.'

He took a bottle from the shelf and two broad-bottomed rummers, poured three fingers of Bourbon for her and three-quarters filled the other big glass for himself, swore because there was no ice container, and instead splashed a little water into both. She was still cold, so she took a long drink from the one he handed her. As the almost neat spirit went down she shuddered; but its reaction was swift and gave her the courage to ask,

'Why have we stopped off here, anyway?'

'See that big crate in the tail of the aircraft?' he grinned. 'That's the reason. It has in it the war-head of an H bomb.'

Realizing that he must have stolen it for some nefarious purpose she stared at him for a moment in consternation; then she exclaimed, 'But why? What do you mean to do with it?'

He swallowed a good half of his drink, set the glass down and replied, 'You're such a smart kid I'd have thought you'd have guessed, after what I told you a few nights back.'

'You . . . you can't really mean that you're going to let it off, here in Switzerland.'

'Sure, honey, sure. It's just that we mean to do. The big bang will scare the pants off the peoples in the West. They'll force their Governments to make a pact with the Soviets to scrap all nuclear weapons. That'll leave a free field for the Russians to go right on with their plans for making the world Communist, without fear of Uncle Sam being able to pull a fast one when he does see the red light. And we'll be made Heroes of the Soviet Union.'

Mary knew that it would be futile either to plead or argue. Even if she could have won Wash over that would now make no difference. Clearly in stealing the bomb he had acted only as the agent of the Great Ram, and he could not be diverted from his evil purpose. While coming up in the cabin of the cable railway she had not dared even to raise her eyes to his; and, with a swift sinking of the heart, she suddenly realized that, now he had got

388

what he wanted from Wash, he might even go back on his agreement to postpone laying a curse on her.

In a low, anxious voice she put that possibility to Wash. But he told her not to worry, because the Great Ram would still need him to fly him on to Moscow.

Shortly afterwards the Chinese cook came in and laid places for three at the long narrow table. Then the stocky, shock-haired Hungarian, Mirkoss, joined them. They exchanged bows and smiles with him but, when the food was served, on account of his presence they fell silent. The meal was simple but good: firm baked lake fish, a ragoût of veal with mushrooms, and a selection of excellent Swiss cheeses.

After it, Mirkoss beckoned them outside and a few yards along the cave, then threw open the doors of two adjacent sheds. Each had only a single bunk. Wash's belongings had been stacked in the one that abutted on to the dining cabin, and Mary's suit-case reposed in the other. They smiled their thanks to the Hungarian, smiled at one another, then entered their narrow but solidly made quarters.

As Mary shut the door her strength seemed suddenly to drain from her. Although she had slept in the aircraft the strain she had been under for many hours had been so great that she felt as if she had not closed her eyes for weeks. There were no sheets, only blankets, on the bunk, but pulling her clothes off, except for her chemise, she crawled in between them and almost instantly fell asleep.

It was late in the evening when Wash roused her to say that another meal was being prepared for them by the Chinese cook. At the far end of her cabin there was a small basin with running water, and above it a nine by four inch mirror. Getting up, she washed and tidied herself as well as she could, then joined Wash in the dining cabin.

He mixed drinks for them, this time having first gone to the entrance of the cave and broken off some icicles to chill the spirit; then Mirkoss came in and the Chinese served them with a dinner of sorrel soup, wild duck and a vanilla soufflé. When coffee arrived Mirkoss declined it and left them, but they sat over theirs for some time drinking with it a Swiss Apricot Brandy that seemed positively the essence of the rich ripe fruit.

They were on their third glass of this delicious local liqueur when both of them instinctively turned round. Their senses, not

389

their hearing, had told them of the approach of the Great Ram, and he was standing silently behind them in the doorway. Ignoring Mary, he said to Wash:

'I do not need your help to-night but I shall require it to-morrow morning. You will be called at first light and we will set to work soon after dawn.'

'Just as you say, Exalted One,' Wash replied submissively; then he added, 'It shouldn't be a long job to fit a coupla time fuses to it. Reckon we could be done and on our way in the aircraft round about midday.'

'It is not my intention to explode the war-head up here,' announced the Great Ram calmly.

Wash gave him a puzzled look. 'Not here! But for why, Chief? Where could you find a site more suitable?'

'In a narrow valley such as this the effect of the explosion would be too localized. The blast could wreck only a few small villages and the fall-out beyond them would be negligible.'

'Hey, have a heart, Chief! That'll be plenty for our purpose. There's no sense in blotting out more folks than need be.'

'Some thousands at least must die if we are to achieve our object of horrifying everyone in the N.A.T.O. countries,' declared the Great Ram in an icy voice.

'But, Exalted One,' Wash protested, coming to his feet, 'you've got the darned thing up here now. I saw Mirkoss's Chinks humping it in. It would be simple to time fuse it to go up a coupla hours after we've quit, but one helluva job to hump it some other place and rig electric batteries to set it off. If it disintegrates a single village that'll sure be enough to scare the pants off every citizen in Europe.'

'There will be no necessity to transport it anywhere. I intend to adapt its case so that it can be launched from this cave as the war-head of a rocket.'

'A rocket!'

'Yes. I had the parts manufactured by a number of different firms, and Mirkoss and I have assembled them here. I have also secured a supply of the latest rocket fuel; so nothing remains to be done but to work out the weight-fuel ratio, now that the weight of the war-head is available to me, and to attach it to the body of the rocket. The calculations I shall do to-night. To-morrow your strength may prove of value in lifting the war-head into position for Mirkoss and I to fix it; and, unless some quite unforeseen difficulty arises, we should be able to launch it on Tuesday.'

'But what's to be your target, Chief? What's to be your target?' Wash asked in a puzzled, anxious voice. 'No one's ever accused me of having a yellow streak when it comes to taking life. No, sir! Not when it's been to forward Our Lord Satan's work, or my own. But to put this thing down on a city doesn't make sense to me. It'll get all the write-up we want without that; and there's mighty few places of any size that hasn't a few Brothers or Sisters of the Ram among its citizens. You sure can't wish to blot...'

'I did not say I intended to drop it on a city,' the Great Ram interrupted coldly. 'But I cannot afford to risk the effect being localized to this one narrow mountain valley and a radius of only a few miles of almost uninhabited country. For a target I have selected the small town of Sannen, in the foothills on the far side of this range. Apart from the mountain areas it is in one of the least populated parts of Switzerland, and almost equidistant from Berne, Lausanne and Interlaken. All of them are a good thirty miles from Sannen, so should not be affected by the initial shock. As for the fall-out, wherever we create the explosion that will be dependent on wind and weather, and Our Lord Satan's will. And now, on this question, you will not presume to argue further.'

Turning on his heel he left them, and for a few moments Mary and Wash stared after him in silence. Then, with a shrug of his great shoulders, Wash said, 'He's right. To put this thing over a hundred-per-cent, there's just gotta be at least one township blown sky-high. Must be, so as the newsreel boys can get their pictures and show the world what nuclear war would mean. And let's face it, honey, what do a few thousand deaths matter, if that insures against millions being slaughtered in a few years time?'

Mary found it difficult not to agree, providing that his basic premises were right. But she still could not believe that the United States would ever attack Russia without provocation, and that if matters were left as they were an all-out war between the East and West was inevitable. She said so, and they argued for another hour, but found themselves going round in circles, so at last broke off and went moodily to bed.

As Mary had slept most of the day she had a thoroughly bad night. For hours she tossed and turned in the narrow bunk, trying to think of some way in which she could get a warning of the Great Ram's intentions to the Swiss authorities; so that, even if they were not in time to stop him launching the rocket, they could at least evacuate the town of Sannen and it's surrounding district. Yet she knew that such mind-searching was utterly futile, because up there in the cave she was as completely shut off from the outside world as if she had been on a desert island in the Pacific. At length she fell into a half-sleep made hideous by nightmare visions of collapsing walls, houses in flames, and screaming, terrified people. Finally her mind became a blank for a couple of hours, but when she was woken by the Chinese cook she had the impression that she had been asleep for only a few minutes.

A quarter-of-an-hour later she joined Wash and Mirkoss at breakfast. They had been up since before dawn working on the rocket, and as soon as they had finished eating they returned to it. Knowing that the Great Ram would be with them, so she need have no fear of suddenly coming face to face with him, she decided to explore the cave.

She found it to be a good two hundred yards in length, curving round to another entrance at its far extremity. Tiptoeing forward to within about forty feet of the opening, she stood for some minutes watching the activity going on there. To one side there was a stack of what looked like oil drums, to the other an open shed housing a glowing furnace at which Mirkoss was hammering on a piece of white-hot metal. Outside in the centre of a broad rock platform lay the rocket, half hidden by a cluster of upright steel girders, a derrick with heavy lifting chains, a pumping apparatus and all sorts of other paraphernalia, among which the Great Ram and Wash were working.

Turning, she made her way back more slowly, exploring as she went the shallow sheds that lined the walls of the cave. Some contained stores of various kinds, including a big cache of tinned food, others were sleeping cabins; and one was obviously the Great Ram's work room, as it had maps pinned up on its walls and contained a table-desk and filing cabinets.

In several places between blocks of two or three sheds there were lower tunnels running in at right angles to the sides of the big one. She cautiously explored them in turn, to find that some of them had pieces of machinery in them. They were all quite short and ended abruptly in a sloping rugged surface; so she thought it probable that most, if not all, of this big hole in the mountain owed its existence to mining operations which had later been abandoned.

Near the end of the tunnel to which the cable railway mounted, she came upon three other cabins of special interest. One was evidently the Great Ram's bedroom, the next a bathroom and the last equipped with wireless apparatus.

The bedroom she did not dare to enter. A glimpse of a small altar in it on which stood a human skull that had been made into a chalice was enough to make her shut the door quickly and pass on; but in the radio room she stood for a long time, wondering if she could possibly send a message by the set. Unfortunately she was totally ignorant of everything to do with such things and had never even learned the Morse alphabet, so she was forced to abandon the idea.

However, the bathroom was a most welcome discovery, as it provided her with the means of whiling away an hour or two and, having collected from her suitcase her toilet and manicure things, she spent the rest of the morning there.

Wash and Mirkoss took barely a quarter-of-an-hour over their lunch, then hurried back to work; so she was again left to her own devices for the whole afternoon. With the idea that she might possibly suborn the Chinese cook, she visited his galley and attempted to enter into conversation with him; but she found that he did not understand a word of English, or French, which was the only foreign language of which she had a smattering. The other Chinese, she concluded, lived down below in the engine-house, and were brought up only when required for special jobs; so it seemed that there was very little chance of her getting a message out by one of them.

Nowhere could she find anything to read, even if she could have settled to it; so in desperation she returned to the bathroom where she spent a good part of the afternoon washing her hair and trying out different methods of arranging it so as to render as little conspicuous as possible the quarter inch of undyed gold that had grown up from her scalp.

Somehow she got through the hours until the early evening and when Wash and Mirkoss had bathed she joined them for dinner. The Hungarian was perforce, as usual, silent, but Wash was nearly silent too, which was most unusual for him; so Mary asked him the reason.

At first he hedged, saying that he had had a long day, and on heavy work of a kind to which he was not accustomed. But when Mirkoss had left them she pressed him further, and he said in a low voice,

'I'm having kittens, honey. The Big Chief's playing some deep game of his own. He's flat lied to me over this rocket set-up, and if he'll do that about one thing he'll do it about another. Could be that now he's gotten all the help he wanted from me, he means to do me dirt.'

'That's bad,' she whispered back with quick concern. 'What sort of lie has he told you?'

'He said he meant to aim the rocket to fall on a little burg called Sannen. You heard him, last night. Well, we worked like buck niggers all day and the rocket's set up. Wants only the right amount of gas pumped in and she'll be ready to go. But her mechanism is not adjusted to send her in the right direction. Saanen is over the range to the west of here. Must be if it's half-way between Lausanne and Interlaken. The rocket is oriented near due north-east, so he must mean to send it some place else.'

'Did you question him about it?'

Wash ran a hand through his almost white hair before he replied in the same hushed, conspiratorial voice, 'Nope. My Satanic name's not Twisting Snake for nothing. Times are when it pays best to let the other feller think he's got away with playing you for a sap. He's more like to show his hand then. Gives you a better chance of saying snap.'

'Have you any idea where he might mean to send the rocket?'

'I had one notion. It can't be right, though. Doesn't make sense. Yet if I were right you and I have got no future. I'd give a mighty fat wad to be a hundred-per-cent certain that I'm wrong.'

'I think you could, without much difficulty.'

He gave her a quick look. 'Tell, honey.'

'While you were all working this morning I explored the whole place pretty thoroughly. Near the far end of the tunnel he has an office. There are maps on the walls and papers scattered over the desk. All his calculations must be there somewhere. If you could get in ...'

'That's certainly an idea. Wonder if he keeps it locked.'

'As he doesn't bother to lock it in the daytime, I don't see why he should at night. Up here there is certainly no risk of burglars.'

'Sure, honey, sure.' Wash gave a sudden grin. 'Then we'll go along presently and have a look-see. Whether he ever sleeps or not I wouldn't know, but there's Mirkoss and the cook, so we'd best give the place a chance to settle down.'

For another hour and a half they continued sitting at the table, occasionally exchanging a remark or taking a sip of the Apricot Brandy, then Wash stood up and said in a whisper, 'Let's get weaving. Go quiet as you can. I'll follow you. Pull up on the outer curve of the tunnel ten yards before you come to his office. Point it out to me as I pass, then keep your eyes and ears on stalks. Anyone coming don't cough; just start walking on again natural. I trained my hearing young on the prairie, so I'll catch your footfalls and be out alongside you time you come opposite the office door. Then if its the Big Chief I'll tell him I was taking you to have a sight of the rocket in the moonlight. O.K.?'

She nodded and he followed her out. The lights along the roof of the tunnel were kept on night and day, and in all the cabins there were pilot lights that gave out a faint blue radiance, like those in the sleepers of International Pullman cars. Very quietly they walked down two-thirds of the length of the tunnel, then she halted and followed his instructions. The door of the office was not locked and he was in there a good ten minutes. To her it seemed an interminable time as she strained her ears for approaching footsteps, and her eyes into the semi-gloom behind her. But at last he emerged, and closed the door gently after him.

Taking her arm, and still walking softly, without uttering a word he led her back to the dining cabin. There, in the brighter light, she saw that his normally ruddy face had gone a queer shade of grey, and that his black eyes held a murderous glint.

'Well,' she asked in a whisper.

He sat down heavily, and muttered, 'What I thought a crazy idea was right. It's all worked out there. He's aiming to put it on Moscow.'

At first Mary did not realize the full implications, so she said, 'I can't help feeling sorry for the Russians; but thank God it's not London.'

For a moment he stared at her then, his voice still low, he broke into a tense spate of words, 'Be your age, woman! The Russians will take it that the West launched the rocket at them. They'll not wait to ask questions. They'll think we've tried to shoot 'em sitting down. Before what's left of Moscow's gone up in smoke they'll press the button. Within twenty minutes New York,

Washington, Pittsburg, Detroit will be just heaps of poisonous ruins – and London too. The West will react with all its got; land-based rockets, rockets from subs and cruisers, H bombs from aircraft. Russia's got subs, cruisers and long-range aircraft too – plenty. I'd give it three days, and every city west of a line Urals, Persia, India will have had it. Tens of millions dead, hundreds of millions dying; the whole of civilization as we know it to hell and gone.'

'Oh God!' she breathed, 'Oh God! Somehow we must stop it!'

'That's easy to say; but you know the man we're up against. I'd never be able to argue him out of anything he's set on.'

'But why, why does he want to do this frightful thing?'

'I'd hazard a guess. Another hunch. But things he's said fit into the picture. He knows that Russian Communism isn't Communism any more. The Soviet is reverting to a bourgeois state. I'd seen that one for myself. It's why I figured it to be the best bet as a place to spend the rest of my life in ease and plenty. But it's no longer good soil for sowing the seeds of the Old religion. And that's all the Great Ram gives a cuss about. "Do what thou wilt shall be the Whole of the Law." As long as there's settled Governments, doing that means risking a stretch in prison. But with a state of universal anarchy; well, ask yourself? Our Lord Satan would come into his own again in a real big way, wouldn't he?'

Suddenly Mary's blue eyes lit up and she stormed at him, 'It's you who are to blame for this! It's you who have made this horror possible! You let him fool you into giving him your bloody bomb. He is a real Satanist. You are not, any more than I am. You've just made use of the cult because it suits you. You only wanted rich living for yourself; to loll around on the profits of girls you have forced into prostitution; to listen to music while fine food is being prepared for you, then take your fill of drink and women.'

For a moment she thought he was going to strike her. But instead he gave himself a quick shake, then seemed to sag, and admitted, 'Maybe you've got something there. The Old Faith is the right one though. Prince Lucifer is the Lord of this World, and those who serve him come out tops.'

'Do they?' she countered hotly. 'Then what about yourself? Instead of being a Hero of the Soviet Union this time next week, you'll either be dead or trying to catch a stray dog to eat.'

396

'There's no going back on what's done,' he muttered miserably. 'It's by Our Lord Satan's will that it should be this way, and we've just got to take it.'

'No.' Mary stamped her foot. 'You can save yourself and countless innocent people. You must sabotage that rocket.'

'I can't. I wouldn't dare,' he protested. 'Just think what I'd let myself in for. If I threw a spanner in Our Lord Satan's work I'd be whipped down to Hell and slow roast while a thousand devils nipped bits off me till the world goes cold.'

'There is a power greater than Satan's that would protect you.'

'Maybe that's what you think. But no one's ever proved it.'

'Yes. I have. You saw me throw that crucifix. It was only a little thing of wood and ivory; but look what it did to your Great Ram. It rendered him as weak as water. For ten minutes he hadn't the power left to harm a rabbit.'

Wash's dark eyes opened in wonder. 'That's true,' he murmured. 'Sure, I saw it happen. Somehow I'd never thought of it like that.'

'Think of it now then. If the Powers of Good can intervene to save an individual, what wouldn't they do to protect a man who saved all humanity? Wash, you must sabotage this rocket. It's your great chance to make a come-back. Every evil thing you've ever done will be forgiven. You could sabotage it, couldn't you?'

He considered for a minute. 'Yeah. Not completely. Now it's been erected I couldn't get at the war-head. But I could drill a small hole in the casing, that wouldn't be spotted. Be large enough though to cause the fuel to leak when it jerked into flight. That'd ensure it coming down somewhere this side of the Iron Curtain.'

With a sudden uplift of the heart Mary realized that he was on the brink of surrendering to her. Grasping him by the arms she pulled him to his feet, gave him a quick kiss on the mouth, and cried, 'Come on then! What are we waiting for?'

As though in a daze he let her pull him out of the cabin. Side by side they tiptoed down the tunnel. When they reached its far end he seemed to have got his wits about him again and to have made up his mind to take the desperate gamble she had urged upon him. As they came level with the pile of fuel drums he said hoarsely,

'Get in among those. Keep watch for me. If you hear anyone coming tap lightly on one of the drums. Stay there till they've passed you, then sneak back to your cabin. If there has to be a show-down I'd as lief have you out of it.'

She pressed his hand and let him go forward, while she crouched down among the drums in a position where she was hidden by deep shadow but could see in both directions. To her left was the empty, dimly lighted curve of the lofty tunnel, to her right and thirty feet away the out-jutting platform of rock with the rocket now standing upright among its vaguely-seen tangle of launching gear.

Beyond it was darkness. Cloud had come down blotting out the stars, and wisps of grey mist swirled about the entrance to the cave. To the right the forge still glowed dully. She saw Wash go into the shed where it stood. For some minutes he remained there, presumably selecting the right tools for the job. While she crouched among the drums she prayed frantically. At last he re-appeared. As he walked towards the rocket she turned to look in the opposite direction. Unheard by her a figure had come into view. Her heart missed a beat. Only twenty yards away, with silent tread, the Great Ram was approaching.

25

Race against time

For a moment the four men in Colonel Verney's office remained stunned by the appalling conclusion they had come to about Lothar's intentions. Then C.B. pressed the switch of his inter-com and said to his P.A. 'Get me No. 10. I want one of the P.M.'s secretaries. On my other line get me one of the Staff Officers of the Chief of Defence. Then get the United States Embassy. All calls top priority.'

In barely a minute the first call came through. C.B. recognized the voice at the other end. 'George, I've got to see the Prime. . . .' 'He is just going in to Cabinet.' 'Then you must hold him for me. Safety of the Realm. A further development of the theft of the secret rocket fuel that I reported to him last week, and a matter of the utmost urgency. I'm coming round at once.'

The second telephone was already buzzing. He picked it up. 'Who's that?' '. . . Oh Stanforth, is your Master in the Office?' '. . . Good. I'm sending a Mr. Sullivan round to see him. Whatever he is doing he must break it off to hear a verbal report concerning the Safety of the Realm. Nothing, repeat nothing, must interfere with your Master's seeing Sullivan at once.'

The first telephone was buzzing again. C.B. gestured to Richter. 'That'll be your Embassy. Over to you.' The American took the call and arranged for an immediate interview with his Ambassador.

Barney had left the room. Now he came back and said, 'I've ordered your car round, Sir. It'll be here in a minute.'

399

C.B. nodded. 'We'll go together. While I'm seeing the Prime Minister, you will put the Chief of Defence fully in the picture and warn him that the P.M. is certain to want him round at No. 10 by the time you have said your piece.' Turning to Richter he added, 'When we are through with reporting we had better rendezvous here to inform each other of reactions. I'll probably be asked to attend a Cabinet. If so, it may be midday before I'm back. But none of us can do any more until we know what decision has been taken on the highest level.'

'Do you wish me to stay here?' Otto asked.

'Yes, you will have this office to yourself. Try to get into touch with Lothar again, and do your damnedest to find out whereabouts in Switzerland this cave is situated.' As Verney spoke he was already hurrying from the room, followed by Richter and Barney.

Two minutes later the American jumped into his Cadillac, and the other two set off for Storey's Gate. There they separated, Verney going through the back way into Downing Street, and Barney into the Ministry of Defence.

Barney was first back. In the P.A.'s office he found Inspector Thompson waiting to see his Chief. Unaware of the possibility that London might be blown to smithereens before the day was out, the Inspector was in high good humour. When they had exchanged greetings he said:

'I've fixed things for Tom Ruddy. He's back in the fight again.'

'Ruddy,' Barney repeated vaguely; then with an effort he brought his mind back to his work of the past two months, which now seemed to have little significance.

'Yes,' the Inspector went on, 'when we raided the place at Cremorne we found a score or more other photographs; different people, of course, but similar to the one they took of him. Last night I went down to Ruddy's place and had a talk with him. I suggested that he should show the whole lot to his missus, including the one of himself and Mrs. Morden, and that I'd vouch for it to her that the whole lot were fakes – composite photographs blended together by a gang of ordinary crooks for blackmail purposes. He agreed, and the old girl swallowed it. So he's standing again and I've not a doubt that he'll be elected as the new boss of his Union.'

'Well done,' Barney murmured. 'How about the bunch of Satanists you pulled in?'

The Inspector grinned. 'Oh boy, what a haul! A strangler who's been on the wanted list for five years, a bank-note forger whose goods we found in his wallet when we collected their clothes, a Czech secret agent that we didn't know was in the country, and a publisher who has distributed more poisonous literature than the Communist H.Q. itself. The rest of them are just degenerates, mostly rich people and well known. Now we've had a chance to check up we've found that it was them and the people in the black-mail photographs who have been paying the fat cheques into the so-called "Workers' Benevolent Institution". So this is going to put an end to one of the biggest sources of the funds used to sabotage British industry.'

'If a lot of them are important people this is going to create a first-class scandal,' Barney remarked.

'It certainly will,' Thompson agreed. 'I've a feeling, though, that the Home Office may decide to play down the Black Magic side of it, because there are names involved that might shake the public's confidence in a variety of national interests. It's probable that the bulk of them will get away with loss of reputation on conviction of simply being concerned in obscene practices.'

'But, damn it all, some of them are Tony Morden's murderers.'

'Naturally, we are going into that, and we shall move heaven and earth to get the goods on those who were concerned in it.'

'We've got the goods already. I brought back from Cambridge-shire a tape recording of a conversation between Mrs. Morden and a Colonel Washington. In it he gave her the Satanic names of the actual murderers and a description of the murder. Among the documents you seized at Cremorne you will find the Lodge's membership book. You have only to look through it to get the real names of those the Colonel mentioned by their Satanic ones.'

'That's splendid news.' The Inspector rubbed his hands. 'Like the strangler and our other beauties, they will be dealt with separately, of course. It will be necessary to take special measures, though. Much of the evidence will have to be supplied by your department, so it is certain that Colonel Verney will ask for these cases to be tried in camera.'

Barney shrugged. 'I'm not interested in providing the public with sensations. All I care about is making certain that these fiends swing; particularly Ratnadatta, and his name was among those given to Mrs. Morden. What is more, according to her, a week ago he was wearing a pair of shoes that he must have taken

401

off Morden's body. They are brown, hand-made by Lobb, and the left one has a bad scratch on the toecap. It is quite on the cards that he was wearing them when I turned him in at Fulham and still has them on. You might check on that.'

'I certainly will. If not, the odds are that we'll find them at his digs. Either way that will put him into it up to the neck. Have you any idea when Colonel Verney will be back?'

Barney was brought back with a jerk to the desperate situation which had sent his Chief hurrying off to Downing Street. He shook his head. 'I couldn't say. But I do know that he is on a top-priority job. When he does come back I very much doubt whether he'll be able to find time to see you.'

Reluctantly, the Inspector stood up. 'Oh well, in that case there's not much point in my waiting. I'll look in again to-morrow morning.'

As he turned away, Barney wondered grimly if there would be a to-morrow morning. Perhaps Ratnadatta and the other Satanists would never be called upon to stand their trial. Instead they might shortly be reduced to a few ounces of ash that by some freak of chance might mingle in the wind with other ash that had once been himself and Inspector Thompson.

Knowing that in C.B.'s room Otto was again attempting to overlook Lothar, Barney remained in the outer office killing time as best he could until the others should return. It proved a long wait but when they did arrive it was within a few minutes of one another.

Otto had nothing of moment to report. He had been able to catch only occasional glimpses of his brother who, it seemed, had spent the whole morning out on the platform at the far entrance to the cave working on the rocket. Colonel Washington and the thick-set man with the black wiry hair were still helping him. Mary had not been visible.

C.B. leaned against the edge of his desk, his long legs stretched out before him, and asked Richter, 'What had your people to say, Colonel?'

The tubby American made a grimace. 'At first they thought I was round the bend, but they couldn't laugh off Washington's having flown out with the war-head. The Ambassador got on the Transatlantic blower. He couldn't raise the President. He's on a golfing holiday; but he spoke with the State Department and the Pentagon. I don't have to describe the resulting flap. Everything has been alerted and some fool has now only to drop a pin for the whole lot to go off. But what was the alternative? At least we'll lose not a second in shooting back, if it does happen.'

'Our Service Chiefs are doing the same,' Verney announced. 'Did your man suggest at any stage that we ought to warn the Russians?'

'Sure; but the Pentagon shot that down. They take the view that Moscow would never credit us with being on the level. They'd believe that this was some sort of a trick. Just one of those things, if you'll pardon me, Colonel, that a whole lot of other nationalities think the British are so good at – putting up a rabbit that will later enable them to say that it was no fault of theirs that the party ever started.'

Verney smiled, pleased that at such a time of crisis his opposite number should have kept his sense of humour sufficiently to deliver that sly crack. He asked:

'How about shooting first? At the Cabinet meeting I've just come from one Minister was very bellicose. He insisted that if we waited for Russia's reactions to Lothar's rocket we'd be blown off the map before we had a chance, and that our only hope of survival was to pull the trigger right away. But, thank God, the others wouldn't hear of it.'

'Same with our folk. First reactions of some of the Pentagon boys was to go to town right away; but the State Department overruled them.'

'Then in the main our Governments are thinking alike.'

'Yes; praise be. When I left, my Ambassador was on his way down to see your Prime Minister. Meantime, he's given me carte blanche on behalf of the United States Government to take any steps I can that might stop it.'

Verney nodded. 'It's the same in my case. I've already been through to the head of Interpol, and our Foreign Secretary is sending an "Immediate" secret cipher signal to our Ambassador in Berne. Naturally the Swiss will give us every possible help, and in the hope that they may be able to locate Lothar's cave I propose to fly out to Switzerland at once.'

'You've taken the words out of my mouth, Colonel. I've already used my Ambassador's name with Pan American at London Airport – quicker than our motoring down to the nearest U.S. air base. They've pushed some passengers off a 'plane and are holding it in readiness.'

'It's a pleasure to work with you,' C.B. smiled. Then he turned to Barney and Otto. I'd like you with me, Sullivan, and you had better come too, Mr. Khune. The nearer you are to your brother the better chance you'll have, I take it, of locating him.'

In such circumstances there could be no question of their delaying to pack bags. As C.B. passed through the outer office he told his P.A. that any communication to him should be made through Interpol H.Q. at Geneva, then the four men hurried down to the waiting cars.

The whole morning had gone in conferences, so it was now well past lunch time and they did not arrive at London Airport until a quarter to three. There they were escorted straight through to the airliner and, shortly after it had taken off, they sat down to a meal. Verney then sent a radiogram to Interpol asking that a senior official should meet them with a car at the Geneva airport.

It was six o'clock when they got in. A thin, dark, brisk-mannered Italian Commandante, named Fratelli, met them and whisked them into the city, then along the lakeside to the fine park in which the International Conference buildings stand. Half an hour after landing they were closeted with Monsieur Martell, the grey-haired Chef de Sûreté, to whom C.B. had spoken on the telephone while still at 10, Downing Street.

For security reasons Martell had been asked only to use all his resources to trace Lothar Khune, Colonel Washington and Mary Morden, with such information as might enable him to do so. Now C.B. put him fully in the picture and, as they were old friends, although Martell showed amazement and consternation, he did not question the statement that the wanted men possessed occult powers.

Having heard Verney out, he said, 'Within minutes of your speaking to me I had these people's descriptions circulated and a big reward offered for information concerning them. But, as you know, we are an international organization, so our main strength lies in the airports and frontier posts. The interior is a matter for the Swiss police. Naturally, I passed the word to my Swiss colleague at once, and for some hours they have been making enquiries. I will get through and see if he has any news.'

For a few minutes he talked on one of his telephones, then he hung up and shook his head. 'As yet, my friend, nothing. Now that May has come the cable railways are being opened up again,

404

but many remain closed all through the winter and are not yet once more in commission. The probability is that it is one such in a sparsely populated area that this man Lothar Khune has made use of while it was deserted, and without the knowledge of the authorities.'

'A check-up must be made on every one of them with a minimum of delay,' said Verney quickly.

'Agreed' Monsieur Martell promptly conceded. 'But remember that so far the Swiss know only that we are seeking three people urgently. They are not yet aware that their lives, and those of millions of others, depend on the success of their efforts; so . . .'

Richter raised a hand. 'Sure, but you will appreciate the necessity for keeping the awful truth from all but the people at the top. If it got out there would be nation-wide panics, thousands of suicides and a leak to the Russians which would probably lead to their opening the ball right away.'

'That's so,' Verney agreed. 'But our Foreign Secretary was going to send a code message to our Ambassador in Berne and instruct him to inform the Swiss Government.'

'Ah!' exclaimed Martell. 'That is better, much better. Realizing the full danger the Government will exert itself to the maximum. By now, perhaps troops may even have been called out to assist the police in their searching and questioning. But all reports will go to Berne. I shall receive them here only later. Therefore, if I may advise, you should proceed at once to the capital. I must remain here to redouble the activities of my own people; but Commandante Fratelli is at your disposal and will open all doors for you on your arrival.'

His advice was sound so they accepted it at once, and a few minutes later he was seeing them off in the car on their way north-eastward. For the first thirty-eight miles their route lay along the north shore of Lac Léman and even their anxieties could not altogether prevent their taking in the beauties of the scene. To one side lay the five to ten mile wide sheet of now placid water, with occasional tree-surrounded châteaux and chalets standing in gardens that ran down to its shore. On the other, the ground rose gently at first, then more steeply, towards the Jura range, the whole being either meadows, in which herds of a curiously mushroom-coloured breed of cows grazed, or orchards. The latter – mainly plums, pears and apricots – were a mass of blossom as, also, in brighter hues, were the chalet gardens of their owners.

Every few miles they passed through a village or small town, each neat, clean and orderly, with gay massed flowers in the beds of its central square. The sight of such peace and unforced prosperity made them more than ever conscious of the incredible evil that Lothar planned to bring upon the world, by turning all this into shambles so that even the few survivors would be forced to live like pariah-dogs in the ruins of what had once been their pleasant homes.

On entering Lausanne they mounted steeply through the streets of the city to come out on much higher ground, from which they caught some panoramic views of the lovely lake before leaving it behind. The road now lay through flattish country, fringed on both sides with orchards and meadows, many of which were a sea of golden dandelions. There were, too, more beautifully kept villages, huge barns with chalet roofs, and often villas in the gardens of which fine magnolia trees were in full blossom; but the light was failing now, taking the colour out of the flowers, and by the time they reached the picturesque old city of Fribourg it was nearly dark. The last twenty miles were soon eaten up and at just on ten o'clock Fratelli brought the car to a halt in front of the Police Headquarters in Berne.

Martell had telephoned so they were shown straight up to the office of the Chief-of-Police. Actually, as Fratelli told them afterwards, the elderly square-faced stolid-looking man who received them was not the Chief-of-Police, but his Deputy by seniority, as the Chief had been involved in a car smash a few days earlier and was in hospital.

The acting Chief stood up, bowed sharply from the waist, and introduced himself as 'Tauber'. He had no news to give them, but said that he had that afternoon been told by the Minister of the Interior of the menace to world peace, and was doing everything possible to trace the people concerned. He added that he had not been informed upon what evidence it was believed that a madman with an H bomb had brought it into Switzerland and proposed to launch it from a mountain cave, and that he was anxious to have particulars.

Verney at once complied, giving him an abbreviated version of the whole story. When Herr Tauber had heard it he raised his grey eyebrows until they almost met the bristling grey hair that grew like a brush above his low forehead; then he said angrily,

'But, Colonel, this is not evidence. It is not even hearsay.

There can be no more to it than the predictions of a gipsy woman who has gazed into a crystal.'

'It's no prediction that Colonel Henrik G. Washington stole and flew off with a nuclear war-head,' Richter rapped out. 'That's a fact.'

The Police Chief grunted. 'I do not question that. But why should he bring it to Switzerland? That he should take it to Russia would make sense or, if he could not fly so far, to Czechoslovakia or East Germany, perhaps, but ...'

It was evident that the bulky, heavy-jowled man had not yet grasped the significance of what he had been told of the intentions with which his visitors credited Lothar; so C.B. interrupted him to cross the t's and dot the i's of the matter.

Tauber shrugged. 'In crooks I believe; in madmen I believe; but not in fairies or magicians. Even to suggest that such people exist, in this age of science, is an absurdity. I have no wish to be rude to this Mr. Khune whom you have brought with you, but in my opinion he is the victim of delusions.'

'We, on the contrary,' Verney declared coldly, 'are satisfied that he is perfectly sane, and may yet be able to locate this mountain cave in which his brother has set up a rocket.'

'Then he will be cleverer than myself and my police. After our Minister had sent for me this afternoon, we studied the maps of the country and listed all its cable railways. On account of Switzerland's unrivalled position as a tourist centre, in the past eighty years or so a considerable number of these railways have been constructed by our excellent engineers. Some are open, others are still shut because the snow at their upper terminals has not yet melted sufficiently for them to be workable. All those either in use or that might have been put into temporary use without the knowledge of the authorities have been inspected within the past few hours. None of them is being put to the use you suggest. The cave you speak of is a myth; a figment of the imagination.'

Otto gave him an angry look. 'I've climbed quite a lot in Switzerland. I've several times seen old ski-lifts and cable hoists that for one reason or another have been abandoned. Have all of those also been checked up as still inoperative?'

'Not the ones in the more remote valleys,' Tauber admitted grudgingly. 'Besides, most of those were constructed by private enterprise so there would be no record of them here in Berne;

407

only at the administrative centres of the cantons in which they are situated.'

Verney sat forward quickly. 'But that is just the sort of railway that Lothar Khune would have made use of. Even if you have to call out every policeman in the country, not one of them must be left unvisited. Just think what it may mean if we fail to lay this man by the heels before he can let off his rocket.'

The Police Chief nodded ponderously. 'Providing you cut out all this talk of Satanism being at the bottom of it I'd be inclined to agree with you. I'm willing, though, to concede that we are up against a madman and, although you've given me no proof of it, accept the possibility that he is in this country. That being so, I'll send out an emergency call for an exhaustive search in all mountain areas. But there is little point in starting it before dawn; because the patrols would not be able to see more than twenty yards, even with powerful torches.'

For a moment everyone remained silent, then Verney said, 'A few hours may make the difference between life and death for more men, women and children than the mind is capable of grasping. Is there no way in which we could identify the probable site of this railway and cave; so that we could raid it first thing in the morning?'

Otto looked across at him. 'In my spirit I've been to the entrance of the cave several times now, and on most the weather has been clear; so I have a good mental picture of the view from it. Do you think that if I drew the sky-line from memory someone might be able roughly to identify the place from which it was viewed?'

'That's a great idea,' Richter enthused. 'Go to it, Mr. Khune, and give us that picture.'

Tauber shrugged, but pushed a sheet of paper and a pencil towards Otto, then lit a cigar and offered the box, and a box of cigarettes, round to the others. They declined the cigars but accepted cigarettes and for some minutes sat smoking in silence while Otto made two false starts then drew a very good picture of a mountain range with a high peak near its centre.

Taking it from him, the Police Chief gave it a quick look, but put it down with a shake of his square, bristly head. 'Gentlemen,' he said, 'no visitor to Switzerland ever sees more than a hundredth part of the country. The great central massif of the Alps covers an enormous area. From Mount Pilatus to the Matterhorn is seventy-five miles, and from Mont Blanc to St. Moritz one hundred and fifty. Between those four points lie hundreds of peaks, innumerable ridges and perhaps a thousand valleys. How could we possibly expect anyone to pinpoint the spot from which this sketch is said to be made? You might as well draw one fir tree and ask us to identify it in a ten-acre fir forest.'

Barney, as the junior member of the party, had so far bottled himself up, but now he burst out. 'No one expects you to, and maybe there's no one here in Berne that could either. But there must be locals who could. I suggest you have that sky-line stencilled immediately and a copy despatched by special messenger to every village police station in the mountain area.'

'Good for you, young man!' boomed Richter. 'He's hit it, Chief. Don't lose a moment. Have every machine you've got put into operation. We'll need hundreds of copies. Then, if you've not men enough of your own, call out Army despatch riders to deliver them.'

'That's it.' C.B. came to his feet. 'We have got to find this place; and quickly. It may be your private belief that we have been made fools of, but there is no getting away from it that an H-bomb war-head has been flown out of England. We believe it to be here in Switzerland, and that it may at any time be used to start a world war. You cannot possibly afford to take a chance on our being wrong.'

Suddenly Tauber's manner changed. The terrible possibilities of the situation seemed at last to have penetrated his thick skull. As he reached for one of the telephones on his desk, he said, 'You are right. It was this talk of a Satanist with occult powers that made me sceptical. But we must spare no effort which might prevent the appalling catastrophe you fear.' Next moment he was giving gruff instructions about mustering despatch riders, and summoning numerous members of his staff.

When he hung up, Verney said, 'It will take several hours to circulate these things, so we had better get some sleep. But I would like to spend the night as near to the possible scene of action as I can. Where would be the most central place for a move either way into the mountains.'

'Interlaken,' Fratelli replied before the Police Chief had a chance to speak. 'It is only about fifteen kilometres from the Jungfrau, and that mountain forms the centre of the main Alpine chain. We will go to the Victoria-Jungfrau. Permit, please.' He picked up one of Tauber's telephones, put a call through to the hotel and a few minutes later reported, 'The manager apologizes that all his best rooms are full, but I have told him that we require only rooms in which to sleep.'

Knowing that such solid types as Tauber were often the most thorough when they got down to a job, and satisfied that he now really meant business, C.B. asked that any news should at once be relayed to him at the Victoria-Jungfrau, then he and his party went down with Fratelli to the Commandante's car.

From Berne they took the road south through a shallow valley for eighteen miles to Thun at the head of Lake Thuner, then for another eighteen miles followed the south shore of the lake as it curved gradually eastward. There was no moon and the stars gave only sufficient light for them to get, first, an impression of country similar to that through which earlier they had passed that evening and, later, stretches of dark water glimpsed between black patches formed by clumps of trees. In the villages few lights were now showing and when they reached the palatial Victoria-Jungfrau it was well after midnight.

In the hotel, blissfully unaware that this might be their last night on earth, many of the younger guests had been dancing. The band had not long stopped playing and there were still quite a number of groups in the lounge, chatting and laughing over last drinks before going up to bed. Few of them even glanced at the little cluster of new arrivals as an under-manager led them through to the restaurant and had a corner of it re-lit for them to make good their missed dinner by a late supper.

Over it, while scarcely noticing what they ate, they speculated in low voices on how long it would take Lothar to adapt the bomb war-head for use on his rocket. All of them hoped fervently that it would take several days, but to have assembled a rocket up in a mountain cave showed that Lothar had either become, or had working for him, a highly skilled engineer; and as by morning it would be forty-eight hours since he had arrived in Switzerland with it, they had to face the fact that he might already have completed the work.

With the exception of Fratelli, all of them were dog-tired and it seemed to Barney that he had only just put out his bedside light when C.B., clad in pants and an overcoat, was shaking him awake.

'Up you get, young feller,' he said. 'Your idea of stencilling Otto's sky-line sketch and circulating it has worked. The local

410

Police Chief has just had word and brought it himself. Several bright boys in the upper Rhône valley are prepared to swear that the central peak in the sketch is the south-west aspect of the Finsteraarhorn.'

As Barney tumbled out of bed, C.B. went on. 'A sergeant at a village called Lax has actually identified the cable railway. Apparently it was a private venture financed in the 'thirties by a crazy Dutchman. He believed that there were valuable mineral deposits in the upper part of the mountains and had the railway constructed up to the cave, with the idea that it would be a good base from which to conduct his operations. There are rare minerals that can be worked up there but the payload was not sufficient to meet the cost of the labour; so the company went bust. The railway has been derelict until a few months ago. Then some solicitors in Zurich, acting for an Hungarian, acquired it for a song. The story was that he intended to build a small chalet restaurant up on the ledge as an attraction for tourists; but the locals say that he is throwing away his money, because it is so far from any of the main tourist resorts.'

The management had supplied Verney's party with tooth-brushes and toilet things from the hotel barber's shop, but no time could be spared for shaving. After a quick wash the five men scrambled into their clothes and assembled down in the front hall. It was a little after six, so the staff were already busy cleaning the public rooms, and the Interlaken Chief of Police, a tall, wiry, brown-faced man of forty, whose name was Jodelweiss, had ordered coffee and *brödchen* for them. Quickly they gulped down the steaming brew and, still gnawing at the crisp fresh rolls stuffed with smoked ham, they followed him outside.

Two cars with police chauffeurs were already waiting there, and there were four more on the road outside filled with police. As they followed Jodelweiss out to the leading cars he was speaking over his shoulder.

'Unfortunately, gentlemen, this place is in a valley on the far side of the great barrier. We shall cross it by the Grimsel Pass – I hope. Normally the pass is not open for another three weeks but this year spring has come unusually early so I think we shall get through. The only alternatives are a long detour to the north, by way of the Susten and Oberalp passes, which are just as likely still to be blocked, or to the south right round by way of Saanen, Aigle, Martigny-Ville, Sion and Brig, but that would mean a run

411

of two hundred and fifty kilometres. If we can cross the Grimsel it is only a third of that distance and we should be there in about three hours; so I feel it is well worth the attempt.'

Since time was so important the others agreed with him and quickly settled themselves in the two cars. As they pulled the rugs over their knees, the klaxons shattered the morning silence and the cavalcade roared away past the still closed jewellers, patisseries, creamery, lace and woodworkers' shops which later in the day would attract many of the temporary inhabitants of this little town that enjoyed such a picturesque setting.

For the first fifteen miles the road followed the north shore of Interlaken's other great lake, the Brienzer See; and now in the early morning light they could appreciate the loveliness of the pale spring green of the beech trees seen against a background of dark pines across a sheet of placid water, beyond which lay range after range of snow-capped mountains.

At the lake's end another seven miles through meadows again dotted with plum, pear and apricot trees in bloom brought them to Meiringen. Beyond the town the road rose sharply, running parallel to the valley of the Aar, through dark gorges, occasional breaks in which offered wonderful vistas of forest and mountain. Ahead on their right reared up, to disappear in clouds, the vast bulk of the Wetterhorn, and to their left those of the Sustenhorn and Dammastock.

Between Guttannen and Hendegg the narrow curving way increased in steepness. The vegetation became arctic in character, on the roadside were high banks of snow and the branches of the trees bent under the weight of it. Still higher up the road became a twisting culvert cut through great cliffs of light-coloured polished granite, and a fresh fall of snow that had not yet been cleared by the snow ploughs brought the car's speed down to near foot pace. But to their relief they got through and gained the top of the pass. From it a marvellous vista spread before them – the sparkling blue lakes of Grimsel and Raterichboden, retained by their huge dams and the miles-wide glacier from which the Rhône rises; then, far below, the green meadows of the valley that the river watered and, away in the distance to their right, the mighty cloud-enshrouded peak of the Finsteraarhorn.

For a few miles the road corkscrewed downwards until they reached the valley with its narrow rushing river and the road and railway that ran beside it. On the valley road were halted a long

412

line of military vehicles – jeeps, light tanks and a small type of snow cat.

As Inspector Jodelweiss's car approached, a short, wiry, leather-faced officer waved it to a halt. When it drew up beside him he said, 'I am Brigadier Stulich, commanding the garrison at Andermatt. I received a signal that an emergency has arisen in which troops may be needed, and orders that a mixed force should rendezvous with you here. I decided to bring them myself. Inform me, please, of the situation and your requirements.'

Jodelweiss introduced the Brigadier to Verney, who was seated behind him, and Verney said, 'Please order your men to follow our cars, Sir, then get in with us. I will explain as we go. Every minute we can save is of importance.'

The Brigadier gave the order to an officer who was standing just behind him, then squeezed into the back of the car with Verney and Fratelli. As they drove on, the former, now refraining from any mention of Satanism, gave the soldier particulars of the threatened danger which, when he learned of it, made even this tough-looking character draw in a sharp breath.

The going was much easier now as the valley road was almost straight, and for fifteen miles they ran down a succession of gentle slopes, passing again through neat villages and between meadows where cattle grazed placidly among golden seas of dandelions. When they entered Lax it was a quarter past eight; so in spite of the long climb and their slow going through the pass they had done the fifty mile journey in just under two hours.

In Lax, outside the village police station, the Sergeant who had reported the cable-railway built by the Dutch mineral prospector in the 'thirties was waiting for them. He was an elderly man with a grey walrus moustache, but bright-eyed and alert. Jodelweiss, the Brigadier, Verney, Fratelli, Barney, Richter and Otto all scrambled out of the two leading cars and crowded round him.

Although still ignorant of the reason for the enquiry circulated the previous night from police headquarters at Berne, he had not let the grass grow under his feet, but at dawn had set off on a recon-naisance. At a hamlet up in the valley where the cable railway was situated, but about five kilometres below it, he had learned that work had been proceeding on the railway for some weeks. During the winter the villagers seldom went so far up the valley, but a number of them had seen aircraft fly in and had assumed that these were bringing the materials with which it was rumoured a

413

buffet to attract tourists was to be built at the top of the railway. The Sergeant had pressed on and found the hangar, but it was securely locked and he had not been able to find out if there was a 'plane housed in it.

Bumping and skidding on his motor cycle he had, soon after seven o'clock, reached the engine-house. Inside it five Chinese, all of whom he described as of the coolie type, had been squatting on the floor of a common living and bunk room eating breakfast. But none of them could answer his questions and it seemed that they could speak only their own language. By signs he had then indicated that he wanted to be taken up to the cave, but they had shaken their heads and begun to show hostility; so he had had no option but to return to Lax.

Immediately the group about him had heard his story Jodelweiss gave him a place in the leading car. The others re-distributed themselves, then the cavalcade set off again, now heading almost due north along a rough road that led up into the mountains, and on which, the Sergeant said, about twelve kilometres distant lay the cable railway.

As the cars wound in and out among the foothills of the chain C.B. wondered anxiously if the old policeman had not done more harm than good by his reconnaisance.

Up till an hour ago, unless Lothar had been keeping an occult watch on Otto, he could not have been aware that they had traced him to Switzerland; but if the Chinese labourers had reported the Sergeant's visit that might have aroused Lothar's suspicions. With luck he would assume that only chance or a routine round had brought a local policeman to the engine-house, but his psychic perceptions being so acute it was possible that he would deduce a warning from it. If so, he was now overlooking their approach and, awful thought, if he had his rocket ready, that might precipitate his launching of it.

When they reached the hamlet Jodelweiss spoke into the car radio. He ordered one of the police cars behind them to stop, and its crew to search the hamlet in case any of the men from the engine-house or cave should have come down there since the Sergeant's visit, and be temporarily hiding in one of the barns. A few kilometres further on, as they came opposite the aircraft hangar, he detached another squad for a similar purpose.

All of them were now craning forward in their seats to catch the first glimpse of the cable railway up which forty-eight hours

414

earlier the stolen war-head had been carried. At length they rounded a last bend and came in full view of it. Half a mile ahead lay the engine-house. Beyond it, in the distance, far up the valley and on its opposite side from the railway, a little group of figures were moving. They were making their way up a broad gully towards a dip in the ridge and were visible only because they had already passed the snow line.

The Brigadier spoke into the walkie-talkie he was carrying, ordering two jeeps filled with ski-troops to go after them and bring them in; but the sight of the group, which was so obviously making off, was enough to tell Verney that his fears had been well founded. The Sergeant's visit two hours earlier must have alerted Lothar to the fact that Switzerland was being combed for him. Since then, no doubt, he would have used his psychic powers to detect and observe the advancing column of police and troops.

Two minutes later the leading cars pulled up outside the engine-house. Their occupants tumbled out. Armed police and troops dashed inside. A Lieutenant emerged again almost at once and shouted, 'The place is empty, but the cage is down here.'

C.B. was staring after the tiny figures that stood out against the snow, and wondering now if Lothar was one of them. Barney tugged at his sleeve and cried, 'Come on, the cabin's here! Come on, or there won't be room for us in it.'

'Half-a-mo', partner,' C.B. replied. 'The bird we are after may have fled the nest. Maybe he's one of those little moving dots up there.'

'He'd never have abandoned his rocket at this stage,' Barney argued quickly. 'I swear he'd die rather. And if . . . if Mary's not dead, she will be with him.'

'If the rocket was all fixed to go, he might have. He could have left it with a time fuse attached to launch it. Anyhow, the rocket is first priority. These cable-railway cages usually hold only four, and the Brigadier told me that he had been ordered to bring explosive experts with him. I'm sorry, Barney, but we must let them go ahead so that they may have the best possible chance to get at that war-head in time to dismantle it. But Lothar is our pigeon, and getting him our best hope of saving Mary. If he is one of those dots up there we must go after him.'

With a murmured apology Barney almost snatched a pair of field-glasses from an officer who was standing nearby. Swiftly he focused them on the distant figures and, after a moment, said,

'There are seven of them. That is two in addition to the five Chinks that the Sergeant found down here in the engine-house. None of them looks like a woman; but in those clothes one can't tell. Anyhow, Colonel Washington's not one of them. I'm sure of that because of his height.'

At that moment there came the sudden crack and roar of an explosion. Its blast flung them both forward on their knees. As they picked themselves up they looked round to find that the engine-house was now a smoking ruin. Shouts and screams were coming from it. Troops and police were running to the assistance of their wounded comrades. For a few minutes everything was confusion.

As the smoke above the wrecked building cleared Barney suddenly shouted, 'Look! Look! There he is. The explosion has brought the murdering swine out to see the results of his handiwork.'

Following Barney's pointing finger, C.B. saw that a figure had emerged from the cave and was now standing on the edge of the broad ledge, looking down through a pair of glasses at the scene of havoc. He, too, had no doubt that it was Lothar.

Richter staggered up to them, his face blackened, his eyebrows singed and his uniform torn.

'What happened?' Verney asked him.

The American was still panting. 'That devil had booby-trapped both the cage and the engine. I chanced to be looking towards the winding gear as a corporal pushed over the lever. Both bombs went off simultaneously. The Brigadier and Jodelweiss were both in the cage. With them and in the freight compartment they had several sappers; bomb experts. All of them are to hell and gone. So are six or eight fellers who were standing round the engine. I was lucky. I couldn't get a place in the cage but I was standing alongside it by the opening. So I was blown clear.'

As he finished speaking Fratelli limped up to them. He had been outside the building but near it, and a flying length of wooden rafter had caught him a nasty blow on his left leg. Otto had escaped altogether, as he had been well away from the engine-house and, already certain in his own mind that Lothar was still in the cave, was staring up at it.

Within a few minutes the last of the wounded had been rescued from the smouldering debris, and a tall, thin Major came up to them. The greater part of the troops were his own men and, now

416

that the Brigadier had been killed, he was the senior officer present. After expressing his fury that the police should have allowed them to walk into such a trap, he demanded to know the object of the operation.

In a low voice Fratelli told him, upon which he promptly declared his intention of having his tanks train their guns on the cave and shell it to blazes. The others swiftly implored him not to, as they feared that the concussion of the bursting shells might set off the H bomb war-head that they believed to be at the far end of the tunnel. It was Verney who said,

'There is only one thing for it now, Major. We have got to get up there by climbing; and the more of us who make the attempt the better, because he may have some means of inflicting casualties on us as we go up. I suggest that you should form your men into groups and send each group up by a different route. Some should certainly be sent round the shoulder of the mountain so as to work their way up, if they can, to the far entrance of the tunnel that can't be seen from here.'

After a moment he added, 'Although we are not equipped for climbing, my friends and I naturally wish to be in on this too. As a number of your men have been wounded perhaps you would be good enough to let us have the loan of their gear.'

The Major agreed, said that he would lead an attack round the shoulder of the mountain on the other entrance of the cave, and detailed a blond, pink-cheeked Lieutenant to look after them. Already most of the injured had had their wounds dressed and, wrapped in blankets, were being made as comfortable as possible in jeeps for swift removal to hospital; so the young Lieutenant was soon able to collect ski-suits, snow-shoes, woollen gloves and caps, and pistols for his charges. Two tracked vehicles came up; the Lieutenant, C.B. and Otto joined the crew of one, and Barney, Richter and Fratelli that of the other.

As they set off Barney glanced at his watch. It had been just on nine o'clock when they had driven up to the engine-house; it was now nearly half past.

It was a beautiful May morning. By this time the sun was well above the ridge to the east, lightening the tender green of the meadows in the valley bottom, turning the flying drops of the cascading river that ran through it into sparkling diamonds and making the snow on the higher levels crumpled sheets of dazzling whiteness.

417

In less than ten minutes the tracked vehicles, which possessed a quite amazing capability to travel up steep slopes, had negotiated the boulder-strewn hillside of coarse grass and carried them up to the fringe of the forest belt. But it was too thick for them to find a way through it. Leaving the vehicles, the two parties and half a dozen others, on average a hundred yards apart, entered the trees and continued the upward climb on foot.

For most of the way the gradient was not less than one in five, and a carpet of pine needles made the going so slippery that it added greatly to their exertions. As they advanced they passed patches of half-melted snow, and every few moments there came a loud rustle, or a 'plop', as the sun's rays caused great lumps of it on the upper branches of the trees partially to thaw and fall to the ground.

When they came out from the trees Barney was sweating profusely, but his two amateur companions were in a far worse case. Eyeing the snowfield, that now lay before them like the roof of a gargantuan house, plump, forty-year-old Colonel Richter frankly confessed that he was in no condition to face it, and declared that if he made the attempt he would only prove a drag on the others. Fratelli, too, decided to throw his hand in, although only because his injured leg was paining him so badly. The others, now reduced to a team of five, roped themselves together, with a Sergeant leading and Barney two from the end. Then they set off again.

Some distance to their left the Lieutenant's team had also emerged from the trees, but its 'passengers' were in better shape. Otto had done quite a lot of climbing on his holidays in Switzerland; while Verney, although he had done no climbing for several years, was an old hand and considerably stronger than anyone might have supposed from a casual glance at his lanky, stooping figure.

Slowly the two teams wound their way upwards, while others to right and left followed other, apparently possible, ways up the mountain side. It was a little after half past ten when the walkie-talkie of the young Lieutenant who was leading C.B.'s team began to crackle. Signalling the string of men behind him to halt, he listened for a few moments, then he looked back and called down to Verney.

'This is for you, Colonel, and for all concerned in the capture of Lothar Khune. It is relayed by our mobile radio unit down in the valley from Police Headquarters, Berne. Soon after ten o'clock Khune put out a long broadcast in Russian and followed it by one in English. He has announced that he, Lothar Khune, is taking steps to-day to bring a New Order into the world for the glory of his master, Prince Lucifer. That an upheaval is necessary in which many must die, but that those who survive will for ever bless the name of Satan. He intends to set the ball rolling which will lead to the establishment of this new order at twelve o'clock precisely.' The Lieutenant paused, then added, 'I don't know what you think, but he sounds completely crazy to me.'

Verney did not reply. By all normal standards, of course, Lothar was crazy, but according to his own lights he was behaving with impeccable logic, and his statement had to be regarded as made by a man terrifyingly and damnably sane.

But that thought no more than flashed across C.B.'s mind. He was gazing upward at the ever steeper ascent, glinting in the sunshine with snow and ice, made perilous by jutting rocks, sheer cliffs and, in places, overhang. So far they had barely accomplished half the climb. By far the most difficult half was yet to come. Since Lothar meant to launch his rocket at midday they had barely an hour and a half left. His heart contracting with despair, C.B. forced himself to realize that they could not possibly reach the cave in time.

26

Deadline – twelve noon.

T HE sight of the Great Ram advancing noiselessly
down the tunnel seemed to turn Mary's blood to water and to
paralyse her limbs. For a few seconds she remained motionless.
With what felt like a physical wrench she tore her glance away and
tapped sharply on one of the fuel drums. The sound might easily
have been made by a falling icicle thawed out at the entrance to the
cave by the heat coming from inside it; but Wash heeded her
warning signal. Stooping, he swiftly thrust in among the paraphernalia at the base of the rocket the tool he was holding.

Kneeling in the narrow, pitch dark space between the two piles
of fuel drums, Mary held her breath. It seemed to her certain that
the Great Ram must have sensed her presence even if he did not
see her and, halting in his stride, would turn and rend her. But on
coming opposite the drums he had rounded the bend of the tunnel
sufficiently to catch sight of Wash. His harsh voice cut the stillness.

'I had a feeling that you were here. What are you doing?'

With a laconic calmness for which Mary gave Wash full marks,
his reply came back. 'Taking a look-see at the rocket. You're an
expert on these things, Exalted One, and I'm a babe. All the same,
I couldn't get it out of my mind this evening that we've got it
oriented wrong.'

The Great Ram had walked on towards him. Now that they
were talking together Mary knew that she ought not to lose a
moment in obeying Wash's orders to leave them to it and get
back to her cabin. If the Great Ram chanced to look round he

420

would see her, but that risk had to be taken as the lesser than his yet discovering her among the fuel drums and realizing that she had been lurking there as a look-out for Wash. Quickly she slipped off her shoes. Then, summoning her resolution, she took the plunge.

As she tiptoed forward her spine seemed to creep. Every second she expected an occult force to be directed at her back – a lightning flash that would scorch, char and utterly destroy her. Into her terrified mind there came again a picture of the Black Imp that had materialized from the Great Ram the first time she had seen him. For one awful moment the sound of the drips from the melting ice at the entrance to the cave seemed to take on a new rhythm and she thought they were the swift, light footfalls of the Imp coming after her. Suppressing a scream of terror, she broke into a run. It was only then she suddenly became aware that she was well round the bend of the tunnel and so must have escaped discovery.

When she reached her cabin she was trembling from head to foot. In the doorway she paused to look back, fearful now that Wash's bluff would fail and that the Great Ram would kill him. If that happened she knew that she would receive short shrift. Any attempt to defend herself would be hopeless but, if she could take him by surprise, there was just a chance that she might inflict some serious injury on him before his terrible power as a destroyer could take effect. But for that she must have a weapon. How, where, could she get hold of one? The kitchen was only thirty feet away. There might be something there.

She tiptoed along, and peeped in. It was deserted but still faintly lit by the small blue pilot bulb. From the cabin beyond it came the snoring of the Chinese cook. As she looked quickly round her glance fell on a saw-edged bread knife that had been left on the table. She would have preferred something more lethal; but it would have taken time to hunt through the drawers, and she dared not linger there. Snatching up the bread knife, she ran back to her own cabin, slipped inside, and shut the door. Still trembling, she threw down her shoes, stepped out of her skirt and, getting into the bunk, pulled the blankets over her.

For some minutes she lay there, her mind a prey to despair and fear – despair of getting the better of the Great Ram and sabotaging the rocket, and fear that his psychic sense would tell him that had been Wash's intention. Then she heard the muffled sound

421

of footsteps and voices outside in the tunnel. She could not catch what was said but they were not raised in anger; so it seemed that Wash had got away with his bluff. Relief surged through her at the thought that he was not dead; that she had not been left alone with the Great Ram and was about to become his next victim.

Wash entered the cabin next to hers. She heard its door slam and a little shuffling, then silence fell. Now she was seized with the urge to talk to him, to find out what had passed between him and the Great Ram, and do her utmost to persuade him to make a further attempt later in the night to sabotage the rocket. But she knew she must control her impatience. To leave her cabin while the Great Ram was still about might prove fatal.

It was as well that she waited. She was lying on her back with her eyes closed. There came a faint sound and she knew that someone had opened the door of her cabin. A sixth sense told her that it was the Great Ram and warned her to keep perfectly still. She felt certain that he had looked in to make sure that she was there and asleep. Now, she thanked her stars that she had obeyed Wash and returned to her cabin instead of remaining among the fuel drums. If her cabin had been empty and she had been found near the rocket, she knew that she would never have been able to stand up to the Great Ram's questioning.

He took a step forward into the cabin. Her heart contracted with a spasm of fear. She was the useless member of the party and he had good cause to hate her. Perhaps he had not just come to see if she was asleep, but had decided that the time had come to rid himself of her. She was still holding the bread knife. Instinctively her grasp tightened on its handle. Had he touched her she would have flung back the blanket and lunged blindly at him. But after a moment he stepped back, murmured a few sentences of what sounded like gibberish, and closed the door.

Sweating from every pore she continued to lie there, still not quite certain that he had left her. It seemed an age before she could summon up the courage to turn her head a little sideways and steal a swift glance from beneath still lowered eyelids. She let her breath go in a great sigh. Except for herself, the faint blue light showed the cabin to be empty.

Once more she resigned herself to wait with patience, until it could be reasonably assumed that the coast was clear. Every few minutes she looked at her wrist watch. Its hands seemed to move

422

with incredible slowness, but minute by minute an hour crept by. Getting out of the bunk, she put on her skirt and cautiously opened the door. No sound came to her and momentarily her hopes soared again. By playing on Wash's resentment at having been tricked by the Great Ram and doing her utmost to strengthen the feeling she had instilled into him that, as a Satanist, he had backed the wrong horse, she might yet induce him to make another attempt to sabotage the rocket and, this time, perhaps they would succeed.

Next moment her hopes fell to zero. The door stood open but she could not pass through the doorway. The Great Ram had erected an invisible barrier there that held her a prisoner more surely than any locks and bolts. Strive as she would, just as had been the case at the Cedars, she could not put a foot over the threshold.

.   .   .   .   .

Only the hands of Mary's watch told her that she had got through the night. Lying fully dressed on her bunk, through parts of it she had dozed; but she had the impression that she had not dropped off, even for a few moments, and certainly her brain had never ceased to revolve round and round the coming day and the terrible fate that it might usher in for millions of helpless people.

On finding that she could not leave her cabin, she had thought of trying to knock Wash up so that he would leave his and come round to her. But the partition that separated the two cabins was made of thick timber. With the handle of the breadknife she had rapped a tattoo on it, but without result. An hour had elapsed since the Great Ram had left them, and from experience she knew how soundly Wash slept. It was evident that he had already fallen into one of his heavy slumbers, and that to rouse him would need violent hammering. The noise that would make would, she felt sure, bring the Great Ram on the scene, and that she dared not risk.

The fact that he had erected an occult barrier to prevent her from leaving her cabin she took to be a clear indication that Wash had not altogether got away with his bluff about his concern regarding the alignment of the rocket. In some way the Great Ram's suspicions had been aroused and, she guessed, they took the form of suspecting the truth – that she was endeavouring to

423

turn Wash against him, and influencing him to interfere in some way with the rocket's proper functioning.

Wretchedly she had flung herself on her bunk, and endeavoured alternately to devise a means of wrecking the Great Ram's plans when morning came, or giving in to her tired mind and, sloughing off all responsibility, get to sleep. She had succeeded in neither.

Soon after seven o'clock she heard the clatter of pans in the galley, but the Chinese cook did not come to call her as on the previous day. She got up, tidied herself as well as she could and again tried to leave her cabin, but found that the invisible barrier still held her back. Half an hour later she caught sounds of Wash stirring in the cabin next door. Shortly afterwards it was swiftly conveyed to her that he was trapped too. She could hear him shouting:

'What goes on here! Master! Exalted One! I'd bust right through this had any lesser Mage corralled me in. But why put me behind the bars? Come on now! Let me outa here. Let me out, I say!'

To his shouts there came no reply. In vain Mary tried to attract his attention by calling to him, but his angry bellows drowned her cries. Nearly a quarter of an hour elapsed before he seemed to resign himself to having been made a prisoner, and fell silent. She seized the opportunity to beat a loud tattoo on the board wall that divided their cabins. After a few minutes he responded with heavy thumps. The planks in the partition were thick, but there were thin chinks between them. By enunciating clearly in a low voice that was not much above a whisper, each could hear what the other said.

Both, by similar occult spells, had been made prisoners in their cabins. Wash said of the previous night that the Great Ram had not appeared to suspect him of a double cross. When he had suggested that the rocket was completely out of alignment if the intention was for it to fall on Saanen, the Great Ram had replied that he had changed his mind and decided to send it in the opposite direction, so that it should fall in the more sparsely populated Bernese Oberland in the neighbourhood of the little town of Ilanz.

That was all very well but, while Saanen lay to the west, Ilanz lay to the north-east, not many degrees off a direct course to Moscow; and, having seen the route and calculations in the Great

Ram's office for the rocket's flight, Wash had not been taken in by this plausible excuse for its reorientation.

He added that both their lives now hung on the Great Ram's having planned that he should be flown out of Switzerland once he had launched his rocket. Where to, remained a matter for anything but happy speculation. Certainly not to Moscow, which by the time an aircraft could reach it would be under heavy atomic attack from the Western Allies; and equally not to any city in Europe, as they would be going up in smoke under hits – or be rendered untenable by near-misses – from Russia's atomic bombardment. Their destination, Wash and Mary unhappily agreed while hoarsely whispering through the chinks between the boards, was probably India or China, and neither had the least desire to go permanently to either.

No one summoned them to breakfast, so they sat on in their respective cabins, occasionally encouraging one another with a sentence or two spoken through the partition. Then, at a little before nine o'clock, the door of Mary's cabin swung open and, with a sudden renewal of her terror, she saw the Great Ram standing looking at her.

'So you thought you could outwit me by seducing from his allegiance that great oaf next door?' he said in his high, sneering voice. 'You miserable little fool. Know now what you have done. With yesterday my use for him ended. I had intended first thing this morning to let him go off in his aeroplane and take you with him. The two of you have found out my real intentions, but I had meant to give him a good reason for not going to Moscow; and there would have been ample time for you to be well out over the Mediterranean before I gave Europe over to havoc. Instead I mean to rescind the postponement of your sentence that I agreed to give him. For the last few hours of your life you may also savour the thought that, through you, this lover of your choice is now condemned by me to the hideous death I intend to inflict on you both soon after midday.'

Mary could take little consolation from the thought that Wash was not the 'lover of her choice', so her heart would not be wrung by the knowledge that she had brought about his death. As for herself, she was not afraid to die, but only of the threatened pain. But a quick death, however hideous, might, she thought, be preferable to being carried off into the unknown by Wash, then abandoned by him to suffer disfigurement and a lingering death from the

425

curse that the Great Ram had earlier decreed for her. She dared not raise her eyes to his and continued to sit on the edge of her bunk as he went on.

'Your insolence in believing for one moment that you could interfere with my plans fills me with amazement. That a creature like you, even aided by that backwoods magician you have besotted with your sex, should pit your puny wits against mine is a supreme impertinence.' Suddenly he gave an eerie cackle of high-pitched laughter, and added, 'How little you can understand the power that I wield. I, the Great Ram, have nothing to fear. No, not even when an army is sent against me. Come, I lift the barrier that bars your door. Follow me, and I will show you how I deal with my enemies.'

As he turned away Mary stood up. Whether she would or not she felt a compulsion to leave her cabin and walk down the tunnel after him. He led her out to the rock platform at which the cable railway ended. Pointing across the valley to a group of tiny figures making their way up through the snow towards a low saddle in the opposite range, he said:

'There go Mirkoss, my cook, and the other Chinese I have had working for me here. You see, I have a care for those who serve me faithfully, even if they are no more than slaves. You and that love-lorn fool, Twisting Snake, would also be on your way out of danger now had you not had the impudence to challenge me.'

Mary found her tongue at last, and murmured, 'But why should they have been in danger if they had remained here? When . . . when your rocket lands on Moscow the Russians will fire back at the American cities and those of the N.A.T.O. countries. They won't waste rockets on Switzerland.'

Again he gave his cynical high-pitched laugh. 'Of course, and I too shall be safe among these mountains; but not in this cave. I have a twin brother: a weak fool with whom I long since quarrelled; yet there remains a strong psychic link between us. A clever Englishman named Verney has used him to overlook me. So they are aware of my intentions, and by one means and another have discovered my retreat.'

At this admission, coupled with Verney's name, Mary's heart gave a bound. Perhaps the spool from the tape recorder that she had thrust on Barney had reached the Colonel and contributed to the hunt that must have started for the missing war-head soon after Wash had flown off with it. If the spool had reached Verney,

426

Ratnadatta, Abaddon, Honorius and the rest of that murderous crew would by now have been arrested. So she would have succeeded in avenging poor Teddy after all. But had she? Within a few hours of the Great Ram launching his rocket London would be laid in ruins. Innocent and guilty alike would perish by the hundreds of thousands. The Satanists of Cremorne would have become cinders long before they could be brought to trial.

She knew that she and Wash would be given no further chance to sabotage the rocket. Now, she could only pray that some fault in its mechanism, some act of God, or even some overweening vanity on the part of the Great Ram himself, would delay the launching. The knowledge that Verney was on his way, and Barney too, perhaps, threw her into a fresh form of agony – for she felt that the strain of waiting and wondering if they would arrive on the scene in time to save the situation must soon prove unendurable.

Hardly had she thought of that before she was relieved from having to face it. Exclaiming 'Here they come! Here they come! I knew they could not be far off,' the Great Ram pointed down into the valley.

At the same moment the distant sound of motor engines was wafted up to her and she saw what seemed from that height a column of toy vehicles emerge from round the shoulder of the mountain. Cars, motor cycles, jeeps and tanks skidded and bumped along the uneven track until thirty or forty of them were visible. When the leading cars reached the engine-house they pulled up with a jerk. A score of figures tumbled out of them and ran towards the building.

The Great Ram gave a sinister chuckle. 'Now, little fool, you shall see how I deal with forces far stronger than yourself when they are brought against me.'

Instantly her joy at knowing friends to be so near was changed to awful apprehension, for it seemed clear that he had already planned to use some form of his evil power for their destruction. Yet he uttered no curse and made no gesture.

Suddenly there came a bright flash, a tongue of flame leapt skywards, and a moment later the roar of the explosion followed to echo and echo back and forth across the valley. Where the engine house had stood there was now a dense cloud of smoke and from it came up thinly the cries of the injured and the dying.

In Mary horror temporarily drove out fear. Swinging round she faced the Great Ram and screamed at him, 'You fiend! You fiend! May Heaven blast you for this murder!'

At that moment, had she had the bread knife with her she would have tried to kill him; but he had come for her so unexpectedly that she had had to leave it hidden under the blanket of her bunk. His only reaction was a scornful laugh, followed by a glance that instantly quelled her and forced her to lower her gaze.

'Come now,' he said abruptly. 'I have work to do, and you shall see me do it. Since you have shown yourself to be one of those who follow the pathetic slave religion started by the imposter Christ, it pleases me that you should hear me announce the death knell of Christianity. If He had the power to preserve it, He obviously would, but He has not; and I intend to show those among His followers who may survive how ill-placed their faith in this self-styled "Saviour of the World" has been. Go in now. You know the wireless cabin. Wait for me there while I watch for a little longer the consternation of those puny creatures down in the valley.'

She knew she must obey him, yet she still had a kick left in her and as she turned to re-enter the cave she burst out, 'You've wrecked the railway, but you've only killed a few of them. And it's certain that with those tanks there are mountain troops. They'll climb up here. For every one you kill they'll call up a dozen reinforcements. You've left it too late to escape. They are bound to get you.'

He tossed his head with the old arrogant gesture. 'Little fool, your persistent blindness to my power becomes almost amusing. Mirkoss and the Chinese I had to send away, otherwise they would have been trapped. But I, the Great Ram, am not as other men. When I will I can call down the cloud to hide the entrances to this cave and halt the climbers, unless they are prepared to risk death with every step they take. The cloud, though, will form no barrier to my sight, and I have long since learned to levitate myself; so I can pass over crevasses that no guide would attempt to cross. I am also impervious to cold; so I shall go upward and make my way unchallenged over the range into another valley where I have already made preparations for my reception.'

To that she could make no reply. It was clear that he had thought of everything. Stumbling a little, she made her way to the wireless cabin and threw herself into a chair there.

The thought that now obsessed her was that Barney might have been with Colonel Verney in the engine-house when it had blown up. She was past tears, but her very heart-strings were wrung with the visual image of her gay, laughter-loving Barney as a broken, twisted body being carried on a stretcher from that still-smoking ruin down in the valley. Her belief that he despised her made no difference to her love for him. And since she had realized, from what Wash had told her, that he must be one of Colonel Verney's young men, although she could not begin to account for such a strange metamorphosis, her love for him, instead of being only an unreasoning passion, had been sanctified by respect and admiration.

For what seemed a long time she sat crouched, wringing her hands, in the wireless cabin. It drifted through her mind that, by ripping at the wires and bending the terminals, she might put the set out of action. But a moment's thought told her that whether he made his proposed broadcast to the world or not did not matter in the least, as that had no bearing on his ability to launch the rocket.

At last he joined her. Waving her from the chair, he sat down in it and began to fiddle with the apparatus. She stood in the doorway, no longer feeling a compulsion to remain with him, but too mentally exhausted to make the effort necessary to break away.

He spent a good ten minutes tuning in to the wave length he required, then began to speak in what she imagined to be Russian. That he should have wished her to remain to hear him she now guessed to be due to his inordinate vanity's demanding the presence of an audience, however humble or unable to appreciate what he was saying, to witness this epoch-making declaration he was making to the world.

Actually he was telling the Russians that their leaders had betrayed the masses by abandoning the Marxist faith of equality achieved through violence, and had become money-grubbing bourgeois intellectuals. He announced the imminent destruction of the régime – although he made no mention of his rocket or the way in which he meant to bring that about – and told the Russians that those who survived the purge he meant to initiate would be given a new chance to be a law unto themselves and enjoy to the utmost all the pleasures this world had to offer. He then went on to talk of himself and the part that, under Satan, he would play in the New Order that was to emerge from the Old.

Although Mary could not understand one word he said, she

felt sure that from his arrogant, ranting tone – which reminded her vaguely of the broadcasts she had heard when a child, made by Hitler – anyone who was listening to him would take him for a madman. That he was mad she now had no doubt, but that did not make him any the less dangerous.

Abruptly he ceased his tirade and again spent some minutes tuning in to a wave length that he evidently considered the best on which to convey his message to the United States and Britain.

He announced himself clearly as Professor Lothar Khune addressing the English-speaking world. To hold the attention of listeners who had chanced to hear him he added that most of them would be dead before the day was out. His theme then was that the Christian heresy had inflicted on the world many generations of senseless self-denial, made an unnatural virtue of celibacy, and denied the people the joy in life which was their birthright; that to bring about a reversal of this unhappy state of things it was necessary for him, Lothar Khune, to act with complete ruthlessness. To destroy the Christian Church root and branch he must also do away with the established governments that supported it. He went on to state that, as they could read in their Bibles, God had given Prince Lucifer this world as His Province. Then he declared that Satan had become weary of the disloyalty of his subjects, so intended to punish them through his servant, Lothar Khune, with a great affliction; but those who survived might look forward to a new era of true freedom and happiness. Finally he declared that on behalf of His Lord Satan he intended to initiate the beginning of the New Era this very day at twelve noon precisely.

Chilled to the heart, Mary heard him out. She knew that almost everyone who had listened to his broadcasts would regard him as a harmless lunatic. But he was not. That he had made them could be due only to a childish vanity – the urge to let people know that it was he, Lothar Khune, who had decreed death for millions and an end to all existing institutions. But he was no mentally ill-adjusted adolescent or madman who did not know what he was doing. He meant every word he said and, short of a miracle, at midday he would launch his rocket.

So pleased was he with himself in his rôle as arbiter of the fate of the world that, having concluded his broadcast, he turned and actually smiled at Mary. As she quickly averted her eyes, he said: 'Twelve noon. That is the time I had already decided upon and I shall not have to advance it by one minute, although by now

430

everything the governments of Europe and America can do against me is being done. The Alpine troops may burst their hearts in their efforts to reach this cave, but when midday comes they will still have several hundred feet to climb. See how perfectly the Lord Satan times matters to ensure the accomplishment of His work and the protection of His servant. Yet you, a woman, a mere piece of flesh designed only as a plaything for men, thought you could thwart me.'

He paused a moment, then added with sudden sarcasm, 'That you are flesh and entirely earthbound reminds me of my duties as a host. Going without breakfast must have made you hungry. It is, too, an ancient custom that anyone condemned to death should be allowed to choose his last meal. In the store next door to the kitchen you will find a great variety of tinned foods. Take what you like for yourself and your leman. Cook him a meal if you wish, while I take my meteorological observations and make the final adjustments to the rocket. You have a little over an hour and a half, which should be ample. He will not be able to cross the threshold of his cabin to eat it. If I removed the invisible barrier I erected across the doorway he might attempt to make further trouble, and it would be an annoyance if I were distracted from my calculations to render him harmless again. But you can pass the food in to him or, if he prefers, give him enough spirits to make himself drunk.'

Having demonstrated his high good humour by according Mary this cynical permission to make the most of her last hours, he lifted his chin and, without a further glance at her, walked off down the tunnel. Relieved of his icy, intimidating presence, Mary's mind became fluid again and she strove desperately to think how she could best employ the limited freedom that he had so contemptuously granted her.

First she ran out on to the rock platform and gazed down into the valley. Over an hour had elapsed since the engine house had blown up. It was now only a broken empty shell from which faint wisps of smoke curled up. The cars and tanks were scattered irregularly round it, and in little groups among them scores of men were standing, their faces all tilted upward as they watched the mouth of the cave. Nearer, she could see several teams of climbers spread out along the mountain side. They had evidently only just emerged from the forest belt and were now slowly snaking their way up across the lowest snowfield.

431

Mary knew nothing about mountaineering, but even the blanket of snow could not disguise the precipitous nature of the cliffs below her. In some places they were sheer, in others slopes led only to outjutting cols that barred further ascent. That there were ways up was evident from the fact that years earlier engineers had scaled these heights and erected the pylons that carried the cables of the now useless mountain railway. But a few moments' anxious scrutiny of the scene was enough to convince her that the Great Ram was right. Two hours at the very least must elapse before the leading teams of climbers could reach the cave.

Wash, then, remained the only hope.

Turning, she ran down the tunnel to his cabin. Grasping the handle of the door she pulled upon it. The door opened so easily that she staggered backwards. He was sitting on the edge of his bunk with his head buried in his enormous hands. At the sound of the door opening, he looked up. Jumping to his feet, he took a pace forward. His eyes lit up and his mouth expanded in a broad grin. Next moment his eyes showed fear and his mouth sagged. On the threshold he had seemed to trip, his hands came up as though to thrust at something, then he staggered back.

Mary shook her head. 'It's no good. He won't let you out. He's making his final calculations, and does not mean to let you interrupt him. But he said I could bring you things: food, a drink. Would you like a drink?'

'Yeah,' Wash nodded heavily. 'Bourbon. Bring me the bottle.'

The dining cabin was the next beyond his. From it she collected the bottle and brought it back to him. He took a long swig, then asked hoarsely:

'What's he mean to do with me? Guess he smelt a rat after all last night and played me for a sucker. But seems you're in the clear. How come you fooled him? Tell, woman, tell?'

'I didn't,' she replied despondently. 'He let me out only because he looks on me as no more capable of harming him than a house-fly. It even amused him to suggest that I should cook you breakfast.'

Wash brightened a little. 'Say, things aren't so bad, then. And I could eat a horse. What are you waiting for?'

She shook her head. 'He meant it only as a horrible joke. He has just announced over the radio to the world that from midday everyone can expect a reign of chaos to begin. Then, as soon as he has launched his rocket, he will settle his score with us.'

'Are you telling me he means to do us in?'

'That's it. Although he pretended not to suspect us last night, he knew all the time that we'd planned to sabotage his rocket. And he no longer has any use for you, because he doesn't mean to leave by 'plane. It's death for both of us unless we can kill him first.'

For a minute they both remained silent, staring into one another's eyes. From about eight o'clock, when he had found himself a prisoner, Wash had decided that it could only be because his treachery had been discovered; but he had counted on still being needed to fly the Great Ram out. Now he realized that, not only was he trapped, he had gambled away his life.

Mary was resigned to losing hers, but still hoped that she could find some means of foiling the Great Ram before he struck her down into oblivion. Alone, she knew herself to be powerless, but if she could free Wash and together they could catch the Great Ram off his guard, they might yet get the better of him.

Suddenly an idea came to her. The occult barrier blocked the doorway of the cabin, but perhaps it did not extend to its sides or roof. In a rush of words she put her idea to Wash. Seizing upon it, he jumped up on the bunk and strove to force up the roofing of the shed. Owing to his great strength the slats ripped from the beams to which they had been nailed, and a gap appeared. But in that part of the cave the rock projected low overhead, so the slat struck against it and the gap where they had broken away was much too narrow for him to crawl through. Yet his effort had proved one thing. He had been able to thrust his hands up through the opening; so no invisible force would have prevented his getting out that way if the gap had been large enough.

Electrified with excitement at the sight of his partial success, Mary cried, 'Try the side wall. Not the one next to the dining cabin. The sideboard backs up against that. You must break through into mine. Throw all your weight against the partition.'

He needed no urging, and charged it with his shoulder. The partition creaked but stood firm. Again and again he threw himself at it, but even under his great weight it did not give an inch. Mary ran back into her cabin and made a quick examination of it. She saw that it was made of stout pine planks that were only about four inches wide, but they were nailed to three-inch

433

square cross battens on her side; so no amount of battering on his could spring the nails that held them. The only hope remaining was to cut a way through them.

Snatching the bread knife from under the blanket of her bunk, she jabbed it into the wood shoulder high, and wriggled it. The result was only a tiny splintered hole and it was obvious that such a tool was hopelessly inadequate for her purpose. All those with which it might have been done speedily were, she knew, in the shed near the rocket, and impossible to get at because the Great Ram was working there. But it struck her that she might find something stronger in the kitchen so, throwing down the bread knife, she ran along to it. The most promising thing she could find was a meat chopper. But after a few blows she abandoned that, as each time she struck with it its blade remained embedded in the wood, and she had difficulty in wrenching it out.

In desperation she reverted to the bread knife and dug frantically at the splintered patch that her blows with the chopper had made. After five or six minutes of stabbing and twisting with the point of the knife, she got the blade through and began to saw sideways with it. As she worked she could have wept with frustration at the seeming hopelessness of the task she had set herself. In ten minutes she had sawed through only an inch and a half of the plank and her wrist was aching intolerably.

Pulling the knife out she darted round with it to Wash and thrust it at him. Easing it into the other side of the slit she had made, he began sawing away with fierce, swift strokes, but he was handicapped by having to work left-handed. Another ten minutes sped by before he had managed to saw right through the four-inch plank.

To get out a piece of the plank another cut had to be made lower down, but while Wash was still working on the first cut Mary had succeeded with the chopper in splintering out another hole eighteen inches below the first.

He got the knife through and continued the painfully slow sawing; meanwhile, she used the chopper to prise the cross-beam a fraction of an inch away from the planks. At last the second cut was completed. He gave a shout, she stood back, then he struck the eighteen-inch length of plank with his fist and it fell at her feet.

So far the job had taken them forty minutes, but now that he was able to get his hands through and grip the sides of the planks the work went much faster. Most men would have found themselves still faced with an hour's work, and perhaps not even then had the strength to force the boards away from the nails that held them; but in Wash's giant arms and shoulders lay the strength of half a dozen men, and after ten minutes of straining, ripping, bashing and kicking, he had made a gap wide enough to force his way through.

Both of them were panting and sweating from their exertions, but he did not pause to rest. Taking her by the arm he hurried her out and turned towards the entrance to the cave served by the cable railway.

Pulling back, she gasped, 'Not that way. He's working on his rocket, making final adjustments to it.'

'To hell with him!' Wash replied tersely. 'We're getting outa here while the going's good.'

'We can't. The cable-railway is no longer working. He blew it up.'

'Then we'll climb down.'

He continued to move forward but she dragged upon his arm. 'Wash, you're crazy! It's like the side of a house. We'd fall and kill ourselves. I've never even climbed down a chalk cliff.'

'Neither have I, but we'll make it someway.'

'There are Alpine troops on their way up, and . . .'

He halted then, towering above her, and exclaimed, 'Troops? How come?'

'We've been traced from England. The Great Ram told me. He has a twin brother who is psychic, too, and located us here. The valley is full of troops. They must know that it was you who stole the war-head, and they'll have found your 'plane by now. Even if we could get safely down the mountain you couldn't escape. It's certain they'll arrest you.'

'That's bad,' he muttered. 'Still, I'd leifer face a court-martial than the Great Ram. 'Sides, they can only jail me, and the jail's not yet made that could hold me for more than a coupla weeks.'

For a second she hesitated. She dare not tell him about the tape-recorder and confess that she had betrayed him. If she did he might kill her there and then, and if she had to die she still hoped that it would not be uselessly, but in an attempt to thwart the Great Ram. Drawing a deep breath she took the plunge.

'It won't be jail, Wash. The British will hang you.'

435

'Nerts! They've no jurisdiction over a member of the United States forces.'

'Maybe not, but they'll get you tried for murder.'

'What in heck are you driving at?'

'You remember the detective who came to the Cedars – Lord Larne?'

'Yeah; but we didn't kill him. He made a getaway after you threw that crucifix.'

'I know.' She strove to choose her words carefully now, so as not to incriminate herself. 'But I told you at the time that I knew him – that he had been accepted as a neophyte by the circle at Cremorne. It's certain that your flying out with the war-head will have sent the balloon up. After that Scotland Yard would not have delayed another hour in raiding the Temple. There must be papers there they will have seized, and some of the Brotherhood will have been arrested. Ratnadatta will have been, for certain, because Lord Larne knew him quite well. The odds are he'll turn Queen's Evidence to save his own skin; and he owes you a grudge. He'll put you on the spot as having taken part in the murder of that other police spy. The one you told me about.'

For a moment Wash remained silent, then his dark eyes narrowed. 'You've sure got something there, honey. If the British have bust that Temple open and got Ratnadatta it could be pretty hot for me. Go or stay put it looks as though I'm for it either way.'

His words braced her for her next effort. They showed that he was coming round to where she wanted him; but before she could speak again he gave a sudden laugh and dashed her hopes.

'We've been talking foolish. When the Big Chief lets off his rocket the past will be washed out. Here in Switzerland I guess we'll stand a better chance of survival than most. But Scotland Yard, Ratnadatta, the air base at Fulgoham – they'll mean as little to us as Noah and his Ark. There'll be no one left to indict.'

To Mary it was a body blow; for in the urgency of the moment both of them had failed to take into account the effects of the rocket and now, by doing so, he had nullified all the arguments by which she had been endeavouring to steer him into attacking the Great Ram. Even so, she made a quick recovery.

'Of course; how stupid of me. But it was you who brought the war-head here. You can't get away from that. And the Swiss must know it. If the rocket is fired you will be accounted guilty of mass murder. They'll not try and hang you but tear you limb from limb.'

He passed a hand over his still sweating forehead. 'Sure, sure. I'd not thought of that. Then I'd best remain here. I've got my gun. I'll shoot it out with them as they come up.'

'No,' she cried, 'That would mean death for certain. If you've got the guts, you can still save yourself.'

'Tell, honey, tell? I like my life.'

'You must face up to that fiend and stop him launching his rocket.'

Wash groaned. 'You don't know what you're asking.'

'He was right, then,' she flung at him contemptuously, 'when he said this morning that you were only a little backwoods magician.'

'Did he say that!' Momentarily Wash's hook-nosed face showed angry belligerence. Then he shrugged. 'Well, maybe he's right. Anyways I'm not in his class. Didn't I try all I knew to break that barrier he put up 'cross my cabin door? No, he's the tops. He'd turn me into a cockroach and stamp on me.'

'All right then! Forget all this bloody magic! You're a man, aren't you, and so is he. You've got a gun. Go down there and shoot him.'

He stared down at her. 'If I could catch him unawares I might. Odds are, though, he'd pick up my vibrations. Then he'd paralyse me before I could get a bead on him.'

She seized the lapels of his jacket and, her face turned up to his raved at him, 'You've got to risk it! Don't you see that it is your only hope! You brought the war-head here believing that it was to be let off in Switzerland, with the result that all such weapons would be abolished and the world relieved for good from the fear of a nuclear war. That's the truth. When the time comes you must tell it and shame the Devil. But there is more to it than that. Much more. You'll be the man who saved civilization. All the evil things you've ever done will be forgiven and forgotten. You'll never be charged with rape, or arson, or murder. Instead you'll be the world's No. One hero. The British will make you a Duke and the Americans a millionaire. Even the Russians will give you the Order of Lenin or something. You'll never again have to run a shady racket to live in comfort. You'll be given lovely homes and lots of servants in all the countries you have saved from untold horror, and be received everywhere like a prince or a bigger than biggest film star.'

Breathless, she paused, for she saw that the picture she painted had rung a bell. Swift as ever to react to fresh emotional stimulants, Wash was smiling, and he muttered, 'Could be; could be. Honey, you're a squaw in a million. I'll do it. Yes, I'll do it. I'll shoot the bastard in the back.'

'Come on then!' She pulled him round to face the other way before some new thought might cause him to change his mind. Glancing at her watch, she added, 'It's twenty to twelve. We haven't any too much time.'

'Steady!' he warned her. 'We'll be walking on egg shells and if we break one we'll get no second chance. Praises be, I was brought up to stalking from the time I was a papoose. Get your shoes off and keep a good twenty paces in rear of me. I learnt early to control my breathing, but he might hear yours.'

As he spoke he was taking off his own shoes. Having done so he got out his automatic, tested the recoil with practised efficiency, and clicked a bullet up into its chamber. Giving her a smile he set off down the tunnel. She walked close behind him till she reached her cabin, slipped into it to collect the chopper she had left there, then, giving him the lead he had asked for, followed him, her heart beating like a sledge hammer.

Ahead of her Wash gave no sign of any tension. He was not walking on tiptoe, but after each medium-length pace was putting a stockinged foot down firmly without a sound. He seemed to glide rather than walk, and in the dim light might have been taken for the dark ghost of some long dead giant.

To Mary, as they advanced, time seemed to stand still. The only sound that broke the stillness was that of the drip of the melting ice at the entrances to the cave. Before she expected him to, Wash came to a halt. Seized with the idea that he had lost his nerve, and needed fresh encouragement, she continued to move forward stealthily. When she was within a yard of him he suddenly raised his gun, took a swift stride forward and fired.

Just in time to see the first phase of the encounter on which so much depended, Mary rounded the curve of the cave. The Great Ram was standing by the rocket with his back turned. As though struck on the head with an invisible hammer he fell to his knees. But he had not been shot. Warned of his danger by telepathy, he had dropped of his own accord a second before Wash squeezed the trigger of his pistol.

438

Its report, in that confined space, was deafening, and reverberated like thunder through the tunnel. In an instant the Great Ram had squirmed round to face the attack. His eyes, now appearing reddish, flashed as though they were rubies caught in a shaft of sunlight. The second bullet tore through the right sleeve of his coat, then he threw up his left hand as though in a futile attempt to ward off others.

But his gesture was nothing of the kind. As he raised his hand Wash's gun hand, too, jerked upwards. The remaining bullets in his automatic sped in a swift fusillade harmlessly overhead. Before he or Mary even had time to move, the Great Ram's body became half obscured by black smoke. Rooted to the spot, Mary guessed what was about to happen. Within seconds the smoke solidified into the Black Imp.

Wash gave a terrified bellow, 'No! No; no!' and turned to run. But in two bounds the infernal creature was upon him. It seemed to dissolve again and, paralysed by horror, Mary saw it streak into his wide open mouth. Next moment he dropped his gun and reeled forward, clutching at his stomach. Wisps of smoke were coming from his nostrils and his ears. His near-white hair was standing straight up on his head; his eyes, suffused with blood, were protruding as though on stalks. He was on fire inside. He emitted one long-drawn scream that ended in a gurgle, then crashed face downwards on the floor.

As he fell his right arm swung out and its fist, tight-clenched in the agony of death, struck Mary sharply on the thigh. The blow caused her to stagger, so jolting her out of the paralysis that had held her rigid with horror. Letting out a piercing shriek she turned and fled.

For the next few moments she had no clear impressions. As though she had been transported by wings she found herself at the far entrance of the cave, brought up short in her flight by the edge of the rock platform. Her first conscious thoughts were that the Great Ram had triumphed and that the sands of her own life were swiftly running out.

A shout from below caught her attention. Looking down she saw four of the teams of climbers all scaling the mountain by different routes; but the nearest was a good three hundred feet below the level of the cave. Still gasping for breath she shouted back. But her cry was one of despair, for the teams were moving upward only at a crawl, and she knew that they could not possibly arrive in time to save her – unless, unless she could find somewhere to hide.

As she looked down she saw that about eight feet below the platform on which she stood there was another ledge. If she could reach it and crouch back against the rock face beneath the overhang she might conceal herself there while the Great Ram, failing to find her at the entrance to the cave, supposed that she was hiding in one of the cabins. By the time he had searched them all there was at least a chance that help might reach her.

Two of the stanchions that supported the terminus of the cable railway were embedded in the lower ledge. Running along to the platform, she threw herself flat upon it, then wriggled backwards until her legs were dangling in space. A few wild kicks and they closed round the stanchion. There followed an awful moment as she lowered herself until she could also grip it with her hands. The ice-cold metal bit into them with savage heat. She gave a gasp of pain, released her hold and slid the last few feet to fall with a bump in the snow. Tears were now streaming down her face but, picking herself up, she scrambled along to the deepest indenture in the cliff wall and crouched down there.

Yet her final bid to outwit the Great Ram was doomed to failure. He had followed her wild flight at only walking pace, but as soon as he reached the rock platform his intuition told him where she was. She had not been crouching beneath the overhang for much more than a minute when she heard him call to her from above to come out.

She tried to crouch further back against the rock, but it was no good. Despite her efforts to remain where she was she found herself standing up and walking forward. The ledge was about ten feet wide. When she had covered half the distance he ordered her to stop, turn round and look up at him. Unresisting now, she did as she was bid.

Tall, dark, saturnine, he stood right on the edge of the big platform looking down at her, his thin mouth curved in a smile. To her amazement his expression was no longer harsh or cynical, but, for the first time she had seen it on his face, a kindly one. And when he spoke his voice was gentle.

'Circe, sometime neophyte of the Ram, I did you an injustice. Although it was impossible for you to defeat me, you have proved a more worthy opponent than I supposed any woman could. It is a tragedy that you should have chosen to adhere to the Christian

440

heresy; otherwise you might have shared with me in ten minutes time the triumph for which I have worked so long. Had we met earlier I would have converted you to the true faith, and done you the honour to allow you to serve me both as a woman and a friend. As it is, in recognition of your courage, I will accord you mercy. Instead of inflicting my curse upon you, or sending my dark inner self to consume you in agony, as I did with the stupid giant you made your tool, I decree for you a swift and painless death. Turn about now and walk forward to the end decreed for you.'

Before Mary had grasped the full significance of his words, she found that she had turned round. An intangible but irresistible force pressed upon her back. She strove to keep her legs rigid and her feet planted firmly, but the pressure against her shoulders increased, bending her forward. To keep her balance she was compelled to put out first one foot and then the other. Two more steps and she was on the edge of the ledge. Immediately below her was a nearly sheer drop of a thousand feet.

In front of her the snow-capped peaks of the range on the other side of the valley glistened in the sunshine. Owing to the clear, rarefied atmosphere they looked so near that she could almost have stepped across to them, but actually they were miles away. Above them puffs of white cloud hung unmoving in a blue summer sky. Her eyes dropped to the green valley, with its toy tanks and tiny figures on the far side of the narrow, rushing stream. Then, much nearer, there were the teams of climbers. They had all halted and some men among them had rifles to their shoulders. One flashed. It was only then her brain registered the fact that they had been firing for some minutes.

Suddenly she realized that they were firing at the Great Ram. A final hope stirred in her. If he were hit she would be reprieved from death. Frantically now she dug her heels into the hard snow and used every ounce of strength she had to throw herself backward. But her effort was useless. All she could achieve was to remain upright. And deep down in herself she knew that the Great Ram would not be hit. The magic aura with which he could surround himself would deflect the bullets.

Still she battled to maintain her balance, pitting her will against his. But his was the stronger. Her head bowed under the pressure so that she was staring down into the abyss. Then, like an officer giving the order to a firing squad to shoot, she heard him call down to her the one word, 'Jump.'

441

She flexed her knees, swayed sideways, threw up her arms, and with a wild cry fell outward into space.

.　　　　.　　　　.　　　　.

Immediately after receiving the radio message about Lothar's broadcast Verney asked the Lieutenant leading his party to circulate to all the other climbing teams an urgent signal. So far the troops had been told only that they were on an emergency operation and must get up to the cave for the purpose of arresting with the least possible delay anyone they found in it. Now they were told that in the cave there was a madman who had stolen an H bomb, and that he planned to let it off at midday. They were then called on to take risks if necessary and make an all-out effort to reach the cave in time. Verney also took it on himself to promise quadruple pensions for the dependants of men who might be injured or killed in the attempt, and rich rewards and honours for the first three teams to reach the cave. They were told, too, that although other teams were on the way to the far entrance of the cave, these had had to make a wide detour before starting their climb, so there was no chance of their reaching the goal first. In consequence, success or failure depended on the teams that had set out on the direct route up from the wrecked engine-house.

There was no more that he could do; yet within the next few minutes it was apparent that the message had galvanized the troops into considerably swifter progress, and his own party resumed the climb at a faster pace.

As the officer or N.C.O. leading each party carried a walkie-talkie set the Sergeant with Barney's team had received the radio message relayed from Berne at the same time as his Lieutenant. The moment Barney heard of it he too realized that only a superhuman effort could enable them to reach the cave before midday, and without waiting for C.B.'s message he urged his party to greater speed.

For the amateurs the pace on the easier stretches became grinding; yet the harder ones caused them more distress from their very slowness on them, and the time it took to cut steps in the ice or plough through patches of soft snow. Many times they slipped and would, perhaps, have fallen to their deaths had it not been for the strong surefooted Alpine troops to whom they were roped before and behind.

442

At times Barney almost despaired of reaching the cave at all. Every hundred feet or so his party found itself confronted with a great mass of overhanging rock, round which a way had to be worked, or a narrow, almost vertical chimney that had to be climbed as the only means of continuing the ascent. In one case they had to cross a glacier and, in another, edge their way along thirty feet of ledge that was in no place more than eighteen inches wide. Not daring to look down, he kept his eyes fixed on the man in front of him, endeavouring to follow his footsteps exactly, but a dozen times his heart was in his mouth and he feared that at any moment he would fall headlong over the precipice.

As they made their way upwards he lost all sense of time until, on coming out from beneath an overhang, he caught sight of the opening of the cave about three hundred feet above him. A quick glance at his watch showed that it was half past eleven. They had, he knew, performed marvels in the past hour, but to scale that last three hundred feet of snow and ice in less than the remaining thirty minutes seemed beyond even the greatest human endeavour.

For a further quarter of an hour, sweating and straining, they toiled on. Then he heard a shout. It came from a member of another party some way to the left of his. The shout was quickly answered by another from higher up. Looking upward, he saw that a woman had emerged from the cave. A moment later he recognized her as Mary. His relief at knowing her still to be alive was so great that, although he waved, for a moment he could not utter a sound. Tears started to his eyes and he was choking with emotion.

Within a few minutes all the men in the climbing teams who were in sight of the cave were staring up at her in wonder, as they saw her run to the cable-railway platform then risk a fall to death by wriggling out over its edge and supporting herself only by a precarious hold on one of its girders.

As she slid to the ledge and picked herself up, Barney let his breath go in a gasp of relief. Finding his voice he urged his team to still greater efforts, but they had covered no more than a dozen paces when Lothar appeared on the upper platform. Verney and Barney both recognized him and almost simultaneously shouted:

'There he is! Shoot him! Shoot! Shoot!'

Some of the troops were armed with Sten guns and others with pistols. Only a few carried rifles, but those who did swiftly unslung them and opened fire. None of their bullets appeared to score a

443

hit and in the next two minutes all the climbers who could see the cave watched with horror as Mary's tragedy was played out.

Verney, Otto and Barney alone among them fully understood what was taking place. But the others realized instinctively that the tall, dark man on the upper ledge was ordering the woman on the lower to throw herself over the precipice.

Barney drew the pistol he had been lent and aimed it at Lothar, then lowered his arm. At that range even rifles were proving ineffective, and a pistol bullet might as easily have hit Mary as the man who was driving her to her death. He closed his eyes for a second. When he opened them again Mary had thrown herself sideways and was hurtling into the abyss.

．　　　．　　　．　　　．　　　．

The parties had started upward again. The rifles had ceased to crack. Lothar had disappeared unharmed into the cave. Barney was climbing now as an automaton. Grief and pain filled his mind to the exclusion of all other thoughts. Instinctively he continued to place his feet in the footsteps of the man ahead and to advance or halt as he was told.

That he should have been robbed of Mary at the eleventh hour caused him a sick misery the like of which he had never before known in all his life. During the past unbearably anxious days he had come to realize that she meant everything to him; that no other woman could ever compensate him for her loss. Almost he had resigned himself to it, believing it next to impossible that the Great Ram would allow her to live after she had thrown the crucifix in his face. Yet he had. Only a few minutes ago she had still been alive, and unharmed. Now she was dead, a broken twisted body grotesquely doubled across some spur of rock, or buried deep in snow, far down below.

The Sergeant rounded a shoulder of the mountain that brought the cable railway again into full view. Suddenly he gave a shout: 'There she is! Blessed God, a miracle!'

The others clambered round the corner after him. He had come out on a humpy ledge of rock broad enough for all his team to stand on. Opposite to them and about ten feet away sagged one of the long swags of triple cable along which the cage of the railway ran. Twenty feet lower down there stood one of the tall T-shaped steel pylons that supported the cables. At the base of the

444

pylon, where snow had piled up, Mary was lying on her stomach, clinging with one arm to the nearest steel strut.

Her sideways lurch as she fell had temporarily saved her. Instead of plunging to the depths she had shot forward beneath the railway terminus platform, hit one of its outer stanchions, checked, slid, bounced, rolled and finally brought up on the drift of snow that had accumulated against the first great pylon some eighty feet below the level of the cave.

'Mary! Mary!' Barney's voice cracked as he shouted down to her. 'Hang on! Can you hang on? Are you all right?'

She squirmed round and her feeble cry came back, 'I've a broken arm. Ribs too I think. But go on up. Twelve o'clock! Twelve o'clock!'

Barney did not need to look at his watch. From the time that had elapsed since he had seen her fall he knew that it could now be only a few minutes to noon. To complete their climb in the tiny fraction of an hour that was left was beyond the bounds of possibility. And the other teams were no nearer to the cave than his.

The Great Ram had won. He would launch his accursed rocket and bring incalculable death and suffering on the world. But for some time at least the mountain areas of Switzerland would remain unaffected. And Mary was lying there still within a hair's breadth of death. To save her was now the highest priority.

Turning to the Sergeant, Barney cried, 'How can we get her up? What's the drill?'

The Sergeant shook his head. 'We can do nothing from here. We must first complete our climb to the cave. From there one of us can be lowered to get a rope round her.'

'But that will take half an hour, longer perhaps,' Barney burst out. 'At any moment the slope of snow on which she's lying may collapse. Anyhow, it's freezing and one of her arms is broken. She'll never be able to hang on that long.'

'There is no other way.' The Sergeant pointed. 'Look for yourself, Sir. We can get down to her only from above. Even if we threw her a rope and she could catch and make herself fast to it, that would not help. If the snow gives or she lets go her hold on the pylon, she would swing out and be dashed to death against the cliff face below us.'

'There is a way,' Barney retorted. 'Quick, give me an extra rope, and lengthen the one attached to me. I'm going to jump to the cable, shin along it to the pylon, and go down to her.'

445

A chorus of protest arose from the five soldiers. They declared that he was mad – that it would be suicide – that the jump was too far for him to catch the cable – that if he missed it the rope could not save him as he, in that case, would be dashed to death as he swung violently against the rock face.

His Irish temper flaming at their opposition, he shouted them down, then bullied them into reluctantly equipping him with ropes in the way he had demanded. Eyeing him with mixed amazement, admiration and distress, they stood back to give him the best run that the ledge afforded. At that moment a single shot rang out, but none of them heeded it. Drawing a deep breath, he took his run and launched himself across the gaping chasm.

He hit the nearest cable with his body. His hands were held open and stretched high above his head. The cable gave under the impact. As it snapped back like a twanged bowstring his body doubled across it, his head went down and he was within an ace of somersaulting over it to his death. But he managed to grab it with his gloved hands and, next moment, was hanging by them from it.

The Sergeant and his men let out a spontaneous cheer, then watched spellbound as he made his way foot by foot along the now sagging cable, expecting every moment that the weight of his body would prove too much for his arms, and that he would drop like a stone into the depths above which he was swinging.

The strain on his arms was terrible. He felt as though they were being dragged from their sockets. But he reached the T-shaped head of the pylon. As he grasped it and clung there panting another cheer went up. For a moment he remained there to recover his breath. Then he scrambled down the steel latticework of which the pylon was constructed.

Mary, half lying on her side, had been holding her breath as she watched him. When he got down to within a few feet of her she breathed again, and murmured,

'Oh Barney, Barney! Just to think you've risked your life for me – even though you despise me.'

'Despise you!' he echoed. 'Oh Mary, Mary, how can you say that? I love you. I love you. And you risked a worse death than a broken neck when you saved me from the Great Ram in the chapel.'

As he was speaking he passed the loop of the spare rope over her head. With a moan of pain she raised her broken arm and got

446

it through the loop. He drew it tight and made it fast to a strut of the pylon. Then he made his own rope fast to another strut and lowered himself on to the snow beside her.

A shiver shook her and she moaned, 'I'm so cold, darling; so cold. I couldn't have hung on for another five minutes.' Yet despite her pain she was smiling.

Even if the snow gave the ropes would hold them now. Taking her in his arms, he said, 'They'll get us up soon, my sweet, and I'll never let you be cold or lonely again.' Then their icy breath mingled as their lips met in a long kiss.

.   .   .   .   .

It was nearly half past twelve before Mary was hauled up to the platform outside the cave, now crowded with the Alpine troops. Yet the rocket had not been fired. As they wrapped her in blankets and laid her gently on a ready-made stretcher, C.B. knelt down beside her, took her hands and chafed them. In a husky voice he said,

'Mary, my dear; I've known a lot of brave women but you are the bravest of them all. Thank God we arrived in time to save you; and may He bless you all your days.'

Her eyes were shining. 'Thank you,' she murmured. 'Thank you. But He's blessed me already. Barney has asked me to marry him.'

'I'd have bet any money that he would,' C.B. smiled. 'It remains only for me to ask His Lordship if he'll have me for best man at the wedding.'

She frowned. 'Please don't joke about it. His calling himself Lord Larne was just a part of his phoney character for the job.'

Verney shook his head. 'You're off the mark there, my dear. He became the Earl of Larne five years ago; but when he came into the title he made a complete break with his old life and decided not to use it in the new one until he had lived down his raffish past. You'll make the loveliest Countess of Larne they've ever had in the family.'

At that moment Barney was hauled up over the edge. After smiling at Mary he turned quickly to C.B. and asked, 'What happened? Did something go wrong with the rocket when Lothar tried to launch it, or was he hit by that single shot I heard just before midday?'

447

Verney came to his feet. 'Neither, partner. That shot was fired by Otto from a pistol lent him by the Swiss. He realized that we couldn't get up here in time and shot himself through the heart.'

'D'you mean he committed suicide in despair?'

'Not in despair. He died a hero's death. I'm sure of it. When the first troops got here they found Lothar lying flat on his face. As he wasn't bleeding they thought he'd had a stroke and undid his tunic. Over his heart there was a great black bruise, as though he'd been kicked there by a mule. Otto knew better than any of us the way in which what happened to one twin could affect the other. By shooting himself he killed his brother with a heart attack.'

After a moment, C.B. added, 'Although there was no thunderbolt or stroke of lightning, I shall always believe that at the eleventh hour, through Otto Khune, God intervened to defeat the powers of Evil.'